THE WAXWORK MAN

Charles Dickens Investigations
Book Eleven

J. C. Briggs

SAPERE
BOOKS

THE WAXWORK
MAN

Published by Sapere Books.

24 Trafalgar Road, Ilkley, LS29 8HH,
United Kingdom

saperebooks.com

ISBN: 978-0-85495-089-8

For Tom

'...so like life, that if wax-work only spoke and walked about, you'd hardly know the difference. I won't go so far as to say, that, as it is, I've seen wax-work quite like life, but I've seen some life that was exactly like wax-work.'

Mrs Jarley in *The Old Curiosity Shop* by Charles Dickens

'In the Chamber of Horrors, there is a novelty as horrible as could possibly be desired — a guillotine — not a mere model, but a real, full-grown, actual workable guillotine and … all the horrors of the affair — the knife, the platform, the very basket into which the head falls; but we were not sorry to see that out of the considerable number of persons who were sauntering among the murderers and victims, staring likenesses of the Mannings, the Rushes, and Thurtells, not one appeared to have any relish for examining the forbidding details of the guillotine... This said Chamber of Horrors is, after all, a nightmare sort of place...'

From *The Morning Chronicle*, 1852

CHARACTERS

Charles Dickens
Catherine, his wife
Superintendent Jones of Bow Street
Elizabeth, his wife
Eleanor and Tom Brim, their adopted children
Scrap, errand boy and amateur detective
Sergeant Rogers
Mollie, his wife
Constable Stemp
Constable Feak
Doctor Woodhall of King's College Hospital
Henry Meteyard, barrister at Lincoln's Inn

IN THIS NOVEL:

Dickens's household at Tavistock House:
Katey and Mamie, Dickens's daughters
John Thompson, his manservant
Betsey Prig, a wax doll, which speaks one word

Dickens's friends and acquaintances from real life:
Mark Lemon, editor of *Punch* magazine
Gilbert à Beckett, magistrate and author
John Forster, friend and first biographer
John Brownlow, secretary of the Foundling Hospital
Edward Laman Blanchard, journalist and author
George Reynolds, journalist
Doctor Thomas Mayo of the Marylebone Infirmary

The Judge's Household:
Judge Fabian Quarterman, known as the hanging judge
Mrs Flint, his housekeeper
Ma Dunk, laundress
Pruey, a servant
Eliza Quarterman, formerly Eliza Clifford, his missing wife
Mr Ebenezer Houndsfoot, the judge's solicitor

Shopkeepers and Manufacturers:
Signor Barone, wax doll-maker
Doctor Kahn, owner of a waxwork gallery
Mr Payne and Mr Jewell, glass eye-makers
Emma Cooper, glass eye painter
Mrs Dryden, fancy goods seller
Mr Thomas Dryden, her missing husband
Mrs Ann Marlowe, oil and colour warehouse proprietor
Seth Marlowe, her son
Alexander Marlowe, her brother-in-law, a bad lot

The Press:
Edward Penman, on the hunt for Alexander Marlowe
Martha Clarke, his aunt, a draper
Mr Crowquill, a journalist

The Witnesses, the Extras, and those just passing:
A man eating a pie at Madame Tussaud's
Doctor Yarwood, Judge Quarterman's neighbour
Doctor Greville, in Southwark
Joshua Munton, known as Munty
Alfred, a crossing-sweeper
Tippler, a cab driver
Simon Holdfast, a locksmith

A boy with a nail in his mouth
Two urchins in a graveyard
A boy with a broken quill pen
A hairdresser with curls
A girl with a coal shovel
An urchin with a message
Two women in black

The Clifford Family, important to the history of Eliza Quarterman:
Lady Julia, a benefactress of the Foundling Hospital, deceased
Sir Henry, her son, deceased
Sir Francis, her grandson, once beloved of Eliza, married to a wealthy brewer's daughter

1: THE CHAMBER OF HORRORS

London, 1851

The rain was coming down as if a barrel of water had been emptied in heaven — several, in fact. Charles Dickens, whose umbrella had inconveniently developed first a rent and then a gaping hole through which the rain poured, slipped into Madame Tussaud's on Baker Street.

It was not far off closing time — about half an hour, by which time the rain might have eased off. He went through the hall, passing by the exhibition of sculpture, and up the wide staircase to the salon.

He'd seen it all before, the Golden Chamber with the tableau of the Royal Family at home with Queen Victoria, Prince Albert and their children and the kings and queens of the past in their robes of state. All those wretched Georges. The ill-tempered one. The mad one. The fat one. George IV in his coronation robes — such opulence was grotesque and ridiculous, he always thought, the tableau including a medieval knight in full armour, and even a Roman centurion. Humbug, the lot of it. Chamber of Horrors.

Just the usual man gazing at the so-called Sleeping Beauty on her couch. They were usually young swains sniggering as they watched her breast rise and fall, thanks to the mechanism within. This one was leaning on his stick, looking intently — he ought to know better at his age. Sleeping — she looked as though she might wake with a kiss, but her waxen lips were another horror.

Dickens rather missed the old lady. It had been worth a shilling to see her. Madame Tussaud had always taken the money and looked you over critically, as if measuring you for the guillotine. She'd died only last year at the great age of eighty-eight. He'd always thought of tumbrils when he'd seen her. She had begun her career in France and had taken casts of the heads of those who were guillotined during the French Revolution, hot off the press, so to speak. Marie Antoinette and her head had been thrown into a handcart and wheeled away to Madame Tussaud and wheeled back again to be tossed into a lime pit. The death heads — a thoroughly mean-looking collection — were to be seen downstairs, and included both those who had perished in the Revolution and those who had condemned them. Among them was Robespierre, who had been finished off by the very instrument that had been used to execute thousands whom he'd sentenced to death, and whose bloodied mouth Dickens always thought was half-smiling.

He paid an extra sixpence for the Chamber of Horrors, that shrine of profound and awful misery, which now boasted the effigies of that murderous pair, Mr and Mrs Manning, whose hanging he had witnessed. The newspapers had advertised a plan of the murderous kitchen, and a plaster head of the victim, Patrick O'Connor, who had been buried under the flags after Marie Manning had shot him and Frederick Manning had finished him off with a ripping chisel. Dickens had been haunted by the sight of the two of them hanging from the gallows at Horsemonger Lane Gaol. *Exorcise them*, he thought, making his way downstairs, *stare them out*. Not that they'd look at you. It was impossible to catch the eye of a waxwork; they always seemed to be gazing at something behind you, and that was a rather chilling notion. Perhaps, when you turned away, they might wink behind your back — wink to that unseen thing they knew was there.

To enter the Chamber of Horrors required the navigation of a dark passage under the guillotine scaffold. The trick was to avoid looking up at the blade — supposed to have been sent from Paris, having done its dreadful work — the blade which you couldn't help thinking might one day drop just as you were passing under. There was a basket of sawdust, handily placed to receive your severed head. Dickens almost started as a tall woman came through. He stood aside as she swept past with a hiss and an angry swish of skirts. He opened his mouth to apologise — though for what, except being about to go in? She hadn't looked up at the blade. A regular, perhaps. Nerves of steel under her black veil.

He went into the passage, glancing at the dingy little cell through the bars of which he saw the shadowy, black-clothed figure of Count de Lorge, imprisoned in the Bastille for offending Louis XV. *Ah well*, Dickens thought, Louis had offended the revolutionaries. The whirligig of Time bringing in his revenges. Too dark, thank the Lord, to see the waxen rats.

The deliberately gloomy lighting gave the chamber an eerie look. Shadows shifted in corners and seemed to shuffle forward to stand by the exhibits as if their dark souls could not leave them, but stayed, hovering indecisively. Hell not very inviting, perhaps. Queer how the figures always seemed to lean forward as if they were about to speak. Not guilty, Maria Manning would repeat. And no one would listen. She was guilty and this was an illusion, if a horrible one. She was looking at something behind him. Dickens moved swiftly on.

Taken from life, Madame Tussaud boasted — not quite. Taken from death. Here was James Rush. Madame had paid seventy guineas to the executioner for Rush's suit — a fortune, yet a bargain, by all accounts. Madame had made fifteen hundred pounds from the exhibition of Rush, who looked what he was in life. A bloated, mean, and arrogant face. He had murdered Isaac Jermy and his son — for money. And he had conducted his own defence, sure that he would be freed. His closing speech had lasted for fourteen hours. No wonder the judge had condemned him to death.

Here was well-dressed, mad Oxford, that simpering boy who had attempted to kill the queen. In Bedlam now. The one-legged sailor, Dennis Collins, complete with wooden leg, who had attempted to assassinate King William IV at the Ascot races. And James Greenacre, a coarse-featured brute, who had cut his betrothed into pieces — her head was found in the Regent's Canal. He was in good company with the dwarfish John Holloway, who had deposited his wife's trunk and thighs in Lovers' Walk in Brighton. The other parts were found in a privy. The inaptly named Daniel Good was another chopper-upper. His fat cheeks and little, pursed-up mouth made him revolting in wax. Two pounds paid for his clogs, so it was said. They were all there: Thomas Wainewright, poet, artist, and murderer; Courvoisier, the valet who had murdered his master; Thurtell, gambler, card-sharp, boxing manager, arsonist, and killer; and Burke and Hare, the body snatchers, modelled from life as the bill poster had it. Hideous in wax. Madame had attended the trial where she had made her sketches. Crime in coats and trousers — more horrible somehow than crime in velvet robes. Because nearer, he supposed. And crime in a nightgown —

Well, not exactly a nightgown, but some sort of bath gown, perhaps, for the revolutionary, Monsieur Jean-Paul Marat, lying in his bath where he had been stabbed to death by Charlotte Corday. Always in the bath, it seemed, for it was the only relief for his loathsome skin disease — leprosy, possibly. He always wore a turban soaked in vinegar, so it was said. Madame Tussaud had been summoned immediately after the murder and had arrived while the body was still warm, the blood still fresh as it looked now. Marat looked gaunt, his mouth partly open in a rictus grin, his hands clasping the knife still plunged into his chest. He didn't look as if he were going to get out of that bath. Madame Tussaud had not brought him back to life, more back to death. His eyes were blank and gazing upwards. Dickens didn't follow that gaze.

He was aware of a noise next to him. A noise like the smacking of lips. Surely not one of the... He turned to see a fair-haired young man with a pimpled face above a red and beefy neck encircled by a blue neck cloth, stolidly looking upon Marat and simultaneously stuffing a piece of pork pie with a brawny ham-like hand into his open mouth. He seemed to be relishing both activities.

'Frenchie?' he asked, jerking his pie towards the body in the bath. At least that's what Dickens thought he said, the word being somewhat mingled with pork pie crust.

'I believe so. Someone important in the French Revolution.'

The young man looked again. 'All that allonging and marshonging, eh? No good came of it, then?'

'Not for him, no.'

'Bad 'un, I'd say, but all of 'em's rum 'uns one way or t'other.' He gestured around the chamber with his pie. 'An every one of 'em 'ung —' smacking his lips again — 'by the neck. Twisted, eh? Seen it. Seen 'im — Manning — go off, an' 'is wife, all in black satin. Looked a picture. French, or Swiss — furrin, anyways. Rum do.' Despite his phlegmatic words, Dickens couldn't help noticing a hand move to the blue neck cloth.

'It was.' It wasn't. It was dreadful, Dickens remembered, and the crowd worst of all, jeering and catcalling, blaspheming and cheering — and eating pork pies, no doubt.

'Better than the Panorama, this. Saw the River Nile there — like bein' in it, but then rivers is rivers. Not much go in panoramas. This, now. What a go is 'uman nature — all sorts, see. Cheap enough, too. Well, I must be off — came in fer a spot o' tea. I've a pickle somewhere — I like a treat.'

He wafted away, leaving a distinct odour of pickle and pork mingled with wax. Marat had not stirred.

Perhaps it had stopped raining. It was certainly time to go. Dickens had no wish to be locked in — certainly not with murderers, not even with the queen. He made to go just as another man emerged from a shadowy corner.

'Neck made for hanging, Mr Dickens — your pie-eating friend. A brute beast.'

Dickens was startled to see a face he knew, a white face like a mask in the gloom, the eyes glittering with what might have been rage. Poor pieman — enjoying his treat. He had seemed harmless enough, hardly deserving of such anger. This was a face he did not particularly want to see. Judge Fabian Quarterman — the hanging judge, they called him. A lot of jesting about drawing and quartering, but it was no joke if you were in the dock. Mr Quarterman generally gave no quarter, not even to strangers, it seemed. However, Dickens only said, 'He was certainly enjoying his tea.'

'Every face here has a face made for hanging.' A sneer and a twist about the lips.

Yours, too, Dickens thought, *for hanging others.* Something cruel in the long face, the thin mouth, and contempt in the long nose, sharp as the guillotine blade. The judge's relish for the hanging trade seemed on a par with the pieman's, despite his silk hat and his fine coat. Dickens took the proffered hand, very long and white and cold as marble. Oh, a gentleman, of course.

'Well, I don't suppose one wants them looking like next door.'

The judge laughed, a sort of dry bark with nothing like humour in it. 'Every one of them deserved it. I hanged Rebecca Smith, so to speak — as wicked a creature as I ever saw — and that wretched female Mary Ann Geering who murdered her husband. A harlot. All harlots. I have my own collection, Mr Dickens, my own artist in wax, much superior to these. I have a personal interest, of course.'

The morbid light of the chamber did nothing for the judge's long, pale face. His black-lipped mouth looked now like the trapdoor of the gallows — all the better to hang you with. His teeth were eerily sharp and yellow in the dark — all the better to eat you with. And those eyes — a glint of ice in the shadows, or glass. A waxwork come to life.

'Oh, indeed,' Dickens said. 'I suppose you would.'

'You must come to see them and take some sherry. My house is just round the corner in Manchester Square.'

'Certainly, certainly — when I have a free moment — I am rather occupied with —'

The strong grip on his arm seemed to compel him to the door. Perhaps the judge had not heard him. In the Grand Hall, he caught a glimpse of the pieman gazing reverently at the Sleeping Beauty, his pickle bulging in his cheek. And then they were going down the stairs.

He was going to take sherry then, it seemed, though he had no wish to visit more waxworks. He'd rather have taken a pie with the pieman. His honest relish had been amusing in its way. There was something rather chilling in the judge's relish for his hangings.

2: SLEEPING BEAUTY

Dickens was not surprised to find that the judge's house in Manchester Square was a gloomy sort of mansion at the corner of the square and separated from its neighbours by a rank-looking garden containing the most melancholy trees and evergreens weeping in the rain. It was very quiet, past the time of the watercarts and old clothes-men, and the organ-grinders and Punch show — though he did not think they would be visitors to the judge. The lamplighter had been, but his efforts were wasted near the corner house where the enfeebled rays seemed to shrink back into the shadows.

They passed into a cavernously chilly hall — he was surprised not to find the judge's own chamber of horrors exhibited there in the shadowy vastness. There was an expanse of dark floor like a trackless desert, and some dark pieces of furniture, spread out as though they dared not mingle. There were empty chairs on which no one ever sat, and various tables of different sizes — one at least for every month of the year — which appeared to serve no purpose, except the one that held a glass dome encasing some rather funereal wax flowers. They all looked as though they had no business there and were waiting for the auction man. There were a few dismal oil paintings seemingly of nothing but murky clouds and gloomy-looking turrets, and what might have been trees, but looked like more black clouds. The judge led him into his library, which did look as though a human being inhabited it rather than the castle spectre. There were a comfortable, leather sofa and two easy chairs by a fire which, however, seemed to cringe at the judge's approach. Nevertheless, Dickens was glad to see more coals put on.

'Sherry,' the judge said. It seemed to be an order and before Dickens could say 'yea' or 'nay', the judge went to a table set with decanters and Dickens looked about him. The glass-covered shelves contained law books by the hundred, all fat with custom and precedent, and cases, and judgements, and sentences — to death, no doubt. No novels, he saw, which was probably just as well. Dickens doubted the judge would appreciate his humorous portraits of the legal profession. On a side table close to the wall were displayed two dreadful casts of peculiarly swollen faces with a twitch about the nose. Taken from death — two hanged men. He was not going to ask who they were. A skull with leering eyes and long teeth completed the trio. He also saw a pair of manacles, a hand in bronze, a plaster cast of Courvoisier, a woodcut depicting an improbably hideous woman — a murderess, presumably — and a woodcut of Eliza Fenning, hanged for murder in 1815. At least she looked human. She had been innocent, as it turned out, too late. He stepped back sharply from something which looked like a piece of dried blue leather. He had a suspicion about that. It was well-known that the skin of the notorious body-snatcher, Burke, had been tanned, and the pieces sold. *Memento mori.* A museum of curiosities, indeed. Mausoleum, more like.

'Ah,' said the judge, 'my cabinet of curiosities. Burke's skin. Sir Walter Scott had a piece. I have the letters of various murderers, if you would care to see them. The skull is Rebecca Smith's — a harlot, of course.'

Dickens let him talk while he sipped his sherry, which would have been very fine if it had not tasted of wax — and, more horribly, of leather. The judge appeared no warmer in the firelight as he expiated on the wickedness of the murderers he had known and dispatched, ignorant, bestial things without which the world was a better place. The women were worst of all. Unnatural hags, every one. Those who excoriated the Law as a murderer were fools and knaves. Be damned to them. Sentimental dolts. The Law had every right to kill where evil had been done. Dickens wondered if the judge had read his own newspaper articles criticising the death penalty. However, it was obvious that he was not expected to reply. This was not a debate, so he offered no comment. The skull and the two death's heads were keeping their own counsel, too. Like the waxworks, looking at something behind him.

The judge rose suddenly to say that he would show Dickens his gallery. He took a bunch of keys from his pocket and chose one to open the door, then took a candle to light their way. Dickens followed his host into the next room, a long chamber, perhaps for dancing once — long ago. The judge turned up the gas lamps. Dickens thought that the room was like a theatre, for at the end was a collection of figures placed on two platforms, as if they were actors waiting for their cue. Actresses, though — they were all women, dressed in black and darkly veiled. They looked like the cast of some Jacobean revenge tragedy. Women in mourning. The groups faced each other, as if they were about to break into the chorus of lament which would begin the play.

If they could speak, perhaps they might explain the meaning of the object which was placed on a higher platform in the centre — something shrouded in black, surrounded by candles in branched candlesticks. The judge stepped up and lit the candles. The effect was certainly startling, if rather macabre. *A coffin?* he wondered. The judge came down to stand by him. His expression had something of triumph in it, though Dickens had kept his lips firmly closed to prevent any gasp escaping.

No doubt that whatever the judge had seen in his face had pleased him.

The judge moved forward to the group on the right. Dickens followed. When Quarterman lifted a veil, he recognised the face. Mrs Manning's chubby features and dark eyes. Hanged for murder. Another face revealed. Sarah Chesham, another murderess. Hanged, too. Judge Quarterman had condemned her. She had been a coarse-looking woman with a big nose in a big face. The nose was large, certainly, and the hair an indifferent brown. Mrs Manning's hair was arranged in glossy ringlets as it had been in life. Rebecca Smith, he thought, as another face was unveiled — she whom the judge had condemned for the murder of her children. He had only seen a crude woodcut in the newspaper. But she was recognisable with her narrow-lipped mouth and a nose like a razor blade. Two other faces he didn't recognise — both unprepossessing, one downright terrifying in its ugliness. A big bruiser of a woman who might have murdered a regiment of dragoons. Odd company, the judge kept. Perhaps the judge had condemned these two. He'd been doing it for years.

They were well done, skilfully modelled and painted, but they all looked the same. No, not exactly, he thought — they had different features, it was true, but there was a blankness about them, an indifference that was unnerving. And something disturbing about the eyes, staring at the opposite group with a kind of cruel glitter. Well, they were murderesses.

'What do you say to my artist? Superior to Madame Tussaud?'

'They are very well done.'

The judge guided him to the other group. Dickens steeled himself not to shudder at the grip of the bony hand on his arm. Did the man think he was going to run out screaming? He wouldn't give him the satisfaction, and, despite himself, he was curious to see what faces would be revealed. But when the veils were removed from the two at the front, he saw identical heads, faces blank with expressionless staring eyes this time. Just dolls in black dresses. He thought there were perhaps three more in the next row and another couple close together in the darkness behind, but who they were he had no idea.

'Well?' the judged asked.

Dickens didn't think these were much to look at. 'They look — like next door, I suppose. Who are they meant to be?'

'Harlots, they were, all of them.' The word came out as a cold sneer. 'Eliza Collier,' the judge continued, pointing to a figure at the front of the group, 'a harlot, rightly punished for her depravity.'

Dickens knew the name of Eliza Collier, who had been poisoned by oxalic acid earlier in the year. The man she had lived with had been brought to trial but acquitted for lack of evidence — the defence lawyers had asserted that she had committed suicide, having been known for periods of deep melancholy. The evidence that her lover had been a drunk and a brute to her did not, it seemed, count for anything. Eliza Collier was a victim.

'But she might have been —'

Quarterman was pointing to the second black-clad figure. 'Eliza Winton, another trollop, a drab.'

Dickens was going to protest that the last-named Eliza had been a victim of her seducer and the hired abortionists who had been tried for her murder, but the judge was pointing to another figure, this one with her veil down.

'A married woman, going abroad in the night, in all her finery, to meet her paramour. A trollop who broke the sacred vow of marriage, and the rest of them, all Elizas, all deceivers, flaunting themselves, selling themselves —' spittle on the thin lips, a gleam of mad rage in the eyes — 'murderers of decency, of the home, of what is right and dutiful.'

The man was mad, Dickens thought, as the judge snatched at the veils of one figure after another. Pretending these dolls were the women he hated, murderesses and victims alike. Ice crept at his neck when he thought which women Quarterman had sent to their deaths because he loathed them. He felt as if he were suffocating — the judge too close to him again, hatred emanating from him as steam from damp clothes, a graveyard smell.

'It has been most interesting, sir, but I must be away. I had not meant to be out so long. My wife —'

'Can you trust her?'

Dickens masked his anger with a fixed smile. 'Certainly, I can. You must excuse me —' But the judge was in his way, that lean, black form towering over him and his breath on his face. Hot breath, that glittering venom in his eyes compelling him to be as mad and bitter as himself. Even the dolls seemed to come too close, their eyes seeming almost alive and somehow knowing. Dickens thought he heard the rustle of a dress in the darkness beyond, but they were all still as statues when he looked again.

'One more,' the judge whispered, 'one more, Mr Dickens. A masterpiece, sir — here.' He mounted the central platform and removed the black cloth. 'Come, see my beauty.'

'Sleeping Beauty,' Dickens said involuntarily. She was. He saw a finely modelled, delicately tinted face, a pale forehead and perfectly arched brows. She looked young and innocent. Her hair was fair and held back from her forehead by a ribbon, though the curls lay on the shoulders of her white silk dress. And there must have been the same mechanism as at Madame

Tussaud's, for her breast seemed to rise and fall. The colour was better than at Madame's, but that might have been the warm candlelight which surrounded her.

'Would you not deem she breathed?'

'"Beauty's ensign yet is crimson on thy lips and in thy cheeks."' Dickens couldn't stop himself quoting; she was like Juliet on her bier. Then he wished he had not spoken.

'Mine, mine. Mine now.'

Dickens heard the greed, the longing, the desire, and saw it in the thin face leering over the sleeping form. Surely, even her eyelids fluttered. And the lips — you knew that Madame Tussaud's Beauty was wax. She was old, thought to have been made in Paris fifty or more years ago, representing Madame St. Amaranthe, guillotined by Robespierre. But you really could believe this young woman was living, her full lips slightly parted. Dickens turned away, feeling like an intruder. He should not be gazing on a sleeping stranger. He took the chance to step away from the judge so that he was free to go.

'A masterpiece,' the judge breathed hoarsely, closing the curtain.

'Yes, yes,' Dickens replied, 'too real, perhaps. What was she? Murderer or victim?'

'Both.'

Dickens was glad to be out of the front door, to which he had hurried with the judge on his heels — and with what he knew was somewhat rude haste. Not that he cared. The man was mad. He had declined more sherry and had bidden the judge farewell with as much courtesy as he could muster.

He took a few deep breaths to get some air into his lungs — cold now, but it wasn't raining. The stars were out and there was a refreshing crispness in the air. He heard the nearby church clock chime and he paused to count the strokes. Good Lord. Eight o'clock. He opened the gate and stepped into the square. A glance back showed him the house in darkness, those crouching bushes and skeleton trees. He imagined how one day, the trees and bushes would encroach on the house, concealing it completely, and the judge would be found dead in his dolls' gallery, still leering over his Sleeping Beauty. *Bluebeard's Castle*, he thought. And then it struck him. Did the judge not have any servants?

Not his business. Time to go home. He looked across the gaslit square. A cab was drawing up on the other side, a muffled face at the window then gone. He heard footsteps behind him as he walked away. He glanced back to see a man and a veiled woman, who seemed to be leaning upon her companion. They paused at the judge's gate. Not his business, either. He hurried on.

A wax doll on the stairs slightly unnerved him as he closed the front door of Tavistock House. The house seemed eerily quiet. Just him and that unblinking creature on the stairs with its smooth wax face and pink lips. It seemed to look down upon him, keeping its secrets like those others. He resisted an impulse to run at it, to frighten it out of its complacency, for it might be someone's darling. He ignored it as he went up to his study.

There was a fire still going, and decanters and glasses winking in the light. Lord, he was frozen to the bone. He poured himself some brandy and stood by the fire. The house was very quiet. He felt as if he had returned from another world — a place of shadows, of ghosts, of creatures poised between life and death, waiting to decide one way or the other. He imagined that doll making up its mind to go downstairs on its little booted feet, shaking its flounces from their long sleep, putting on a bonnet and pelisse, and simply going out of the front door and never coming back.

He tossed back his brandy. Nonsense. What was he thinking? He couldn't stop himself. He went out to look down the stairs. Damn it — the doll was gone.

He went into the drawing room, which was empty. Where was everyone? Then he saw her. Someone had placed the doll in a child's chair, and there she sat, still gazing with that smirking air of self-satisfaction. One of the maids had picked it up, probably.

Time, he thought. Where on earth? Oh, Lord, the pantomime. That was where they all were — where he should be. He had forgotten. No wonder he felt guilty. That wretched man, Quarterman and his grotesques. Damnation — and he'd promised. Not too late — he might make it for the second half. He turned to go just as a voice said, 'Papa.' Dear Lord, who the devil? He turned, but there was only Mistress Simper leaning forward. He remembered — she had two words and 'papa' was one. 'Good night,' he said and flew downstairs.

John Thompson, his manservant, materialised in the hall. 'Oh, I beg pardon, sir, I didn't know you were here.'

'I shouldn't be. Find a cab, John, to Drury Lane.'

3: A MISFORTUNE OF ELIZAS

Dolly, it seemed, was everywhere. Now, however, at breakfast, she did not look quite so pleased with herself, nor had she anything to say. Someone had removed the flounces and the ringlets had been much disarranged. There was a good deal of waxy chest showing. No boots, either. Just little wooden feet — stumps, really.

'Betsey,' Dickens's daughter Mamie announced, 'I'm making new clothes. I'm giving her to Lally for her birthday. She likes the name Betsey.'

'Trotwood?' he enquired.

'Silly Pa, Miss Trotwood's an old lady. Just Betsey.'

'Prig,' Katey said.

Mamie did not condescend to answer. Dickens turned his laugh into a cough. Prig, indeed. Betsey Prig was Mrs Gamp's nursing friend, and very unprepossessing, being deep of voice and bearded. Katey Dickens was watching him with a wicked glint in her eye; she had no time for dolls and when she did, there was a fierce discipline to be meted out. Katey had probably left Betsey Prig on the stairs in the hope that she might tumble to her death.

Rather cheered by Betsey Prig's fall from serene perfection, Dickens went into his study. The queer sensations of the previous night had subsided. He had made it to the pantomime, slipping into the box and taking his seat behind his friend, Mark Lemon, whose bulky form obscured his entrance. All other eyes were on the stage, those of Catherine, his wife, Lemon's wife, Nelly, his two daughters, Lally and Betty, and his own Mamie and Katey. He hadn't missed much. E. L.

Blanchard's usual star-crossed lovers, Prince Bluecap and Princess Saccharina, had overcome their trials in the shape of a cruel father and the wicked rival, Grimgruffin. Mechanical dancing fairies had intervened. A talking dog and various vegetable characters, including King Cauliflower, had played their parts against a background of grottoes, caves, and palaces. Tiptop had been the verdict of his party, and no one had commented on his late arrival.

And John's appearance in the hall last night and the maid tidying up had explained the disappearance of the doll. The judge was welcome to his dolls. Dickens would not be going for sherry again.

He set about his letters before he went to his office in Wellington Street. Mrs Gaskell first. He had some explaining to do about a ghost story he had written which had just been published in *The Keepsake* — a promise to a friend. The tale had been inspired by a story told to him by Mrs Gaskell about a woman haunted by a face. He had stolen the idea, he'd have to admit that, but, after all, ghost stories were common property. He'd written one about a man who'd seen the ghost of his twin brother, a story which his friend, Doctor Elliotson, had appropriated for a book about the processes of the human mind. Dickens had assured Elliotson that the story was true. Strange things happened; it was not entirely surprising that a grieving brother should see the ghost of his twin. A twin would be your other self, surely. A phantom of the mind.

Who could say what lay in the mysterious recesses of the mind? He thought of the case of the artist, Ferrars, which he and Superintendent Jones had investigated. Ferrars, from Venice, a man who was obsessed by a woman with red-gold hair, a man whose mind was so possessed by this memory that he went mad. Dickens had seen how the man had not known what he was doing — as if he were in some trance-like state in which his rational mind slept and some unconscious mind took over. Madness, possession — Judge Quarterman, obsessed by the women he had dispatched to the gallows. There was a study for Elliotson.

Not that Quarterman was any business of his just now. He needed to write to Mrs Morson at the home in Shepherd's Bush. He'd arranged for a young woman called Eliza Clayton to be taken in from Coldbath Fields prison. It was an unusual case. Eliza Clayton was a widow and somewhat educated. More so than most of the young women at the home, who were generally illiterate. She was a proficient seamstress and could embroider, and he thought she deserved a chance. He'd thought of the actress, Eliza Clayton, now appearing at the Princess's Theatre to great acclaim, and there was her namesake, so humble and grateful. Miss Coutts would not want a widow, but he'd have to persuade her.

And there was the key for Frank Stone, his next-door neighbour. He took the key from his desk drawer and wrote a note explaining that it was the Right-of-Way key for the garden … *a Bluebeard sort of enclosure, but perfectly…*

He was going to write 'harmless'. Odd how the Bluebeard image had come again. Judge Quarterman and that Bluebeard's castle in Manchester Square were haunting him. Like the bill which lay on his desk from Cubitt, the builder, for the repairs to Tavistock House, so long that it would take Babbage's Calculating Machine to work it out. He composed a note to Superintendent Sam Jones at Bow Street, confirming that they would dine at The Ship in Gate Street that evening, and wrote an order to Mr Ellis for some dozens of bottles of port. And then it was time to go to the office in Wellington Street. The house was quiet. No one was seated on the stairs.

At Wellington Street the newspapers were laid out for him. The front page of *The Morning Post* gave an account of the triumphal progress of Louis Kossuth, the Hungarian revolutionary, now a refugee, touring England and greeted rapturously as an advocate of freedom for the working classes. Kossuth, whose fame was such that his waxen effigy was already on display at Madame Tussaud's. Not, of course, in the Chamber of Horrors. No rapturous cheers for poor Eliza Smith — that was a scandalous story from the St. Pancras Workhouse where the young woman had died of tuberculosis and the workhouse master had been accused of violating her person, as the report had it.

The ladies were out in force, he noticed, with their new works. Mrs Trollope's *Family Mysteries* in three volumes; Miss Jewsbury's *Marian Withers*, in three volumes, too — he liked Miss Jewsbury. She'd written for *Household Words*. He had asked her for more, but she was proving elusive. Miss Jewsbury's friend, the poet, Eliza Cook, was advertising her weekly *Journal*.

Time he was out in force with his new novel — the first number scheduled for February. Too soon to be advertising. He'd wait until he was certain of the title. Never mind Miss Cook's *Journal*. Time, too, that he got on with the Christmas number of *Household Words*.

He folded the newspaper but was stopped by the copy of *The Globe* beneath. Good Lord, it seemed that every packet ship, brig, barque, collier, sailing ship and steamer was named *Eliza*, if not *Eliza Ann*. The world was suddenly full of Elizas, and they were, indeed, an unlucky tribe. Eliza Bigge had murdered her only child, Eliza Cooper had been charged with keeping a brothel, and here was a phrase to conjure with — *Eliza Jordan,*

31

a nymph of the pave, was placed at the bar before the Lord Mayor on a charge of stealing a watch…

The nymph, described as a haggard young woman of twenty-five, denied the charge, swore she had never met the victim, who must have mistaken her for someone else, claimed she was innocently strolling along another pavement entirely, and was remanded — to a sylvan grotto in Coldbath Fields prison, probably along with the other wood nymphs and water sprites whose fairy qualities were usually heavily disguised under layers of paint and garish satin. He could well imagine what the grim old judge might have made of Eliza, the nymph, and of the missing Eliza Irwin whose indignant husband had inserted a notice in the newspaper to the effect that he would not be held responsible for any debts she might contract. She had deserted her hearth and her husband — the tone of the notice suggested that Mr Irwin was not a man of easy temper —

Good Lord, Eliza. Quarterman's wife had been an Eliza. It had been years ago — twelve or more. He hadn't known the judge then, but there had been gossip that she had left him for a lover, only weeks after their wedding. However, she had never been found. He thought about the judge's Sleeping Beauty. Was she Eliza Quarterman restored to him in wax? She would never run away again.

4: A DREADFUL FACE

'Amen to that,' Dickens said, raising his glass to Superintendent Jones at The Ship tavern, where they were having a snug little dinner, as Dickens called it. Little was hardly the word, since after a gargantuan leg of braised lamb with oysters — enough for ten strong men — Mr Stagg had brought in the apple pudding and cream, to which they could not do any kind of justice.

The occasion was the satisfactory conclusion of what Dickens called The Elephant Case. His "amen" had been in response to Superintendent Jones's heartfelt wish that the jury would be convinced by the evidence and send the perpetrator of the murders to perdition where he belonged. He had shown no remorse. Two elephants which had been passing along the quayside at St. Katharine's Dock, minding their own business, had found themselves embroiled with a key witness.

'And long life to our pachyderm collaborators,' he said.

'Amen to that, too.'

'A night out, Mr Jones, is what is called for.'

Jones noted a sly smile and a mischievous glint in Dickens's eyes. *What now?* 'This is a night out.'

'Ah, but I had an idea — a treat for Posy, for Scrap, for Eleanor and Tom, your Elizabeth, Sergeant Rogers and Mollie. Elephants at Astley's, I wondered. I should like to see the happy couple again.'

'I've had enough of wild beasts. Thank you, all the same.' A violent gang of feral boys had been accomplices to the murderer, and particularly obstructive.

'*Box and Cox* at the Adelphi Theatre? Two gentlemen mired in a comedy of errors.' Jones groaned. 'No mires, then. Ah, well, let me see. *The Road to Ruin* at The Olympic? *Circumstantial Evidence* at The Strand Theatre — very good reviews —'

Jones laughed. 'You're making this up.'

'The newspaper, Mr Jones. All there, as true as the steamship timetables.'

'Don't remind me. All that chasing about the docks — like herding cats, trying to round up those women.'

'Not *Dick Whittington*, then, at Sadler's Wells? *Harlequin Charley* at The City of London — opens in a dismal swamp, apparently, the abode of the Demon Vice.'

'I've had enough of vice and swamps, too, and mires, now I think of it.' They had spent a night on some freezing marshes in pursuit of the murderer.

'Waxworks, then. Five bloomer costumes on display. Something for the girls. For the boys — Chamber of Horrors is still sixpence.'

'"I have supp'd full —"'

'Droll, Mr Jones, so not *Macbeth*, but these children deserve a show of some kind.'

'Oh, all right. *Harlequin Charley* — for your sake.'

'A hit, a very palpable hit, Samivel. But my preference is for —'

They were never to know what Dickens's preference would be, for the door opened and an apologetic Rogers came in. 'Sorry, sir, sorry, Mr Dickens —'

'What?' Jones asked.

'Suspicious death, sir, Sir Fabian Quarterman.'

'Good God, the judge,' Dickens said. 'I know him — I —'

'Why do you need me?' Jones asked.

Rogers looked uncomfortable. 'Someone saw Mr Dickens going into the house with the judge last evening. I thought if there was anythin' suspicious, you'd want to know.'

Jones looked at Dickens. 'Oh, I do. Prime suspect, eh? That's handy. Knew him well, did you?'

'No, I didn't, and he was alive when I left him — well, as much as one could ascribe life to the man. How did he die?'

'Well, that's it, it's hard to say — I mean, there are no signs of a struggle. He wasn't stabbed or shot. You'll have to see for yourselves. It's his face. I don't know — looks like a man what was frightened to death.'

The waxen ladies turned on him? Dickens wondered as he paid the bill and then hurried to catch up with Jones and Rogers. The Beauty recalled to life. He shivered when he thought of that and remembered his idea that the judge would one day be found dead, still leering over his doll.

On the way to Manchester Square, Rogers explained that the judge's housekeeper, Mrs Flint, had returned this evening from a visit to her sister in Lambeth. She had let herself in as usual by the back door. Nothing was different in her kitchen, except that she noticed that the judge had not been served his tray of cold cuts — she had left instructions that the girl she sometimes employed would take up the tray to the dining room at seven o'clock, and then she could go home and return in the morning to cook breakfast for the judge. It was a long-standing arrangement — the girl, Pruey, was a good girl. Slow, but reliable. She lived with the laundress who did for the household, one Ma Dunk —

'Never!' Dickens said.

Rogers grinned. 'What she said. Course, I didn't question it in the circumstances.'

'No other live-in servants beside Mrs Flint?' Jones asked.

'No — the judge didn't need much looking after, it seems. Very sparin' in his habits. Didn't like strangers and left the household matters to Mrs Flint. She wasn't that surprised about the supper — he didn't always eat regular. He hadn't told her he didn't want breakfast, but, again, he might have made another arrangement. He sometimes went out early. Liked a long walk, apparently. Never told her what he was doin' or where he was goin' an' she didn't ask.'

'No one there when you visited, Charles?'

'No, I remember thinking it was odd, but then the whole place is odd. He has his own waxworks museum. I met him at Tussaud's, and he invited me to view his collection.'

'Where he was found, Mr Dickens — queer business. Them figures, they're all —'

'I know, Rogers, but we'll let Mr Jones see for himself.'

The judge lay as if he had fallen just at the end of the Beauty's dais, his nightcap askew, and his nightgown stained with vomit. Dickens thought how absurd he looked — fallen from the dais and from the icy heights of his lawyer's dignity. The waxwork women all seemed to be leaning forward, looking down at the fallen man — they looked like a gaggle of gossips at a street accident. If the superintendent said, 'Come along ladies, make room,' he thought they would scuttle away.

He went to look, and almost recoiled from the face he saw beneath him. The judge was not leering now — the mouth was open in a snarl of terror, the eyes wide and staring, the skin cold and grey as ashes. What on earth had he seen? Dickens looked at the Beauty and gasped.

'What?' Sam Jones asked.

'The Beauty — that's what he called her,' Dickens said, pointing to the recumbent figure. 'Her eyes are open. She was asleep —' he saw Jones's startled look — 'I mean her eyes were closed as if — well, she looked — you know that figure at Tussaud's, the one that seems to breathe?' Jones nodded. 'She was like that. It just startled me — as if she'd seen him.'

'Perhaps he opened them — some mechanism, like the breathing one?'

'She's not breathing now,' Dickens realised. 'Someone tampered with it? It looks different now — just a doll. She looked all too real last night.'

'Was the door to this room locked?' Jones asked the sergeant.

'No,' Rogers said, 'but the front door was locked. Mrs Flint checked after she found him. See, she came upstairs from the kitchen to find out if the judge was home, still puzzled by the tray and no sign of breakfast having been made. She went into the library and saw the sherry glasses and then the open door to the —'

'Chamber of horrors,' Jones said, looking about him. 'Did he lock the door when you left this room?' he asked Dickens.

'I don't remember. I was so intent on getting away from him and his dolls.'

'What time did you leave?'

'At eight o'clock. And he locked the front door. I heard him. Then I went out into the square. I saw a couple pause at the gate. Are they the ones who saw me?'

'It was a neighbour who saw you going in.'

'There was a cab, too. I noticed someone looking out, just a face muffled up, but I couldn't tell if it were man or woman.'

'The judge — was he ill?' Jones asked, as he stared down at the body. It was true there was no sign of a struggle. *Apoplexy?* he wondered.

'No — just mad. You know who these figures represent?'

Jones shone his lamp on the nearest. Dickens almost gasped again. For a moment, he thought she looked — well, gloating somehow. The mouth looked different. More open, as if she were about to throw back her ringleted head and laugh uproariously. The lamp moved and the impression was gone.

'Mrs Manning, I believe, and this is —' Jones moved his lamp to another figure, and Dickens thought he caught a glint in Sarah Chesham's eye — you couldn't catch the eye of a waxwork — 'Sarah Chesham. The judge sentenced her to death, I remember.'

'Yes, and these two —' Dickens turned to the opposite blank-faced group, on which Jones shone his lamp. All the veils were raised. 'Supposed to be Eliza Collier and Eliza Winton.'

Jones stared at him. 'But they were victims of injustice. Eliza Collier was probably poisoned by her common law husband, and poor Eliza Winton — she died because of a botched abortion. The man who seduced her and arranged it got away with it. What's it all about?'

'It was as if he hated them; he seemed enraged by them, and he had no pity for the victims. All harlots, he said. He had a woodcut of Eliza Fenning among his collection of death masks. She was innocent. He had a bit of Burke's skin on display out there in the library.'

'Dear Lord, that's grotesque. What about this one — the Beauty?'

'I wondered if she were to do with his wife. I remembered this morning that about twelve years ago, he married a young woman, thirty years or more younger than he. Eliza something or other. The story was that she left him after mere weeks of marriage — went off with a young man. Nothing heard of her again.'

'Who was she?'

'I don't remember, except that she was called Eliza. Hence the victims here. He said they had murdered decency and duty. The Beauty was murderess and victim.'

'What do you remember about the couple you saw?'

'Veiled woman, leaning on the man. I didn't pay much attention; I just wanted to get home. His wife, I wonder if she —'

'Has come back after twelve years? Bit of a leap, Mr Charles Dickens, even for you. What'd she come back for?'

Dickens thought of the faces he had just seen. They knew what had happened — dumb witnesses. They couldn't tell, but they knew. 'Revenge,' he said.

Jones raised his eyebrows, 'You think someone did for him?'

'Look at his face. I wouldn't be surprised if one of these sprang to life to see him off. This place gives me the shivers. It's like being surrounded by ghosts.'

Jones looked at the figures. True, they looked a bit eerie in the dim light, but as for coming to life, it was just the thing a novelist would think of. He turned to practicalities. 'We'll have to see what the doctor says about cause of death. You've sent for someone, Rogers?'

'Yes, sir, Mrs Flint's gone for a Doctor Yarwood — lives across the square. The judge's doctor is in Wimpole Street — not that he ever saw much of him, according to Mrs Flint. Just a check-up now and again.'

'Doctor Yarwood can give us a preliminary verdict. Apoplexy, I'm wondering.'

They heard footsteps outside and Mrs Flint ushered in a cheerful, brisk-looking man of middle years who stopped at the threshold, looking at the pageant of figures.

'Good Lord,' he said, 'what's this all about?'

'You didn't know the judge?' asked Jones.

'Only by sight — not the sociable type, but I'd heard he had some sort of macabre collection of waxworks. Bit grim, ain't it? Let's have a look, then.'

Doctor Yarwood examined the corpse. 'Nothing to say how he died — no wounds. Apoplexy, I should think.'

'Would that make him vomit?'

'It can do.'

'The expression on his face. What do you think of that?' asked Dickens.

'Well, the acute pain of a seizure, say, might well contort the features at the moment of death. If he was looking at this lot — that's Mrs Manning, isn't it? Peculiar things to keep about you. Still, it takes all sorts. He's quite cold. Rigor mortis starts at the face, so that may well explain the expression. It's difficult to say when he died. It usually begins three hours after death, and he's quite cold and stiff now, so we can guess at twelve hours ago or more, which would make it —'

Jones looked at his watch. 'About six o'clock in the morning, or earlier.'

'In the small hours, yes, or even midnight. It's not possible to be certain, I'm afraid. No one in the house to give you more information?'

'No, he was alone in the house — as far as we know. His housekeeper had time off. She only came back a couple of hours ago.'

'Nasty shock for her.'

'It was. Seizure, you think?'

'Probably, but a full post-mortem will tell you more — if he's been poisoned, for example, which might account for the vomit. I can't tell you that. I'll leave you to it.'

With that, he bade them a breezy farewell. Rogers was detailed to speak to Mrs Flint about the girl, Pruey, and why she hadn't served the cold cuts for the judge's dinner and hadn't made his breakfast. He would also arrange for the mortuary van to take the corpse to Doctor Woodhall at the hospital in Portugal Street. Jones continued to look at the contorted face on the ground, wondering about poison and anyone who might have cause to loathe the judge. There were plenty, probably.

Dickens was staring at the victim figures. 'I think there's one missing from the victims' side.'

'What?'

'I thought there were two at the front, then another three and two close together at the back, where there's just one now.'

'Are you sure?'

'There wasn't much light, so maybe I'm wrong. They were all veiled.'

'Did the judge tell you who made them?'

'Not Madame Tussaud, but there are plenty of wax artists about. I saw the Montanari wax figures at the Great Exhibition, but I shouldn't think Mr Montanari would be making murderesses or victims. He's moved his exhibition to Charlotte Street. Plenty of visitors, I should think. He was a medal winner. There's Pierotti in Oxford Street — they display life-sized models. Sarti's in Regent Street — he of the Moorish Venus. Grimaldi at Greenwich Fair and beyond — the Croydon Fair's on now. Always waxworks there.'

'Waxwork exhibitions in Lambeth and Southwark, wax doll warehouses, tailor's dummies, milliners' models — dear Lord, there's any number and everywhere. Not that it matters, unless we find out that he was murdered.'

'Someone could have been here.'

'We can't prove that. The house doors were locked. The judge was in his own waxwork museum, and he died there, and we can't say for certain when he died.'

'What was he doing down here in his nightclothes?' Dickens asked, but then he answered his own question. 'Mad. I wouldn't be surprised if he spent nights down here just gazing at them.'

'And you can't say for definite that there is one figure missing.'

'True, Mr Jones. The whole thing is unnerving. Maybe I'm imagining things — that meeting with him was a chilling business. Very unsettling, and this lot — I keep thinking they're going to walk out.'

'Perhaps your missing one did,' Jones joked.

'Don't,' said Dickens, thinking of Betsey Prig eyeing him beadily from the stairs.

'We'll see what Doctor Woodhall has to say. If it was a seizure, then there's nothing more we can do, even if he did have a late-night visitor — other than you, of course.'

5: OF WILLS AND CODICILS

The verdict of the court on the sudden death of Judge Fabian Quarterman was "Visitation of God". Doctors Yarwood and Woodhall had agreed that there was nothing suspicious about the death. Doctor Woodhall explained in some detail that the cause of apoplexy was the accumulation of phlegm in the viscera, which accumulation might stagnate in the cranium where it caused a softening of the brain. Dickens wasn't at all surprised at that — softening of the brain was about right. Doctor Woodhall further explained that an apoplectic seizure would be characterised by the cessation of the function of the senses and of voluntary movement. The judge's own doctor from Wimpole Street — another brisk individual — had confirmed that he rarely saw the judge and when he had last seen him, over a year ago, he had been his usual uncommunicative self. There had been nothing to show that anything was wrong with him. Nothing was said about the expression on the judge's face. Sam Jones had been present at Doctor Woodhall's post-mortem and had reported to Dickens that the dead man's face had been simply a dead man's face, all trace of terror gone.

'The sudden onset of pain and rigor, as Doctor Yarwood thought,' Jones had told him. 'The law is quite clear on the matter. Homicide can only be attributed if the death results from bodily injury, occasioned by some act — by force, or by poison, or by some mechanical means. It doesn't matter what he looked like.'

Mrs Flint gave her evidence, as did Pruey, the hired girl, who explained rather haltingly that she had taken up the tray to the dining room. She had heard voices in the library, so she'd taken it back down. When she heard the front door close, she thought the visitor must have gone so she took it up again. The judge was in the hall and told her he didn't want anything, and she needn't worry about breakfast as he would be leaving the house early next morning. Then he went upstairs. She had nothing to say about the judge's demeanour — the word defeated her. 'Was he behaving in an unusual way?' counsel simplified. She didn't see much of 'im, couldn't rec'llect if she'd ever spoke to 'im. Didn't think nothin' about 'im. When recalled, Mrs Flint agreed that the judge sometimes left his food, did not have much of an appetite, and did sometimes change his plans. It was not for her to question his ways.

Dickens merely reported his meeting with the judge at Madame Tussaud's and his tour of the judge's waxwork gallery. No, he had had no idea if the judge were ill. He had seemed well enough, though Dickens did not know him intimately. He did not mention his idea that one wax figure was missing.

'Best left that way,' Jones said, after the verdict was brought in. 'There's no point in fuelling speculation and rumour. The newspapers are full of lurid details about his waxworks. Quite a few have offered Mrs Flint money to let them have a look round.'

'Has she?'

'She says not, but who knows? In any case, the newspapers always find things out somehow, and we don't know who's been in that house over time. Doctor Yarwood knew, so maybe the doctor's wife, maid, boot boy, dog. Anyway, it's over and I'm quite prepared to accept "Visitation from God".'

'The Devil, more like,' Dickens responded.

'No evidence of that, I'm glad to say. And unless a black-gowned waxwork comes calling to confess, then it's over.'

'Droll, Samivel, very droll, but you're right.'

'Back to Bow Street for me. A little matter of a double murderer nicely tucked up in the cells. I'm hoping that Constable Stemp has loomed over him menacingly enough for a confession.'

While Superintendent Jones was listening to a murderer's confession to the killing of his employer and the assistant who had tried to intervene, Dickens was thinking about arsenic and the number of murders by that poison in the last few years, the subject of his article for *Household Words*. Poisoning, a fiendishly sophisticated means of murder, he'd always thought, especially when the poison was administered over a period of time. Mrs Barber, for instance, had got her brother to purchase arsenic, which she'd then given to her husband by degrees. Mrs Hathway, landlady of the Fox beerhouse, had done likewise — a lot of wives were murdering their husbands, it seemed. Mrs Mary Ham had married suspiciously quickly after the death of her husband. Mrs Cage, too, had been remanded for the poisoning of her spouse. Granted, husbands were also doing it. The seventy-year-old Mr Harris had murdered three wives, but here were Ann Fisher and Catherine Foster, both handy with the white powder. Mrs Foster had administered arsenic to her husband after only three weeks of marriage.

Dickens couldn't help thinking about Eliza Quarterman, that young wife who had fled after only weeks of marriage? Had she returned to Manchester Square? Obviously, she hadn't slipped the judge a glass of port laced with arsenic, but had she frightened him to death, a black-clad waxwork come to life in his chamber of horrors? And had she then opened the eyes of the Sleeping Beauty so that she could see the horror? Not, of course, that he knew that the veiled woman and her companion had gone into the judge's house. They'd paused at the gate, but that might not mean anything.

He thought of those figures. Mrs Manning gloating, the glint in Sarah Chesham's eye. Maybe the glass eye had briefly caught the light of Sam's lamp. And the rustle of a skirt. Perhaps he had imagined them. He hadn't mentioned those impressions, even to Sam Jones. He was still not sure if there had been one figure missing, and no one had found a black-clad waxen victim in Manchester Square. He supposed that someone could have slipped through the back garden with the figure in his arms. Unwieldy, though, and why would Eliza Quarterman or anyone else steal a waxwork figure? Unless you wanted your victim of injustice back?

Dickens gave up on murder for the time being and turned his attention to the scraps of advertisements from a German newspaper, submitted by a contributor. Light-hearted and amusing, just what was needed as an antidote to poison. 'Brighten it, brighten it,' were his watchwords to Harry Wills, his sub-editor. He couldn't help chuckling at the officer of state who wished to marry "a beautiful and accomplished lady with eight hundred florins." Very exact. What had the officer to offer the wealthy young lady? And, indeed, the same might be asked of the sixty-five-year-old Imperial Army officer who wished to marry "without hesitation". Ah, he was offering his pension of four guineas yearly. No wonder the "well reflecting persons" were required to pay the postage when replying — with all dispatch, of course. A suitor in a hurry.

Had the long-faced judge advertised for his bride? Dickens wondered. He could hardly imagine any very delicate wooing had gone on, nor could he imagine a young woman of fortune throwing her portion away on a cadaver. Still, it was a truth, he reflected, that many a disagreeable man succeeded in matrimony where a perfectly decent young man of moderate means might fail.

The evening brought a dinner at the Rainbow tavern in Fleet Street, where Dickens found himself seated next to Gilbert à Beckett, magistrate and author, who had recommended a poor tramping girl to Dickens's home for fallen women. À Beckett enquired after the girl's progress.

'A decided success — which I never doubted. She is even beginning to make out her letters and is most anxious to please. I catch her sometimes smoothing down her dress and looking in wonder at it, as if she cannot believe it is hers. I wish I could say the same about some of the others.'

'I saw that case of Martha Williamson — two months at the House of Correction.'

'I was sorry for it, but she was bent on absconding — and with two dresses and various other clothes. I don't think we could have done anything more with her.'

'Some — many, I suppose — you can't. I had a case yesterday of a young woman who had robbed a five-year-old child of its clothes. Left the poor creature nearly naked in an alley, and she'd done it before. Hard as nails. Not that the boys are any better. Fagin's gangs are still abroad.'

'In the wildernesses of Southwark, no doubt.'

'Wilderness is about right. It's a depressing business, all these abandoned children, young girls kidnapped into brothels, boys ensnared into robbery. Thirty-five houses were broken into by the so-called Window Gang. Most of them were about fifteen, and one was as young as twelve. Another lot, the Twentyman Gang, as they call themselves, were living under the railway arches — three were apprehended and the rest, the Lord knows where.'

'I sometimes think it surpasses all understanding. Crime, starvation, and misery in the richest city in the world.'

'And you'd like to think the higher classes would know better. There was a doctor who attempted to murder his wife — threatened to cut her throat and tried to strangle her. Only married a few weeks. A respectable young woman, very pretty and well-mannered, but he insisted that he had raised her from the gutter to the dignity of a lady.'

'Pity he wasn't a gentleman.'

'No, he wasn't. He was a brute.'

A few weeks again, thought Dickens. Here was an opportunity to ask about Quarterman. 'Did you know Quarterman?'

'Of him, of course. Died of apoplexy, I read. All that stuff about his waxworks in the papers — very odd. Mind you, he was a queer bird. Didn't have much heart. Awful to women, especially those who transgressed. He'd have made short work of Martha Williamson. Transported, she'd have been, as soon as you could say knife. If that poor tramping girl of ours had been up before him, he'd have had her down as a girl of low character — off to the House of Correction. Did you know him?'

'He showed me his waxworks — don't ask me how I came to be there. I didn't want to be, but somehow, he wouldn't take "no" for an answer.'

'Murderesses, the papers said.'

'Some were, but some were just blank faces. He kept pointing to them, telling me one was Eliza this and another, Eliza that, all victims of some injustice, and I remembered that his wife was called Eliza and that she left him.'

'I heard that story from a Doctors' Commons man who knew it all. I tell you, Dickens, it's an extraordinary tale. You could turn it into a novel — now he's dead, I might do it myself.'

'She might be alive. She was much younger, I believe.'

'Thirty years or more. She was about twenty-one, as I remember.'

'Grim — he was in his fifties. Not an attractive bridegroom, I shouldn't think, even twelve years ago. Who was she?'

'That's the remarkable thing,' à Beckett replied, filling their glasses. 'She was a foundling.'

'What? From Coram's?'

'The very same. However, when she married him, she was Eliza Clifford, taken in by Lady Julia Clifford, of Cleeve Abbey. She'd been left as an infant at the Foundling Hospital by her mother. I don't know the details, but as was the usual procedure, she was fostered out to a woman in Kent, to be returned to the hospital at the age of four or five to be educated and trained for service. However, Lady Julia, a benevolent sort of middle years, took a fancy to the child, a pretty little thing, apparently with something of breeding about her.'

Dickens could believe that when he thought of Quarterman's Sleeping Beauty — there had been delicacy and refinement in that almost living face. 'That was unusual, I think, from what I know of the hospital's system.'

'Lady Julia Clifford, Dickens, very well connected and charitable. I shouldn't think she'd brook any opposition.'

'I suppose not. Lady Julia became fond of her, I suppose.'

'She did, having only a son, but Lady Julia died when Eliza Clifford was about twenty-one and, unfortunately, Lady Julia's son and heir, Sir Henry, a miserly sort of fellow, found himself with a very pretty young woman he didn't want. Nor did his wife. Not a beauty, the wife, it was said, but she had money, of course. The plan was that Eliza should be sent to be a governess. Up to the north country, as far away as it was possible to send her.'

'And the judge stalked in, on the look-out for someone to raise to the dignity of being his wife.'

'Exactly. A complication for the heir was that his own son was rather too much interested in his pretty cousin — or whatever he called her. Now, an alliance with an orphan who really belonged to the Foundling Hospital was not what Clifford had in mind for his heir.'

'Didn't Lady Julia provide for her?'

'Some jewellery, but no annuity to support her, or cash legacy. Lady Julia died suddenly, so her intentions were never known. Perhaps the great lady assumed that her son would provide, or she liked the idea of an alliance between her grandson and Eliza. Whatever she assumed or wanted, Eliza got nothing to maintain her.'

'Did she return the young man's affections?'

'Not known.'

'But there was talk that she went off with a lover.'

'So there was, but young Mr Clifford married elsewhere. Daughter of a country gentleman down in Kent and a brewer. And you know what they say about brewers.'

'Never met a poor one.'

'I don't know why it should be a crack thing to be a brewer; but it is indisputable that while you cannot possibly be genteel and bake, you may be as genteel as never was and brew.'

'Avaricious crew, the Clifford heirs, it would seem.'

'I'd say so, but nothing to say that Lady Julia's grandson didn't keep up any clandestine relationship with Eliza.'

'What was said about her to the judge?'

Gilbert à Beckett laughed. 'No one dared. There was talk, of course. I mean, married for a matter of weeks and then she's gone. Never to be seen again.'

'He didn't murder her, did he?' Dickens thought about that hoarse voice that had said the law was right to murder when evil had been done.

'The story was that she had been seen with a young man in Kensington Gardens. That's how the love story got about, but no one mentioned murder. I suppose you're thinking of those wretched waxworks and all those murderesses.'

'Quarterman said that the Elizas were debauched and degraded and deserved their fate. Deserved to be murdered.'

'That's a chilling thought. Have you mentioned this to your friend, the superintendent?'

'No, I didn't think of it until now.'

'Well, the house in Manchester Square will be emptied and sold, I imagine, so if —' à Beckett grinned at him — 'if there is a skeleton mouldering in some gloomy cellarage tucked in with the judge's port…'

'You think it's a mad idea.'

'I grant you he was a very peculiar man, especially about women, but murder? Anyway, the case is closed. Natural causes, I read. If there is a skeleton in his cupboard —'

Dickens grinned back. 'Cellarage.'

'Wherever — the house clearance people will find it, and you can read it in the papers like the rest of us.'

They were joined by Dickens's friend, John Forster, and the talk turned to the interminable case in Chancery of Jennens v Jennens — Jennens, the richest commoner in England, had left a fortune fifty-five years ago and the arguments about who should get what were still going on.

'And the lawyers getting fat, and the immediate heirs dead and gone,' Dickens observed. His interest lay in the fact that the first chapter of his new book concerned the fictional case of Jarndyce v Jarndyce, but only John Forster knew that. Forster had acquired for him a pamphlet dealing with the Jennens case — every detail about the wrangling over the will pertinent to his own imaginings.

'Day?' he asked, picking up the threads of the talk, and hearing a name he knew.

'Charles Day — the blacking man,' à Beckett said, 'died in 1836 and left a fortune. Another case that's gone on for years.'

'Money to be made in blacking, I daresay, providing you don't have to dirty your hands.' Which the young Dickens had, pasting labels onto blacking pots for Mr Day's rivals, Warren's Blacking at Hungerford Stairs and The Strand. Forster knew about that, too.

'Charles Day had one daughter and three illegitimate sons. Perfect case for a lot of wrangling. The daughter eloped with some bounder called Horatio Clagett, who contested some codicil to the will. Charles Day was blind, so he couldn't have attested the codicil, or something of that kind. They're still at it. Seventy thousand pounds in costs so far. And all the servants and the blind people to whom he left money are still waiting for their pennorth.'

'Or dead in direst poverty, or labouring in some other blacking pit. The doom of English wills, eh?' Dickens thought of Eliza Quarterman again and Lady Julia who had not provided for her. If she were alive, she might inherit the judge's fortune. Dickens had no doubt that he had made one. He had been a lawyer. Jennens had been known as "the miser of Acton". Quarterman was probably the miser of Manchester Square.

'What have you for me for *Household Words*?' he asked à Beckett, wanting to change the subject, and rising to go.

'Ah, a pretty little tale of the vanishing orphan, perhaps.'

6: A BLANK CHILD

Clagett — what a name. Horatio after Nelson, Dickens supposed, and to mitigate the ridiculousness of the last name. A bounder after money, à Beckett had said, and Lady Julia Clifford's heir another miserly wretch; the grandson, a rake, perhaps, betraying the beautiful Eliza with the brewer's daughter. Eliza must have been illegitimate, or she would not have been placed at the Foundling Hospital.

Vanishing orphans, illegitimate children, contested codicils, forged wills, lovers separated, unsuitable marriages, secrets long kept, and people thought you made it up. You didn't need to. It was all in the papers every day. The novelist's job was to turn the eye of fancy on the tale, apply patient and continuous energy, and grind out sparks from the blade, however dull sometimes.

And grind he must, for he had his own tale of secrets to spin. Why, he hoped his readers would wonder, did the usually glacial Lady Dedlock faint at the sight of the handwriting on some papers brought by the lawyer, Mr Tulkinghorn, papers pertaining to the case of Jarndyce v Jarndyce?

"Faint," my Lady murmurs with white lips, "only that; but it is the faintness of death."

What is it that makes her feel as if death is upon her? Dickens thought. His eye of fancy conjured Lady Dedlock's fine face, not in its heyday, but still pretty enough to make her the cynosure of fashionable eyes, those fashionable eyes which follow her every stately gesture, who know her every move, but who do not know nor can yet guess at her secret. That secret whispered upon the tainted wind of Tom-All-Alone's, that fevered lane where Death peers in through the gaunt eyes of discoloured shutters and an unnamed man lies waiting for him.

Dickens put down his pen and shook the sand onto the blue paper. He looked at the name which gave him the subject of his next chapter. More secrets. Esther Summerson, the orphan of his book, was to appear very soon, brought up by a grave and strict godmother. Esther Summerson, who had never heard of a mama or papa. A blank child as yet, with no history written upon her. Nobody's child, according to English Law — the sins of the fathers visited upon the heads of their innocent children. And the mother's — her false step, the doom for herself and her child. He thought of Eliza Quarterman, a blank child received into the Foundling Hospital. Only then would she have been given a name.

Suddenly decisive, he went out, locked his study door, went downstairs, took his coat, hat, and stick, checked the weather, left his wounded umbrella behind, and was at the gates of Tavistock House in two minutes. He was stopped by the sight of a man on the other side of the road. He was back. The foreign gentleman with a beard who had persecuted him at Devonshire Terrace — a gentleman who left notes, signing himself "a fellow man", and asked on several occasions for twenty pounds. Dickens had thought he'd seen him off. Superintendent Jones's Constable Stemp had done the honours. Dickens had not cared to look, but whatever the timber-framed constable had done or said had evidently persuaded the foreign gentleman to depart — without his twenty pounds. Yet here he was again at Tavistock House. Mind, a lot of people knew where he lived. He was angry at himself for hesitating, but he had no wish to be accosted again. Just then a cab rolled up, and when it was gone, so was the bearded fellow. Someone else, probably. Just a man with a beard.

He walked briskly, bound for the Foundling Hospital where he hoped to see John Brownlow, the secretary whom he had known since he had lived in Doughty Street just round the corner from the foundlings and rented a pew in the hospital's chapel. John Brownlow's name had its echo in kindly Mr Brownlow, the rescuer of Oliver Twist — another orphan, another blank child whose name was not his own. John Brownlow had been a foundling, too, and had been given a new name. He had risen to become Secretary of the Foundling Hospital in 1849. A good man, who might be able to give him some information about Eliza Quarterman, though, of course, she might not have been an Eliza then.

His way took him into Great Coram Street, named after Thomas Coram, the sea captain who had begun it all. He'd had no children of his own but, moved by the plight of the thousands of destitute children in eighteenth-century London, he had fought Church and State to get his hospital started. Passing the Russell Institution, where Bakewell's new electric telegraph had been demonstrated a week or so ago, Dickens reflected that it was a pity someone couldn't have telegraphed that great dust heap of imbeciles in Westminster about the epidemic of scarlatina in the slums of Little Coram Street, where children were dying in hovels in which thirty or forty people were crammed into a few rooms, or they might have signalled the truth about the prostitution in Hunter Street and Brunswick Square where the nymphs of the pave plied their trade at the very gates of the hospital. Cholera was on the increase, too.

Orphans being made, he thought, with every step he took.

An hour later, Dickens found himself at the top of Essex Stairs, looking over the river to Southwark and thinking about the church of St Saviour, the name of which he had just seen on a metal token left with a three-month-old child once called Mary-Anne Benson, christened in the Foundling chapel as Eliza Scott, probably named, John Brownlow had told him, after the author, Walter Scott.

Such had been the practice in those days to give the foundling a virtuous name in the hope that in its future life that virtue would be maintained, assisted by the education given by the hospital school, and sustained by the regular and nourishing diet. The virtue of little Mary-Anne's mother had certainly been compromised, according to the record so meticulously kept. The woman asking for admittance of the infant submitted a petition to the hospital and was interviewed. She was required to name the father of her child and to give some idea of what had become of him — the petitioner must have been deserted, which the record showed was the case of Eliza's mother, Alice Benson. It was a familiar story. Seduced by a gentleman, she had claimed, a man who had promised marriage and simply vanished. His name was Alexander Marlowe. The enquiries of the then Treasurer's Clerk had confirmed Miss Benson's story that she was in respectable service in Nelson Square and that her employer had confirmed that Alexander Marlowe had lodged there. He had been a young gentleman of means, and she thought he had gone abroad. However, after little Eliza had been christened at the Foundling Hospital, nothing further had been heard of either parent, even though enquiries after a child's health could have been made at the hospital on Mondays.

Dickens thought of the scrap of material that had been with the token — a little bit of flowered cotton. A young woman's Sunday dress, perhaps, worn to walk out with the lover who had deserted her. Where had that hopeful girl in her best gown gone? He looked down at the scummy water slapping at the stairs. Into the river, as so many lost girls still did?

They had talked of Eliza's good fortune and the mystery of her subsequent disappearance, Mr Brownlow expressing his sadness at the outcome, and wondering if she might have been better served by returning to the hospital to be educated there. While Lady Julia lived, Eliza would have known a protected life, would have had the example of her benefactress to guide her, but an ambitious marriage perhaps was beyond her scope. A quiet life of charitable works might have been more fitting. The girls educated at the hospital were trained for industrious lives and taught to conduct themselves honestly and soberly.

To know their place, Dickens thought, but he didn't say so, merely observing that he supposed even some of the industrious girls might succumb to the temptations of the wicked world, though, of course, he had read the advice given to the foundlings as they were leaving to take up their lives of service, and he did not doubt that most of them heeded it.

Mr Brownlow agreed that most did. The hospital kept in touch with the foundlings to ensure that they were behaving as they should — though in the case of Lady Julia's protégée that had not been possible. Lady Julia had wished, it seemed to him, to erase Eliza's past. He did not know if this were a wise thing — the foundlings were taught never to be ashamed of their time at the hospital, but to thank the good Providence of the Almighty that they were taken care of, were able to lead useful lives, to be honest, laborious, and diligent. As they departed for their useful lives, they were advised always to behave justly and carefully, especially towards their master and his family. Some, of course, cast away their chances. He had heard only some months ago of a young woman who had left her employment and simply vanished. Yet her employer had treated her well.

Looking again at the swirling river, dark and unfathomable, racing to the freedom of the sea, Dickens reflected on the mysteries of human nature. Just as the river kept its secrets, so did every heart. He remembered the hospital chapel, seeing the orphans ranged tier by tier in their uniforms, each face too far away to tell one from another, just pale ovals in the half-light. It was all very well to think of each blank child waiting submissively for the impress of duty, obedience, and usefulness to be hammered into it like the image of the church on a tin token, but suppose that heart raged within, hated submission and bore it only until its chance came to fight for its freedom. Such was the case with some of the girls from the home in Shepherd's Bush. He thought of red-haired Isabella Gordon, long departed — full of fire, but not to be tamed. But she had come from prison, so it was not so surprising. Mr Brownlow's missing girl had had the long years of the hospital's teaching, yet, released from confinement into yet another servitude, she had broken free.

And what of Eliza Quarterman? Had she, too, exchanged one servitude for another? And had she then broken free to vanish like the other foundling because the judge had wanted a wax doll for a wife, to mould to his own design, a toy to say only, 'Yes, sir,' at his command? She had escaped him, and he had replaced her with a waxwork figure which lay submissive to his touch, breathing and opening or closing her eyes at his command.

He thought of the waxwork Beauty. If that had been Eliza Quarterman, he could not imagine her over there in the wilderness of Southwark, where he had lived in Lant Street as a boy when his father had been in the Marshalsea, the debtors' prison. Perhaps she had fled with a lover to some quiet country village, some place by the sea, or abroad, living in quiet seclusion as a married couple under yet another name. He rather hoped so.

7: SOME DETECTIVE

The illustrator, George Cruikshank, had been on Dickens's mind as he had walked back from Essex Stairs. He had looked at William Hogarth's portrait of Thomas Coram in the Foundling Hospital while he was waiting for John Brownlow. Coram looked every inch the sea captain he had been, a man of action, sitting upright in his red coat, his sturdy legs apart, buckled shoes firmly planted, a globe at his feet, a sun-burnt face, and his rather pugnacious chin and wild white hair in contrast to the dignified and bewigged gentleman in the other portraits. The eyes, though, what was it about them? Something melancholy, hurt, even, Dickens thought. Coram had had a difficult childhood, he remembered, as had Hogarth, who perhaps saw something in those brown eyes that spoke of the neglected child. Both had been driven to fight their way through the world. Well, Dickens knew about that, and Hogarth had seen all the filthy life of the streets way back in the 1730s. It was there in his pictures, *The Rake's Progress* and *The Harlot's Progress*; one set depicted a gentleman rake who ends up in Bedlam, the other an innocent young woman driven by poverty into prostitution. *The Marriage Settlement*, too — all those men in silk and velvet, haggling over the price of the bride. He imagined Lady Julia's heir and the judge doing just that.

Critics called George Cruikshank the modern Hogarth. He had illustrated *Oliver Twist*; his engravings included Bill Sikes hanging from the chimney pot over Folly Ditch in Southwark. Southwark again. The place was haunting him. Dickens had thought of Cruikshank when hurrying along Holywell Street;

he had seen a drunken man lying in the gutter, berated by his wife while a couple of children sat on the pavement sucking stones. Cruikshank's series of engravings entitled *The Bottle* had been based on Hogarth. Now, Cruikshank was a leading light in the Temperance League. Dickens didn't expect to see much of him, especially as two of his fellow temperance advocates had had some very critical words to say about Mr Charles Dickens who did not support the total abstinence principle. He thought money might be better spent on clean water and houses fit to live in — in Southwark, and St Giles's, and Clerkenwell, and Little Coram Street, for that matter, and the other fifty thousand miseries which were the wretched causes of drunkenness.

All that, he thought, and memories of Lant Street and the Marshalsea, Eliza Quarterman, and the judge in his chamber accounted for a night of restless dreams. He had been looking at Cruikshank's cartoon, *I dreamt I slept at Madame Tussaud's*, in which Napoleon danced with Madame while Henry VIII and Queen Elizabeth looked on. Queen Victoria was there, too. Only, in his dream, Thomas Coram played the fiddle and Mrs Manning danced with her husband, who wore a noose around his neck. Madame Tussaud had stared through her eyeglasses at the bewigged and capering judge in his nightshirt, leering horribly at his black-veiled partner. He had woken up at that point. *Haunted*, he thought, turning over in the narrow bed in his dressing room. The new baby was due in March, and he liked to leave Catherine to sleep in peace. He lay awake for ages, his hands folded meekly on his breast, and composed himself to think about Esther Summerson's story, but it was a man dropped senseless in a fine library who appeared, and a veiled woman lay in the mud by an iron gate over which a faint lamp burned. Dickens rose before dawn. He remembered the waxworks dancing in his dream, but he did not know that he had dreamed the end of his novel.

At Wellington Street, he took down his copy of Burke's Peerage. On his way to the office, he had thought about the young man who had supposedly been in love with Eliza Quarterman. How had he fared with the brewer's daughter?

Lady Julia Clifford's son and heir was dead, and his son and heir, now Sir Francis Clifford, was safely entitled and ensconced in Cleeve Abbey. Married in 1839 to the former Miss Henrietta Marchmont, only daughter of Mr Henry Marchmont, gentleman — brewing not mentioned — of March Place, Kent, and Clara, daughter of Sir Gilbert Murray, baronet. Title on the mother's side for the brewer's daughter. Good enough, then. Prolific, Lady Julia's grandson. Seven children, one son and heir, also named Francis, six daughters, unnamed — they wouldn't count, Dickens supposed. Son and heir born in 1840. A man with his quiver full. Hardly likely to be dallying with Eliza Quarterman in Kensington Gardens. Hardly likely to be skulking about Manchester Square in league with his former love and frightening Judge Quarterman to death. He put Mr Burke back on the shelf.

Dickens turned his attention to the newspapers. Waxworks again — on the front page of the *Morning Advertiser*. Well, they had been quick. The judge's replica in wax was now in the Chamber of Horrors — the notorious hanging judge who had died in his own private waxwork gallery, where, the newspapers reported, he had exhibited a parade of nefarious murderesses. The old scandal of his marriage had been disinterred, so, of course, the new waxwork had drawn the crowds. Dickens thought of his pie-eating friend. He'd have been there chomping on his pickle.

Dickens couldn't help it. He was curious. He wanted to see how Tussaud's had modelled that long, drawn, white face. Would it show what he really was, or would he be just a bland representative of the law, the judge in his dignity, wearing his wig and his robes? Not the absurd man in his nightshirt and cap — the man to whom justice had returned terror for terror. *Robes and furred gowns hide all*, he thought. Shakespeare had it right. In his stained nightgown, the judge had been only a man with spindly legs and corns on his toes.

He worked until late afternoon and then slipped out in his long coat and low-crowned hat. He had no wish to explain why he was going to the waxworks in disguise, and he thought the crowds might be fewer by then. It was dark already and raining again. Dickens went downstairs to the Chamber of Horrors where, fittingly, the judge had been placed with some of the victims of his severity. He had certainly been a horror in his life. No sign of Mr Pieman, but there was a woman gazing upon the judge. A woman wearing a black veil. Like the woman he had seen that first time when he had met the judge down here. Someone who had known him? The woman who had once been his wife coming to look upon the husband whose death she had brought about?

She stood so still that she might have been a waxwork herself. He remained in the shadows. At last, she turned away from the judge. Dickens didn't move. She passed him. He heard her go up the stairs.

He had to look. A lamp went out, but he saw something that made him recoil, for just at that moment the judge's face seemed a haggard mask of terror, the mouth drawn back in the snarl it had worn at the instant of his death. Only the eyes were expressionless. A movement behind made him turn. A man standing behind him with a bunch of keys.

'Closin' time, sir — you'd best be quick. You don't want to be locked in wi' this lot.'

'No, indeed, I'm going.'

Dickens glanced back. The judge stared beyond him into the dark, his face a bland mask, his mouth closed. Bland, blank, dead. An empty page, but the memory of that terror he had seen in the judge's gallery and imagined in the dark just then, renewed his conviction. Whatever the inquest had concluded, someone had been there on that night. A woman in black whose skirts had rustled.

He darted back under the guillotine and up the stairs. There she was, making her way to the exit. He darted through the crowd of people leaving, and looking up and down Baker Street, he caught sight of her heading to Portman Square. He followed and saw her turn into Seymour Street, which was busy. He tried to keep her in sight and then he thought he'd lost her, but there she was again, crossing into Duke Street, where she stopped by a very respectable-looking house. Suddenly he was exposed, standing and staring. She lifted her veil and stared back at him. Though she was at a distance, he could tell she was suspicious. He walked towards her, but she didn't move.

'Are you following me, young man? If you are, then I must warn you that if I see you again about these parts, I shall summon a police constable.'

He did feel a fool. 'No, not at all. I was looking —'

'For an elderly gentlewoman to prey upon, I daresay.'

He saw that she was elderly and with a rather commanding presence. 'I do beg your pardon. You see, I saw a lady I knew at the waxworks,and I thought you were she — I mean, you—'

'Waxworks, indeed. Vulgar displays for vulgar people.'

With a final icy glare and a decisive nod of her head, she turned from him to open her front door. At least she hadn't hissed at him. There seemed to be rather too many ill-tempered women in black veils about. Lost his youthful charm, he supposed, and then again, he didn't look much like a gentleman in his present outfit. Better move on before she did call a constable. Imagine being marched to Bow Street in handcuffs. Superintendent Jones might well raise an eyebrow. And what had happened to his quarry he had no notion at all. He must have lost her somewhere along Seymour Street. Following the wrong woman. Some detective.

8: A SEVERED HEAD

'What are you skulking about here for?'

Dickens hadn't intended to go to Bow Street, but here he was outside the police station, and here was Sam Jones smiling down at him. 'I wasn't skulking. I was merely hesitating. I was wondering if you might care for a chop.'

'I've just come from Wellington Street. Mr Wills said you'd gone out — he didn't know where —' Jones looked at the hat and coat. 'Up to something?'

'Just out and about. What did you want me for?'

'Someone got into the judge's house.'

'Robbed?'

'The victims have vanished, except for one — without a head.'

'Good Lord, Sam, no one saw anything?'

'Mrs Flint, the housekeeper, locked the place up and moved out, but Quarterman's lawyer asked her to keep an eye on things. The front door was open. Once again, no sign of forced entry. Mrs Flint took one look at the headless figure and went for a constable.'

'Someone has a key, surely.'

'Looks like it. I asked Mrs Flint about the judge's keys. They were in his bedroom, and she passed them on to the lawyer. I asked her to have a look to see if there was anything else missing — silver or whatever. She says not, and his safe is locked. She doesn't know what he kept in there. Money, papers — a matter for his lawyer. Anyway, I thought you'd want to have a look. I wondered if there was anything different about the murderesses — anything missing.'

It was an alarming sight. No wonder Mrs Flint had fled. Just for a moment, as Dickens's eyes adjusted to the gloom, the figure seemed to loom horribly. And then came the realisation that it was headless, its arms reaching out in supplication, as if searching for its head. He couldn't help thinking of Madame Tussaud's guillotine.

'I can't say which one she is. Quarterman only mentioned the names of Eliza Collier and Eliza Winton, and they looked the same — in black, and even when he snatched the veils off, I couldn't tell one from another.'

'I wondered if someone might be having a joke at our expense. It's all been in the papers. It'd make a good story for someone,' Jones said.

'Keep it going, you mean. "Waxworks stolen. Police baffled." I can imagine it.'

'Well, I am baffled. Somebody must have brought a cart into the mews behind to take them away, but nobody saw anything. It must have been the middle of the night. The judge didn't keep a carriage, so no reason, I suppose, for anyone to be around the back of his house. And leaving one headless — that's a bit disturbing.'

'A severed head, eh? Bit of a shock if you found that while fishing in the canal,' Dickens said, thinking of James Greenacre.

Jones read his mind. 'Greenacre, eh? Nasty surprise, true, but this does make me wonder if you were right about one of the figures being removed when we came on the night of the judge's death. Someone's up to something.'

'The judge's victims taken from his clutches, so to speak. Saving them, in a way — from more humiliation, from public display. I'm assuming they were to be sold.'

They went in and Jones opened the wooden shutters to let in some light. The Beauty was still there. The candles were snuffed out. Her eyes were closed again, but she did not breathe. Not Sleeping Beauty, just a doll. The judge had deceived himself. She had deceived him. He looked at the murderesses again. They looked the same, though their eyes were blank now. Nothing to see.

'I think the murderesses are all still here. It's a rum do, Samivel.'

They walked over to the victims' platform and in the light of Jones's lamp, Dickens could see where the dust had been disturbed by the sweeping of the dresses as they had been removed.

'No footprints?'

'Partial, here and there. No boot marks — took them off, probably. And you can see faint marks in the dust where the ladies' feet were placed if you look closely.'

Dickens took the lamp and tried to count the pairs where shoes had rested, but they were blurred now. He moved to the back of the platform where he had thought there were two figures, though there had only been one figure when he and Jones had viewed Judge Quarterman's body. It looked as though two had stood here. Perhaps that one really had been taken on the night of Quarterman's death. He inched to the edge of the platform where he could see how the skirts of a dress had disturbed the dust, and he lowered the lamp to try to see more clearly. Then he saw it — the faint impress of a heel at the edge of the platform. He knelt and there it was, a toe mark where someone had stepped off the platform. And he thought of the rustle of a dress in the dark.

'What do you see?' Jones asked, stepping forward.

'The print of a woman's shoe or boot. It looks as though someone stepped off this platform, a real someone, not a wax doll. I did count two that night. Someone was hiding here but she'd gone, of course, when we came to look at the judge's body. And I did think I heard the rustle of a dress, Sam, but then I thought I'd imagined it. Did she come out to confront him? Imagine thinking that one of your victims had come to life.'

'Unless it was someone else. Someone quite innocently in here and not necessarily on that night. Mrs Flint, perhaps.'

'Not to do her dusting, I see.'

'That girl, Pruey, or someone else to whom he showed the waxworks.'

Dickens smiled. 'Devil's advocate.'

'I have to be. In any case, even if someone lurked here to confront him, it wasn't technically murder. The crime is theft.'

'The judge saw, Sam. Remember his face. I think someone came here and frightened him to death, and though I think he was a dreadful man, nevertheless, there's black work here.'

Jones saw in his mind's eye the judge's contorted face, the body in its nightshirt sprawled on the floor, and he thought of the missing head. 'All right, I'm willing to consider it. Someone connected to the victims, maybe. Those names he gave you — there must be relatives, friends — witnesses from the trials. It was Quarterman who directed the jury to a verdict of suicide in the Eliza Collier case, though there was clear evidence that the man she lived with had threatened her many times. There was a sister, as I recall.'

'A woman's footprint, Sam.'

'Or a man with small feet — I'd not be surprised to find a kind of miniature Quilp in here. The place is a horror.'

Dickens had to laugh. It was true. The grotesque Daniel Quilp was just the sort to be keeping company with the judge. 'True, my noble patriarch, but suppose it is a woman's print. Which Eliza?'

'Quarterman presided at the trial in Eliza Winton's case a few years back. I remember it because the abortionist was found guilty of manslaughter, but the lover, Thomas Dryden, got away with it. He denied criminal conversation with her. Her father gave evidence, but the judge dismissed it.'

'I wonder who the others were supposed to be. Any more Elizas you can think of?'

'I think we've enough to be going on with, but I'd like to know who made them. Somebody must have brought them to the house for the judge. Maybe he or she fancied having them back.'

'Mrs Flint might know.'

'We'll ask — we'll also find out if she remembers going into the exhibition, or if the girl, Pruey, ever did. I'll ask the beat constables to keep an eye on the house. If someone comes calling again to pick up Mistress Headless here, we might nab him — or her. And I'll report it to Quarterman's solicitor. He ought to get a move on and get the house emptied and the locks changed. I have Mrs Flint's key for now.'

'Any heirs?'

'Don't know. I suppose he made a will — he was a lawyer. I shouldn't think he left all his worldly goods to his errant Eliza.'

'Ah, the other Eliza — the Beauty. Eliza Quarterman. I found out about her.'

Jones looked at him quizzically. 'Why am I not surprised?'

'You will be when I tell you. She was a foundling.'

Dickens told the story, and he had to confess that he had followed a black-veiled woman all the way to Duke Street, and she had threatened him with a constable.

'You saw a black-veiled woman looking at the waxwork of the judge and you thought that she might be Eliza Quarterman — after all these years.'

'Well, now you put it that way … but I did see a black-veiled woman near the judge's house on the night I came with the judge, and there was one coming out of Tussaud's Chamber of Horrors when I met him.' Dickens looked again at the headless figure. 'Another Eliza, I'll bet, whoever she is.'

Mrs Flint lived not far away in South Street. She remembered an Italian man coming with one of the figures, but that was maybe a year back or more. Signor somethin' or other. She couldn't really tell what he was sayin'.

'Not Montanari?' Dickens asked, and seeing her blank look, he tried, 'Sarti? Pierotti?'

She couldn't remember. Yes, she explained to Jones, she was occasionally asked to do a bit of dustin' in the waxworks chamber, but the last time had been when the Italian came.

'I don't think he wanted me in there, really, not that I wanted to go in. They're creepy things,' she said, 'in all them veils, but the judge liked them. Not for me to wonder, sir. He paid me well an' it was an easy job. Most of the rooms in the house is shut up. I didn't see much of him, really. He wasn't one for idle talk, an' it suited me to get on with my work, an' he didn't mind me takin' the odd night off. Pruey had her orders not to disturb him.'

'Did Pruey ever go in there?'

Mrs Flint looked uncomfortable. 'Well, yes, she pestered me. You know what young folks are — readin' them penny dreadfuls, an' a locked room, of course, an' Ma Dunk liked a gossip. Folk knew that he had the waxworks an' those other things, an' Pruey was wild to see 'em, but not for long, I said — just to stop her goin' on. Gave her a fright, I can tell you.'

'Did the judge ever show the waxworks to anyone — a friend, or guests, perhaps?'

'Only his friend that was a lawyer who sometimes came, an' I daresay they went in there, but I only served the dinner in the dining room. They'd sit in the library all night. Not that he's been here for months.'

'No ladies came?'

'Oh, no, sir, there was never ladies invited.'

'Any visitors in the last few weeks? Anyone whom you didn't know?'

'No, sir.'

'Delivery men — anyone you didn't recognise?'

'The coal's due, sir. We have a delivery each month, from Mr Reid on the Strand. Always the same man, an' the milk girl comes from the dairy just in East Street. She doesn't come into the house.'

'And the butcher? The baker, perhaps?'

'No, I do all the shopping.'

'Isn't that a bit unusual?' Dickens asked, thinking of all the people who were constantly coming and going to the three large houses in the terrace where he lived.

Mrs Flint seemed to find it difficult to answer. 'You see, sir, the judge, he was very close. I don't think he liked people. I think he'd have managed without any servants if he could have. He was very frugal in his habits... I don't think he liked spending money, 'cept on — well, you know — the figures.'

'You don't know if he had debts or if he'd been worried about money recently?' Jones asked.

'I wouldn't know, sir. He did sell some things, bits of silver, you know, trinkets I used to polish. I asked him about a little gold enamelled box that was missin'. He was very short with me, said he'd no need of such fripperies. He wanted things plain and simple. The safe was kept locked, but I know there was things in there. He showed me a diamond cross once. It belonged to his mother. I don't think he'd have sold that. He was an odd man, I suppose, not very sociable.' *Neither was his furniture*, Dickens remembered. Mrs Flint was continuing, 'An' some folks like to keep their money — they like to know it's there. I'm a careful woman, myself. Servants have to think about their future, specially at my age.'

'And you have enough now that your employer is dead?' Dickens asked.

'Oh, yes, sir, I'll be comfortable with my sister.'

'Just to go back, Mrs Flint,' Jones said, 'when you went in the chamber to dust, did the judge give you a key?'

'No, I had one myself with the keys to other rooms and the back and front doors. They're kept secure in my own parlour, sir.'

'Did you ever meet the judge's wife?' Dickens asked.

Mrs Flint looked astonished. 'Oh, no, sir, that was before my time. I knew about it. Ma Dunk liked a gossip, as I say, but I wasn't to be drawn into that kind of talk.'

'What kind?'

'Well, she left him after a very short time an' was never heard of again, so you can imagine that people gossiped. What had happened to her an' that — whether he'd…'

'What?'

Mrs Flint reddened and rubbed her hands on her apron. 'I don't like to repeat it, sir. It was all nonsense. Penny dreadful stuff…' She was aware that the two men were waiting. She was bound to tell them. 'Whether he'd done away with her. That Pruey was always askin' if there might be a skeleton in the cellar. Stuff an' nonsense, I told her.'

Dickens almost blushed when he thought of what he'd said to Gilbert à Beckett on the same theme. He was no better than that Pruey, it seemed.

Jones didn't look at him, only saying, 'Well, they know now that there was no skeleton anywhere. Some of the wax figures have been stolen, so I must ask you to give me all your keys —'

Mrs Flint was indignant now. 'You're not sayin' —'

'Not at all. The place needs to be secure. I'll be asking Judge Quarterman's lawyer to get the locks changed. There's still some valuable stuff in there. Someone got in, Mrs Flint, someone with a key. What about Pruey? Did you give her a key to get in when you were away?'

'We had a system, you see. I'd put the back door key in the wash house for her and she'd leave the key there in a drawer when she left, you see. I mean, no one would know, and it was there when I came back that night. I don't think anyone could have taken it, sir. It didn't happen often.'

'What about the yard door? Did you leave that open for Pruey?'

'Oh, no, sir, I had to give her a key to that, but I didn't want her to take a house key away — Judge Quarterman wouldn't have liked that.'

'And you have the yard key back now?'

Mrs Flint's hands went to her apron, and she blushed again. 'Oh, I forgot, sir. I didn't think with all the to-do. I am sorry, sir.'

'That's all right, Mrs Flint. We'll go round there and collect it now.'

Jones meant to reassure her, but he couldn't help thinking that Pruey had had access to Mrs Flint's keys on the night of the judge's death, and the yard key since, and that footprint suggested that someone had been there.

'I wonder if whoever was there intended to harm the judge, and nature did it for her,' Dickens said, echoing Jones's thoughts.

Jones gave him a wry look. 'Or him.'

Ma Dunk's house was just a step away from Mrs Flint's house, in Paradise Yard — which it wasn't — a small, terraced house with a mean-looking expression in its small windows, but neat enough. There'd be a yard at the back with a wash house, or a cellar where the copper for boiling and soaking the washing would be kept, Dickens thought, remembering the house in Camden Town where he'd lived as a boy. Their next-door neighbour had been a washerwoman, a stout, good-natured woman who had the look of a suet pudding kept under a damp cloth. She'd steamed like a pudding, too, on cold winter days when he'd watched her stumping along Bayham Street with her basket.

A rather lumpish, steaming Pruey answered the door, her arms and hands red, her face flushed and her hair damp and curling under her cap. Her mouth formed an alarmed 'Oh', as she saw Superintendent Jones and Dickens on the doorstep and recognised the tall policeman from the inquest. The smell of household soap wafted at them as she opened the door wider to let them in to the front room, which was full of baskets of dirty laundry and clean laundry draped over a fireguard and hanging from rope lines strung across the room. There were a couple of flat irons standing upright on the table, something white in the process of pressing, and another iron sizzling on the hot plate by the fire which was blazing. The smell was of hot iron and wax for the starch, the jelly-like substance made of melted wax and borax quivering in bowls on the table.

Pruey looked helplessly at them. There was nowhere to sit, since every chair was stacked with ironed clothes. 'We're that busy, sir, 'aven't time ter sit down.'

'Is Mrs Dunk available?'

'Down the cellar where the copper is. She's amanglin' the sheets. 'Ave I ter call 'er?'

'We'd be obliged.'

Pruey shrieked down the stairs, 'Visitors, Ma!'

A hoarse voice cried back, 'Not in!'

'Perlice, Ma, perlice 'as come!'

There were a few moments' silence, and then a good deal of huffing and puffing announced Ma's ascent up the steps. Her scarlet face wreathed in a steam cloud emerged, as if she were some female devil come from the underworld, bringing with her the smell of boiled lime and gunpowder — the latter for skying the copper. Dickens remembered that from Bayham Street. He'd thought the house was blown up.

She was a tall, stout personage swathed in an apron with a scarf tied round her head. Dickens noted the meaty smell of her and the beefy arms — big muscles for mangling and handling the heavy sheets. She carried her copper stick for stirring the laundry, but was otherwise unarmed, and her smile seemed amiable enough in her big, coarse face. However, her dark eyes flashed a wary glance to Superintendent Jones. Just a second of calculation, perhaps. But then they were the police — not necessarily welcome visitors, even for the innocent.

'Oh, Superintendent Jones, I remembers you from the inquest. What can I do fer yer? We've 'eard about all them stolen waxworks. It's a queer do an' no mistake.'

The voice of someone who might have swallowed gravel, Dickens thought.

'Did you ever see the judge's waxworks?'

'Saw Mrs Mannin' an' that Rebecca Smith brought in — nasty-lookin' objects. Yer could tell what they was, but I didn't see the others. Give yer the creeps, an' Mrs Flint was very careful about that — more than her job was worth to be lettin' folk in there.'

'But she showed them to you, Miss Pruey?'

'Mrs Flint wouldn'ta, 'cept the silly piece kept mitherin'. 'Ad nightmares after,' Ma Dunk answered.

'Didn't niver want ter go in again.'

'Told 'er it served 'er right — not your business, I said, what grand folks spends their money on.'

Now for the difficult bit, Jones thought. The matter of the key. Best tread carefully. 'Have you been back to the house since the judge died?'

'Oh, aye — 'ad ter get the laundry as usual. Last lot, God rest 'im,' Ma Dunk said piously. 'Yer niver knows the day, do ye? Don't matter if yer 'igh or low, yer can't avoid the reaper. Queer sort, though, that judge, not that I ever sees much of 'im, but Mrs Flint did all right there. Very comf'table. Serpose she'll stay with 'er sister now — she'll 'ave savin's. Give us a few bits, too — good of 'er. Old shirts an' that — come up lovely, they 'as. Good bit o' scrubbing an' a darn — good as new.'

'You didn't see anyone hanging about?'

'Yer mean any likely lad plannin' on stealin' them dolls?'

'I do.'

'Didn't notice, sir. There's mews round the back where I goes in, an' there's allus folk about durin' the day, but yer know 'ow it is, sir, yer just don't pay attention — thinkin' about the laundry or the rain, or a nice bit o' mutton fer roastin'.'

'What about you, Pruey? Did you ever see anyone in the yard, for example where Mrs Flint put the key for you?'

Pruey blinked, and blinked again. 'No, sir, see, the yard door was allus kept locked.'

'Mrs Flint gave you the key to get in that night the judge died?'

A simple question, but Jones noted how her eyes slid to Ma Dunk before she answered, 'Yes, sir.' Blinking.

'And you still have it.'

'Oh, lor, so we do,' Ma Dunk said. 'Forgot all about it. We're that busy, sir. It'll be in the scullery — best yer take it, sir. We'll not need it agin.'

Noting the slide of her glance to Pruey, Jones said quickly, 'I'd be obliged, Mrs Dunk, if you'd fetch it.'

While Ma Dunk went for the key, Jones asked Pruey again about any strangers, but Pruey — very slow and blinking — didn't think so. There was the coalman, grooms from the carriage houses in the mews along the way, the milk girl, but she knew them.

'And no one came to the house on the night you were to take up the judge's supper, apart from the person you heard in the library?'

'Jest 'eard them voices. Wasn't my place ter go in the library.'

Ma Dunk came back with the key, which she was rubbing on her apron. 'Sorry, sir, it's been in with the soap in a dish.'

Jones thanked her and took the key, giving Dickens a quick glance as he did so.

The constable, a guileless sort of fellow, asked, 'Mrs Dunk, ma'am, I wonders if yer knows whether the judge 'ad a mother, or a wife mebbe — someone 'oo might 'elp us?'

'Old feller like 'im with a ma? I don't think so. Old as the 'ills, 'e woz.'

'Beg pardon, ma'am, I wozn't thinkin'. No wife, then?'

''Ad a wife — wife wot left 'im, an' woz niver seen again. Folk talk, see, when yer goin' in an out with laundry, an' there was them as said 'e done 'er in. Niver believed it, o' course, sir. Wouldn't repeat such a thing. Told our Pruey it woz all nonsense.'

Dickens and Jones walked away from Paradise Yard. 'Dunk, forsooth — I still can't believe it. Mind you, there was a Mr Dunk, hop and seed factor in Southwark, now I remember,' Dickens mused.

'Never mind Southwark,' said Jones. 'The comic vaudevilles don't know what they're missing in you.'

'Box and Cox, eh? What do you make of our Mrs Bouncer there?' Dickens asked.

Mrs Bouncer was the unscrupulous landlady in the farce that Superintendent Jones had declined to see. They hadn't got to see *Harlequin Charley*, either. *No need*, Jones thought, as he grinned back at Dickens.

'Those keys interest me,' said Jones. 'Pruey had access to them in Mrs Flint's parlour. It's easy enough to take an impression from a bar of soap, or they could just have lent them to someone who wanted to get in and offered enough money. Why not? And even if they know more than nothing, Ma Dunk's not going to tell us.'

'Not quite the woman that Mrs Flint described. Ma Dunk liked a gossip, according to Mrs Flint, but, of course, Ma Dunk wouldn't repeat what was said about the judge and his wife. A pattern of virtue, Ma Dunk.'

'That girl's under her thumb. I noticed how she looked for permission to answer, and Ma Dunk wasn't very keen to leave Pruey alone with us.'

'She took a long time to answer a simple question,' Dickens added. 'The portrait of a blinking idiot. Something not right.'

'But then again, Mrs Dunk might just be your run-of-the mill hard-faced woman whose instinct is to keep the police at a distance,' said Jones. 'She'll have some racket going, I'll bet. Nice line in second-hand clothes, I'd imagine. There'll be cast-offs and items that go missing from the weekly wash.'

'My friend, Mitton, who had chambers in Barnard's Inn, had a laundress who used to pawn his clothes. She worked out a very cunning system. Always kept one piece of property in pledge and redeemed it for another when she knew he wanted whatever it was — a country jacket, for example. I can see her face now — sharper than a serpent's tooth. Now, what was her name? Betty? Bess? Or maybe —'

Jones laughed. 'Don't. I think we might eliminate the coalman — no coal dust. The milk girl didn't go into the house. We've only Ma Dunk and Pruey with possible access and according to Mrs Flint, some Italian came once last year, and the friends or relations of the missing Elizas, who may or may not exist at all — not exactly much to go on.'

'Eliza Quarterman might have had a key —'

'No more. Mrs Agnes Stagg at The Ship Tavern has the sweetest sound for me just now, so what about that chop? And let's talk about anything but Eliza anybody.'

Sweet was not the adjective Dickens would have used for Mrs Agnes, whose temper was very often uncertain — at best frowningly irritable, at worst enough to curdle milk — but he only said, 'Lead on.' A glass of pale ale might be safe enough.

9: WAXWORK MANIA

There was no occasion for Superintendent Jones and Charles Dickens to speak of any Eliza for some days. Superintendent Jones had a moment of anguish which interrupted his relish in Mr Daniel Stagg's succulent lamb chops when Mrs Agnes, wife of, called out the dread word in the snug bar of The Ship Tavern. However, no one answered, and Mrs Agnes bustled away to seek out the recalcitrant bearer of the name. Who she was, they were never to know. It was the first and last time Mrs Stagg was to utter the word. Her next display of temper was directed at a Polly, a harmless-looking damsel with surprised blue eyes, who answered by hurtling into the bar and knocking over two stools and dropping the milk jug. She was never seen again, either.

In the days following the theft of the waxworks, Sergeant Rogers was on the hunt for an Italian artist in wax, of whom there were rather too many if you included Montanari, Pierotti, Sarti — no go there — and the Italian tailors and the Italian milliners, and the Italian warehouses who imported wax goods of every kind. Constable Stemp found the milk girl and the coal man — blameless — and Constable Feak on his innocent beat kept his eye on Ma Dunk's laundering premises.

Superintendent Jones had quite enough on his plate. Robbery with violence; pick-pocketing — two ten-year-olds; assault; fraud — two Italians; obscene publications in Wych Street; even bigamy — an Irish man; more fraud — two French wine importers. Vinegar, more like. A German before the magistrate on a charge of beating and starving a servant girl — remanded. Constable Stemp had collared Teddy, the

83

Spaniard, a notorious dog thief — denizen of St Giles's in fact, not Madrid — and the expensive dog he was walking. Spaniels were Teddy's speciality — geography hazy. All the world seemed to be committing crime in London, including an American man who had fatally stabbed a sailor in a pub brawl.

There was always murder. There was a dreadful one in Marylebone. A husband murdered his wife, but she was a Margaret. Another poor Margaret, Mrs Blakemore, murdered her child and killed herself, but nobody called Eliza was murdered. An unnamed young woman was pulled out of the water by Waterloo Bridge — an attempted suicide, possibly, and a man was found drowned at Hungerford Bridge. No one saw anything. Accident, murder, suicide? Impossible to say. He might have fallen in. The weather was dreadful. Fog everywhere — so dark and wretchedly sulphurous; no wonder people were killing themselves or other people, even if accidentally. One cab driver had run over a young woman, and another had been killed when his cab turned over. None of this was unusual, of course, for November, or for most months for that matter, Superintendent Jones thought resignedly.

And then something very unusual began — what the cheap newspapers and running patterers gleefully reported as 'Waxwork Women Mania', 'Waxworks Walking', or 'Wizardry', or 'Witchery' — no end to their alliterative ingenuity. The reference was to the mysterious appearance of black-gowned wax figures. The first was found at the door of a wax chandler's shop in Duke Street, just below Manchester Square. The shopman who was opening up thought she was a customer. Candles wanted, perhaps, or black sealing wax — there was a funereal air about her black veil. When she didn't answer his several polite enquiries, he called his boss. Deaf as a post, they thought. The shopman was sent for a policeman to take her into custody. Number two was waiting by an undertaker's premises in Maiden Lane — Biers and Graves, Mistress Martha and Mistress Sarah, who were quite unmoved by the visitor. *Mistresses of death*, Dickens thought, but did not say, nor did he comment on the names when Jones told him. Mr Jones was not in the mood for witticism, because number three was discovered gazing into the window of a toy shop in St. Martin's Lane — at the wax dolls, of course.

'Two or three more to come and one head. Someone's making a fool of us,' Jones said to Dickens as they gazed upon the ladies who were reclining in various attitudes in a cell at Bow Street with their headless companion, their faces all alike in their blandness, and giving nothing away. Dickens couldn't tell if they were part of the judge's collection. He heard the growing irritation in Jones's voice — understandable in the circumstances, given the headline which he had foretold, 'Bow Street Baffled'; however, he tactfully forbore to mention that, merely observing a little facetiously that something would turn up.

Something did, but not before the enterprising Mr Springthorpe, whose waxwork exhibition was now showing at number 393 the Strand, had the ingenious notion of arranging a group of black-clad wax ladies outside his premises — at least Mrs Manning, Rebecca Smith and Sarah Chesham were recognisable, but a number of humourists reported the sighting at Bow Street and the newspapers had a field day. Mr Springthorpe's ticket sales soared, as did those of Napoleon Montanari, whose wax figures had won the medals at the Great Exhibition. His shop in Soho was packed. Superintendent Jones was not particularly amused by the wax dummies in the hairdresser's shop window on the corner of Bow Street and Little Russell Street. The usual simpering pink-clad miss with her golden tresses was now draped in black and her improbably red-lipped swain removed to be replaced by another wax woman in black. And another crowd. What larks!

Pedlar dolls were everywhere, too — every street seller was cashing in with trays of hunched little figures in red shawls and bonnets. Cheap to make — just a crude wax head on a wooden stump. More elaborate Arab pedlars in turbans and coloured robes and beads. There were pen-wiper dolls whose red petticoats served to wipe your pen, pincushion dolls carrying baskets, sewing companion dolls stuck about with pins and needles, baby dolls, some swaddled, some naked — and, apparently, unashamed — seemingly untouched by the raw November weather. There were also dolls in white smocks tucked into paperboard boxes horribly resembling miniature coffins, dolls with hard black eyes, and wax angels for the Christmas trade looking distinctly unimpressed by the world into which they had descended.

Whatever the size, they all had that rather cold and curiously indifferent gaze which looked beyond you, Dickens thought, as he dodged past an importunate cross-eyed seller who offered him a cross-eyed wax doll for which he was to cross her palm with a silver sixpence. And they never smiled.

The city seemed to be gripped by the waxwork mania. A drunken Irish woman was brought before Gilbert à Beckett charged with attempting to destroy the wax figure of Mrs Manning at an exhibition in Lambeth — she had thrown her clog at it. Mrs Manning's nose was badly bruised. She bore the indignity stoically. The proprietress soon got over her indignation when her ticket sales rocketed. Middleton's waxwork exhibition in Blackfriars Road caught fire — which served them right, Superintendent Jones observed testily. Same when Ogleby's wax and spermaceti works in Paradise Street,

Lambeth, burnt down, though he managed a grin when Dickens uttered the word 'Inferno'. And when Mrs Peachey, artist in wax to Her Majesty, reported the theft of a wax bouquet from her premises in Oxford Street, Mr Jones didn't care at all. A box of wax candles arrived at Bow Street — *to lighten their darkness*, so the impudent message went, and a box containing the wax hand of a woman was sent by a well-wisher, addressed to Superintendent Jones of Bow Street, the black-edged card expressing condolences for his loss and offering to give him a hand. Not funny — well, it was, but the joke was wearing decidedly thin.

But Dickens couldn't help laughing uproariously — though not in front of Mr Jones — when he read that on Wednesdays henceforth, according to the advertisement, in consequence of repeated applications from ladies of quality, Doctor Kahn's celebrated Museum of Anatomical Wax Models would open for ladies to attend. He wondered what the ladies would make of the Venus Medici and her exposed intestines. Ah, a professional lady in attendance to give the necessary explanations. Nothing to call a blush into the cheek of a young person, he hoped, but then he had seen the waxwork Samson at Simmonds's with his huge gaping torso revealing his innards and rather too much of his outer parts. Viscera, accurate in every detail, Mr Simmonds had boasted. A sight to make any strong man shudder.

It was the said professional lady, in the highest of dudgeon, who reported to a passing policeman — Superintendent Jones's Constable Dacres — that a female figure in black had been placed in Doctor Kahn's porch and that it must be removed forthwith, and no, she had no idea how it had got there, and no, he could not enter on a Wednesday — only ladies of quality admitted. Constable Dacres, somewhat cowed, and to much cheering by passers-by, took hold of the lady waxwork and carried her to Bow Street.

Dickens kept a straight face as she was manhandled to her cell, but then he was astonished to see that there were seven there already, all with the same expressionless faces. 'Lor, Sam, is this a joke?'

'Someone's leading us a dance — there's no way of knowing which belonged to the judge. One thing, though: these heads, they're made of what is called over wax —' seeing Dickens's face, he explained — 'I called in the hairdresser to have look, the one on the corner.'

'Ah, the one with the black-gowned figures in his window.'

'I thought I'd rattle his bones a bit — serve him right for getting in on the act. I wanted to know if these heads are professionally made. They are, but he didn't think by an artist of the Tussaud calibre — you can get these from any doll manufactory and paint them up. Over waxing just means that they are made of something like papier-mâché or wood. And the paraffin wax is painted on. The point is that they are not made of poured beeswax like the ones of the murderesses. They're cheaper.'

'Now I think of it, the judge's murderesses were different — much more finely done. The victims were — well — like next door, I said to him. He ignored me, of course — too busy itemising their harlotry. Two different makers?'

'Could be. However, Mrs Flint didn't remember anyone but the Italian coming with figures, though I suppose she wouldn't know all the comings and goings.'

'And Quarterman was a secretive devil.'

'And we've no way of knowing whether any of these are the judge's. Any joker could have made them. This one has painted eyes.'

Dickens looked again. 'So it has. And not very convincing. Not one of the judge's, I shouldn't think — I'm sure they had glass eyes — so some of the ones we have now are the work of a prankster, perhaps. No witnesses, I suppose?'

'No — they appear in the mornings, so it happens in the night, in the early hours when no one's about. I tell you, if any more come, I'll burn the lot, and case closed. I can't think what else it is. But I suppose no harm's being done, and everyone's enjoying it — except me. As if we haven't enough to deal with. I'm considering going out in disguise. And the judge's death is being linked to it, of course. The stray waxworks a visitation of God, some supposed cleric has written in the newspaper. And the story about his wife. Nothing more on her, I suppose? Not that I want to know.'

10: FOR SALE

When he was not viewing the ladies in their cell — a dozen by now, with the addition of some children's dolls of the Betsey Prig tribe, brought in by variously indignant or amused citizens who had found them on their doorsteps or perched on windowsills peering in like inquisitive neighbours — Dickens worked on his Christmas piece for the extra number of *Household Words* to come out in December and set his teeth to brighten it. Though he couldn't help laughing at the ridiculousness of the waxwork mania, he did sympathise with Sam Jones. The wretched fog coming down was a blight on the city and it wouldn't help Sam if waxen ghosts in black loomed up in innocent gardens, or even the hallways of respectable citizens, or in graveyards, for that matter.

It all seemed harmless, and it would pass, no doubt, as crazes often did. He thought of newspaper headlines he had read; apparently, there had been a mania for waistcoats for ladies last year. What had happened to that? 'Flounce Mania' — another headline he'd seen. There didn't seem to be a more than usual number of flounces on dresses that passed him on his own stairs, Betsey Prig excepted. 'The Bloomer Craze' — learned ladies giving lectures, satirical squibs in *Punch*, bloomer demonstrations, bloomer waxworks, and bloomer balls, plays, and pantomimes. Where would the ladies in trousers be next year? On balance, he thought he'd prefer the flounces. A craze for vampires at the theatre a few years ago — that had passed. But then he thought of the 'Poison Mania' headline — that epidemic of arsenic he'd been writing about. It had passed, but, after all, poison was a very different matter from flounces and stage vampires with paste fangs. Murder had been done.

And, he admitted to himself, there was a lingering sense of something darker beneath all the waxwork business. A woman had reported that a man in a mask had leapt out at her from a doorway. The mask was found — a mask of Mrs Manning, and a noose beside it. That wasn't funny. That black-edged card sent to Sam, the kind that invited you to a funeral — if a joke, a rather macabre one. That hand in its box had looked too much like a dead one on its cotton wool bed. The judge's distorted face came back to him like the memory of a dark dream, and he couldn't quite shake off a feeling of unease. A visitation, certainly. Someone had been there; someone had looked the judge in the eye, and the old waxwork himself had seen retribution.

A rustling skirt in the dark. A footprint in the dust. Eliza Quarterman's?

Judge Quarterman's house was emptied, and no skeleton was found in the cellarage, or in any locked chest or cabinet, so Superintendent Jones told Dickens, who noted the satirical look in his eye. Sam Jones had known what he was thinking. No one was seen lurking near the house. The judge had kept some pieces of silver in his safe, which the solicitor opened and took charge of as well as the judge's papers. The will left his house and its contents, including his library of books, to his friend at Doctors' Commons — who didn't really want them, having plenty of dusty law books of his own. But he was glad to get the money and was ready to retire to Broadstairs on it. The house was sold, and the contents went to auction, on which day, the judge's solicitor, Mr Ebenezer Houndsfoot, arrived fleet of foot at Bow Street in the afternoon to speak urgently to Superintendent Jones.

At the same time, having finished his work on Christmas trees and other festive accompaniments, Dickens found himself in need of a brisk walk, despite the fog, and in need of a companion. Chatham Place was his destination — the premises of Mr Jas. Oiley, auctioneer. He had foreseen the destiny of those heavy pieces of furniture, after all. No harm in taking a look. He took Scrap with him — no need to mention it to Mr Jones. And Scrap, who was always ready for action away from the stationery shop where he was sometimes behind the counter and sometimes out and about on errands, was perfectly delighted to see the waxworks and to look out for a lady in a black bonnet and veil.

Detecting was the real business of Scrap's life, and Mr D. always had somethin' interestin' on the go. Didn't miss much, Mr D., though he 'ad some queer notions. In the street, pickin' their way through the blasted fog an' all the mud, he suddenly said out loud, 'Megalosaurus,' and Scrap made the mistake of stopping to say, 'You what?' an' some old cove walked right into them. 'Vagabonds,' the cove muttered. Course, Mr D. laughed an' said, 'Dinosaur,' a bit too loud, an' the cove turned round an' shouted, 'Impudent rascal!' Then, they'd to wait in a doorway while Mr D. wrote the word down on a bit o' paper. Scrap didn't find out until much later about the Megalosaurus — not until the first number of *Bleak House* came to the stationery shop in its familiar green cover. An' only he, Scrap, knew how it had come about. He practised the word so that he could say it — casually, o' course — when the moment came. And it was a triumph when Mrs Jones an' Eleanor looked at him open-mouthed. Mr D. just winked. He remembered, o' course. Well, they both did — a bit of a bad business, what happened after. For all of them.

There was quite a number of black-veiled ladies going into the auction rooms just off Chatham Place, by Blackfriars Bridge — perhaps they didn't want to be seen ogling the waxworks, or the body-snatcher's bit of skin. Neither did Charles Dickens wish to be seen ogling anything or anyone, which was why he wore his spectacles, his old long coat, and low-crowned hat. Just a clerk, perhaps, looking to pick up a bargain. No one especially interesting to look at. His son with him, perhaps, a nice-looking boy, respectably dressed, too. They did look at the curiosities, and even Scrap, who had seen many horrors in his short life, recoiled a moment from the piece of Burke's skin. Dickens had whispered his reply to Scrap's question.

'Blimey, Mr D. 'Ow'd they do that?'

This was not the time to go into detail about flaying and the turning of Burke's skin into a notebook as well as cutting up pieces and dying them blue for sale, so Dickens merely murmured, 'You don't want to know.'

They stared at the death masks. Blank-faced, eyeless, but still something brutish in the thick waxen lips and spread noses, Dickens thought. What a strange man, the judge, the company he kept while sipping his sherry. Those two gazing at him. Did he shake the bronze hand as he came from communing with his Beauty and her companions in death?

'Murderers?' Scrap asked, pointing. 'Them the rope marks? Rum things to keep at 'ome.'

'He was a rum sort of man. I should think they were murderers, but I don't know who. Never mind them, keep your eyes on the ladies with veils.'

Easier said than done, however. The auction was crowded with plenty of people who had not come to bid, but, caught up in waxworks mania and rumours about the judge's death, to see the parade of murderesses. *Huddle*, Dickens thought. They looked somehow sheepish now rather than sinister, though their eyes still stared at something in the distance. However, there were those who couldn't resist a feel of the black satin which had gone out of fashion after the hanging of Mrs Manning, or the touch of a waxen cheek or stiff ringlet. Checking they were dead, he supposed. There was no gloating or glinting eye, and the stiff skirts rustled only at the touch of an inquisitive finger. Maybe he had imagined all that — something eerie in Sam Jones's lamplight and the judge's dreadful face.

The old hands — an auction was always a good show, especially when there was a whiff of murder about the proceedings — surged to the front as one of Mr Jas. Oiley's minions reverently filled the water glass on the auctioneer's pulpit. They knew it was going to start soon. The judge's chairs were packed with bonnets, veils, caps, toppers, long coats, short coats, coats shiny with wear, velvet collars, fur mantles, pelisses, patched shawls, and further back, the rest of the audience perched on tables, bedsteads, bookshelves and handy stacks of carpet. There was even a plump cherub with a runny nose and dangling legs upon a marble pillar, propped up by a greasy-looking man in a napless hat with a catalogue in his hand and a pencil behind his ear. The abandoned head of Julius Caesar — or whoever it was — lay on the pillow of another iron bedstead. How are the mighty fallen. And, His Honour, the judge — his household gods trampled, as it were, under the feet of commerce and scandal. Then there was a hush as the great man, Mr Oiley, ascended and took his bow. He wouldn't disgrace the boards at Drury Lane, Dickens thought.

From his pulpit, genial, red-nosed Jas. Oiley (Auctioneer, Valuer, Coffin Warehouse) — a man of many parts, enjoyed himself hugely, detailing the histories of the ladies, as he called them, to his laughing customers who enjoyed themselves hugely, too. Mrs Manning came first, manhandled by a burly porter. 'Ah, Madame Marie, *allongez, ma petite*, don't be shy,' Jas. called out with facetious familiarity and an execrable accent. Mrs Manning was Swiss. French, Swiss, all one to Jas. 'Not so cocky now, are we?' She wasn't. She looked distinctly dusty and a bit frayed at the edges, like a worn-out cook. She wouldn't have liked that, nor the laughter which greeted Jas.'s comic sallies. Jas. put on quite a show. The murderesses were soon dispatched, however, with the representative of Tussaud's purchasing the lot, including the Beauty. They'd be turned into something else. Rebecca Smith melted into some portly princess, perhaps. When the skull, the death masks, the bronze hand, the woodcuts of the murderer, Courvoisier, and Eliza Fenning, and the suspicious piece of blue leather came up, Tussaud's paid a good deal for them, too. 'See you again, ladies. Be good girls, now,' Jas. Oiley joked as he bowed them away to cheers from the crowd.

Dickens kept his eye on the back of the room, for there were still people examining the furniture, the silverware, the china, and the books which would come up in the afternoon. He was amused to see Scrap lurking about the tables, casually inspecting various pieces of silver with the air of a man who could tell a piece of plate from the real thing. Most of the black-veiled ladies had departed, having seen the show. It wasn't worth staying, Dickens thought. Then he saw a tall, black-veiled lady at the door — no way of knowing if she were the one who had hissed at him at Tussaud's, except the similar height. Nevertheless, he waited. Scrap had seen her, too, and he waited, still apparently weighing up the value of a silver box.

She passed by Scrap and made her way to the wall and, lifting her veil so that she could see, raised her eyes. Dickens edged his way over to stand by Scrap, who seemed to show him something of interest on the table. Simultaneously he managed to peep over the boy's shoulder to see what the lady was looking at. He thought he recognised some of the muddy oil paintings. He couldn't imagine anyone buying them unless for the frames, and then he saw what he had not seen before. The woman was looking up at a portrait. Something about her stillness and the set of her shoulders suggested that she was looking intently. He dared not take off his spectacles, but surreptitiously shifted them down his nose a little. He was too far away to see clearly, but he could tell it was the portrait of a man. He motioned Scrap to go nearer and melted away into a group who were still examining the items on the table.

Scrap sidled up to the woman and was gazing up. 'Who was he, then?' he asked the woman in his respectable voice, giving her his best smile and wide-open blue eyes. Just a curious lad.

As she turned, the veil came down, but she answered in a low voice, 'Judge Quarterman, I believe.'

'Did you know him?'

'I never knew him,' she murmured and turned to go.

Dickens watched as she made her way to the door. Scrap joined him, whispering the name of the man in the portrait. 'Said she never knew 'im.'

Knew of him, though, Dickens thought. They kept a discreet distance as she went down the stairs and to the front door. Scrap darted ahead. Dickens saw him disappear. Now he hurried and gained the street in time to see a black-clad lady crossing the street to the cabstand opposite, but then there were two more hurrying across. He saw Scrap at the cabstand, and a lady enter a growler — a closed four-wheeler cab. Scrap perched on the back, as urchins often did. The going was slow, and Dickens followed as the cab turned into Chatham Place and turned right. It had to be going across the bridge — into Southwark. The traffic was stalled at the entrance to the bridge — the crush waiting to cross and the fog slowing everything down. Link boys had materialised like genies from lamps — extraordinary how they possessed themselves of their flaming torches, ready to hire themselves out as guides for sixpence. There was a smell of burning pitch and tar to add to the sulphurous fog.

Even going at footpace, Dickens kept Scrap and the cab in sight as the cabs, carriages and assorted carts moved off. An omnibus blocked his view as he stepped onto the bridge, and then everything moved forward. He could hear foghorns and steam whistles sounding their mournful warnings from the river below, where the sky now seemed to rest on the water and only faint lights were to be seen. Ahead along the bridge, the gas lamps loomed and vanished as he passed, and the torch lights flared. He quickened his pace to overtake the omnibus. He wanted to keep his eye on Scrap — not that he could come to any harm at this pace.

He heard the wild neighing of the horses first and then almost immediately the crash and thud, followed by the shouts and high-pitched screaming. The sound of terror. On his side the traffic stopped, though it was still grinding its way on the opposite side, coming from Southwark. He tried to run — oh, God, not the cab Scrap had perched on. The press of people was too thick. Somewhere ahead, other people had stopped. An omnibus had stopped, too, people standing upon the knifeboard on top, craning, shouting, and gesticulating; a man was alighting from a two-wheeler cab, another climbing onto the parapet, clinging to a lamp post; a laundry woman with a large basket dumped on the pavement got in his way. Link boys ran through, waving their torches — people shrank back as the flames passed. Dickens pushed his way through, hearing the roar of police rattles and imagining Scrap crushed under the wheels.

A cab had turned over onto its side, one hind wheel shattered. An omnibus coming from the opposite direction had shoved into it, its fore wheel broken, its horses rearing and bucking, a policeman trying to grip the reins. Passengers were being helped away by passers-by, some still on top, clinging on. One man was on the ground, and another was helping him up. Another policeman was still swinging his rattle and shouting for room. The cab horse was down in the broken shafts. A big, capable-looking man in a leather apron with his sleeves rolled up was tending to it, a link boy holding his torch aloft. A woman standing a little further off with a boy — a boy with blood on his face.

Dickens managed to reach them. Scrap looked a bit dazed, and the woman was holding a bit of cloth to his head.

'Ain't nothin',' Scrap said, seeing Dickens's shocked face. 'Jumped off when I 'eard the bang. 'Bus crashed into the cab, knocked it over. Me, I just tripped an' knocked me 'ead.'

'He's all right, I thinks,' the woman said. 'Jest a cut — 'eads allus bleed a lot.'

'The woman?' Dickens asked, looking at the overturned cab. He recognised the driver by his many-caped coat and the whip lying by him. He was stretched out where he had obviously fallen unconscious.

'Don't know,' said Scrap, 'underneath, I bet.'

'She couldn't have survived that,' the woman said, 'poor thing.'

One of the policemen had organised a gang of men to lift the cab now the man in the leather apron had released the fallen horse from the traces. On the count of three, the gang — made up of rough jackets, frock coats, caps, toppers, gloved hands, raw hands, men of all types suddenly brought together in their rescue effort — made to lift.

Someone must have heard Dickens, because the cry went up, 'Woman under!' and with a tremendous heave, the broken cab was raised up to a great cheer from the crowd. The cab was shoved aside, and the crowd fell silent at the sight of the prone figure in the light of the torches and the policemen's lamps. The spread skirts told it was a woman. A tall man stepped forward and Dickens heard him say that he was a doctor. The tall man knelt by the body.

'Don't move,' Dickens said to Scrap as he took off his hat and spectacles and walked forward. 'I have brandy,' he added, taking the flask from his pocket.

The man looked up. 'Mr Dickens,' he said.

Dickens recognised Doctor Mayo of the Marylebone Infirmary. 'Doctor Mayo, is there anything to be done?'

'No, sir, she is dead. I'll have her taken to St Bartholomew's, though how in this fog, I don't know. I daresay I can commandeer a cart when the police have moved everyone on.'

St Bart's at Smithfield. Dickens thought quickly. 'What about King's College? Fleet Street might be quicker.' It wouldn't be, but Sam Jones could take a look at her there.

'It won't matter to her. However, I'll have to see the other casualties. If you could stay on guard for a while, I'd be grateful.'

Dickens agreed and signalled to Scrap, who, when he saw that she was dead, took off his cap for a moment. Dickens looked down at her. The veil was still over her face — like the woman in his dream, lying in the mud. He saw the mud on her black skirts, which were rather worn. He didn't think she was My Lady Disdain from Duke Street. But she had looked at Judge Quarterman's portrait with quiet concentration. It would not be seemly to lift up the veil. He would have to wait until he and Sam Jones could get to King's College Hospital before he knew if she were Eliza Quarterman.

11: LADY ON A GRAVE

Late afternoon and Constables Stemp and Feak, picking their way through the fog and the dark past St Giles's Church on their way to Bow Street, heard the shrieks and the running feet. Two ragged urchins hurtled out of the church gates to be stopped in their tracks by Stemp's solid form blocking the way. Feak's lamp showed two dirty faces and two pairs of wild eyes under two seemingly identical thatches of matted hair.

'What's all the racket?' asked Stemp, keeping a firm hold on the smaller figure. They'd seen two coppers. Their instinct would be to flee. Feak took the other.

'Seen 'er, seen 'er, copper — dead she is, lyin' there just dead on a grave.' The speaker was a boy of about ten years.

'Touched 'er, touched 'er 'and — cold as an eel in a bucket.' A girl's voice this time. The policemen's lamps revealed the ragged shawl and skirt.

'Seen 'er earlier wiv a feller. Then she's lyin' down on the slab —'e 'ad 'is 'ands on 'er — now she ain't movin'. Dint answer when we asked 'er woz she awright.'

'Murdered 'er, I reckons, the feller did it.' The girl wasn't frightened, but then a dead body in a graveyard was not perhaps that unusual in this benighted world that was St Giles's. Bodies were always being dug up and re-buried, even those who were recently interred. The place was always flooding. The neighbours in Cook's Row which abutted the cemetery were always complaining. A woman had found a head in her garden once, and the residents had seen parts of bodies and shrouds being tossed into wheelbarrows. And murder, too, was not uncommon hereabouts.

'Where?' asked Stemp.

'Over there — off the path. Near the 'ouses. Angel on the grave — big 'un, pointin' up.'

Leaving Feak to keep hold of the urchins, Stemp went into the churchyard. His lamp showed the thick green-brown fog wreathing the gravestones in a particularly unearthly way, as if the souls of the dead were rising from their putrid habitations. Not that Stemp felt it so. He was used to fog and to graveyards. Fog was a nuisance that got in the throat and on the chest and made it hard to see your way when you were followin' someone on the lurk. Fog bred crime — robbery, garrottin', knives in the dark, sneaks in the back yards of respectable citizens, an' that was annoyin' for a copper doin' his duty. There were a lot of angels pointing upward, but he could see the faint lights of the houses to his right. He couldn't hear anything; however, when he groped his way further across, he saw a tomb with a pointing angel, and there seemed to be a figure lying down. Getting closer, he saw the skirts hanging down. A woman, then.

A glittering pinpoint as he lifted the veil which was draped over the face. His lamp picked out a staring blue eye, an eye that was just glass in the expressionless face, which the kids would not have seen. He knew what it was but touched the face, just to be sure. It was made of wax. And there was one eye missing.

As he went back to Feak and the ragged witnesses, he wondered about the man the kids had seen with the figure. Someone who had stolen the judge's waxworks or just another joker? It somehow didn't seem like a joke, Stemp thought. The others had been comical in their way — outside shops, or that museum, an' even the dolls and the candles. But that hand in the box. And now a graveyard and what had looked like a dead body. That bothered him. A sign of something worse to come? *Well*, he thought, *let's see what the kids have to tell about the feller.*

Their playground was the graveyard and the nest of miserable alleys which twisted their way around the great church. A place of crime and poverty where the residents emptied their chamber pots in the street; where lodgers burnt their straw beds in the night to kill the lice; where there might be ninety lodgers to a house and one privy; where prostitutes and burglars plied their trades; a place of fever and smallpox; a place where two ragged urchins were unmoved by death or by murder.

Neither of them went to school — not even the ragged school; sometimes they went out beggin'; sometimes they went scavengin' for food; sometimes they jest 'ung about. Watchin', see. Dug up the graves in there — yer could see 'em. Legs, an' arms, and 'eads sometimes. Give yer the creeps. Niver seen anythin' like that woman. Nah, they dint go 'ome afore dark. Nothin' ter do there. Ma wozn't never 'ome. Dint 'ave no pa — couldn't remember no pa. Liked the streets at night best. Folk 'ad baked taters, eels, fish an' sometimes yer got a bite. Sometimes a cove would drop 'is tater, an if yer woz quick… Anyways, liked ter see' wot woz doin'. Liked a fight in the street or a fire. Old Ma Nolan burnt ter death last week.

'And what was doin'?' Stemp asked, patiently. 'You saw a man and the woman.'

'She dead, then?' the girl persisted. 'Did 'e do her in? Tol' yer 'e done 'er in.'

'It's not a woman. It's a waxwork. Someone 'avin' a joke, I daresay.'

''Eard about it. Waxworks all over town, they says. Cor, we got one. Can we 'ave another look?'

Stemp glanced at Feak. 'No, the constable 'ere is goin' to 'ave a look, an' you can tell me about the man.'

'Nasty bleeder wot tol' us to git outer it or 'e'd give us somethin' we wouldn't forgit. We woz only 'avin a laugh when we saw 'im layin 'er down. Knowed wot 'e woz up ter. Seen it afore — couples priggin' on a grave. Sometimes watched fer a laugh. Sed woz 'e payin' the lady?'

Stemp asked, 'When was this?'

'Dunno. We runs off an' when we comes back, there she is, still lyin' on the grave, still as a corpse. 'Nother o' them bleedin' waxworks, yer says? Thought she was a dead 'un.' There was regret in the voice.

'I 'eard the clock,' the boy said, 'but can't say wot time. More than wunce, I thinks.'

'What about the man? Can either of you say what he was like?'

'Big 'un. Collar turned up, black 'at, gloves. Beard an' a big gob — saw that. Growlin' like a bear. Big gnashers like the bogeyman, like that feller wot murdered 'is wife in Church Street. 'Anged, 'e was. Liked ter 'ave seen that.'

'You 'adn't seen him before?'

'Dunno, couldn't really see much. Best ter scarper.'

'Get off 'ome then yourselves, an' quick. You don't want to see him again. Where do you live?'

'Wot about a reward, copper? They gives rewards fer information.' The girl held out a dirty hand with black and broken nails. *Thin as a bit o' string*, Stemp thought, *and probably not long for this world or any other*. Stemp had daughters of his own. He also knew what it was to be poor and to have no hope.

He fished in his pocket for a threepenny bit. ''Ere — that's all you're gettin'. Now, be off with you.'

He remembered when it was too late that the girl had not given an address. Maybe they hadn't one. Just lived any place they could. Not that it mattered. They didn't know anything. And the description of the man — they might have made that up. He went to join Feak at the graveside. He looked a little white about the gills.

'Creepy old place, an' this is even creepier. It's just a head, Stemp, I think. I mean, there's no wax body — it's just sort of shaped like a lady.'

Stemp did know, for the waxworks that had come in were much the same, their heads and shoulders made of waxed papier-mâché and their bodies, arms and legs made of linen firmly padded, shaped and neatly stitched. He prodded the body and felt the lumps and bumps. It felt softer, clumsier, like a bolster, and he heard paper crackling. 'Did you look?'

'I didn't like ter. I mean, what if someone saw? What'd it look like? Me liftin' a dead woman's skirt.'

'Maybe the head what was missin' from the judge's house. Nothin' else found?'

'Couldn't really see. What'll we do with her?'

'Arrest her. You take one arm and I'll take the other.'

Their prisoner was perfectly quiet as they escorted her back to Bow Street. No one paid any attention. Arrests, even of quietly veiled ladies, were common in St Giles's.

Superintendent Jones, summoned by Sergeant Rogers, came down to survey the prisoner and to hear the story.

'Just a head?'

'We 'aven't looked, but the body feels like some sort of bolster — softish an' lumpy. Paper in it, too. Not like some of the others,' Stemp explained. 'Didn't want ter be seen liftin' the skirts.'

'This man they saw, do you believe it?'

Stemp thought. 'Don't know about the description. Sounded a bit of a fairy tale ter me — bogeyman, big mouth an' gnashers, but I reckon they did see a man layin' 'er down, an' I believe they did think that it might 'ave been a man with a dollymop. They've seen that before.'

'No one else about, I suppose.'

'Couldn't see a thing in that fog, an' I didn't 'ear anythin'. I mean, 'e only 'ad ter take 'er by the waist an' walk 'er in there. Anyone seein' 'em woulda thought what them kids thought.'

'And they had no idea of the time?'

'I don't think time means anythin' to 'em, sir. The boy 'eard St Giles's clock, but 'e couldn't say 'ow many strokes. Couldn't count, I suppose.'

'There was folk passin', sir, gropin' their way in the fog, but no one stopped ter care about a copper an' two nippers,' Feak said.

'It's different, sir, I think, from the others. Don't seem like a joke like some of 'em. I mean, I sort of thought the graveyard might mean somethin'. Mebbe just the place, though, in the fog.'

'You mean putting the figure on a tomb might mean something more sinister?'

''E was serious, I reckon. 'E threatened them kids. That head, do you think it was from the judge's house?'

'Could be. You can have a look about that graveyard when it's light tomorrow. See if he left anything — and we'd better take her out of the way before anyone starts talking. See if she fits that body we've got.'

'Search 'er, sir?' Stemp grinned, taking the lady in his arms.

Superintendent Jones grinned back. He always relished Constable Stemp's dry humour, but before he could reply, a constable came hurrying in.

'Bad accident on Blackfriars Bridge, sir — collision between a cab an' omnibus — cab goin' to Southwark —'

On which portentous word, two other people came in, somewhat bedraggled and begrimed. Superintendent Jones was not a bit surprised, and he couldn't help enjoying the look of astonishment on Dickens's face as he contemplated Constable Stemp, who appeared to be embracing a one-eyed woman in black.

12: NO NAME

'You followed another woman in black?' Superintendent Jones had left the others to examine the head and its sacking shroud while he listened to the newcomers. Dickens was looking rather dishevelled, his face black with smuts, and he noted the cut on Scrap's head — to be dealt with when he had heard the full story. Dickens had told him about the auction and the woman who had stared at the judge's portrait, and that he and Scrap had followed her cab onto Blackfriars Bridge. The detail about Scrap's perching on the growler had been omitted.

'But the woman said she hadn't known the judge,' Jones pointed out reasonably.

'Ah, well, she wouldn't have known him really, would she? Maybe she was saying that as a wife, she hadn't —' Dickens saw Jones's sceptical eyebrow — 'But it was going to Southwark, so I wondered —'

'I wish you wouldn't. You don't even know if Eliza Quarterman is in Southwark. Twelve years, Charles. She might be anywhere.'

'She might be in the mortuary at King's College Hospital.'

'The veiled one is the casualty, I take it.'

Then Superintendent Jones listened to the account of the accident, Dickens's meeting with Doctor Mayo, the eventual lifting of the fog, the clearing of the bridge, and the removal by cart of the body to King's College, where Doctor Woodhall was to perform the post-mortem, and Dickens's idea that Superintendent Jones might like to —

'Er — investigate,' he finished.

'I will — on the condition that if she is not Eliza Quarterman, you swear that you will not follow any more women in black veils, young, old, with a stick, without, in a cab, or on foot. Not in any cart or carriage — two-hander or four —' he raised his hand before Dickens could interrupt — 'or by railway train or steamboat. And that goes for you, too,' Jones added, looking at Scrap.

Dickens had to laugh, but he promised. However, he couldn't help asking, 'And if she is?'

'I haven't the faintest idea. I'll only know that she has perished in an accident on Blackfriars Bridge. How far across the bridge?'

'Not far from the Bridge Street side.'

'Pity it wasn't the Southwark side, then it wouldn't be my business at all. As it is, and since you have so thoughtfully arranged her removal to King's College, I've not much choice.'

They went out into Bow Street, where Jones turned to Scrap. 'You'd better get off and see Mrs Jones about that cut. I won't ask how it happened.'

Scrap would have liked to know if the woman was this Eliza Quarterman, but he was too wise to linger. He had recognised Mr Jones's "I mean it" tone. Anyway, he thought, let Mr D. explain. He could take the blame. Mr D. did. Without prevarication. Mr Jones tutted, and Mr D. also kept wisely silent until they arrived at King's College Hospital in Portugal Street, just below Lincoln's Inn, only a few minutes away. Dickens and Jones knew Doctor Woodhall and his mortuary very well. Doctor Woodhall was not surprised to see the superintendent again, having spoken briefly to Dickens about the dead woman from Blackfriars Bridge.

'She was crushed under the cab — broken pelvis and legs, and injuries to the chest,' he told them, indicating the covered figure. 'It is doubtful that she could have survived those injuries. The actual cause of death was suffocation. She was trapped under the cab for some time, I believe.'

'About twenty minutes to half an hour, I think, by the time the police organised men to lift the cab.'

'What age do you think she was?' Jones asked.

'I should put her at fifty years, or more. She has had a hard life. No wedding ring, but she has borne a child or children. There might be family somewhere.'

Too old for Eliza Quarterman, Dickens thought, who would now be in her thirties. Had he and Scrap followed the wrong woman in that crowd outside the auction house? Very likely. It was becoming a habit.

'Any identification?' Jones asked, looking at the clothes on the table.

'Nothing,' Doctor Woodhall's mortuary assistant answered. 'There are no labels on the clothes and no laundry marks. Nothing in the pockets except this key — unusual design.'

Dickens took the key and they looked at it. It was about three inches long and was made of iron, with a wrought circle on the top in which there was a cross. It looked more like the key to a church than to a house.

'It doesn't look like the keys Mrs Flint gave us — not the judge's front or back door,' Dickens said.

'Nor the yard key.' Jones turned back to Doctor Woodhall. 'If you'll keep her for a few days, we'll advertise. Someone might come forward, and there'll be the inquest on the accident.'

Dickens examined the clothes. The black dress and cape were worn but carefully darned in places. The leather of the boots was old but polished to a shine. Warren's Blacking, perhaps, or Mr Day's, he of the chancery suit. The soles had been mended and there was mud on them from the streets, and mud on the black skirts and on the white petticoat, but the cotton was clean and smelt fresh. A woman with not much money, but neat and clean.

Cold as any stone, and as mysterious. Whoever she was, she had taken her secrets with her. She had gone into that inscrutable dark, too deep for sense or sound, the dark from which no word could come. If no one claimed her, then it would be a pauper's grave.

Outside the hospital, Jones said, 'Too old for Eliza Quarterman, I imagine?'

'I should say so. I don't think she was the woman who looked at the portrait. Pity. Nor can I say if she is the woman who passed me at the waxworks.'

'I should give up following women in black if I were you,' Jones observed drily. 'One of them might turn on you one of these days.'

'A hit, Samivel, a very palpable hit — straight to the heart.'

But Samivel was striding on, seemingly oblivious to the wound he had inflicted on his amateur detective. Dickens had the last laugh, however, as he hurried to catch up, almost tripping on the ladder of a billsticker who was wrestling with the flapping folds of a sheet which he was attempting to stick on the wall. The billsticker cried out, but Dickens held onto the ladder while the man managed to complete his task. Sam Jones came back, and they both looked up to the poster. Two words in letters a foot long asked, *WHERE'S ELIZA?* Dickens read the phrase aloud.

'Dunno,' the billsticker answered without looking down, 'missin', I supposes.'

Dickens affected to help Jones away. 'It's the name, sir!' he shouted to the man. 'It always brings on his fit!'

Another mystery, Dickens thought, and the next time he passed down Duke Street on his way to Lincoln's Inn, the poster had blown away. Eliza blown away on the wind.

13: MR HOUNDSFOOT'S NEWS

Dickens and Jones looked at the clothes which had been removed to reveal the stuffed coal sack which had been the body. The dress gave nothing away. It could have come from any second-hand clothes shop or market stall, as could all the other black dresses on the other figures. No labels, of course, and no laundry marks giving a useful name. The contents of the coal sack were laid out on a table that had been put in the cell to which the wax head had been conveyed. It lay there, too, its glassy eye giving it the cock-eyed look of a winking barmaid who knew that her customer had had enough, but the empty space on the other side kept its secrets and the blank face told nothing. It could have been the anonymous face of any of hundreds of servant girls or seamstresses whom you saw in the street, though, of course, the popular prejudice ran in favour of two eyes for most mortals. And it had a wooden post below its neck.

'That post maybe slotted into the shoulders. It did have a body. A glass eye, too. The head from the judge's house?'

'I should say so — it fits on the headless body,' Jones said.

The rags were remnants of clothing dirtied by coal dust — torn, grubby shirts, bits of old petticoat and drawers; part of a moth-eaten shawl, the colour of snuff; what looked like old rags of sheets and pillowcases; some greasy bits of cloth, and even a remnant of a horse's nosebag. They could have come from any old rag-shop or dust heap. There was wrapping paper, too, which Rogers had smoothed out for them to read the lettering. They made out the partial words: *The Lond-n Soa-Comp--y*, *mfctr*, *Wax Cand---*, *oils and soa--*.

'Wax,' Dickens said. 'That company is in New Bond Street.'

'And every grocer, chemist, and candle shop in London,' Jones said. 'They all buy in bulk.'

'Woolley's in Denmark Street — they sells wax in bulk, sir. Know a fellow there,' Stemp said. 'Denmark Street near St Giles's Church.'

Jones thought about that. 'Discreet enquiries, Stemp. Anyone who once worked in the wax figure trade, for example, or anyone suddenly missing from work — you know the sort of thing. The story about the graveyard will have got out by now. With any luck, it will just be taken as part of the jokery, but you might hear something.'

'What about the maker?' Dickens asked when Stemp had departed.

'Rogers found a Signor Barone, who —'

'Ah, Serafino —'

'Sera — what?'

'Signor Serafino Barone, Mr Rogers, High Holborn, 129, only begetter of the speaking doll —'

Rogers opened his mouth. Superintendent Jones could only manage the faint words, 'Oh, no, not speaking — no —' He only recovered himself to ask, 'Why didn't you say?'

'Oh, Mr Dickens, if you knew how many Italian places we've been to!'

'No, well, I didn't think. Toy dolls, you see, not life-sized figures. Two feet tall at the most. Ladies of distinction, dressed in the height of fashion. I have one at home —' seeing their still incredulous faces — 'not mine, of course, though she does call me Papa. Name of —'

'I really don't want to know,' Jones interrupted.

'It's not — ah, never mind, but Signor Barone does only make toy dolls. He is an artist, and I can't imagine him making

114

the kind of dolls you've got in the cells. He makes speaking dolls, too. There's a secret to the talking mechanism which he won't reveal. It's a family business — wife, son, daughter-in-law. Exports to America and the Continent. It's a good business.'

'Which is now closed. It seems that Signor Barone has returned to Italy — oddly enough on the day of the judge's death. Give Mr Dickens the details, Rogers.'

'The workshop's all closed up. I spoke to a fellow at a neighbouring place. Said he hadn't seen the signor, though he had said he was going to Italy an' was thinkin' about closin' the business. Said he did occasionally make life-size figures — for wealthy clients. That's why I wondered.'

'We need to get in there, Rogers. On the quiet, I think. All this waxworks stuff in the papers and now this head in a graveyard — some journalist'll get onto it. Later on, I'd say. Rogers, get a man to keep an eye on the workshop until we get there. If there's any more wax figures in black lurking there, I want this caper stopped.'

Dickens and Jones went up to Jones's office, where there was a selection of newspapers laid out with *The Police Gazette* on top.

'Research?'

'It will be, while we're waiting for Stemp to come back. But first I need to tell you about Mr Ebenezer Houndsfoot —'

'Ah, sniffed out something, I take it.'

'Indeed, he has. He's the judge's solicitor. He came in earlier with some news which made me think about who might have wished to harm the judge.'

'I'm all agog.'

'You remember that the proceeds from the house and the goods therein went to his friend at Doctors' Commons, and there was a legacy to Mrs Flint of one hundred pounds. Mr Houndsfoot dealt with all that, but he was puzzled by the judge's bank statements. He was never a spender, but over the last six months on a regular basis, large sums of money had been withdrawn — three hundred pounds each month, and nothing to show for it. Nothing new in the house. No pictures, no curios, or trinkets, other than the silver that was kept in the safe and bought years ago, according to the receipts. The judge was a careful man — noted the price of everything he had bought. Pity he didn't note down the name of whoever he gave that money to. And that diamond cross Mrs Flint spoke about was missing from the safe.'

'Blackmail? He was selling stuff, too, according to Mrs Flint. Needed cash to pay the blackmailer? And Mrs Flint mentioned a gold enamel box. Gave them in lieu of cash? Did the solicitor say there was anything different about Quarterman, anything to suggest that he was worried, anxious, distracted in the last months?'

'Never saw him. Mind you, no one saw much of him. Mrs Flint said that the Doctors' Commons man hadn't been for months.'

'And I can't say that the judge looked frightened or worried when I met him at Tussaud's. Angry, if anything. Bitter, certainly.'

'Someone knew something about him, about his wife?' Jones speculated.

'Good Lord, Sam, you don't think... I mean, there was gossip. Mrs Flint, Ma Dunk and Pruey had all heard rumours. And Quarterman said to me that the law was right to murder when evil had been done. He was the law — a law unto himself, perhaps.'

'He thought so in court. He must have been paying someone and Mrs Flint never knew where he was going. Long, solitary walks. Off to meet his blackmailer, maybe.'

'If the judge had murdered Eliza Quarterman, then perhaps he had an accomplice. Someone who turned up again wanting more.'

'Never thinking he'd die of fright, but now he's dead, why not leave it alone? Why keep drawing attention to the case? The inquest verdict was quite clear. The judge wasn't murdered.'

Dickens thought about that. 'Unless none of the waxworks you've got is to do with the judge's death. They were stolen for a crazy joke and we're on the wrong track. The footprint in the dust is someone quite separate.'

'I don't like that mask business. Of Manning, the murderer. And a noose. That poor woman was half scared to death, and there was this last figure in the graveyard and the man who threatened those two children. Even Stemp thought there was something sinister about that. He thought the graveyard might mean something.'

'I see that. Leaving a waxwork at the wax chandler's, the cab stand, the toyshop, and that Anatomy Museum is a lark. I can imagine someone enjoying himself hugely, especially as it escalated and then the candles came in and the toy dolls, but the mask of a murderer and the figure on a grave, that is more macabre. And that black-edged card with the wax hand.'

Rogers came to say that he had dispatched a constable to Signor Barone's shop with instructions to keep watch on the alley behind. 'Thought it more likely that someone might sneak in the back way.'

'Good, we'll wait for Stemp. In the meantime, I thought we'd have a look for Elizas remanded in Newgate, trial to proceed at the Old Bailey, or, of course, Eliza victims in those cases.'

'The blackmailer connected to an Eliza victim?' Dickens asked.

'I did wonder. The *Gazette* will give us names and we can then look at the newspaper reports, which will tell us if Judge Quarterman presided.'

'Eliza Collier's case was January this year,' Rogers said, 'an' Eliza Winton in 1846 — p'raps we should concentrate on the years in between.'

The turn of Mary-Anns and Marys, Dickens thought, who were out in force on the pages he turned, stealing bonnets, buttons and butter, caps — lace, silk, calico; gowns and guns; cheese, chops — and choppers, though that was a Mary-Ann with her husband; shoes, shawls, shirts; a salmon; a pig's cheek; a haunch of mutton; rope; rags — dear Lord, anything that was not screwed down, though a Daniel Proud had managed to steal a street door. He ignored the Eliza who had stolen two teaspoons. Mary Fuzzle — could that be? — had stolen some lemon peel and flour. Birthday cake? Angela, Georgina, and Belinda Waxman were remanded for assault. Should that be waxmen? Waxgirls? He did not read out the name. Three savage sisters, it seemed. In another life, they might have been the Three Graces with those poetical names. Woollens, watches, wooden boxes, and heavens, another Eliza had stolen a widgeon — bird-fancier, then? It was going to be a long night.

It was. All that could be heard was the turning of pages and the occasional intake of breath. An Eliza found, perhaps? But no, a sigh would follow. Only another teaspoon, or a tippet, though Rogers was heard to chuckle, and when Dickens and

Jones looked up, he couldn't resist reminding Superintendent Jones about the man who stole a shotgun and shot himself in the foot. 'Lived just off Pepper Street.'

Dickens grinned. 'Southwark.'

'And no Eliza in the case,' Jones countered.

'Wife was a Charlotte,' Rogers said. 'Beefy sort o' lady. Inspector Wells over there had an idea she might have shot him, but the husband was more frightened of her than the police. Six months, he got.'

'And a life sentence with Missis,' Dickens said.

They bent to their task again. It was Rogers who found Eliza Parr. 'Should have thought of her, sir. 1847. Lived with a man called James Munton in Golden Lane. They had a new baby that died of a wound in the throat, and James Munton's son said he saw Eliza Parr harm the child. The evidence was conflictin' with some neighbour sayin' that James Munton had beaten Eliza Parr an' that he'd admitted he'd harmed the baby. They swore that Eliza wouldn't have done it. She loved the child, but in the end, she was transported, and James Munton was hanged. Now, the judge, who was Quarterman, referred to a previous case involving Parr. She'd had another baby that died an' she was had up before the magistrate. She was acquitted of harmin' that child, but o' course, the jury would have thought of that, an' she wasn't married to Munton, nor to the other child's father.'

'Sounds like just the sort of Eliza Judge Quarterman would have taken against,' Dickens said.

'I don't know what happened to the son. He'd have reason to hate the judge. Can you recall his name, Rogers?'

'No, I can't.'

'See what you can find in one of the newspapers. Mr Dickens and I will look at the Elizas we know, and who might have been harbouring a grudge against Quarterman.'

'What happened to that fellow you mentioned who was acquitted, the one who'd seduced Eliza Winton?'

'Thomas Dryden. He was a bad lot, but in court he came over as the gentlemanly type. Of course, Judge Quarterman fell for that. Mrs Dryden had some sort of business — a prosperous shop selling fancy goods. Very genteel. She stood by him, said in court that Eliza Winton was a customer of hers —'

'An' what would a poor barmaid like Eliza Winton be buyin' in a fancy goods shop?' Rogers asked.

'Quite, but she insisted that there was nothing going on between him and Eliza. They'd tried to help her — they'd given her money, and Eliza Winton had gone to the abortionist. Nothing to do with them. They didn't care tuppence about a dead girl. And neither did Judge Quarterman.'

Jones found the newspaper report of the Eliza Winton case, which he handed to Dickens. 'Hm,' Dickens said after a minute or two. 'Her father didn't know of any other lover, but that doesn't mean she didn't have one. And the woman who carried out the abortion was transported. Any relatives there, I wonder?'

'I doubt they'd be liberating Eliza Winton's wax effigy, and Dryden had every reason to be grateful to the judge.'

'Parr,' Rogers said. 'Found it. The son was Joshua Munton, aged fourteen at the time. Eliza Parr came from Hampshire. The lad testified that Eliza Parr and his father had lived together for a couple of years. His father had brought her home to live with them. He didn't know where his mother was.

Course, there's no reference to any family that Eliza Parr had. I don't know — it doesn't seem likely that the son would be stealin' waxworks. He might have blamed the judge for his father's bein' hanged, but they were all dirt poor, Mr Jones. An' the Colliers, if you remember. Collier was a drunk.'

'There was a sister.'

'There was. Now, she was a respectable woman — lived out beyond Holloway, a blacksmith's wife. Can't see her doin' it, either.'

'Good thought, Alf. I can't imagine Eliza Winton's father stealing waxworks, either. He lived at Walworth, as I recall. Shoemaker, I think. Respectable man.'

'I can't see the people we're talking about doing it,' Dickens said. 'Leaving the waxworks here and there. It probably turned out better than they could have imagined. It's annoying, I know, but ingenious, really. Witty, even. Think about the person who dressed up as one of the judge's waxworks and waited there until I'd gone. That's ingenious in its way, certainly elaborate.'

'Blackmail requires imagination,' Jones said. 'You've to think what might hurt your victim most.'

'Choose the thing which could be true. It's deniable, but there is the possibility that it could have happened. Mud sticks and all that.'

'There was that clergyman, a single man,' Rogers interrupted, 'who was lured to a brothel supposedly to attend to a dying woman. Course, there was nobody dyin' — a lot of women undressed an' their pimps tellin' him to pay up or they'd tell the newspapers. He wasn't havin' it an' they were had up for attempted blackmail an' found guilty, but there were them as wondered. Had to leave his parish.'

'And supposing the judge was being blackmailed about murder, he could deny it, but where was Eliza Quarterman? Nobody could say. He wouldn't want the story brought up again. And if he had done it, he'd certainly pay up,' Dickens said.

Jones took a pencil and wrote for a few moments, then he looked at what he had written. 'So, we have a possible murder, possible blackmail; one faint footprint in the judge's chamber of horrors, possibly a woman's; a collection of unidentifiable waxworks, some — we don't know which — stolen from the judge; one wax head from a graveyard; and an unidentified woman in Doctor Woodhall's mortuary. Thomas Dryden who had every reason to be grateful to the judge — unlikely; Eliza Collier's sister, respectable wife of a blacksmith — unlikely. And Eliza Parr's stepson whose father was hanged, though he did give evidence against Eliza Parr —'

'Thin, though, sir — I mean, if you're thinkin' someone's doin' all this because of Eliza Parr, who had nothin' an' was nobody. An' as Mr Dickens says, it's all a bit elaborate for such a poor lot.'

'Not much left then, is there?'

'Nothing will come of nothing,' Dickens said in Shakesperean mode.

'Very helpful. Much obliged, I'm sure. Let's do something practical. Tomorrow, Rogers, you can go to Walworth about Eliza Winton's father, Inspector Grove can go up to Holloway, and Stemp can set about tracing Eliza Parr's stepson. He can start with those neighbours. For the Lord's sake, let's eliminate somebody, anybody.'

Stemp returned to tell them that he had met his acquaintance in St Giles's, but he hadn't heard anything to the purpose — the usual comings and goings from any business. No one in particular that the man could remember. The story of the waxwork in the graveyard was much talked about, but people thought it all a joke.

As they made to leave for Signor Barone's premises, Constable Feak came in with an interesting snippet of information.

'That Ma Dunk an' Pruey, seen 'em in a cart driven by a young man, goin' down Paradise Street towards where they lives in that yard. Young man drops 'em off by the 'ouse an' makes 'is way along up by the burial ground. Didn't see 'im come out.'

'Good, Feak, you can investigate tomorrow when it's light. We're off to a doll shop. Bring your lamp.'

14: ARTIST IN WAX

Feak guarded the front door and Stemp stayed in the yard with his truncheon at the ready. Jones's keys opened the back door of the workshop, and their lamps first revealed a huge pot-bellied stove, unlit now, cauldrons of various sizes, and huge earthenware jugs. They could smell wax, paint, and glue.

In the next room, the lamplight picked out the shelves of faintly glistening wax heads atop little torsos in serried ranks. Some heads were made of papier-mâché, some of plaster, and all were horribly bald like the shaven heads of lunatics. Boxes of blue glass eyes winked back at them, coldly knowing, and there was a table on which a headless thing lay, its body apparently swaddled in calico, its leather arms at its side. Its terrible flatness, Dickens thought, gave the impression of an Egyptian mummy. A row of similarly swathed dolls were on a shelf, looking out at them with glittering eyes. A Lilliputian chamber of horrors.

Certainly, a maker of dolls, the signor, but these were, as Dickens had said, children's dolls waiting for their dresses or their sailors' outfits. They were the same size as Mamie's Betsey Prig, whom he hoped had packed her portmanteau and departed for the Lemon household. There was no sign of any adult-size figures or heads. Dickens and Jones crept into the next room, where there were some finished heads, beautifully painted, but they were still dolls' heads and shoulders waiting for their other parts to be assembled, and presumably waiting for their Day of Judgement, when a little girl would love them or not. Dickens thought of his daughter Katey. Her judgement would be a raised eyebrow and the curl of a lip.

He lifted his lamp to have a close look at one of the wax heads. It seemed to him very like the Beauty. There was the same delicate tinting of the cheeks, and the lips were slightly parted, as if she might speak. The shoulders were beautifully modelled, but that was the end of her. Dickens wondered if Signor Barone had perhaps been specially commissioned to make the life-sized models for the judge. It was possible, if the money was good.

'That one looks like the judge's Beauty,' he whispered to Jones, who raised his lamp, too. 'I wonder if the signor made her.'

They moved into the next room, where there were shelves full of fabrics, laces and ribbons, and little shoes and boots made of felt or leather. There were elaborately flounced dresses — that mania was still about, then — capes, velvet cloaks, fringes, lace collars and beads, and there were wigs, mostly ringleted, mostly blonde, but some brown or auburn, and more bald heads, but everything was on a miniature scale, including the shelf of finished dolls in their court dresses. Waiting to be presented to Her Miniature Majesty, perhaps.

Beyond the door was a space which turned out to be a hall from which a staircase ascended. In front of them was another door which they found led into the shop front, where there were finished dolls looking out into the street. At nothing, Dickens hoped.

Rogers kept watch at the bottom of the stairs while Dickens and Jones went up to where Signor Barone must have lived before his precipitate departure. One of the doors was open and as they stood waiting and listening, they heard the faintest of whistling, followed by a grunt and then rustling. Someone was asleep.

Nothing for it but to exploit the surprise. Jones kicked open the door and shouted, 'Police!'

There was a thump and a cry, and in they went to see a fully dressed man on the floor, tangled in a blanket, his mouth open, and his dark eyes wide and frightened. Dickens recognised him as Signor Barone, albeit unusually dishevelled and discomposed. He was a man who normally had the seraphic composure of one of his dolls.

'*Dio mio*, you scare me to death. What do you want?'

'Signor Barone?' Jones asked.

'Who else? It is my house.'

Dickens tried to remember his Italian. '*Scusi il disturbo*, Signor Barone, *vorremmo* —'

Scrambling to his feet and kicking aside the blanket, the *signor* interrupted, 'Signor Dickens — why do you bring the police?'

Dickens explained in English about Judge Quarterman's waxworks. They wanted to know if the *signor* had made them.

'I did not wish to do it — to make murderesses. Ugly faces. That is for Madame Tussaud. *Dio*, my wife, she did not like them, but the judge — a wealthy man. He offered a good deal of money, and I wished to go back to Italy. We all wished to go. I have taken my secret mechanical voice to Italy. We have taken a fine workshop in Florence, so the money is good, and no one would know. I will pack up here and take my stock with me.'

'Did you make the Sleeping Beauty?'

'That was different — that was art. I copied from a little painting he had. I made her breathe, but not speak. He did not want that. She was beautiful, but the judge did not say who she was. Signor Dickens, he was a strange man — not *sympatico*, but if he wanted wax dolls, I made them. I did not ask why.'

'Judge Quarterman had other wax figures. Their faces were all the same.'

'No, no, he gave me engravings of the faces he wanted. I knew which was Mrs Manning — I made six of them. I did not want to know who they were. Only six.'

'Do you know of any other waxworks artist whom the judge might have approached?'

'No, he spoke only of the ones he wanted. Why do you wish to know all this?'

'The judge is dead,' Jones told him, 'and some of his other waxworks have been stolen. I'm trying to find out who made them.'

Signor Barone crossed himself. '*Dio*. You think I took them?'

'It was a possibility, but I realise now that you did not. My apologies for disturbing you.'

Signor Barone looked at the tangled blanket on the floor. 'You gave me a scare, coming in the night. That was necessary?'

'I am sorry, sir, but someone has been placing waxwork figures all around the town. It was necessary to do it quietly — possibly to find the waxworks and put a stop to whoever it is.'

'It is a joke?'

Jones didn't want to tell the *signor* anything about murder. He only said, 'Possibly, but I need to find out who is doing it. It is a nuisance.'

'I am an artist, *signor*. I do not need cheap tricks to sell my dolls —' bowing to Mr Dickens — 'dolls for the best families. I am the only maker of the speaking dolls. It is my secret, which I dreamt of for many years. I make them say "mamma" and "papa". I once took a lady to a party and made her speak on the stairs. A young man turned white — he thought it was a spirit —' Dickens could well imagine. He had heard that slightly ghostly, apparently disembodied voice in his own drawing room. He had a chilling image of all the dolls in the cells at Bow Street suddenly crying out the name of the blackmailer, all the dolls in London joining in some unearthly chorus of accusation.

However, he concentrated on Signor Barone, who was still speaking. 'But there are others, of course, who make fine dolls. The best are Signor Montanari in Soho and Signor Pierotti. The English ones are not so fine. Signor Haggett in Cheapside, Signor Brogden in Hatton Garden, and more, I think.'

'Thank you, Signor Barone. We will ask. I wonder, though, if you would oblige me by coming to Bow Street to look at the dolls we have. You might be able to tell if they are made by anyone you know.'

'At this time? I have come from Italy this evening.'

'It would be very helpful, sir.'

'Very well. I will not sleep now.'

At Bow Street, Signor Barone looked at the wax figures critically. 'Anyone could have made these — they are made by an apprentice, perhaps, someone who knows something about the modelling, but is not an artist. It is not my work, nor that of Signor Montanari or Signor Pierotti. Our work is the finest in London — this is crude. Look at the faces. The painting is flat; it has no life, no shade, no skill. The wax is too yellow. It is fairground work.'

The *signor* was an enthusiast. What they had not known about the making of fine wax dolls, they knew by the time he had departed. Signor Barone used real hair inserted with a special needle — unlike the wigs of the captured dolls — or sometimes the softest mohair. He also used the finest silk and lace, seed pearls for caps, and only glass eyes, never painted ones. So, the figures with painted eyes could be eliminated — some joker, as they had thought. The judge's murderesses had had glass eyes, as had the two victim faces Dickens had seen. Judge Quarterman would not have accepted anything less, he thought, but he had accepted the yellowish faces of the victims. Who had persuaded him to buy those inferior figures?

When, at last, Signor Barone departed, Jones said, 'Well, I suppose we've eliminated him, but we're left with any number of possibilities. Someone knew enough about the wax figure trade to make them for Judge Quarterman, or to get hold of them.'

'One of those eye men any use?' Dickens suggested.

That was the only nugget of useful information from the *signor*'s treatise on doll-making. It seemed that there were only two makers of dolls' glass eyes in London. The *signor* bought his from the one in Chandos Street, and the other was in Earl Street. Superintendent Jones hardly dared contemplate the manufacturers of medical glass eyes. Or taxidermy. Grim thought. Chandos Street it would have to be tomorrow, first thing.

'Ye who have eyes and see not,' Dickens murmured as he parted from the Superintendent at Tavistock Square, to which the latter replied drily, 'I have ears and hear not,' before marching away smartly.

'Tomorrow, and tomorrow!' Dickens called after him, but Sam Jones was gone, leaving Dickens to contemplate the blind windows of his house. Good Lord, after midnight.

15: A PAIR OF FRIGHTENED EYES

Five hundred and seventy-six thousand eyes — not that they were all staring at Dickens and Jones, for which small mercy they were grateful, though there were enough gazing up at them from opened boxes to create a dizzying sense of unreality. Mr Payne, the dolls' glass eye-maker of Chandos Street, proved as loquacious an enthusiast as Signor Barone, and if he had been made in the image of a waxwork doll, he could not have been less useful. He had, it seemed, one hundred years in the trade. His grey beard suggested so, but it was his father who had served the first sixty years, and Mr Payne, the younger, had served a mere forty — which forty seemed a very long time to his listeners.

Twenty-four thousand dozen pairs of eyes could be manufactured in one year. There was a kind of madness in his glittering eye, Dickens thought, as Mr Payne lifted the lids of box after box of eyes and gave them — not that they wanted it — the staggering total of five hundred thousand etcetera… They were transfixed in wonder, like the Ancient Mariner's wedding guest. Six shillings for twelve dozen pairs of common eyes. Four pence a pair for good ones. Blue eyes most in demand. Her Majesty, blue eyes, did they see? They did, though Mr Jones's grey ones closed for a moment. Eyes exported to America. Eyes made for a French house in Le Havre. Black eyes always for South America.

Dickens managed a glassy-eyed nod. Mr Payne was gratified, taking up a blue eye in his delicate fingers with the air of a connoisseur selecting a particularly choice sugar plum. 'What we call common eyes, sirs, made of hollow glass, enamelled and painted blue or black — blue mostly. That's what the lads an' girls are workin' on.' He pointed to the nearest table where three young ladies were bent to their task, paint jars to hand and brushes working. They looked up at the visitors and Dickens saw two pretty, smiling faces. Mr Payne explained, 'These three are working on what we call a natural eye — very delicate work, for the iris must be correctly represented. Emma, bring the eye you're doin'.'

Emma seemed rather reluctant. Perhaps the work was difficult and did not bear interruption, Dickens thought. However, she came and held out the eye, though hers remained downcast. The light on the glass made it glint all too realistically. There was even a slight touch of green near the pupil in the centre of the painted blue iris, which had a darker circle around it. It was very finely done, and Dickens said so. Emma went silently back to her place at the table.

'The *signor*,' Mr Payne continued, answering one of Jones's introductory remarks at least, but his point was to explain that Signor Barone had placed an order for £50 for natural eyes. Signor Barone was an artist, o' course. Mr Payne had made eyes for the Montanari family, who were waxwork makers. Bigger eyes, o' course, an' a lot o' delicate work. Now, Madame Tussaud's, they had their own —

Superintendent Jones came out of what had seemed to Dickens like a glaze-eyed trance and hastily interrupted, 'Yes, indeed, Mr Payne. However, I wished to know if you have had a new customer recently for a small quantity of natural eyes, say, over the last year — a private individual, for example.'

Mr Payne's customers were known to him. He could supply the superintendent with their names, of course, and the addresses of the warehouses and shops he dealt with. The superintendent expressed his gratitude and suggested that Mr

Payne might send a messenger with the list to Bow Street as soon as was convenient — though never, was his inward hope. With that, Dickens and Jones departed before Mr Payne could expiate any further on his eyes, or anybody else's. Dickens glanced back as Jones preceded him through the open doorway. Mr Payne was replacing the lids on his boxes; two of the young ladies were busy at their natural eyes. One pair of eyes was looking at him. *Distinctive eyes, hazel,* he thought, with what looked like a dark stain in one iris, in a thin face with two hectic spots on the cheeks. Frightened eyes. He turned away quickly. *What was worrying her?* he asked himself.

'I suppose we'll have to make our way to Earl Street,' Jones said, 'but the thought of —' Seeing Dickens's abstracted air, he asked sharply, 'What?'

'That girl, the one who showed us the natural eye, she was watching us as we were leaving. She looked frightened. Payne said they made eyes for waxwork figures, too. Five hundred thousand eyes, Sammy, my lad, easy enough to slip a few blanks in your pocket and then paint 'em up for someone.'

'It would be. I don't suppose you saw what colour eyes the victims had?'

'Too dark — just a sort of glitter in the candlelight. Glass, though, I'm sure. Is it worth pursuing young Emma?'

'I'll put a watch on her —'

'Scrap — he'll be waiting for something to do after... I shouldn't have let him perch on that cab.'

'I don't suppose you could have stopped him. He'll keep himself invisible watching the girl, but, of course, she might be selling them on her own account to small doll-makers who won't be wanting to buy by the dozens. Still, she might be a lead. Someone made those Eliza figures for Quarterman, and he didn't want anyone knowing who it was.'

'Man of many secrets, the judge.'

'Damn his eyes, and Mr Payne's.'

Dickens laughed, 'And Mr Earl Street's, too.'

'Let's get on with it.'

An hour later and none the wiser, they returned to Bow Street. Mr Earl Street, who was really the amiable Mr Jewell, had greeted them in his office where only a few boxes of glass eyes, fortunately with their lids closed, were on his desk. He laughed very loudly when Jones said they had come from Mr Payne's establishment.

'You'll not want to see my samples, then.'

'No, sir, we are fully apprised of the intricacies of the manufacture and sale of dolls' eyes,' Jones had told him and then had repeated his enquiry about a newish customer for a small order of natural eyes, to which Mr Jewell had shaken his large head and informed them that customers rarely came in off-chance, and if they did, it would be with references which told him which house they represented. And he knew all his customers — he could let Mr Jones have a list if he wanted. When asked if there were any pilfering of eyes, he readily admitted that there could be, but the numbers would be so small as to be worthless — a few pennies from a cheap doll-maker, but more trouble than they were worth. He trusted his workers and he had sharp eyes. In any case, cheap doll-makers generally painted the eyes. It was faster and their customers weren't so fussy.

'So,' Dickens observed, as they went up the steps of the police station, 'Miss Emma, if she is stealing, might well have someone other than a cheap doll-maker —'

What Mr Jones thought of that, he had no time to utter, for Constable Feak was waiting to tell them the latest startling news. Sergeant Rogers and Constable Stemp were already at Paradise Street — a stone's throw from Ma Dunk's laundry in Paradise Yard, in the vicinity of which Constable Feak had been looking for a driver and his cart when a young man had appeared, shouting for a policeman.

16: CLEAN LAUNDRY, AND DIRTY

The corpse of the young man lay in Burying Ground Passage, a crooked little alley off Paradise Street, which led to the Marylebone Workhouse. The geography was grimly apt, Dickens always thought — out of the workhouse, through the passage, into the burial ground hard by, and off to Paradise when the day came, if it ever did for the jumbled residents of the crowded graves. The passage abutted the graveyard, where the body had fallen onto the muddy stones. The smell of blood mingled with the stink of urine. He had been stabbed in the back.

A young man, in his early twenties, Jones thought, not well-dressed but not dirt-poor, either; brown jacket and black trousers, a bit shiny with wear, a coarse woollen scarf now stained with blood, a rough cap that had fallen off, to reveal rather lank brown hair, scuffed boots a bit down at the heel. Nothing to suggest, however, that he had been worth robbing.

'Nothing to say who he is?' Jones asked, somehow knowing the answer.

'Nothing in the pockets of the jacket or trousers as far as I could tell, though I ain't moved 'im at all,' Stemp said.

'What did the witness have to say?'

'Peter Larkins — I took him home,' Rogers answered. 'He was a bit rattled. Just a lad taking a shortcut from Crawford Street. Lives in South Street with his ma. Got the impression they are respectable folk. His mother didn't like him going that way, near the burial ground, but he often did it.'

'What was he doing in Crawford Street?'

'Harp lesson.'

'What?'

'Said they were respectable — he's learning to play the harp.' Rogers grinned. 'Miss Stringer at number twenty-four, so he says. I'll have to check, of course.'

Dickens couldn't help laughing. 'The name or the address?'

'I don't think he's anythin' to do with it. Sensitive type, I'd say. His ma was all of a flutter. Couldn't get him inside fast enough. He'll have taken to his bed by now. He said he didn't know the man — almost tripped over him. Thought he was a drunk, then he saw the blood.'

'He didn't hear or see anybody?'

'Only when he ran out of the alley to get help. He saw a couple o' people passin' an' then he saw Feak, who shouted for Stemp.'

'More likely he went out at the top of the alley towards the burial ground. It would be quicker that way. He was probably gone before Mr Larkins arrived. We'd better get the body out of here. Mr Dickens and I'll go up to the workhouse and organise a cart to take him to the infirmary there. Stemp, you stay with the body, and Rogers and Feak, you'd better get on with enquiries. Anyone saw the victim, knew him, the usual thing. He didn't drop from the sky.'

'The laundry, sir, Ma Dunk. I was lookin' about that little court behind Paradise Street, and I saw the girl go out with a basket o' laundry and 'eard 'er shout somethin' back ter the ma, so she was in.'

'Paradise Street, and South Street where Mrs Flint lives, and Manchester Square where the judge lived,' Dickens said.

'All very suggestive, perhaps. Let's not disturb Ma Dunk just yet — let's just see if we can find out who he is first.'

A single stab wound in the back which had penetrated the ventricle of the heart. What the workhouse infirmary doctor called an 'absolutely mortal wound'. The cleanness and regularity of the stab wound, its form and depth suggested a long single-bladed knife. But as there was no knife left at the scene of the crime, that information was not much use, considering that long single-bladed knives were found in abundance in homes, butchers' shops, ships, docks, fishmongers, factories — including wax and tallow factories — in short, anywhere a policeman in search of a murderer might care to look. And just as unhelpful was the fact that there was nothing on the body to tell them who the victim was.

He was about twenty years old; his outer clothes were unremarkable, his face was unremarkable — one of the unremarkable poor whose lives passed without notice. *A poor, bare, forked animal*, Dickens thought as he looked down at him. His life appeared to have had no meaning, though his death had. A murder always meant something, however unpremeditated it might have been. A random act of violence had a meaning. It meant rage against one who had harmed the desperate perpetrator, or madness, or despair, even hatred of the world and its injustice. Something in the murderer's sudden eruption had a cause. And if it were not a random act, then someone had wanted this man dead. Someone hated or feared him, and, besides, there was one remarkable thing about him.

'Remarkably clean linen,' Dickens observed. Unusually, the shirt and underclothes were clean.

Jones lifted the shirt to his nose. 'Starched, too, quite fresh. And a laundry nearby. Friend of Ma Dunk's, perhaps.'

'Good Lord, Sam, The London Soap Company — that paper stuffed into that coal sack found on the grave in St Giles's. Soap. Rags of old clothes.'

'And a cart, Charles Dickens, a cart carrying Ma Dunk and Pruey, driven by a young man.'

'Disappearing up by the burial ground. Ma Dunk up to her elbows in it.'

'And further, maybe. Things are moving.'

Indeed, they were. 'Found him,' Sergeant Rogers said, as Dickens and Jones arrived back at Bow Street, 'an' the cart.'

'And he is?'

'Known as Munty by the fellow at his lodgings. Some old-timer having a smoke on the steps. Description fits our man, an' accordin' to the old timer he sometimes drives a horse an' cart, fetchin' an' carryin'. Has a girl, too —' Rogers paused to enjoy his coming sensation — 'name o' Pruey — laundress, it seems.'

'Oh, well done,' Jones said. 'How d'you find the lodging?'

'Me an' Feak went down the alley by the burial ground, turned off into another street that goes nowhere an' there was a sign for lodgin's and the old fellow sitting outside. Asked him about the horse and cart, an' he says there's a stable a bit further along in Bird Court — an' there was the cart. Out at night sometimes, Mr Munty, bringin' stuff back to the stable. Didn't know what Munty was carryin' but they were awkward things to handle, an' there were two women that helped him. Sometimes they carried them out again an' loaded on the cart. Deliverin', he supposed. The old fellow hasn't much to do but watch what's going on — and, no, sorry, sir, he couldn't tell us when he saw Munty out at night, or where they went.'

'Anything in the cart?'

'Best bit, sir.' Rogers held out his hand. Dickens and Jones saw just the one shining blue eye. They thought they knew where the other was — in a wax head found in a graveyard.

'An eye for an eye,' Dickens said, looking at it. 'Natural.' Mr Payne's lesson was not about to be wasted; the iris looked very realistic. 'One of the judge's figures, surely. The natural eyes are the expensive ones.'

'That one-eyed head Stemp found?'

'Right, sir, it matches the eye in that head Stemp found. An' there's more, sir. The old cove told me that his pal, Munty, was meetin' a gent on a bit o' business at that pub, the Yorkshire Stingo — money in it.'

'Didn't say who, I suppose?'

'No, sorry, sir, but our Munty dressed himself up a bit, apparently.'

'Munty,' Dickens said.

'As in Munton, perhaps, the Parr case. Joshua Munton, the son who testified against Eliza Parr, and whose father was hanged for the killing of the baby. We need to find out. A call on Ma Dunk and Pruey.'

Constable Box had joined them and Ma Dunk answered the door, up to her elbows in suds and much else, no doubt. Her smile was just a fraction too late; her eyes had given away her alarm first, but Superintendent Jones chose to take the smile and to ask with grave courtesy if they might come in. Dickens adopted a look of undertakerish solemnity and what he hoped was the right degree of pity for those who were to receive the bad news of the sudden death of a friend. They'd worked out their strategy on the way. Dickens was to keep his focus on Pruey.

'The sympathetic touch, I think, constable, for a pretty young woman,' Jones had said.

'Pretty hefty.'

'I'll deal with the harpy. She'll be the handful.'

Both took off their hats, Dickens holding his at his breast and bowing his head, as they stepped into the hissing, steaming parlour still swathed in damp sheets and shirts. Pruey was at her ironing. Dickens looked at her with what he hoped was sympathetic solemnity. He didn't think they knew yet, but Ma Dunk certainly had something on her conscience — a threadbare thing, he'd bet, more a matter of self-preservation than remorse for any ill-doing.

'It's about Munty, Mrs Dunk — he's dead, I'm afraid. My condolences.'

Ma Dunk opened her mouth, no doubt to deny all knowledge of such a person, but, again, she was a fraction too late. Pruey gave it away. The iron dropped with a thud onto the table; there was the stench of scorched linen and a scream as she sat down heavily on a stool from which the freshly ironed linen toppled. Pruey knew him, no doubt; her hand went to her mouth and her eyes started from her head.

Superintendent Jones was faster than Ma. 'I beg your pardon, Miss Pruey, for breaking the news so suddenly. Some water for the young lady, constable.'

Dickens obliged, handing her a tin cup from the table and remaining protectively beside her while she gulped and sobbed at the same time. Ma Dunk snatched up the hot iron and stood with it in her meaty hand. Jones wondered if she might hurl it at them and make her escape. Her eyes were darting from them to Pruey. She did not look pleased.

'Betrothed, were you?'

Pruey's hiccupping sobs were stopped by the suddenness of Jones's question. 'Not 'xactly, sir. We woz keepin' company.'

'His full name is Joshua Munton?'

Pruey's glance swivelled to Ma, who looked at Jones. He could see the calculation in her eyes. How much to reveal? He waited.

'Yes, sir,' Pruey answered.

'What's 'appened to 'im?' Ma asked.

'Murdered, Mrs Dunk, I'm afraid —' Pruey let out a wail, which was cut off by a look from Ma and followed by another hiccup. Jones ignored her. 'Naturally, such a thing must be investigated, so I should like you to tell me all about Mr Munton. How did you come to know him?'

'Jest a neighbour, sir, lived in lodgin's an' Pruey got ter know 'im.'

'What work did he do?'

'Jest labourin', sir, hereabouts.'

'Where? I shall need to contact his employers, of course.' Sam Jones's voice was still mild, and Ma Dunk was still wary, but he would lead her where he wanted her to go.

'Dunno, sir, I mean, 'e'd be casual like — a bob or two 'ere an' there. 'T'ain't allus easy for poor folks ter get work. Me an' Pruey, we fed 'im an' that. Nice young feller. Can't imagine 'oo'd want ter 'arm Munty. Didn't do no wrong to no one. I'm that sorry, but there's some terrible things go on. Some terrible folk about. Why, poor Mr Black up in Edward Street 'ad 'is rats stolen, an' some of 'is ferrets. Worth a good bit, them creatures — sells 'em to military men.' Ma was getting quite comfortable now in her virtuous sorrow at the world and its crimes. 'Yer'll know Mr Black, sir, calls hisself rat and mole catcher to 'er Majesty. 'E 'as a cart with two rats an' a crown on it —' a gravelly chuckle now — 'yer can't but laugh at 'is cheek, but a crime's a crime.'

Dickens had often been amused by that cart — seen frequently outside the Coach and Horses in Marylebone High Street with the cages of rats. He tried not to look at them. Sam Jones did know of Mr Black, and he'd read about the case, but if Ma Dunk thought to create a jocular distraction, she'd have to think again.

'Ah, a cart. Mr Munton drove a cart, I'm told — your cart kept in Bird Court.'

Ma Dunk's mouth was still open. Dickens thought of bared fangs, and the attempted smile didn't reach her hard eyes, but she was game enough. 'Oh, aye, sir, well, 'e did, yes, the laundry baskets, see, sir, a bit 'eavy fer Pruey sometimes. Give 'im a sixpence fer 'is trouble.'

Jones very much doubted stout Pruey's frailty. 'Nothing else but laundry?'

'No, sir, though I serpose Munty mighta borrowed the cart ter do a bit o' business.'

Jones's voice took on a harder edge. 'What business would that be?'

'Well, folks sometimes need a cart, yer knows, sir, if they's movin' 'ouse or somethin'. I says ter Munty that 'e could use it if 'e wanted to earn an extra bit. No 'arm, sir, in that. Jest wanted ter give 'im a leg up, didn't we, Pruey, love?'

Jones turned to Pruey love. 'And you helped Munty, so I'm told, on the nights that he had to bring stuff to the stable and sometimes when he was out on deliveries. Awkward sort of goods to handle, I'm told.'

Pruey blinked, looked at Dickens and blinked at Ma, who looked at Jones, her mouth and eyes working on her reply.

'And you, Mrs Dunk, you were seen, too, helping to unload your cart and to load it again. Now, I ask you again, what business?' They were both silent. 'Perhaps this will stimulate your memory.'

Jones held out his hand on which lay the one blue eye, winking, it seemed, in the firelight's flicker. Pruey gasped. Ma Dunk just stared. He waited. The silence gave them away.

'It's from a waxwork figure, one of the ones stolen from Judge Quarterman's house — a house for which you, Miss Pruey, had a key to the back door and the yard key, which was here for some days. You had access to Mrs Flint's keys. You knew which key unlocked the waxworks room because you had been in there.'

Pruey still stared at the eye as if mesmerised, then she looked up at Jones's implacable face. 'Munty said, well, Munty asked — I dunno, Ma said —'

'Mrs Dunk, Mr Munton said, and you said?'

'Jest a bit o' business. Munty 'ad a pal what wanted them figures. I mean, the judge 'ad no need of 'em — stingy ol' beggar. Mrs Flint got an 'undred quid an' me an' Pruey left without a customer — they woz only a lot of ol' trash. The pal thought 'e could get a bit fer 'em…'

'And the name of this pal?'

'Jest Tom, sir, knowed 'im only as Tom — never saw 'im, though. Munty's pal, see.'

Dickens thought of the two he'd seen outside the judge's house and took a shot in the dark at Pruey. 'Now, Miss Pruey, we knows that someone went inter the judge's house on the night of 'is death, someone with the keys you had given him. That person — or persons — knew that Mrs Flint was away. Who was it, Miss Pruey? Yer'd best tell us, yer knows.'

He hit his target. Pruey blinked and blinked, her terrified face turning red and then white, and her mouth opening and closing in the manner of a hooked fish as she looked at Jones. Ma Dunk was, at last, speechless.

'Who?' Jones asked. The sharp one. The frightening one.

'Mr Tom, see, 'e came ter the back door — I woz jest goin', an 'e wanted ter — 'ad business with the judge. No 'arm, 'e said, only a little talk. I woz ter go 'ome.'

'Just Mr Tom?'

Jones noted Pruey's blink. 'Yes, sir.'

'And the deliveries, Miss Pruey, where did you go with Munty after you had loaded up the cart with those waxworks?'

Pruey looked at them with wide eyes now. 'Dunno, sir.'

'You don't know where you went?'

'Dark, see, sir, didn't know where we woz. Took an age an' I was cold, sir. Couldn't tell, sir — jest a place where Mr Tom woz.'

''Ouse? Shop? Church? What kind o' buildin'?'

It was quite clear that she had no idea. Even the word 'building' seemed beyond her understanding. 'A place, sir — behind big places wot woz all dark. Place like a stable, sir, an' I eard 'orses. Mr Tom an' Munty took them figures in, an' I woz ter stay with the cart. Then me an' Munty came away. Dunno wot Mr Tom did.'

Dickens thought of warehouses, abandoned ones, perhaps, where stolen goods might be kept and no one any the wiser. He turned his kindly eyes on Pruey. 'The river, Miss Pruey, anywhere near the river?'

A light went on in her darkness. 'Sees the water, sir, an' then we goes under an arch inter a tunnel, I remembers, where there woz people an' 'orses. Could 'ear the water.'

The Adelphi? he wondered, thinking of the grand buildings close to the river, under which there were passages and tunnels and wharves and warehouses nearby. He'd wandered into those arches as a boy when he was free after a morning at the blacking factory by Hungerford Stairs. It was the haunt of tramps and labourers, carriers and carters, watermen, lightermen, dredgermen — all the human flotsam and jetsam of the river. He remembered watching some coal-heavers dancing outside a pub, the Fox-under-the-Hill. A blacksmith in the arches and stables and warehouses.

'Was it a long way from 'ere?'

'Dunno, sir. When we came out, we stops fer a drink at a pub an' a bite o' somethin'. Munty's treat. 'E's good ter me, is Munty — 'e ain't done no —' She remembered he was dead and burst into sobs again.

'Now, now, Miss Pruey, don't take on. Try ter remember the name of that there pub where yer 'ad the nice treat.'

'Coal 'eavers, they woz in there, all singin' — it woz nice there.' And she sobbed at her loss of Munty and that one nice evening which she'd never have again.

Dickens gave a brief nod to Sam to indicate that he had an idea where Pruey's stable might be.

'And neither of you said anything about the cart, the keys, or the visitor at the inquest,' Jones said.

'Wozn't asked — I wasn't in no tunnel. Ain't nothin' ter do with me.' Ma was recovering her composure enough to give another gravelly chuckle. 'Visitation of God, them lawyers said. I wozn't visitin' when the ol' skinflint copped it. Served 'im right.'

Jones wiped the smile off her toothless mouth as he explained that they were to be taken into custody under the provisions of the Larceny Act, 1827, which provisions had, he must tell them, abolished the difference between petty larceny and grand larceny. Thus — he shook his head regretfully —

the waxworks were not, in law, a lot of ol' trash. Two years in the House of Correction — with hard labour.

'And the Malicious Injury to Property Act, sir, if yer don't minds my mentioning it.'

The superintendent did not. 'Two years more, Constable Box. Very good.'

The speechless and very much cowed prisoners were escorted from their premises. Ma Dunk had run out of steam.

17: A DEATH AT HUNGERFORD BRIDGE

The inquest was adjourned pending further enquiries by the police, but the coroner gave a melancholy sigh. He knew that such killings were often never solved. A shabby young man found stabbed in an alley was not an exceptional matter, except for the proximity to Paradise Street and Manchester Square, which Superintendent Jones had wished to remain confidential for the moment. He explained to the coroner that he did not want the newspapers to get hold of that information — there had been enough sensational reporting of Judge Quarterman's death. The coroner agreed and the verdict was that the young man, known as Munty, had been killed by person or persons unknown in an alley near the Marylebone Workhouse and he had been pronounced dead at the workhouse infirmary. The police would be pursuing further enquiries.

Ma Dunk and poor Pruey, who reminded Dickens of a bewildered ass led by the nose to a new stable, were remanded to await their trial for being concerned in a burglary committed in Manchester Square. Superintendent Jones's dressing up of the charge had elicited the reluctant confession that they had mentioned the possible murder of the judge's wife to Mr Tom but had not loosened their tongues on the matter of pal Tom's identity. Pruey's inarticulate portrait of a dark-haired man, usually dressed in a brown suit was not much help, though she did manage to suggest that he had been a toff. Nor had the prisoners been able to supply any further information about Munty, from which byways he had come into their lives. At least, Pruey hadn't. Jones was not at all sure about Ma Dunk, who, he had observed, had recovered something of her insolent composure. Better to go down as an ignorant accomplice than a principal. 'She'll survive,' he said to Dickens, 'in the House of Correction, or anywhere. Tasmania, preferably.'

But poor Munty, Dickens observed to Jones, mother unknown, father hanged. Destined for a miserable life and even more miserable death, but that was the way of things, he reflected, in the environs of the Marylebone Workhouse, the infirmary, the graveyard, in St Giles's, Clerkenwell, Belle Isle, Limehouse, Wapping, in Southwark and Lambeth, or in any blighted region of the city where millions dwelt in shadows, came out blinking into daylight, and vanished into twilight, leaving no trace upon the teeming earth.

Superintendent Jones listened patiently to these lyrical observations before returning to practical matters. 'Of course, we don't know if he was coming or going in that passage.'

'Anyone remember him at the Stingo?' Dickens asked.

'Of course not — always packed, the Stingo, but if he was coming from there, he could have had money on him. Could be robbery.'

'Whatever it was, it was murder, and there is his connection to Judge Quarterman and Ma Dunk.'

'True, though nothing doing at the Adelphi arches, I'm afraid,' said Jones. 'That place never sleeps, but I'll bet you were right. The ideal place to hide your stolen goods. Who'd notice a cart with goods on it?'

'Indeed. No handy severed wax head or glass eye to be found, I suppose?'

'Nothing yet. I've still got men there, but needles and haystacks come to mind. And Mr Tom, of course. Not the couple you saw outside the judge's house, it seems.'

'Ah, my leading lady in the black veil — a wild goose chase all that, I admit,' Dickens conceded. 'But, Sammy, I beg you, grant me, there was someone in the judge's waxworks chamber when I was there; I heard the dress rustle and there was a victim waxwork missing.'

'I grant it, Mr Dickens. Pruey insisted that only Munty's pal, Mr Tom came; therefore, we're thinking that she who left her footprint arrived earlier while the judge was out meeting you at Tussaud's. She could have had a key; easy enough to take an impression from a bar of soap. I noticed Pruey blinking when I asked if only Mr Tom had come. Pruey could have let her in.'

'I saw someone come up in a cab. Mr Tom, maybe?'

'Watched you go and slipped round the back,' Jones suggested.

'Where Pruey was on her way out. The judge had told her he didn't want anything more and went upstairs — to bed? He was in his nightshirt when we found him.'

'This Tom waited with the waxwork woman until all was quiet, then brought the judge down, forced him, probably, and the waxwork came to life.'

'And, Sammy, my lad, they did have keys because the judge's keys were in his bedroom,' said Dickens. 'He definitely hadn't gone down voluntarily to spend the night with his waxen ladies. They went to get him from his bed. I didn't like the man, but woken up, manhandled downstairs in his nightshirt, bundled into the gallery... Dear Lord, it is grotesque.'

'They wanted more money, and they didn't bargain on him dying of fright.' Jones paused. 'And yet, I still can't understand why they didn't leave it at that. They must have seen the inquest verdict. They'd got away with it. All this pantomime with waxworks. They might just as well have left a trail of blood.'

'Well, they have — Munty's blood,' said Dickens. 'Mr Tom murdered him? Munty knew too much?'

'Might have. Still, the name "Tom" interests me. Thomas Dryden, alleged paramour of Eliza Winton, is the only Tom we know of connected to Judge Quarterman. By the way, Eliza Winton's father is dead, so we can rule him out of any desire for revenge against the judge. And Eliza Collier's sister is still a blacksmith's respectable wife beyond Holloway, according to Inspector Grove. The sister also told him that Eliza Collier's common law husband is dead of drink. Good riddance, his epitaph, with which sentiment I cannot help but agree in the circumstances.'

'But Thomas Dryden got away with it — he's no cause to hate the judge.'

'I know, but he and Munton are linked to the judge,' said Jones. 'Maybe Dryden recruited Munton, knowing he had cause to hate the judge because of his father's hanging. Not a coincidence, surely. Ma and Pruey admitted that they'd talked to Mr Tom about the judge's wife and murder, and someone was directing Munton, Pruey and Ma Dunk to steal those waxworks, someone with a brain.'

'And imagination,' Dickens added. 'I mean, thinking up the idea of frightening him with what appeared to be a live waxwork, and then leaving waxworks about the city. Whoever it is, he's having the time of his life.'

'And remember, it looks like blackmail. If it is, and Thomas Dryden's just the type, he doesn't have to have any particular feelings about the judge. The money's the thing.'

'Was Dryden part of his wife's business?' Dickens asked.

'Ah, a gentleman of private means, apparently. I had the impression of a man who hadn't done an honest day's work in his life. He liked the cards, the horses, anything that might make quick money. Rogers is on the hunt for him.'

'Could the wife be the woman who left the footprint, I wonder?'

Their pondering on that idea was cut short by the entrance of Rogers, who came, he said, from Mrs Thomas Dryden's fancy goods shop. 'A rum do, sir; you remember, there was a man drowned at Hungerford Bridge a few days after the judge died. Inquest verdict was unknown man — buried in a pauper's grave. However, an' this is the interestin' bit, he turned out to be Thomas Dryden.'

'Hungerford Bridge, a stone's throw from the Adelphi arches,' Dickens said.

'Thought o' that, Mr Dickens, an' the name "Tom", sir, that Ma Dunk and Pruey talked about.'

'How did they find out?'

'Notices roundabout — aged about thirty years, brown plaid suit, distinctive silk waistcoat, silver tobacco box, initials T.D. an' after the inquest, a couple of fellows came forward with the name. One, an Edward Penman. Said he'd known Dryden a bit from the Retailers' Association. Left his address if they needed him, but he'd be away on business. Dryden played cards with the other one at the Cyder Cellars. Police know him.'

'That sounds like Dryden,' Jones said.

'Police went up to Mrs Dryden's premises. She hadn't seen him for six months or more — upped and left her for some other woman.'

'Pruey mentioned a brown suit and that Tom was a toff,' Dickens remembered. 'And Mr Tom to his subordinates — he was a toff, by their standards.'

'And a silk waistcoat sounds about right for Dryden. Any sign of foul play?'

'I went off to see the river police at Hungerford Bridge. Constable tells me Dryden was pretty much bruised an' battered, but then he'd been buffeted by the water an' smashed against the brick tower. Inquest gave it as an accident. No one knew what he was doin' there an' Mrs couldn't help. Not that she cared. She'd a man there. Cigar on the table and a jacket on a chair. I didn't see him.'

'What did she say about the burial?'

'They told her about the pauper's grave up in Adelaide Street, but she wasn't a bit interested. Nothin' to do with her, she said.'

'No point in exhuming him,' Jones said. 'We've nothing to connect him to the judge's death, and there's no saying that we'd find an injury consistent with murder, but it's mightily coincidental that Thomas Dryden and Joshua Munton, both connected to the judge, are now dead in suspicious circumstances. Pruey's description wasn't much use.'

'Those kids in St Giles's graveyard, sir, the girl said the man had a beard.'

'Big mouth and big teeth, as I remember. Stemp thought it was a fairy tale. I know Dryden was battered about, but send a constable back to Hungerford Bridge to get as good a description as he can. I want to know if he had a beard.'

'Could have been Dryden in the graveyard,' Dickens said as Rogers went out.

'If it was, it means that someone else is directing it all. Munty and Dryden surplus to requirements now, maybe. But who?'

They brooded on that unfathomable question until Dickens asked, 'What about Dryden's other woman? No one reported him missing.'

'Hm, she must have had a reason for not coming forward.'

'Lord, Sam, Chandos Street, not far from Hungerford Bridge,' Dickens said. 'Mr Payne's glass eyes, and there's Emma of the hunted stare.'

'And right next door to Maiden Lane, home of the Cyder Cellars, and where the second wax figure turned up. Suspiciously coincidental again.'

Dickens had a thought. 'That eye you showed Ma Dunk — let me look at it again.' Jones took it out of his pocket. Dickens examined it closely. 'Emma painted this. Look — that little bit of greeny-yellow near the pupil. It's almost the same as the one she showed me. Could Emma be Thomas Dryden's lady friend?'

'We need to find her. Scrap was watching her. Rogers will know where he is. He'll be back in a minute.'

'Of matters coincidental, I wonder — humbly, and with my usual bashfulness — about blackmail and the judge's presence at Madame Tussaud's and who he might have been meeting there. Mere speculation, of course.'

Jones grinned. 'You saw a woman in a black veil coming out. A secret tryst, you think?'

'Just the place our imaginative blackmailer would choose. He or they knew about the judge's waxworks. How fitting to send a woman in a black veil to collect the money.'

'Emma?'

Dickens thought back to the woman who had emerged from under the guillotine. 'I don't think so. I got the impression — brief though it was — of an older woman. I can't say why, just an impression of someone taller than Emma, bigger, not a slight girl like her. Confident, too. She didn't look up at the blade — you know the guillotine —' Jones nodded — 'and angry, I thought, as she swished by me. I assumed because I was in her way, but maybe the judge refused her demands.'

'But it's odd, don't you think, that the angry woman who met the judge for blackmail purposes as we're speculating, then visited Tussaud's to look at the waxwork of the judge and afterwards went to look at the portrait at the auction?'

Dickens thought about that. 'It is odd. More than one black-veiled woman? Different reasons for being at Tussaud's. One bent on blackmail, the other, a wife bidding farewell to a husband. Dare I speak the name?'

'I'll say it. Eliza Quarterman.'

'I'll admit her story haunts me. Scrap and I followed the wrong woman in the cab, so Eliza Quarterman could be alive, Sam. Not necessarily to do with the blackmail, but —'

'You want to find out and you'll not be satisfied until you do, so go back to Southwark while I pursue the matter of Thomas Dryden and the young woman from Mr Payne's manufactory, if Scrap has managed to find out something.'

Rogers returned to answer Jones's immediate question about Scrap. 'Sent him to Chandos Street this afternoon —' his usually cheerful face clouded — 'no sign of him.'

Jones looked at his watch. He didn't need to say anything. Dickens took up his hat and stick and Jones put on his coat. As they went downstairs, Dickens couldn't help remembering a death at Hungerford Stairs. An old grey on the stairs of the derelict blacking factory, looking at him as if it remembered a boy with blackened fingers who pasted labels on blacking pots, a boy whose heart was broken. Another boy whose heart had stopped, a boy encased in mud as though already in the shell that was brought later by the mortuary men, a drowned boy with blackened hands. Jemmy, who had been murdered. A sky marbled with red and purple and the river coloured green like poison, slapping at the pillars of Hungerford Bridge where now a man had drowned, a man who might have been murdered. Sam Jones glanced back at him. He was remembering, too.

18: A LESSON FOR SCRAP

He was there, a very ragged, weary-looking figure trudging along Bow Street. Rogers vanished back into the station. Dickens and Jones appeared to be in earnest conversation as he came up to them. They could tell by his despondent face and hunched shoulders that things had not gone well.

Superintendent Jones merely said, 'We were wondering where you'd got to.'

'Food and drink are needed, and immediately. Forward into Covent Garden, my boys. Chops on me.'

Scrap, who was always hungry, brightened, and within fifteen minutes, he was tucking into a succulent steak and kidney pie and Dickens and Jones were eating their chops in the Piazza Coffee House. A hot cup of coffee had restored Scrap while they waited for the food. They only knew so far that Scrap had followed Emma from Mr Payne's factory down to Hungerford Stairs.

Knife and fork dispensed with, and the last crumb of pastry chewed, Scrap was ready to tell his tale.

'She goes down to Hungerford Stairs — you know where them old factories are.' Oh, yes, they knew Hungerford Stairs. They nodded. 'She waits there. Lookin' about as if she's waitin for someone, then I follows her along by the Adelphi arches an' she stops there. Thinks she might go in, but she goes on to Waterloo Bridge an' I follows 'er across.'

'Into Southwark,' Dickens couldn't help saying.

'Turns off by the theatre — I remembers that from when we went to the pantomime.'

'Victoria Theatre, into what's called the New Cut. Market there?' asked Dickens.

'Right, an' across the big road what goes up to Blackfriars Bridge where the cab crashed. Turns right onto a widish road — don't know what it's called.'

Dickens was with him every step of the way. 'Gravel Lane.'

'Few twists an' turns an' factories an' then what looks like a chapel or somethin', where she stops for a minute or two, lookin' about 'er as if she can't decide what to do. Then she seems to make up her mind an' turns back the way we came. I steps out of my doorway an' then I knows I've made a mistake.'

'How so?' Jones asked.

'Shoulda known it. Someone watchin' 'er go back along the street. Me, I was too busy keepin' 'er in me sights. Could kick meself — I mean, me, not realisin' we was bein' followed.'

'Who?'

'Well-dressed cove, tall, black coat, silk 'at, beard, but I couldn't really see 'is face. Stick what 'e's leanin' on, watchin' Emma. Noticed 'im, see, by them gardens. Didn't think anythin' then, but 'e's watchin'. I daren't move. Jest loungin' there. I knows 'e's got a choice — me or 'er, cos 'e musta seen me followin', but from when I don't know. Can't believe I was such a fool.'

'What next?'

'Emma goes along, all unknowin'. 'E tips is 'at to me, so I knows then. 'E'd seen me, an' 'e's kind of sayin' you can come if you like —'

'You didn't?' asked Dickens, horrified at the thought.

'Nah, I ain't such a fool as that, Mr D. Came back by Southwark Bridge an' by St Paul's — long walk, but 'e didn't follow, sure o' that, at least. But I'll know 'im again an' 'e won't know me. I'll make sure o' that.'

It was true. Scrap, the other day the modest, polite son of the clerk at the auction, had turned himself into the raggedest, filthiest urchin for his day's pursuit. His own mother wouldn't have known him. Not that he had one, except Mrs Jones, who would have known him anywhere, and Dickens, who knew Scrap's eyes as well as his own, and his gait, and his hands, but the cove in the black coat might be fooled, whoever he was. Not Thomas Dryden, though, Dryden buried in a pauper's grave. Someone else behind it all.

'Didn't care, that cove, I could tell. Somethin' about 'im — 'ard to say — didn't belong in them streets — like 'e was a toff who thought it was all a joke. Well, I wasn't laughin', but I saw 'im follow Emma out of the lane an' that's it. Sorry, Mr Jones.'

'No, you did well, Scrap,' said Jones. 'That young woman, Emma, who makes glass eyes might well have something to do with it all. You saw her waiting by Hungerford Stairs near the bridge where a man was drowned — a man we think is connected to the waxworks business, and she lingered by the Adelphi arches where Pruey who worked in the judge's house sometimes was seen with Munty, the man found dead in Burying Ground Passage. They are all connected.'

'A joker,' Dickens said, 'a man who is amused even when he's spotted following a young woman.'

'Having the time of his life, you said, the one who left waxworks for us to find,' said Jones. 'Clever devil, that's certain, but who? Who was blackmailing the judge?'

Dickens was thinking of a young woman going all the way to Southwark. When she went down by the workhouse, she knew where she was going and then she changed her mind. To see someone? 'What was Emma doing in Southwark?' he asked.

'It's a long walk. And then she stopped at the chapel or whatever place it was. Some connection there?'

'Stemp had better go and see the other two girls — find out what they know about her and whether her home is in Southwark.'

'An' that impudent cove?' Scrap was still nettled at being mocked.

'Someone from the judge's past, I'm guessing. Someone who had cause to —'

'Make him suffer,' Dickens said, 'toy with him, squeeze him for money, make that appointment at Tussaud's, send a black-veiled woman to collect the money, yet he seemed angry more than anything when I first met him there.'

'And so was the woman. You could be right about him refusing to pay any more. Thought he could face down a woman, and they turned the screw on him.'

'That makes sense. They went to his house to show him that they'd make him pay. Humiliate him by dragging him from his bed in his nightgown. Terrify him with a waxwork come to life. Our someone didn't mean murder, then. And then the judge was dead.'

'And Thomas Dryden and Munty knew all about it. Pruey said it was Dryden that she let in. He'd not want them talking.'

'That young woman, then,' Scrap said, 'Mr Rogers said you thought she might be in with this Thomas Dryden, an' if she was… 'E was after 'er, Mr Jones, an' I made it easy for 'im. If 'e's done for two people already…'

Jones put his hand on Scrap's shoulder. 'I know, Scrap, but it happens. It's happened to me and Mr Rogers, and Constable Stemp. We make mistakes. Even Mr Dickens here, who's usually right about a cove.'

Dickens grinned at Jones. 'And Mr Jones is always right, Scrap. There was a lady once. She told me something and I should have told Mr Jones — it was evidence — and he said what he's said to you. It happens, and I had to accept that I'd made a mistake.'

'We mean to do the right thing,' Jones continued, 'but we don't always know who we're dealing with. Your cove was one step ahead. We thought we had the evidence that Thomas Dryden was our man. We couldn't have known he was already dead. You know enough about murder cases now, Scrap. It doesn't always go our way. Now, get off to Norfolk Street.' Giving Dickens a meaningful glance, he added, 'Mr Dickens will go with you.'

Scrap was silent for a while as they walked up towards Oxford Street. Thinking, Dickens knew. He kept quiet. Scrap was like him, he often thought, mostly optimistic, but not one upon whom the world's cares and errors sat as lightly as his dress — and that wretched urchin outfit was light enough. Scrap would learn from his mistake. Not that it would never happen again. Mistakes were bound to happen, especially in the present circumstances in which Sam Jones's "clever devil" was their adversary, but Scrap would accept his mistake, though Dickens hoped it would not be the burden of the missing Emma's death. That was the trouble with getting involved with murder. It led into so many obscure byways to get lost in; into so many hidden corners where danger lurked; it led to the brink of precipices over which you were terrified to look, but you must, for the truth might be there and you had committed yourself to Sam Jones. And Scrap had committed himself, too.

In Newman Street, Scrap spoke. 'Didn't think enough about Emma. Thinkin' about me, about 'ow clever I was bein'. She'd never see me, I thought, an' all the time 'e was there…'

'There's a wisdom of the head, Scrap, and a wisdom of the heart. Your head was working out how to accomplish your task. Head over heart for a while, but your heart was, as it always is, with Mr Jones and how you could help him. We're all complicated, my boy. Proud of what we do well, and sometimes forgetful of others, but life brings us up short. There's a choice, Scrap. Accept the mistake, but don't believe you won't make another. They'll leave their marks like scars, and from time to time, you'll feel the hurt, but that reminds you of where you went wrong.'

'But, if that young woman…'

'He didn't know you. He knew her and he wanted her for some reason. He was following her, and he probably would have done so even if you were not there. And he may have found her, but that won't be your fault.'

They reached the Joneses' house. 'What 'ave I to do now?' Scrap asked.

'Come with me to Southwark tomorrow morning. Respectable tradesman's lad. Blackfriars Bridge — not Waterloo. Eleven o'clock, if you will.'

That cheered him up. Scrap touched the scab on his temple. 'Best walk, though, 'adn't we?'

19: INTO THE WILDERNESS

Seventy thousand people in London rose every morning without the slightest knowledge of where they would lay their heads that night. This was according to a young journalist, George Sala, who had just left Dickens's office in Wellington Street, having delivered a manuscript, one of a series in which Sala described the lives of the poor and dispossessed from Westminster to Whitechapel. Dickens had admired 'The Key to the Street' immensely and regarded the young man as a very good acquisition for *Household Words*. He looked forward to reading the next instalment, but later. Scrap would be waiting.

Seventy thousand, he thought, hurrying downstairs, seventy thousand houseless souls, and that might well be an underestimate. Who could count the true number? He wondered about Emma, the glass eye painter. Where had she lain down in Southwark last night? Eliza Quarterman, too. Odd how Southwark seemed to be drawing him. A place he knew too well. A place he did not care to frequent too often.

Such poverty there still, and in those long-ago years when Eliza Quarterman had been born to her vanished mother, and he'd had the key to those streets when he had lodged in Lant Street in the house of Archibald Russell, a decent man who had been kind to him when his family were housed in the Marshalsea Debtors' Prison. He remembered vividly the beggars, the loiterers, the slinkers, the visitors waiting in the queue for admittance, the hungry eyes, the cast-off clothes — so wretched, patched and ingrained with dirt that they couldn't have fetched a farthing even at a rag fair. The sleepers in doorways, under the railway arches, under carts in the Borough market with rotten cabbage leaves for a pillow, or a pile of hop sacks for a bed. The houses like packing cases full of fever. Broken doors and windows, the dilapidated staircases glimpsed in passing, the stink of a thousand crammed breaths streaming into the gutter, rolling out of doors and windows and broken chimney pots like foul smoke, gushes of unwholesome sewer smells, more rotten cabbage, and greasy mutton, the shabby little taverns filled with raucous laughter and mad music, reeking of tallow and gin and stale beer. The smell of the leatherworks and the tanners, and the sawmill. His attic room had overlooked a timber yard, and beyond he had seen the crook-backed chimney tops and cracked back windows from where poles jutted, and lines of laundry fluttered like the ruined flags of wrecked ships.

Gravel Lane, and then somewhere about Union Street, where he thought Scrap had seen Emma loitering until she'd made up her mind. All mean streets, sometimes lit by an occasional oil lamp and even meaner alleys lit by nothing at all. Hog Yard, Dog Yard, Goat Yard, Middleditch, Backditch, Deadman's Place, Dirty Lane, Black Boy Alley, Black Horse Court, Blackman's Place. The map was in his head.

He reached into his pocket for his gloves and felt cold metal — the key they had taken from the dead woman at Doctor Woodhall's mortuary, the key which he had not given back to Sam Jones. He looked at it again and remembered the sign of the golden key, a large wooden emblem above a locksmith's shop in Mint Street not far from the Marshalsea. He had wondered as the child he was if Caleb Holdfast — the name came to him in a flash — had the key to the prison, and was it as big as his sign? If anyone might recognise this unusual key, then surely it would be a locksmith. Caleb Holdfast, indeed. He might still be there.

Scrap was waiting at the end of Blackfriars Bridge with the news from Bow Street that Emma Cooper, as he'd found her full name to be, had not turned up for work that morning. Constable Stemp had asked a few questions which elicited that Emma had worked for Mr Payne for about six months, but the two young women who also painted the natural eyes couldn't tell him much about her. Kept herself to herself did Emma, jest got on with the paintin'. Niver spoke much. Stemp was directed to her lodgings where the large, square-jawed landlady proved almost a match for Stemp's solid height in the ferocity of her indignation. Niver 'eard of no Emma Cooper. Respectable 'ouse, she kept. Her lodgers niver 'ad no dealin's with coppers. The door had slammed shut. A young woman who had something to hide might very well give a false address. Stemp stumped back to Bow Street.

Scrap's optimism had returned. Another jaunt with Mr D. was always welcome. 'See if we can find that place where I sees 'er — I remembers the factories. Not far from them.'

They retraced his steps to Gravel Lane, where they saw the drug mills and Scrap pointed out the mouth of a narrow alley into which he thought he had followed Emma, but there was no building like a chapel, only a huddle of houses and small shops and then another maze of alleys, which defeated Scrap and even Dickens. They eventually found themselves in Mint Street, a narrow lane lined with more poky shops, dirty windows and lodging houses, and with great oak beams stretching from one side to the other, buttressing the taller buildings. There was a vacant lot boarded up — no doubt a house had tumbled down, unable to bear the weight of its packed inhabitants. Its neighbour now leant precariously into the space. Near the end of the street, Dickens stopped when he saw the golden key and the legend above the door which read *Simon Holdfast, Locksmith* — son, perhaps?

'What do we want a locksmith for?' Scrap asked.

'This.' Dickens held out the iron key with its circle and cross. 'It was found on the woman in the cab.'

'But she wasn't Mrs Quarterman,' objected Scrap, 'too old, you said.'

'I know, but I wonder why no one has come forward to claim her. It's an unusual key and while we're here, I might as well ask if Mr Holdfast recognises it.'

The workshop was exactly as he remembered. There was a little forge inside the smoke-blackened room where a boy sucking on a very large nail was at work on the bellows. There were keys on the workbench, fragments of iron, half-finished locks, various tools, more keys on shelves and great bunches of keys dangling from the ceiling, some so large that they might have been the keys to the kingdom of heaven, though, on second thoughts, the keys to hell and death seemed more likely. The keys to heaven would surely be brighter than these rusty articles.

'Mr Holdfast?' he enquired of the smoke-blackened boy.

The boy kept his comforting nail in his mouth, out of which came what Dickens deciphered as the word, 'Keys.'

Well, they knew that. Cross Keys? he wondered. There was a pub of that name round the corner. Apt, he thought, asking, 'The Cross Keys?'

''Igh Street. Thirsty.' And with that terse information, he turned back to his bellows.

The Cross Keys on the High Street was one of those brown, low-browed, dingy, furtive-looking pubs which looked as if it wished to scuttle away, perhaps down the opposite passageway — that which, as Dickens knew very well, turned into Angel

Alley — a very squalid angel — which led to the spiked wall, all that remained of the Marshalsea prison. He could smell it, even taste the roasted corn, that substitute for coffee which, of course, cost less than the real thing. He could feel the stale air as if it gathered about him now in the open street; he could taste the ashes from the fire, and the rancid butter. Supper in the Marshalsea.

Brown inside, too, The Cross Keys. The smell was of beer, grease, tallow and sea coal and the air was thick with smoke from the fire and the clay pipes, and the smell of sawdust which had been sprinkled on the floor, now mingled with mud from the heavy boots which had come and gone throughout the morning. Whether Mr Holdfast, locksmith, had trodden through, it was hard to say. There were a good many working men leaning at the bar, drinking deep.

No use wondering. Dickens went to the bar and simply asked if Mr Holdfast, locksmith, were present, in answer to which the landlord pointed at a table in the corner. No one wasted words in these parts, it seemed. Taciturnity, the daytime habit. Garrulity came out at night, probably when tongues and tempers were loosened by more drink and fists curled round broken bottles.

The man at the table wore a leather apron and a coat of some drab fustian cloth. He wore a blue belcher handkerchief around his neck and a pair of spectacles pushed into his thick hair, and Dickens noticed the slender, if rather dirty, fingers which were wrapped round the ale pot. Not a brawler, Mr Holdfast. He'd need his delicate fingers for his work.

'Mr Holdfast?'

A straight look from two surprisingly blue eyes. 'Who wants 'im?'

Dickens didn't want to give his name. 'It's about this key. I wonder if you made it.'

The locksmith looked at the key in Dickens's open palm. 'Pa's work. Old chapel up in Union Street by Redcross Street an' the Crossbones — ladies run it now. Paupers' place.'

Clearly that was the end of the conversation. Mr Holdfast turned back to his pot and Dickens and Scrap made their way into the street.

Scrap's eyes gleamed. 'Chapel, Mr D., chapel. What's Crossbones?'

'Burial ground — dreadful place. Worse that St Giles's.'

It was. Worse than anything, Dickens reflected as they walked up to Union Street. The Single Woman's Burial Ground, it had been called, which meant the unconsecrated burial ground of prostitutes for three hundred years. They buried the so-called "Winchester Geese" there — the young women who had lived in the stews of Southwark on land that had been owned by the Bishop of Winchester; a place of stench and filth that he had avoided as a boy. There had been enough to see in the streets. Poverty and debauchery festering in the unlit, crowded alleys where the people lived like beasts. Only John Forster knew the story of the Marshalsea, but even he could not know what the twelve-year-old boy had seen late at night on his way back from supping with his family in the prison. Such things of which he could not write or speak. Alleys used as privies, naked children, half naked men and women copulating, girls of ten or eleven years already practised in luring young men, older prostitutes ready to importune a boy. Men, too, from whom he had fled, not knowing what they wanted, but knowing that it was corrupt. He had been ashamed when he went back to school, ashamed to have seen what he had seen, what his schoolfellows had not.

Sam Jones knew what abandoned children saw, and Dickens thought that only Sam Jones really understood the battle he had fought to extricate himself, to rid himself of the taint of poverty, filth, and corruption. And Scrap knew. The three of them knew — it was there in those brief exchanges of glances when they found themselves in some back alley and heard the screams and wild laughter, the groaning of beasts, the bare-breasted women fighting, the bruised, misshapen children, and all the feral eyes glaring, glittering and hungry. Despair and sin written upon every iron face.

Scrap knew. He just nodded. 'This chapel, then, we'd best 'ave a look.'

The corner of Redcross Street and Union Street and another narrow street where a little ecclesiastical building occupied a space between a charcoal burner's workshop and an empty shop with broken windows. It looked like a forgotten chapel of ease or a mortuary, though Dickens didn't remember a mortuary connected to the burial ground, only the stories of women tossed in there for centuries, and later, the undeserving poor, those outcasts whom nobody thought it worthwhile to bury with dignity or compassion.

'Could this be the place where you saw Emma?'

'Can't be sure, Mr D. I went round in a lot o' circles to find my way to Southwark Bridge an' now I can't tell.'

The heavy door looked like that of a church or chapel, and the keyhole certainly looked as if it might take the key with the cross. There were lights on within, though the door was closed. There was nothing for it but to knock and then to listen to the echoes falling through the air, and to wait for footsteps, perhaps. Dickens used his stick, and they stood still, waiting. The sound of a key turning in the lock.

A woman looked out at them, a tall, thin woman in a plain black gown, unrelieved by any trace of white lace or cotton collar, except that she wore coarse apron. Dickens knew she wasn't the woman who had come out from under the guillotine, but she could have been the slender woman who had looked at the portrait. A woman with thin, delicate features, pale blue eyes, even paler lips, but lips with a trace of fullness left. Time and suffering had etched this face on another face — that of a lovely girl with the same pale forehead and arched brows. Delicacy, yes, but there was steel there, too, he thought. She stood very straight and unsmiling.

20: PAUPERS' KITCHEN

The unsmiling woman was looking at Scrap. 'I know you. You were at the auction. You asked me about the judge.'

Scrap bowed. 'Yes, ma'am.'

She looked at Dickens then. 'I know who you are, too, Mr Dickens. Who does not? Were you there at the auction with this boy? I saw you at Madame Tussaud's where the judge was exhibited. And you gave evidence at the inquest. I read about it in the newspaper. What is this about?'

'I came to ask you something.'

'About the judge? I went to the waxworks to see if he were really dead. I am ashamed to say that I was glad. He has haunted me, and now I am free.'

'You are Eliza Quarterman?'

'Mrs Clifford now.'

'After Lady Julia.'

Eliza Quarterman gave a rueful smile. 'Why am I not surprised that you know it all? I suppose I half expected you, having seen you twice already, though I do not know how you found me. No one knows who I am — who I was. What is it you want of me?'

'This key — it was found on the body of a woman who died in a collision on Blackfriars Bridge. I was there.'

Eliza looked at it for a second or two. 'Ah, then you had better come in, though I haven't much time. We feed the poor, and it is nearly the hour for their meal.'

They stepped into a gloomy vestibule and were led into what looked like an old school room, in which were arranged benches at rough deal tables set with spoons and tin beakers.

There was the smell of some sort of stew and bread. A woman was finishing the setting at the furthest table. She vanished into another room when she saw there were visitors.

'My assistant,' Eliza said, 'she helps with the cooking. We are given money by some local businesses, and medicines from the workhouse infirmary. One or two doctors help us from the infirmary and from St. Thomas's. We give succour mostly to vagrant women and their children, of course, and any stray children, anyone in need of hot food, orphans, runaways, the lost and forsaken. We ask no questions, Mr Dickens. We have no rules, though we are willing to advise, but if a woman wishes to move on, we will not force her to go to the parish, or to the workhouse, or the Magdalen Home, and we never ask for names. We do not preach here, nor do we teach.' A slight smile played at her lips as she looked at Dickens. 'Punishment, redemption, obedience and submission are the business of others.'

'You knew the woman with the key?'

'I gave it to her. We went together to the auction to look at the portrait for different reasons. She had a daughter long ago, a daughter who was buried in the Crossbones ground. You can guess what she had become — after she came out of the prison to which she had been sentenced by the judge. We had seen in the newspapers that he was dead. She wanted to see him, and then she went away. I had given her the key, but I did not ask where she was going. The key was my pledge — she could return if she wished.'

'You knew it was she in the accident?'

'When I came back, she was not here and I was not really surprised; then I read about the accident. I did not know her real name. It is better that she was never known. She was entitled to her secrets and I to mine. No good would have come of my identifying her. That is all I have to tell you.'

'And you, will you not tell me your story?'

'You know it already. You know all about the Foundling Hospital, I'm sure. What else is there to tell? That part of my life is over. The present matter of a hot meal is my business now. You can hear our guests at the door.'

'We'll stay an' help, ma'am,' Scrap put in, 'an' then mebbe Mr Dickens can tell you what we needs to tell you. See, there's things goin' on to do with the judge an' the waxworks, an' we could do with your help. There's a runaway, I think, an' I've somethin' to put right, ma'am. I made a mistake. So, if you could just —'

Whatever Eliza saw in Scrap's earnest face made her relent. 'You'll have to wash up, too.'

'Used to it, ma'am. Turn our hands to anythin', me an' Mr Dickens, an' 'e's very good with kids. Got a house full of 'em. I'm not so bad meself. They call me Scrap — 't'ain't my real name, o' course.'

Eliza smiled, a rather lovely smile, which told Dickens what she might have been. She opened the door, and the sweepings from Hog Lane and Dog Lane and all the streets that Dickens had walked filed in. Sliding, furtive eyes, hunted and haunted ones, red-rimmed ones, the clouded eyes of a bent old woman led by a blue-eyed girl. The hard eyes of a few feral boys, eyes that were temporarily softened by the presence of Eliza, who would give them food and ask nothing of them. Mostly women, as she had said, some with small children and some with babies, and a scatter of other children whose homes had no food to offer. And those who had no homes but the stones of the streets and alleyways. All in rags and ingrained dirt. The other nameless woman had come out with a stack of tin plates.

172

'Our visitor will carry the stew.' No names, Dickens noted as Eliza directed him into what proved to be a rudimentary kitchen. He returned to the largest table in his shirtsleeves and with the steaming cauldron. The well-behaved guests sat down quietly. Eliza and Scrap delivered the plates of food, Scrap choosing first a table of wretched boys, and making sure the smallest received their due, but they showed no curiosity about the new waiter, nor about the man who was ladling out the stew. They wolfed down their portion and waited to see if there were any more. The women were equally silent, but they smiled up at Scrap, who ruffled the scanty hair of babies and toddlers. He paid no attention to the smell and the dirt or the running noses and scabbed cheeks. Dickens saw how Eliza watched him with a smile. If she were to tell her story, she would tell it to Scrap.

When the cauldron was empty, the diners filed out past Eliza and Scrap, who stood at the door. The women bobbed a curtsey, and the boys bowed to Eliza as they left, with a 'Ta, miss, an' sir.' The very faintest flicker of belief in humanity left, kept alight by such as she. Dickens was clearing the tables.

Eliza let her nameless assistant go and they set about the washing up and putting away plates and tin mugs. The cauldron was left to soak in soapy water. Dickens noted Eliza's swiftness and efficiency, and her work-worn hands with their clipped nails. Her clothes were well-worn, too, patched and darned in places. *Serviceable*, he thought, remembering the white silk that the Beauty had worn — her bridal gown, perhaps.

Dickens oiled the hinges of the creaking back door and fixed a gas mantle while Scrap brought in more coal and chopped some wood. Eliza made tea when they had finished their chores and they sat by the old pot-bellied stove.

'Thank you, both, you certainly can turn your hands to anything,' she said as she watched Dickens replenish the stove with coal. 'Now, you had better tell me how I can help you.'

She listened while Dickens told her about the story of the stolen waxworks, the blackmail, and their great friend, Superintendent Jones of Bow Street. He left out the murders for the time being. When he had finished, she asked if he had thought she had been at the judge's house.

'I confess I did wonder, because I became so sure that one of the waxworks had moved and then we found the woman's footprint. However, the superintendent didn't think that the woman who had visited Tussaud's to look at the waxwork and who had looked at the portrait was the same one who had been involved in the judge's death.'

'He was right. I went to Tussaud's because I wanted to see what he looked like — whether the waxwork would truly show what a wicked man he was. It did not, of course, though I recognised that thin mouth and that nose down which he looked so often at his new wife. However, if, as you say, he was terrified to death, then that is dreadful to contemplate, and blackmail for my supposed murder…'

She looked away from them into some distance, Dickens thought, some distance where pain resided. She had thought it was over with the judge's death, and he had brought back her pain by coming here to talk of blackmail and murder.

She turned back to them. 'What an irony — he would have killed me had I stayed. There was cruelty in him, and if he had not murdered me, I would have died in the end of grief and shame. But I am alive and the life I chose, punishing as it may be, has been a better life than that of a chattel.'

'Them women an' kids, ma'am, you do good to them. I was one o' them once, on the streets, no home to go to, an' good

174

people took me in. The world was not as bad as I thought, an' there's good folk as well as bad.'

'So there are. And it is good that you have found good friends, including Mr Dickens, I see. Many do not… But why, Mr Dickens, why did the judge pay blackmail money when he knew he hadn't murdered me?'

'Frightened of the scandal, I suppose. Whoever the blackmailer is, he was clever enough to know that the judge would not want his past raked up. The judge could not prove that you were alive.'

'And you have no idea who he is?'

'None whatsoever. Someone from his past, perhaps, who held a long-standing grudge. Someone who hated him.'

'Apart from me. I didn't hate him. I was frightened of him. It was a kind of torture —' the steeliness returned to her mouth — 'but enough. I wasn't there, Mr Dickens. I can tell you nothing more.'

'There is more, I'm afraid. There have been two murders which we believe are connected to the judge's death.'

'This is dreadful — murder, but how connected?'

'The victims are connected to the judge because of the sentences he handed down to —'

'Women,' she interrupted. 'I read of him sometimes in the newspapers. A harsh judge to unfortunate women, especially young ones. Judge not that ye be not judged — a text, of course, that did not apply to him, but I know no one connected to him that way. I know nothing about murder.'

'There's a girl, ma'am,' Scrap said hastily, 'what I was followin' yesterday, an' I think she was goin' to come here, but she changed 'er mind. Then someone followed 'er an' I lost 'em.'

'And she is to do with your case?'

'We thinks so — name of Emma Cooper. Worked for a glass eye-maker up in Chandos Street. Painted what they calls natural eyes.'

'Painted?'

'Yes, an' she's missin'. Someone was followin' me followin' 'er. Should 'ave noticed, so if you knows anythin' — she might be in danger, an' it'll be my fault.'

Dickens wasn't surprised that Scrap's appeal moved her when she turned to him and said, 'Describe her to me.'

Dickens answered. 'Very slight, fair hair, hazel eyes with a dark stain on one iris.' He saw the recognition in Eliza's eyes. 'She looked frightened when I saw her at the glass eye workshop.'

'I know a girl with those eyes and with that name, but whether it is her true name, I cannot say. She was a foundling — as I was, brought up to obedience and industry. A girl with some artistic talent who was fortunate enough to be placed with one of our benefactresses, Mrs Beddows, who runs a fancy warehouse.'

'Selling?' asked Dickens.

'Decorative items, fancy goods — glassware, china, workboxes, dolls, wax flowers — they are in fashion. Apparently, Her Majesty —' her eyes widened — 'oh, waxwork... I can't imagine ... but you think Emma is connected to it all. And she has disappeared. You said she might be in danger.'

'Can't say for sure, ma'am, but the feller I saw after 'er — somethin' about 'im — somethin' not right.'

'Why did she leave Mrs Beddows?' Dickens asked.

'She fell in love.'

'With whom?'

'I don't know. A gentleman of means, she called him. I couldn't ask his name. There are no names here, but I knew what that meant. It was not for me to judge her, but as gently as I could I tried to explain that she must be cautious. His intentions might not be honourable. I know what can happen, Mr Dickens — young women, girls ruined by so-called gentlemen, unwanted children, disease, and then the Crossbones cemetery, but he promised her jewels and fine dresses and, of course, she was tempted away. She could not know that there can be too heavy a price to pay for such things.'

'How did she meet this gentleman?' Dickens asked.

'She was restless and dissatisfied before. Her employer, Mrs Beddows, is a kindly soul, but as with many who extend the hand of benevolence, something is expected, even demanded, in return — submission and gratitude, for example. Emma was not to forget her origins — the hands that raised her up might easily dash her down again —'

As she paused there, Dickens wondered how far Eliza was talking about herself. The Clifford family had raised her up. Her obedience in the matter of marriage was the gratitude and submission demanded, or exile to the north as a governess. She was not to forget her origins — marriage to a Clifford was out of the question. He dared not ask about that.

Eliza continued, 'Mrs Beddows is a pious woman. Emma was brought here to help — to be reminded what she came from — as if she would ever forget. It was too much for her. I think she resented more servitude. I understood her longing for freedom. How was she to know that freedom does not always mean riches and fine dresses? The man bought goods from Mrs Beddows, I think — a businessman, Emma said.'

'How long had she worked for Mrs Beddows?'

'Two years. She came straight from the Foundling Hospital at the age of fifteen. Mrs Beddows reported her disappearance to the hospital.'

Mr Brownlow's missing foundling, Dickens thought. He had been right. The blank child was not, in truth, blank, a waxwork to be moulded and painted in the desired image of meekness and submission. Wax figures had no heart beneath the casing of linen or canvas. A human heart beat in the child and beat more fiercely under the continued yoke of discipline, forced obedience, and, perhaps, the weight of expected gratitude. It was no wonder Emma Cooper had broken free.

'Is there anyone at Mrs Beddows's establishment who might know something, or anyone who came here and to whom she spoke?'

'I doubt that Emma would have told any of Mrs Beddows's workers. They are trained to piety and obedience, and I don't think she would have spoken to anyone here. She did not like coming — the people frightened her. I saw how she shrank from the women, from the smell and the dirt.'

Dickens tried another approach. 'Is there anyone — from the past — whom you remember, who might have cause to hate the judge and might have harboured a grudge?'

Eliza remained silent, looking down that perspective once more, he thought, which perhaps opened up to reveal at the end of it, a little likeness of a face — the rumoured lover, perhaps, or further back, the grandson of Lady Julia Clifford. He dared not ask. When she turned back to him, something flickered in her pale eyes. Fear, perhaps. Doubt, certainly. He had struck a chord. She knew someone.

'There is someone, someone I thought was gone from my life forever, but who returned, a ghost, I suppose, or something like it. A name which I had thought to find on a grave, but I found a person in a grave of a kind.'

21: SHADES OF THE PRISON HOUSE

'Dead to the world,' were Eliza's first words after they had waited for her to continue. She stopped again and looked at Scrap. 'This is a long story. More tea would be welcome, if you would oblige, Scrap.'

Scrap obliged and they heard the tap running in the kitchen.

'This is a dreadful story, Mr Dickens. You have told of such things, I know, but how much is that young boy to hear of it?'

'You heard him say what his origins were. He has seen and heard far too much for a boy of his age, but it has been tempered by the goodness of his friends, Superintendent Jones and Mrs Jones, and Sergeant Rogers and his wife. Scrap lives with them now, but Mrs Jones's house is his second home. What you say cannot harm him now, or ever. His feet may have been sunk in the deepest mire, but his heart is one of the purest I know. And one of the truest.'

Eliza smiled at his words. 'And yours, I think — where your friends are concerned. Your books do not lie. What comfort they give to the poor — to know that someone cares about their blighted lives. Had I had a friend such as you when I was a young woman…'

'I am here now if you need a friend, and Scrap is here —' he echoed her own word to that poor dead woman on the bridge — 'whose pledge, once given, will not be broken, nor mine.'

Scrap returned with three tin mugs of tea as Dickens was speaking. 'What you tells us, ma'am, we won't be tellin' anyone, 'cept what Mr Jones needs to know, an' you can trust 'im with your life.'

'I'll trust you both, and you must trust that I am telling you the truth as I know it. Mr Dickens knows all about the Foundling Hospital where I was given up by my mother, whose story is the one I feared for Emma. I expect you know that story, too, Mr Dickens. My mother never reappeared after she had given me up, but I knew her name, and when I came here, I looked for her. My own detective work, Scrap, and I made mistakes and found the wrong people. I had money from the jewels I sold, the valuable jewels Lady Julia Clifford had given me, and I knew that my mother had given up a token with the name of St Saviour's Church impressed on it. I started there and found the record of a child with my mother's name born in the parish to a cobbler and his wife in 1804. I was born in 1820 to a girl of sixteen, whom I thought might still be alive. Her parents had lived in poor circumstances in Axe and Bottle Court in the shadow of the Marshalsea prison. You know it?'

'I do — the debtors' prison.'

'It was to Axe and Bottle Court I went to discover that my grandmother had been taken to the workhouse. She was a very sick woman. She hardly knew what I was trying to tell her — that I was the granddaughter given up to the Foundling Hospital. I wanted to know what had become of my mother. Goose, she told me. I thought she was just babbling until I found out later about the Winchester geese, the prostitutes buried in the Crossbones cemetery — you know what kind of a place that is?'

'Yes,' Dickens said gravely.

'A place not fit for any human creature to be laid to rest. Nothing to mark the passing of any pauper or ruined girl. Whatever my mother had done, she deserved better than that.'

'It is a stain on our city,' Dickens said. 'There is a commission set up to look into the state of graveyards. I have given evidence. I trust — I hope — that Crossbones and many others will be closed.'

'I hope so, too, Mr Dickens. The poor old woman — such pain in her eyes when she spoke of it as she drifted in and out of the shadowy world she inhabited. Sometimes her eyes fixed on me with recognition, and she said my mother's name as if she thought I were she, the girl she had lost. So sick, she told me, her poor, pretty girl, so changed. I found out later — I have lived here long enough — what disease had racked that girl's face and body.'

Eliza sipped some of her tea. Scrap put more coal into the stove, and in the flicker of firelight, Dickens saw the sadness in her face. Neither Scrap nor Dickens spoke. The day was waning, but it was better to sit in the shadows which settled about them and to listen.

'I went back each day to take what comforts I could. She remembered the child given up and at times she wept. I tried to tell her that the child had been loved by a good woman, but I don't know if she understood that. I could only hold her wasted hand and hope that there was comfort in my presence, even if she did not really know who I was. I was there at her end.'

'The workhouse was the grave you found?'

'Her grave is in St Saviour's, where I put a headstone — a simple one. Just her name and some words to say that she was a good wife and mother. It was the only way I could give some remembrance of my own mother. My grandmother told me a name before she died, the name of a man. I think you know it already. The name is Alexander Marlowe, and I found him in another grave.'

'Your father.'

'I had not asked about him, but from her broken words I had pieced together the story of a girl seduced and then abandoned by a gentleman, but who he was or where he had gone, I could not tell until she talked of a prison. One evening when she seemed to be sleeping tranquilly, she opened her eyes and said his name quite clearly, and then she seemed to fade again and I heard only snatches of words. "A ghost," she said. I wondered if she were seeing someone from the past in her last hours, whether it was true, as some say, that the ghosts of the dead come to take us. Before she fell into that last sleep, she muttered about the marsh and the sea. Again, I thought she was seeing something beyond this life, but later I realised that she meant that prison near where she had lived.'

The air felt close for a moment and the shadows moved as if, Dickens thought, the crowded ghosts of those miserable years gone by leaned in to hear what he might say. Scrap looked at him, but he could only say the two words: 'The Marshalsea.'

'I did not know if she meant that Alexander Marlowe was a prisoner then and if he were the ghost who had returned; it could do no harm to find out. When I looked down at the old woman in her workhouse bed, I felt such an emptiness, such loss, and such loneliness. I belonged nowhere. The Clifford family had abandoned me. I did not belong in that house in Manchester Square, which would have been my grave. I thought perhaps that I could belong to someone — that there might be some feeling in the poor prisoner for his returned daughter…'

She did not look at them, but Dickens could tell by the twist in her lips that she was thinking that she had been wrong, and when she looked up again, she said so.

'Not immediately. He welcomed me and the comforts I took. He liked his tobacco, his bottle of wine and his cold chicken, and his cards — bad luck had put him in there, he explained. He had been in there about a year. I deduced that perhaps my grandmother had seen him — he was the ghost returned. He was very sorry for my mother, and the child, of course. He would have stayed with them but for his infernal luck. What he wanted was a fresh start — if only he had the means to get out, but that would never be. He had to accept his cursed fate. But he was glad to see me. Perhaps one day we might settle in a little house together. I believed him, Mr Dickens, because I wanted to. He was my father. Of course I must care for him. He would live a better life. I could redeem the time. I know better now… I have seen in so many cases that food and medicine are as much as can be done. That is why here at the kitchen we never preach, and we help beyond the bodily needs when it is asked for. I learnt a lesson then — a hard one: we cannot change people by wanting that change for ourselves.'

'Learnt that, ma'am, a bit before you. My pa was a brute — never could understand it then. Jest thought a pa was supposed to care. Now I knows it ain't always the case. Some folk'll go their own way. Born that way, I suppose.'

'You're very wise, Scrap. Perhaps I would have done better if I had known someone like you.'

'Give up on him, did you?'

'I should have, but I went on blindly believing. I kept only one ring from Lady Julia and sold the rest to put money into his hands to get him his release, and I never saw him again.'

The glow from the stove faded, and the shadows deepened as they sat for a few moments. It was a terrible betrayal, Dickens thought, especially after the Cliffords had abandoned her, and the marriage to the judge. What pain she had endured, yet here she was, giving her life to the outcasts.

'Did you look for 'im?' Scrap asked.

'He told me that his father had been a prosperous businessman in Leicester Square who had left a fortune to his brother. He told me that they were all dead and the money gone out of the family, but I went to Leicester Square, and I found Ann Marlowe, wife of George Marlowe, who was Alexander Marlowe's older brother, dead by then, but Ann was running the business. Of course, it was still there. It is an oil and colour warehouse, supplying materials to artists — paints, oils, polish, candles. When I thought of Emma working in wax, of course, I thought of him. Alexander Marlowe trained with a wax modeller whose business was next door, but he did not wish to be a tradesman, and when the father died, he took his inheritance and went to live elsewhere. Ann told me that she had quarrelled with her husband more than once because he had given money to his brother. She knew that he would always be coming back for more, but eventually he simply vanished from their lives. Ann advised me to give him up — a bad lot, she said, and he was.'

'Did you remain in touch with Ann Marlowe?'

Eliza smiled then. 'I did. I do. She is a strong woman, a stern one in her way, but one of the good people of this dark world, and she supported me. I found work at the Magdalen Hospital in Suffolk Street here in Southwark. You know what work they do —'

'A refuge for fallen women.'

'Yes, I thought of my mother and how she had been buried in an unmarked grave, and in unconsecrated ground, and how I might have been just such a one if it had not been for Lady Julia Clifford. They were good people at the refuge, but they demanded penitence and religious discipline, and if a young woman could not conform, she had to leave. I set up my kitchen, with the help of Ann Marlowe, for those whom no

185

institution could help. My poor grandmother might have avoided the workhouse had someone given her a hot meal and a few pennies.'

'And Mrs Ann Marlowe could tell you nothing more about Alexander Marlowe?' Dickens asked.

'Nothing, except she remembered him as a tall, handsome, well-dressed man, not at all like her husband. I could see myself that he had once been handsome. In the prison, he was somewhat ragged, and yet, there was a gentlemanly air about him always, which charmed me, as it had charmed my mother, I suppose. I could see what he might be in fine clothes. But it was in his eyes. What I took for shame when his eyes slid away, was calculation...'

'Borrowing eyes, sharp and speculative as to your softness.'

'How acute you are, Mr Dickens.'

'I have seen those eyes — measuring if that softness might be of advantage.'

'I know it now. I know that even the moisture in his eyes meant only to get what he wanted. I don't know where he went.'

'He couldn't be the man who tempted Emma Cooper away?'

'I doubt it, Mr Dickens. I don't think he would have stayed in Southwark, near the prison. He had money to go where he was not known.'

'Could 'ave been the man that followed Emma,' Scrap said. 'Tall man — an', ma'am, somethin' — I can't explain it really, somethin' cocky about 'im. 'E tipped 'is 'at ter me an' laughed.'

'I can imagine him doing that, but I can't imagine how he is connected to Emma.'

'That is for Superintendent Jones to find out,' Dickens said. He saw how weary she was and felt it was time to go, but he was uneasy, too. If Scrap's cocky gent were Alexander

Marlowe, had he seen the lady who ran the paupers' kitchen? Would he know she was the daughter whom he had betrayed?

As if she read his thoughts, Eliza said, 'He would not know me.'

'Does he know the name, Clifford?'

'He knows it all. I trusted him, you see, at first. I told him how the judge had mistreated me. He was outraged. He talked of the judge, too, many times. He was on my side, of course. The judge was a scoundrel — a man who deserved —' her hand went to her mouth — 'to be punished.'

'I must advise you to take very great care. Is there anyone whom you can trust to protect you if he were to come here?'

She smiled at that. 'My neighbours are my friends, Mr Dickens. There are plenty who would serve me if I asked, though in ways that your Superintendent Jones might not approve of.'

'Then, please ask, I beg you. And if you hear anything of Emma Cooper, if she returns to you, then you will send a message?'

Eliza promised to do both and took Dickens's card. The key turned in the lock as they left her to take the long road to Bow Street.

22: MUSEUM PIECES

Superintendent Jones and Sergeant Rogers listened to the story of the former Mrs Quarterman told by the second incarnation of Box and Cox, Scrap interpolating his trenchant comments into Dickens's narrative. 'That toff — time to wipe the smile off 'is dial.'

When the recital had finished, Jones commented on the interesting detail about the oil and colour warehouse and the wax modeller next door. 'Marlowe was training with him, you say?'

'Upped and left when his father died. Signor Barone said the figures we have are apprentice work.'

'Thirty-odd years ago, though, when he was an apprentice.'

'I know, Sam, but Marlowe knew all about the judge from Eliza Quarterman. I'll bet he read up on his cases. Not that it would be to avenge his daughter's suffering.'

'Could 'ave been that Marlowe,' Scrap said. ''Ad a beard, same as that cove in the graveyard.'

'That's a fair point. Thomas Dryden had no beard, according to the constable who fished him out of the water.'

'And there's the young woman, Sam.'

'Right, that does make it more urgent. Mrs Ann Marlowe's oil and colour warehouse, then.'

'I'm thinkin', sir,' Rogers offered, 'whether it might be worth Scrap an' me goin' back to the eye factory. There'll be other folk that know Emma Cooper. Somebody might have seen where she went after work.'

Leicester Square, the haunt of snakes — real and human ones — and sea monsters, sorcerers and giants; ladies with two heads, or none at all; sheep with six legs or only one, dogs who could tell the time; acrobats and jugglers and fortune tellers; jacks of all trades, performing in the streets or at the Panorama where all the known rivers of the world were displayed, including the pieman's River Nile; waxworks, of course; card sharps, sharks, pimps, and the haunt of yet more nymphs of the pave; coffee houses, wine shades, gambling dens in cellars. Every language spoken and every kind of crime committed. The world lived in Leicester Square, swirling round Mr Wyld's dream of the world, his great globe itself, made of lead, sixty feet in circumference, and within all the wonders of the known world, the world turned inside out, and all for a shilling.

And in Leicester Square was once the Sybil Office at number fifty-four, so Dickens reported to Superintendent Jones as they stood contemplating the crowded street.

'Sybil Office — saw the future, did they?'

'Home of a Consul of Levant, way back, so they say.'

'No one there to tell us the whereabouts of Mr Alexander Marlowe, I suppose.'

They walked along until they came across Marlowe's Oil and Colour warehouse, where a tall young man was putting up the shutters outside. A long-established business. Dickens noted the sign above the door where the name *Ann Marlowe and Sons* had been painted over another name — the blurred remnants of what might have been a *William Marlowe*, and you could see the faint outline of another *S* which had once been added to the faded word *Son*. Mr Alexander Marlowe painted out, perhaps.

'We are looking for Mrs Ann Marlowe, sir.'

The young man turned a pleasant face to them. There was an ease and grace in his manner, surprising in a shopman, Dickens thought. 'My mother — she's inside. Who shall I say wants her?'

Dickens gave his card and asked the young man to tell his mother that they had come from the paupers' kitchen in Southwark. He thought it better not to mention Eliza's name.

The man came back to show them into the neatly ordered office of Mrs Ann Marlowe, who dismissed him rather curtly, Dickens thought. Mrs Marlowe, dressed in severe black, was standing behind a portentous desk. She looked what she was — a very capable businesswoman. No curls or lace caps, or jewels, just a masculine gold watch worn on a heavy Albert chain round her neck. Time, Dickens thought, would not be wasted by Ann Marlowe. She came straight to the point.

'Is there something wrong in Southwark?'

No name, Dickens noted. He'd made the right decision. 'No, Mrs Marlowe, I left your friend in good health.'

'I know who you are, of course. This gentleman?'

'Superintendent Jones of Bow Street.'

'Police? Then what?'

Jones had the measure of her, too. 'Alexander Marlowe.'

'He's back in Southwark?'

'We think he might have been.'

'Your friend told me all about him,' Dickens said, 'and there's a young woman known to her who was followed to the chapel by a man we think may be Alexander Marlowe.'

'It's to do with Judge Quarterman's death and the theft of the waxworks. You know about all that?' Jones asked. She nodded. 'Two murders have been committed. We came to ask if you have seen or heard anything of him lately. I know it is a long time since he deserted your friend.'

'You think he has to do with the murders?'

'In all honesty, Mrs Marlowe, I don't know yet. I take it you haven't seen anything of him?'

'Not for years, sir. He was a bad lot. Charming, of course. Had his mother round his little finger. Her favourite son, of course, and my husband was worth ten of him — twelve years between those boys. She lost other sons, so Alexander was kept in cotton wool. He was thirteen when I married George. Course, that silly woman didn't want George marrying and having children to take Alexander's inheritance. I put paid to her nonsense.'

I'll bet you did, Dickens thought, noting the thrust of her handsome chin and the flame in her eyes. A formidable enemy to Alexander Marlowe. Perhaps she had routed him altogether.

'I knew he'd go wrong… Seth, my older son, looks just like Alexander. I keep him on a tight rein. No favouritism. They can have their due when I'm gone and not a minute before.'

'What did Alexander do with his inheritance?'

'Spent the lot, I should think. It was Eliza who told me he had been in the Marshalsea. I wasn't a bit surprised. He was always one to take what he wanted, and he was given it by his foolish mother. He had a tutor — imagine, a tradesman's son! Oh, they thought he'd go to Cambridge, be a fancy lawyer. Too much hard work, that. Then he'd be an artist, so another tutor, then a sculptor, if you please, and then he'd work with Mr Flack and we'd be opening a waxworks — better than Tussaud's, of course. But he wanted everything yesterday. Never thought you had to work for it, but then he was never taught. A wastrel.'

'When did you last see him?'

'Long before Eliza found me. Way back. I didn't know about her then. Oh, I felt for her — poor girl, after that marriage to the judge, and then thinking she'd found a father. Not that we'd ever known about any child. He'd just left 'em behind and moved on to greener pastures. I told her to forget all about him, live her own life, and she has. I help her out with money for the kitchen, but I wish she'd give it up. That place — round there, it's a swamp and no mistake, but sometimes I think she's making up for something. I can't imagine what.'

'Was he in funds, then?'

'Yes, very much the prosperous gentleman — silk hat, embroidered waistcoat, lavender gloves. Some rich woman, I'll wager, but it didn't stop him observing how well the business was doing and telling me that he was entitled to some of my profits. Family business, he said, but he'd had his inheritance and spent it. It was a deal of money, I can tell you, and me and George took on the business. We thought we'd go under. Killed George, but I was determined to go on, and I branched out into more of the artists' supplies. Mr Landseer, Mr Stanfield and others from the Royal Academy come to us. I built up this business. I was having none of his impudence and I told him so. Sent him packing.'

Completely routed, Alexander Marlowe. He'd have found an easier means of living, though. Dickens wondered who the rich woman might be. A procession of them, probably. The word "impudence" struck him, however. 'Laughed at the world and its cares, I daresay.'

'Everything was a joke. He'd laugh at a funeral going by. Laughed at folk — even his mother. You always thought he was laughing at you, as if he knew something about you that you didn't know yourself. Liked a practical joke, so long as someone else was made a fool of. Mouse in the teapot. Salt in the sugar. Tar water in the wine, that sort of stuff. Always laughing at his brother, not that George saw it. Fond of him, he was, but I put a stop to his tricks. Me and George fell out over him more than once in the early days.'

'Mr Flack, the wax modeller, will he remember Alexander Marlowe?'

'No, that business has gone. James Flack died and that was the end of it.'

'And you have no idea how he made his living in the period after he left with his inheritance?'

'No — as I said, living off his fancy women, I should think.'

And that was that, Jones thought, as they left her. Seth, the young man who had let them in, was waiting to show them out. He stepped onto the pavement after them.

'I was listening. She treats me like a fool sometimes. I'm still putting up the shutters and doing as I'm told. As if I hadn't the right to know when a policeman comes calling. I heard you ask about Alexander Marlowe. I remembered him coming that time. I remember because it was like looking in a mirror. Of course, she bundled him into the office, but I insisted on knowing who he was. Anyway, the point is that I think I saw him very recently.'

'Where?' asked Jones, studying the face intently, though he knew Dickens would remember it. Eyes of a lightish brown flecked with gold, long dark lashes, smooth skin with a fresh colour, high cheekbones, a long straight nose, and a finely modelled mouth. Altogether a handsome young man. Surely not at all like the man in St Giles's graveyard.

'At the anatomical museum — Doctor Kahn's on Oxford Street. I'm interested. Should like to have worked with James Flack who was next door, but, of course, Ma wasn't having any of that. I saw him as he was coming out. I'd have known him anywhere — like seeing myself, only older, of course. He didn't see me, and I was too shocked to do anything. Didn't tell her — let sleeping dogs lie. Is it any help?'

'It is. When was this?'

'March, I think, maybe April, before the Crystal Palace Exhibition opened, I know that.'

'One last thing. Did the man you saw have a beard?'

'No.'

'The man of two faces,' Dickens observed as they walked away. 'Well, we know what he looked like — surely not the man at St Giles's.'

"Seven hundred models," so Doctor Kahn boasted on his poster, "illustrating every part of the human frame in health or disease." Handing over two shillings, Superintendent Jones hoped he would not have to see them all, certainly not the diseased ones. One or two bodies at a time, stabbed, shot, drowned, beaten, or poisoned was enough for him. And post-mortems were a necessity, not entertainment. There were rather too many gloating faces in the queue — they'd be off to the freak show at Croydon Fair next.

Jones and Dickens moved through the porch where the wax figure had been found, and they walked under the dignity of the Corinthian columns and passed the poster advertising Doctor Kahn's lectures. Naturally, the exhibit which greeted them was an enormous human eye, fit for a giant — blue, of course, fashioned from wax and fitted with a glass iris. Thick red veins discoloured the white of the eye, which stared menacingly at them. Dickens thought of Frankenstein's monster.

'Good Lord.' Jones looked at Dickens, who seemed to be cupping his ear with his hand. The next exhibit was a large wax ear. Jones couldn't help grinning, though the next sights were no laughing matter.

A cross between Madame Tussaud's and a charnel house. Glass cases full of what looked like severed heads and hands complete with leaking bloody veins; lungs, hearts, kidneys, livers, and other unidentifiable parts suspended in spirit. Brains and open mouths with cavernous larynxes. Teeth as big as tombstones. More heads, which looked as though they had been cut down from the gallows too soon. Foetuses at every stage of development, and that was before you came to the full-sized figures. A Brobdingnagian chamber of horrors this time.

Dickens's old friend Venus Medici was still there, lying in that slightly provocative position with one arm above her head as if she were expecting a lover, not the anatomist. She was not unlike the judge's beauty, though; her eyes were closed, her hair luxuriant and glossy, her face with that faint blush. Mind, he thought, if she woke up, she'd be blushing even more at the sight of her own lungs, liver, spleen, intestines, large and small, and bladder on display. All eighty-five pieces of her could be taken to pieces for detailed examination. Her companion, Apollo Belvedere, also displayed his luxuriantly crimson arteries and his creamy intestines — a lot of muscle and sinew, too. Plenty of other waxen or leather models as well, to teach the eager student the workings of the human body.

'At least they're not diggin' 'em up nowadays,' Dickens murmured, thinking of Burke and Hare grubbing about in graveyards.

'That's a mercy, but I don't want to see seven hundred of these. Let's see if we can find where Doctor Kahn has his bloody chamber,' Jones said as they stepped smartly past the line of waxworks showing, it seemed, the whole progress of humanity from the earliest origin to the present.

'Not got very far, have we?' Dickens said, noting that the modern specimen had the same blank look of the Neanderthal. The same flat nose, too. Jones merely cupped his ear.

They hovered by a door which indicated that medical students and practitioners could enter to make a close study of diseases, dissections, and medical practices. A young man with a kind of writhing motion, Uriah Heep come to life, accosted them. Only another shilling to see the private parts, he told them, winking when they denied that they were doctors. 'Sssyphilitic parts,' he hissed, but before they could refuse such a horror, they were elbowed aside by a very eager customer. He might have been a medical man, of course.

At length they found a perfectly ordinary young man who guided them to Doctor Kahn's office into which they were invited by the stocky, round-faced, twinkling-eyed medical man who professed himself delighted to meet Mr Dickens, whose works he had read in German, of course, when he had studied medicine under the great master, Herr Professor Döllinger. And, Superintendent Jones of Bow Street, of course. Yes, he remembered the discovery of the wax figure in the porch, but he had not seen it. He could not help the police about that.

Jones explained that they were searching for a man called Alexander Marlowe in connection with the matter of the stolen waxworks.

'No, no, no,' exclaimed the doctor, 'impossible. Herr Doctor Marlowe is a most respectable member of the clergy, a Doctor of Divinity.'

'Ah,' Jones said neutrally, 'how do you come to know him?'

'I met him only on a few occasions. Here we execute orders for wax models — you may have seen the advertisements —

for medical practitioners, or students, or those who wish to be enlightened as to the workings of the human body. How much sin and error, my dear sirs, might be avoided were men — and women — brought to an understanding of their structure. My pamphlet, here, *The Shoals and Quicksands of Youth*, may be of interest to you. My argument is —'

Another Mr Payne, Dickens thought, and before they could be sucked down into Doctor Kahn's quicksands, and forbearing to snatch the thing from the outstretched hand, he said, 'I should be greatly interested to take one with me.'

'And Doctor Marlowe, the clerical gentleman?' Jones asked.

'Yes, he wished to open a collection of his own in Knightsbridge, where he had leased premises. He sought my advice and naturally I sold him some figures, which he said he would have his artist paint for him. They were not intended for medical purposes. Religious themes, he told me, intended to remind the viewers of the teachings of the Bible.'

'Female figures?' asked Dickens.

'Yes, yes, he intended to present Ruth amid the alien corn, Naomi, Esther turned into a pillar of salt, and other representations of women of the highest virtue. And a nativity scene, he thought, for Christmas. He thought his premises in Knightsbridge might attract those visiting the Exhibition. It was to be an antidote to the riches displayed, a reminder of the Lord's truth.'

'How many did he want?' Jones asked.

'Six to begin with. He has placed an order for his nativity scene, which is ready for collection.'

'Not delivery?' asked Jones, already certain of the answer.

Dickens noted the first flicker of alarm in the doctor's eyes as he explained that Herr Doctor Marlowe had collected his figures in a cart. The final bill would be settled when he returned for the nativity figures.

'I doubt that Doctor Marlowe will be collecting his nativity order, or paying his bill,' Jones said. 'I doubt that he is a doctor of anything.'

'But he was —'

'Perfectly respectable, I'm sure. A tall man, hazel eyes, clean shaven, very charming, always smiling, I'm guessing.'

Astonishment mingled with alarm now. 'He is not what I thought?'

'He is not, but if he should return, then you must contact me at Bow Street immediately, and you must not tell him of this visit. Now, one last thing: these premises in Knightsbridge, do you know where they were?'

'Herr — he — Marlowe showed me an advertisement from a newspaper. Premises to let, suitable for a waxworks exhibition. It did not say exactly where, but there was an agent, though I do not recall the name. Holborn Bridge, I think.'

They left Doctor Kahn at his desk, no doubt contemplating his loss, though judging by the press of people gazing at the exhibits, he would get over it. Dickens and Jones hurried past a clergyman gazing at Venus Medici in appalled fascination, his fingers steepled and tapping. Counting up to eighty-five, perhaps. Passing the mute mouths, the deaf ears, and the all-seeing eyes, they were out in the street in a few moments.

'So, that accounts for the victim figures in Judge Quarterman's gallery, and the rest, he could pick up at any warehouse and leave for us to find.'

'And some of those toy dolls that came in were the work of pranksters. He'll have enjoyed that.'

'Herr Doctor Marlowe, indeed. I'm inclined to think that mask of Manning and the noose were also some other joker in on the act.'

'He's leaving clues, Sam, leading us by the nose. Duke Street just below Manchester Square, the figure that was here at Doctor Kahn's, St Giles's, St Martin's Lane, Maiden Lane, the Adelphi arches. He's the Pied Piper, and we're following. The other prank figures must have been icing on his cake. He was waiting for us to work it out.'

'He meant for us to come here, and what we find out won't worry him because he won't have leased those premises. Nevertheless, I'll send someone to find the agent at Holborn Bridge — just in case.'

'But where next? And where is that poor young woman, Emma Cooper?'

23: A LETTER FOR MR DICKENS

A solitary figure stealing away through a twist of alleys where only a single gas lamp flickered, and where the very silence listened to the ghostly footfall, its breathing, perhaps coming in fearful gasps; eyes watching, knowing that this was not a suffering, fellow creature, but an outcast thing, throwing its monstrous shadow on the dead wall of the night, afraid only for its own safety...

Dickens laughed to himself, holding his pen up for a moment. A murderer from the imagination of a would-be contributor to *Household Words*, and nothing wrong with that. Readers wanted a thing of terror, a slinking thing, the bloodied knife, or the pistol, or the secret vial in his black-gloved hand, a thing that came in the dark up the panelled staircase to turn the silent key to the room in the turret where the innocent sleeper lay. He put down his pen.

And what did he and Sam Jones have? A man who walked in broad daylight, a joker, a man who tipped his hat to invite his pursuer to join the chase, a man whose breath came in laughter, and they were no nearer to him than if he had been that slinking creature with a monstrous shadow on a wall. Of course, he had not leased any premises in Knightsbridge, nor, they were certain, had his artist painted the noble features of virtuous women. Neither was there any news of Emma Cooper, last seen in Southwark. He wondered if it might be worth returning to the Foundling Hospital. Mr Brownlow would have details of her parentage, though her mother might be dead, might be lying like Eliza Quarterman's mother in the Crossbones, or gone away.

It would be worth it, he decided. If there were no trace of the mother, then that would be that. They would have to hope that Alexander Marlowe had not caught up with her, or that she might turn up at Eliza's kitchen, for that must have been her intention when Scrap saw her. She had been looking for him at Hungerford Stairs, and she'd looked at the Adelphi arches. Perhaps she didn't know that Thomas Dryden was dead. If she had been supplying Thomas Dryden, living with him, then she would have thought he'd abandoned her. She'd stolen for him and was frightened. Eliza might have been the only person she knew who might help. But she had changed her mind for some reason. Shame, perhaps.

He would go when he had finished the present task, which was to decide if the story of the sleeper in the turret was suitable, and whether the slinking murderer had been caught. And how might it be pertinent in the present circumstances. They could do with a hint from someone — anyone. He could call at the office on his way and take the story with him. He took up his pen again just as there was a knock at the door and John, his manservant, came in with a parcel.

'This came for you, sir, left in the porch. Someone knocked, but there was only a cab going away outside the gates by the time I answered.'

John went away, leaving the parcel. Dickens looked at the handwriting, but he didn't recognise it. *An early Christmas present?* he wondered, cutting the string to reveal the box inside. He removed the inner wrapping.

Well, he thought, *at least it isn't a hand or a bit of someone's innards*. It — the thing in the box — was a wax flower, a red wax flower, looking like a bloodstain on the white wrapping. Another piece of theatre, but the joker knew that Dickens was in it, and he was daring enough to come right to his door.

What might that mean? And there was a letter, or rather a paper, since it began with no salutation:

'I had no thought of encompassing his death. Neither did the idea come upon me at once, but by very slow degrees, presenting itself at first in dim shapes at a very great distance, as men may think of an earthquake or the last day — then drawing nearer and nearer and losing something of the horror and improbability — then coming to be part and parcel, nay nearly the whole sum and substance of my daily thoughts, and resolving itself in a question of means and safety; not of doing or abstaining from the deed…'

Of course, you recognise these words, sir. They are yours. You are a student of murder, nay, a solver of murder, you and your colleague, Superintendent Jones of Bow Street. Well, I suppose this is in the nature of a challenge. You know now that the writer has not abstained, but has he — or she, perhaps — resolved the question of means and safety? What means? Ah, that is for you to discover. And safety? Is the writer so safely hidden from those brilliant eyes of yours that he may never be discovered? A dim shape at a distance? Or drawn so near that he has been in your very sight, yet not recognised even by your penetrating gaze?

Where's Eliza? I think you know now.

The memory of a bearded man up a ladder and a flapping poster flashed into his mind. And a bearded man outside the gates of Tavistock House a couple of days after the judge's death, a cab rolling away, a cab drawing up outside the judge's house in Manchester Square, and a man tipping his hat to Scrap. That billsticker whose face he had not seen, and two words in one-foot-high letters: *WHERE'S ELIZA?*

Oh, yes, Alexander Marlowe had followed them everywhere. He must have seen Dickens at the judge's house that first time. Dickens had seen a face staring at him from the cab. *Cab*, he thought. John had seen a cab roll away just now. He looked at his watch. Alfred, the crossing-sweeper would be there now. He never failed, whatever the weather. A twenty-year man was Alfred, his pitch having been bequeathed to him by his father, and he didn't miss much. If a stray dog were to appear, Alfred would know about it. He returned dogs and cats to the householders in the square, even stray children sometimes. He might have seen the visitor with the parcel, and he just might have seen the bearded man outside Tavistock House whom Dickens had thought was the foreign gentleman who had sent the begging letters asking for twenty pounds.

He was out of the house in two minutes. Alfred was at his post, taking his hot tea, which had probably come from one of Dickens's maids. His household had instructions to provide for Alfred, especially in the cold weather, for he was a man subject to a bad chest when the wind came from the north, bringing a touch of Siberia with it, though he was wrapped up well. Dickens recognised his own scarf and an old coat with a few stains of white paint, the evidence from a previous case in which a workman had flung a pot of paint at the murderer. Dickens had been in the way. And he noted the umbrella leaning against the post, the very umbrella with the rent in it that Dickens had used on the day of his visit to the judge's house. Now mended, he saw, with a rather fetching scarlet neatly inserted into the torn silk.

Alfred had seen the man come up in a cab and dash through the gate to the porch and dash back again to his cab.

'Saw 'im come back, clear as I sees you, sir. Tall feller with a beard. Toff, I should think. Sees 'im afore.'

'Do you remember when?'

Alfred looked to the heavens, as if the answer might be written in the louring sky. 'Today's Friday, ain't it?'

'It is. The umbrella, Alfred, when —'

'Wife mended it — done a lovely job. Mr Thompson gave it ter me, sir, said it wasn't no use ter you.'

'You're welcome to it, but when did Mr Thompson give it to you?'

''Eavy rain coupla weeks ago — that's when I saw 'im — the toff. You came out, feller waitin' fer someone, I thinks, an' you stops an' looks, then a cab comes an' 'e's gone. Stranger, see, so I notices. Rain came later, though, an' Mr Thompson gives me the umbrella — knows my wife'll mend it. Same feller, Mr Dickens.'

The day he had been to the Foundling Hospital, Dickens thought. 'And the cab driver, anyone you know?'

'You knows 'im, sir, wears a plaid shawl about his neck. Leather cap with flaps. Stand at Euston Square.'

'Tippler?' Dickens asked, thinking of the driver with his tartan muffler and the great red nose like a burning lamp which accounted for his name. Dickens usually avoided taking his cab. It was too often a corkscrew ride.

'That's the feller — gives me a nod an' a tip of 'is whip. Picked the feller up at Euston, mebbe. Didn't see where they went.'

Dickens gave Alfred his customary tuppence and went back to the house for his coat. Tippler would surely remember the man who had delivered a parcel to Tavistock House and who had returned to the cab.

The waterman by his post in Gordon Street told Dickens that Tippler would be back about lunchtime to leave the cab under the waterman's protection while he went to the Drummond Arms for refreshment. Reg'lar as clockwork, Tippler woz, it seemed. Allus at 'is table by one o' the clock.

Dickens looked at his watch. Only eleven o'clock. Bow Street, then. Sam ought to see the letter.

24: BAD BLOOD

Sam Jones read it. 'He intended to do it — to kill the judge,' he said, passing it to Sergeant Rogers.

'He pondered the means and came up with the devilish idea of frightening the man to death with a moving waxwork. He knew the judge would be terrified. Perhaps he knew that the judge had a weak heart,' Dickens said.

'Safety, eh? There wasn't a mark on the judge. No one could say he'd been murdered, but he was.'

'Can you be frightened to death — in law, I mean?'

'Remember that elderly housekeeper in Princes Square?'

'I do — when we were looking for Cornelius Mornay's killer. The housekeeper who died of fright.'

'So the inquest concluded, though at the time no one was had up for the burglary at the house. However, a couple of years ago two burglars were convicted of the manslaughter of another old lady who died of fright. Transported, they were.'

'But what you said about homicide — if there's no bodily injury —'

'But there is — his stroke. At the time, there was nothing to say that anyone had been near him, only that you thought a waxwork was missing, but now we know differently — and if you recall, the law refers to an injury occasioned by some act, by force —'

'They forced him from his bed and down the stairs, and she, Mrs Dryden, the waxwork, came to life.'

'The act, then. Homicide, it is. It had better be.'

'There was a bearded man near my house a couple of weeks ago. I thought it was that begging letter fellow — the one that

Stemp frightened off — and Alfred the crossing-sweeper tells me it was the same man who brought the parcel and letter this morning.'

'And the beard's back, the bearded man who followed Scrap —' Jones stared at Dickens — 'and where's Eliza? A joker up a ladder. Oh, he's a wit all right. Here, there, everywhere.'

'At Tussaud's, as well. When I passed through the Grand Salon, I saw an older man looking intently at that figure, Tussaud's Sleeping Beauty. I'll bet it was him.'

'Beard?'

'I think I'd have noted that or remembered when I saw the bearded man outside my house. We didn't see the bill-sticker's face.'

'Puts it on and takes it off when it suits him. But it doesn't matter where he was. He's nowhere now that we know of.'

'I found out the cab driver who drove him away. Name of Tippler — to be found at the Drummond Arms near Euston at one o'clock precisely.'

'We'll pay a visit. But before we do, Rogers has news.'

'Lad at the eye factory saw Emma Cooper with a man. Toff in a brown suit. Few weeks ago, so I'm thinkin' Thomas Dryden. The lad saw 'em going into a house in Porter Street. House with a green door, he says. He was on his way home — lives in Grafton Street, so off we went, Scrap an' me. Respectable-looking house. Scrap's waitin' there.'

'Let's get going, then.'

Scrap, who had been loitering in a doorway opposite the house with the green door, reported that no one had gone in or come out of the house while he was waiting. He and Rogers went down the little alley at the end of the terrace while Dickens and Jones went to the green door. The house looked well cared-for, the steps clean and the brass knocker polished.

No one answered. Jones knocked again. Silence. They went round the back to find Rogers and Scrap standing outside what must be the yard door. Rogers gave Scrap a leg up so that he could see into the yard, but there was nothing to see.

'I can drop down,' he said, 'see if I can open this door.'

A moment later they heard the bolt sliding, and the door opened wide enough for them to slip in. Jones's skeleton key opened the back door into the kitchen. A kettle sat on the black range, but the ashes were cold in the grate. There was a loaf of bread on the table — stale, a knife in the butter, a cold teapot and a cup and plate. Beyond the kitchen there was a sparsely furnished parlour with another table and a couple of chairs, one pushed back as if the sitter had stood up suddenly.

And what was on the table suggested that the sitter had simply abandoned what she was doing and left. There was a paintbrush on a saucer, the blue paint hardened now, another saucer with green paint, and another with white, a few little glass globes, waiting to be painted, and one painted blue like the common eye which Mr Payne had shown them, not yet refined into a natural eye by the skilled Emma Cooper.

'Well, that confirms that she was in on it,' Jones said. 'Let's have a look upstairs. See if there's any trace of Dryden.'

They passed through an empty hall and glanced into another room, which was also empty. Upstairs there were three bedrooms, only one seeming to have been used, as there were sheets and an eiderdown in a tangle on the bed. A wardrobe door hung open, but there was nothing inside, and all the drawers in the chest were empty. Jones opened the window shutters.

'Looks like Emma Cooper left in a hurry,' Dickens said.

'Frightened when Dryden didn't come back, I wonder? And nothing of his. Maybe he'd planned to abandon her.'

Rogers was looking under the bed. 'Something here,' he said, dragging out a rather worn leather suitcase. There was a tarnished brass plate on the top. Rogers looked closely. 'T. D.,' he said, 'Dryden's.'

He opened it to take out a man's shirt, a silk cravat, a silk handkerchief with the initials again, a pair of kid gloves, a tortoiseshell comb with a silver top, and a penknife with a mother-of-pearl handle. 'Very fancy.'

'Fancy goods,' Dickens said. 'He bought fancy goods from Emma Cooper's employer. Had a taste for the good things in life.'

'Like Marlowe — birds of a feather,' Jones said, 'but nothing of Emma's. Anything more under that bed?'

'Nothing.'

'What was Emma Cooper wearing when you saw her, Scrap?' Jones asked.

'Grey coat an' dark bonnet — 'ad a bag, though, I remembers that now you ask. Nothin' special — what you'd carry your shoppin' in.'

'Maybe she took everything that she had away with her,' Rogers said. 'She wasn't comin' back, not after Dryden didn't come back an' you an' Mr Dickens were at the factory.'

'Dryden thought he was coming back, having left his fancy goods here.'

'Emma Cooper's employer, Mrs Beddows, sold them to Dryden for his wife's shop. He left her six months ago, when the blackmail started. When Dryden must have got involved with Alexander Marlowe, the length of time Emma was working at the eye factory. Somehow, Marlowe got to know them all — but how?'

'Mrs Dryden's shop,' Jones said, 'Marlowe found Dryden at the shop, maybe. Marlowe was a natty dresser, according to Ann Marlowe.'

Dickens thought for a moment. 'Rogers, you said she had a man there. I know you didn't see him, but could it be —'

'Marlowe?' Jones finished the question. 'You asked earlier if she could have been the woman who left the footprint.'

'Ann Marlowe said he had a trail of women — usually rich ones. Mrs Thomas Dryden must be doing all right.'

'Hard as nails, that one. Didn't care tuppence for Eliza Winton, nor that Dryden was dead, if you remember,' Rogers put in.

'I do. Lord, we didn't ask you — where is that fancy goods shop?'

'John Street in —' Rogers's face changed.

'Marylebone — not that far from Manchester Square,' Jones interrupted.

'And Ma Dunk's laundry,' Dickens said.

'I didn't think of it, sir, at the time.'

'No, why would you? She didn't seem all that interested in her husband, but now … hm…' Jones paused. 'Charles, the woman you saw with the judge at Tussaud's — you thought she was older than Emma Cooper, taller and more substantially built. Rogers, you've seen Mrs Dryden —'

'Handsome, I'd call her, an' big built — you'd not think she was a girl.'

'Somebody as hard as nails collecting the blackmail money, hiding in the judge's waxwork gallery, watching him die. Somebody as hard as nails not turning a hair at her husband's death,' Dickens said.

'Because she had thrown in her lot with somebody who seemed a better prospect than Dryden — the husband who had betrayed her over Eliza Winton, whose abortion he'd procured. Marlowe all charm, and money with it.'

'Told you I'd know 'im again — an' he won't know me,' Scrap piped up suddenly. 'Know that cocky smile anywhere.'

'You and Stemp, then, go and keep watch. If you see him, straight back here. Rogers, you wait while Mr Dickens and I go to see Mr Tippler. With any luck, he might have taken Marlowe right back to John Street.'

The lamp of Tippler's nose was a sure guide to his whereabouts, all afire with carbuncles of a very swollen appearance. It was the only glowing thing in the benighted chamber that was the parlour of another beetle-browed, brown-stained pub, the Drummond Arms. The fire was a meagre thing of a few damp sea coals and about as effective as Bob Cratchit's fire on Christmas Eve.

Tippler recognised Mr Dickens, whom he acknowledged with a nod, but he slipped a sideways look at the taller man, and Dickens noted that he squared his considerable shoulders and his capacious nostrils dilated as if he had scented danger. Tippler had reason to fear for his licence.

Tippler had unwound his plaid shawl all the better to drink deeply, but he put down his tankard like a man realising he had possession of something he didn't want. A purple tongue flashed out to lick the thick, dry lips.

'Mr Dickens, yer honour.'

Superintendent Jones was almost distracted by the nose in all its fiery glory. He didn't know if you could have gout of the nose, but he'd seen a man with gout of the eye — red and inflamed like Tippler's. He didn't look as if he could see a yard in front of him. He shouldn't be driving a handcart, never mind a cab, but he'd deal with that later.

Dickens was staring, too, but not at the nose. He was staring at a clean white collar and shirt front, partially revealed by the removal of the shawl. Darned in places. Second-hand, maybe, but certainly freshly laundered. Jones almost started when Dickens said, 'Your very good health, Mr Dunk,' as he put down the tot of brandy he'd bought at the bar, having observed to Jones that such a thimbleful could hardly make any difference to Tippler's driving habits.

Tippler's hand went to the glass and withdrew as if scorched. Jones noted the trembling. Tippler Dunk, forsooth. How did Dickens know? Then he looked up from the hand and saw the clean shirt. He took in the big coarse face and the sliding eyes. Brother? Dress up Ma Dunk as a man and there'd be Tippler, or — a figure in a graveyard with a wax woman in her arms, a wax figure packed with wrapping paper from a soap company. Soap, not wax, of course, had been the clue. Ma Dunk's voice, too — coarse as a dock worker's. And Dickens had seen a cab roll up to the house in Manchester Square. Driven by Tippler Dunk? A muffled-up face at the window. The same passenger as the one who'd left the parcel for Dickens?

Jones was aware of hoarse breathing and the fact that the three of them were still staring at the brandy glass.

'Drink up, Mr Dunk,' he said. 'Steady your nerves.' It went down in one gulp, but Tippler Dunk's hand still shook. 'Superintendent Jones of Bow Street investigating murder. Ma Dunk, laundress of Paradise Yard, on remand with Miss Pruey. Bow Street wondering about your connection. Clean shirt, Mr Dunk.'

'Sister,' Tippler's voice emerged as a hoarse whisper.

'Passenger to Mr Dickens's house — left a parcel.'

Tippler's story, a gasping, halting account, told of Mr Marlowe whom he sometimes picked up from his sister's house. Took him to various places, Manchester Square, the Adelphi, Old Slaughter's private hotel in Seymour Street — Dickens blinked; Jones did not — and to a shop in John Street — fancy goods.

'And this morning?'

'Euston Square.'

'Taking the train, was he?'

'Didn't say — I ain't no pal of 'is.'

'Pal of your sister's, Mrs Dunk?'

'Dunno — gent, see, Mr Marlowe, 'ardly likely ter — did 'is washin', prob'ly —'

'I don't think your sister is on remand for doing a gentleman's washing, nor Miss Pruey. A matter of murder, as I said: Judge Quarterman in Manchester Square, Joshua Munton, and Thomas Dryden — all dead and Mrs Dunk knew them all, and you, I rather think, have been ferrying the murderer around London. Accessory, we call it, accomplice, possibly. Up to the magistrate. Your cab's being looked after, I take it, so we'll get off to Bow Street, unless…'

Tippler slumped on his bench. His clown's face seemed to have fallen in; even his nose had gone out, though his eyes were still red raw. He resembled now a deflated shadow of sturdy Ma Dunk. Dickens went to get him a pot of ale — he'd be no use to them without, and he wouldn't be driving his cab again. Not today, not ever, probably. He was hardly capable of walking to the door, never mind Bow Street.

They waited while Tippler drank up and some colour returned to his cheeks. 'What else did you do for Mr Marlowe other than driving him?' Jones asked.

'Didn't do nothin' — only wot Melia asked. I'd ter be ready if I woz wanted. See, Melia, she's wot yer'd call a force o' nature — allus bin a strong woman, so yer does wot yer bid an' yer asks no questions. Leastaways, not me. Honest, Mr Jones, yer honour, I ain't no part o' murder — jest a cabbie. Niver knowed wot Melia woz up ter —'

'But she was often up to something,' Dickens said. 'What sort of things?'

'She liked — well, she did a lot o' laundry fer folks. Good 'ouses. 'Elped 'erself very often. See, Melia thought we woz 'ard done by, an' some folks 'ad more than wot woz fair. Careless, too, she said, leavin' things about, puttin' temptation in poor folks' way. I dunno — she don't seem ter be like other folk, but then 'ow could she be? 'Ow could I be?'

'Why is that, Mr Dunk?'

'In the blood, prob'ly.'

'Blood?' Dickens asked, intrigued now. Brother and sister bound by some terrible curse, it sounded like.

Tippler drank more ale. 'Melia saw 'er at the judge's — our ma — she woz Biddy Ross —' the nostrils flared for a moment — 'an' yer knows 'oo she woz, I'll bet, Mr Copper.'

Dickens had a sudden memory of a coarse wax face — a bruiser of a woman who might have murdered a regiment of dragoons. Biddy Ross in the judge's chamber. No wonder Ma had connived with the judge's blackmailers and hadn't cared a jot about his death. "Served him right" had been her verdict. He remembered the gravelly chuckle.

Jones knew all about the Biddy Ross case. She had been hanged for murder in 1822, when her daughter was sixteen and Tippler, only twelve. It had been a horrible case, not the least because of Biddy Ross's reputation. She had been a thoroughly bad woman — originally from Ireland — who had been a drunk, too, a street brawler, a thief, and as cruel a creature as ever lived, according to the evidence presented in court — a robber of children, a skinner of cats, and a vengeful fury. She had murdered an old woman, one Caroline Derby, aged eighty-four, who'd lodged with the family. Melia, the daughter, Tippler, the brother — Reggie then. No father, of course. In court, neither child could recall a father. Sometimes men lodged, but they didn't stay — Biddy Ross was too handy with her fists. Melia, now Ma Dunk, had worked the streets, and Tippler was a potboy in a pub. Neither of them knew anything about the murder. The old woman had been in the house all day. They went to their night work, and she wasn't there the next day. Melia put on a very good show of innocence for the court.

Another pot of ale and a piece of pie this time livened Tippler for a while. 'Clever, our Melia, an' a good-lookin' girl wunce, 'an'some built.'

Dickens could believe the latter. Built like Chaucer's miller now and capable of breaking any door with her head. Dickens and Jones did wonder how much she had known about the murder of the old woman. Tippler looked very shifty when they asked, preferring to move on with his tale, and then there was the matter of three very recent murders. Bad blood, maybe.

Pretty, clever Melia was actually co-habiting with a sailor named, appropriately, Dunk, and quite inappropriately, Ambrose — known as Patch. It seemed he had piratical ambitions. Two perfectly good eyes, though. As handy with his fists as Biddy Ross, but conveniently not in residence at the time of the murder of the old woman to whose money Biddy Ross had taken a fancy. A grant was given to the poor orphans, raised from a fund for the houseless and destitute administered by a clergyman, and with this unexpected good fortune, Melia and Tippler decamped from the purlieus of Limehouse. Dunk gave up the sea and they opened a lodging house and a receiving business near the London Docks. Money to be made from shipping — as in shipping stolen goods in scuttle boats. Dunk was drowned in a whirlpool of flying fists, stamping feet, wild eyes, tattooed arms, broken bottles, and a knife in the back. Buried at sea, so to speak. Melia and Tippler moved on before the police could ask too many questions about the body in the river. An obliging publican had suggested that Dunk lived at the lodging house just off Anchor Lane.

Money in her purse, the Ross name left behind, respectable lodgings, laundry work, head down for the time being, carrier work for the lad, Melia lived a quiet life near Smithfield Market and when a butcher came calling, she was quite willing to oblige, and when Tippler met the shrewish daughter of a cabman, she let him go, knowing he'd be looked after in the manner to which he was accustomed — kept in his place. The butcher burst a blood vessel, father cabman likewise, and Ma Dunk — bigger, coarser, and nobody's sweetheart now — set up in Paradise Yard with the butcher's leavings and Tippler inherited the shrewish daughter, the cab, and the bottle, and the bad blood still flowed in Ma Dunk's veins.

'Who's Pruey?' Dickens had asked, noting that the name had not been mentioned.

Tippler looked blank before saying, 'Oh, the girl — butcher's girl. Simple, that one, an' she'd nowhere ter go. Melia 'ad 'is goods an' 'is money.'

Like Eliza Quarterman and Emma Cooper, Dickens thought — orphaned, left with nothing, passed on to whomever might provide a roof. Girls' lives cheap as oysters and crushed underfoot.

They gave Dunk a blanket in the cell and Rogers found a cushion for the big head. He couldn't help feeling sorry for the man who was brought stumbling and shambling back to Bow

Street. Dickens and Jones thought he probably didn't know about murder. Tippler was a drunk, probably a thief, but he had been bullied all his life by women who were cleverer than he and had no more conscience than the stone walls of the cell. And he wouldn't be driving a cab again.

'Bad blood,' observed Dickens, as they made their way to John Street and Mrs Thomas Dryden's fancy goods shop, hoping that Alexander Marlowe had not removed himself by train from Euston to some other part of the breathing world.

'I wonder, did Alexander Marlowe know that Ma Dunk's mother was a murderess and that her waxen effigy was displayed in the judge's gallery?'

'The stars knew, perhaps. Some fatal conjunction bringing together all those tainted with murder. Bad blood calling to bad blood.'

25: SOMETHING IN THE CELLARAGE

Constable Stemp was out at the front of Mrs Dryden's shop, keeping an eye on the premises from another shop doorway. The fancy goods shop was closed. No one came in or out, but there was light showing through the shutters on the first floor. Someone was in, and if that someone came out — Mrs Thomas Dryden or Alexander Marlowe, for example — then he'd follow. Feak was round the back with Scrap. Feak's instructions were to follow if someone came out the back way.

The back of the shop and the rooms above were in darkness. Scrap strolled along, kicking stones, just a lad with nothing to do, but his eyes were on every back door. He heard the scrape of a boot on stone and turned to see Alexander Marlowe just a few yards away, standing still as if he had materialised from the earth. Scrap opened his mouth to cry out for Feak, but he was too late. The man tipped his hat, smiled, and said, 'We meet again,' and was past him, shoving him out of the way and running down the alley in the opposite direction from Feak, who turned just in time to see Scrap fall. He ran, too, not pausing to look to Scrap, who was also getting to his feet.

Marlowe was gone, of course, into the nest of alleys at the top of the alley, towards the cemetery and Burying Ground Passage where Joshua Munton had been found. Marlowe would know his way about there, Feak thought. He stood uncertainly at the top of the alley. He heard footsteps and looked to his right, where a man in a top hat was coming towards him, followed by a woman with a child. He stepped out to ask if they'd seen a running man, but they hadn't. No one had passed them. No use chasing about the alleys.

Marlowe had escaped. He turned back, but Scrap was nowhere to be seen. *Gone to get Stemp*, he thought, and went that way himself.

Scrap picked himself up. Only his pride was wounded again — by Mr Impudence. 'Ow 'e'd like to knock that topper into the gutter with its owner. But 'e'd come from somewhere. 'Ad to. Wasn't a bloomin' magician an' it wasn't the Arabian Nights what Mr D. was so fond of. 'E was real.

The back door to Mrs Dryden's premises was firmly shut. He tried it, but the next back door opened at his touch. Not on the latch. Then he was in a yard, the yard behind an empty house, and right next to the wall abutting Mrs Dryden's yard, there was a trapdoor, the kind you emptied the coal down. He lifted it and saw not a coal chute but a set of stairs. He listened first, but there was no sound. Halfway down, someone — Marlowe, he calculated — had left a lantern in which a candle still burned. 'Ta, very much,' he murmured, but he paused to listen before he took the first step. That Mrs might be down there — mind, 'e could deal with her. An' Marlowe couldn't 'ave got back down. Could 'e? Scrap thought about the empty house. Nah, 'e'd run off.

There was no sound coming from below as Scrap crept down the stairs to pick up the lantern. The door at the bottom of the stairs opened a little at his tentative touch. Still no sound. He pushed it wide enough to slip in and raised the lantern to look about him. Just boxes, a mangle, buckets, a trunk — and someone seated in the far corner. Someone who had not moved or looked up as he came in.

While Scrap was staring at the motionless figure, Superintendent Jones and Dickens were contemplating Mrs Thomas Dryden — certainly handsome built, but without the coarseness of Ma Dunk and very well dressed in her outdoor clothes and carrying a portmanteau. Dickens saw the startled glitter in Mrs Dryden's eyes as he stepped into her premises, emerging from behind Mr Jones. She looked for a moment like a woman caught out. She must have seen him at the waxworks, Dickens thought. She looked like a woman who might hiss. He saw how her nostrils dilated as she breathed a quick, alarmed breath. And if she were the woman in the judge's waxwork gallery, she had seen him when he had looked upon the murderesses and victims for the first time. When he had heard the rustle of a skirt.

Superintendent Jones asked courteously for a word concerning her dead husband, and she led them into her parlour, by which time she had recovered her composure. *Cool customer*, Dickens thought, but they knew that. The woman who had possibly frightened Judge Quarterman to death. However, he noticed that her gaze flickered to him from time to time, as if she couldn't stop herself, and it flickered to the door. Was she expecting someone?

Jones began mildly enough, expressing his condolences about her husband's death. She bowed her head. Mr Jones wondered if she could tell them anything about a Mr Alexander Marlowe. Mrs Dryden looked regretful. She did not know any Alexander Marlowe. She had no knowledge of her husband's friends, or his life after he had left her for … for another — lady. It was a painful subject upon which she preferred not to dwell. He was gone and she must bear it. Her handkerchief dabbed at her eyes, but Jones could see no moisture there. If they were finished, she said, she had an appointment to keep.

Jones looked at the handkerchief and thought of the pauper's grave in Adelaide Street and a man's jacket on the chair. They always overdid it, the widows who encompassed their husband's deaths. He remembered very pretty, delicate Mrs Emmeline Woods whose husband Reverend Mr Woods had taken poison — oppressed by his many cares, so his widow had averred, lace at her dry eyes. She had been very convincing, but her little hand had put the arsenic in his tea. A freshly laundered handkerchief, he remembered, embroidered with the initials, "E.W.". He took another tack.

'Mrs Dunk is your laundress, I believe.'

The hand that held the handkerchief tightened. Her eyes flicked to Dickens, who was simply standing still, ready to meet that look whenever it came his way. Then they flicked back to Jones. 'She is. What has she to do with my husband or his friends?'

'She has a brother, a cabman, who brought Mr Marlowe here — more than once.'

'I'm sure it is possible. However, as I have said, I do not know him. He may have come here to see my husband. A good many people came to see him.'

'Mrs Dunk was laundress to Judge Quarterman. You remember him, of course. It was he who acquitted your husband in the Eliza Winton case. The girl who died because of a botched abortion.'

The blood rushed to her face then. 'That was nothing to do with me. I don't understand what all these questions mean.'

'Judge Quarterman was murdered. Your husband was involved in it with Alexander Marlowe. Miss Pruey, who lives with Mrs Dunk, let two people into the judge's house on the night of his death, a man and a woman, a woman in a black veil whom Mr Dickens saw at Madame Tussaud's, a woman who had been meeting the judge. I believe that woman to be you.'

Mrs Dryden stood up then, looking from one to the other and to the door. She was rattled now. 'He couldn't have seen me — I wasn't wearing — I don't know —'

The shout startled them all. It was Feak who hurtled in to tell them that Marlowe had appeared in the alley at the back of the shop where he'd been waiting. He'd followed Marlowe and lost him, and Scrap had vanished.

Jones turned to Mrs Dryden. 'The man you don't know — been calling, has he?'

Mrs Dryden didn't answer. Feak was instructed to stand guard outside her parlour. Jones didn't think she'd be likely to jump from a first-floor window.

'You don't think he's taken Scrap?' Jones asked.

'Couldn't 'ave done. Scrap was just gettin' to 'is feet as I was runnin' after Marlowe, an' when I came back, Scrap was gone. Mr Stemp's lookin'.'

They rushed out through the back door into the alley. Stemp was calling out, and then he appeared at the next yard door. 'Trapdoor to a cellar. Steps. He's gone down. I was just goin' when I heard you. This way.'

Stemp called out for Scrap, and there was an answering shout. Jones went down, followed by Dickens. And they saw the black-bonneted figure, too. A waxwork, of course, and there were more than the one. And underneath some sacking in various tea chests there were more heads, rather grim-looking, bald heads, unfinished faces and blank eye sockets. Heads overpainted with wax like Judge Quarterman's victims.

'Gave me a turn, she did,' Scrap said, pointing to the bonneted figure, 'but I guessed when she didn't move.'

'Kept his stock here,' Dickens observed.

'We'll see what Mrs has to say about that.'

Stemp shut the trapdoor and shot the bolts. They returned to Mrs Dryden's house.

'Bring a cab to the front of the shop,' Jones told Stemp, 'and you can escort her back to Bow Street. Handcuffs, I think. That'll make her think. Put her in a cell and leave her.'

'With Mr Tippler fer company, mebbe.'

'We'd better not go that far.'

Mrs Thomas Dryden swore that she knew nothing of what was in the cellar, but, holding her lace to her now wet eyes, with handcuffs on her wrists, mute and meek, she was removed to the cab. As it moved away, Dickens saw her shattered face looking her last on what she had lost. She had something to cry about now.

26: WAIF AND STRAY

A search of Mrs Dryden's rooms revealed nothing of Alexander Marlowe's presence. Dickens and Jones were not at all surprised, but Scrap was determined to open every cupboard door and drawer in the kitchen. They heard the sound of doors banging and the rattle of cutlery as drawers were pulled out. Hoping to find a handy diary or letter with a convenient address, Dickens thought. Some hope. But they left him. If anything were to be found, Scrap would find it.

As Dickens and Jones went through the bedrooms and attics, Dickens wondered what Marlowe had intended by his visit to Mrs Dryden's house.

Sam Jones wondered, too. 'I can believe that she thought she was running off with him, but I cannot believe that he would scarper with her. He's a user of people. Think of Munty and Thomas Dryden. We presume he'd finished with them.'

'Perhaps we've saved her life,' Dickens said.

'That's a chilling thought,' Jones said as they went downstairs to retrieve Scrap.

'Unless he knew we were here. Tippler dropped him at Euston Square. Only a minute or two to come back to see what I did after his message had come. He's not going anywhere. He's having too much of a good time.'

'Well, we've got her. She might tell us something. A night or two in the cells concentrates the mind wonderfully.'

Dickens grinned, and then he thought of something. '*Where's Eliza? I think you know now* — that's what he wrote. I didn't think then, but, Lord, Sam, he knows. I'll bet he knows where Eliza Quarterman is.'

'Get over there and warn her. He probably won't go there, but just in case. I'll get back to Bow Street and I'll send Stemp. He'll meet you at Waterloo Pier. Don't go without him — he doesn't know where that chapel is.'

It was dark now and the river black and swollen, mists rising to meet the lowering cloud mass, the moon's eye shrinking to blindness, the inflamed eyes of warning lights menacing near, like so many Cyclopes. The frozen air cut at their faces, the reflections of the lights of the bridge shivered in the choppy water, and the police boat heaved on the swell. Two burly policemen pulled at one set of oars, Stemp and Dickens at another, and Scrap was in the bow, his face tight with anxiety. *Lost 'im twice*, he was thinking. There wouldn't be a third time.

Crossing the Styx, Dickens was thinking, Stemp in his great pea-coat like the hefty ferryman, Charon — with clothes on, sensibly in this weather. Off to that blighted underworld which was Southwark in the dark. He was glad to know that Stemp was with them, looking as if he could row any number of sullen and wrathful sinners to their doom. What about a laughing one? As long as it wasn't his doom, or Scrap's, for that matter, he thought, as the Styx tossed a filthy wave about their feet. An hour or more of this and he'd be glad to land at Barge House Stairs or the entrance to Hell — whichever came first.

The stairs came first, greasy with slime, but they scrambled up and were away towards Union Street and Redcross Street in minutes. Stemp kept his distance, but they could hear his firm tread behind them. It wasn't Marlowe Dickens was afraid of, it was the denizens of Southwark spilling out of pubs with their broken bottles or sneaking out of passageways with their coshes or garottes. They waited at the corner of Redcross

Street, where the Crossbones cemetery lay, unconsecrated, under the black sky. A few flickering lights could be seen, and the odd shadow flitted in and out of the lights. Some outcast being buried or dug up. Some grave being made ready for a second guest — or third, or twentieth. Vapours rose like phantoms coming out of their graves to haunt the night — and the day. Many a gravedigger had died from the poisoned air from the decomposing bodies. A grave-digger burning straw, perhaps — they did it to dispel the noxious air.

Across the way the little street was in darkness. Dickens realised that he didn't know if Eliza Quarterman lived in rooms in the chapel. She'd spoken of neighbours, which might suggest she did, or certainly nearby. He'd have to knock, and if there were no answer, they'd have to ask at the charcoal burner's premises or a house further down.

Scrap crept forward and slid along the pavement. He disappeared briefly into the dark mouth of the little street. Then he was back, whispering, 'Somebody there, lyin' down in the chapel porch. Woman — sees the skirts. Can't tell if it's Mrs.'

Dickens couldn't answer and they waited, hardly daring to breathe, while Stemp crossed the road first. When he reached the narrow entrance, he dropped down as if to tie his bootlace. He looked about him and slipped down the street. He was soon back and beckoning them over.

'Emma Cooper,' Dickens said, looking down. She appeared to be asleep, curled up on the steps in the shelter of the porch. He saw how exhausted she looked, her thin face very pale and dark bruises under her eyes, a fresh bruise and a cut on her cheek. Stemp's lamp picked out the blood that had run down from the cut. She looked half-starved, too. She had gone missing on the day they'd been to the glass eye factory. That was — what? Four days ago. Seen by Scrap two days ago. Frightened and nowhere to go in this benighted land. Her skirt was muddy, and her coat sleeve torn. Whether she had been attacked or had just collapsed there, it was hard to say, but her breathing was shallow and when he felt for a pulse, it was very faint. He moistened her lips from his brandy flask and was relieved to hear her moan.

'Bag's missin',' Scrap said. 'No bonnet, neither. Robbed, mebbe.'

Not Marlowe, then, Dickens thought. The joker wasn't the robbing type, and Dickens couldn't believe he would have left her here. No, this looked like a street crime.

Stemp stayed with Emma as Dickens and Scrap went to see if there were any alley or passage which might take them round the back of the chapel. A narrow alley presented itself a few doors down, and they saw the bulk of the chapel rising above a wall with a door in it. A locked door — Eliza had taken his advice — but it was the work of a moment for Scrap to scramble to the top of the wall, and Dickens heard him drop down on the other side. In the quiet, he heard the faint tap-tap of a hand on glass, then a door opening, footsteps, a bolt sliding, and there she was in her apron, telling him that she would open the front door so that they could bring in Emma Cooper.

'I have soup. Scrap can fill the stove and make a fire.'

Stemp lifted Emma into the vestibule from where they went through the canteen and into the kitchen where Dickens had ladled the stew. They then moved into another small room, where there was a bed and a few pieces of furniture and Scrap lighting a fire in the grate.

Dickens and Stemp stood back while Eliza examined Emma Cooper.

'She is exhausted, I think, and bruised. Someone has hit her, and she has fallen. Doctor Greville will come. He lives in Blackman Street, number 90. He is a good man.'

Stemp accompanied Dickens to find Doctor Greville, whose lack of surprise at finding Charles Dickens on his doorstep in the company of a policeman was explained by his telling Dickens on the way that Eliza had told him of Dickens's visit and her precautions against the possible advent of Alexander Marlowe on her doorstep.

'We're old friends,' he said, 'and she trusts me not to ask questions. I respect her privacy, but I've kept an eye on the place. She does a lot of good hereabouts, and she doesn't ask questions of her customers, either. Sometimes it's the best way. A plate of hot food is more use than scripture.'

'Water, too,' Dickens said, 'hot or cold. How can any man's soul rise above the filth and degradation in which he, his wife and his children are mired? Give them cheap, pure water and wholesome air. And the plate of stew, of course. I was not diminishing the work of the kitchen.'

'I know. I read your speech on sanitary reform back in May. I've been into every foetid court you describe here in Southwark, but tell me, the injured young woman —?'

'One Emma Cooper, known to the kitchen, who was seen near the chapel some days ago, then vanished, only to turn up again, almost unconscious, bruised and nearly starving. Robbed, I think.'

Dickens and Scrap waited in the dining hall by the stove while Doctor Greville and Eliza saw to the patient.

When the doctor emerged, he told them that her injuries were not serious. No need for hospital, but she was very weak, chilled, and feverish.

'She has been very frightened, I should say, but with warmth, rest and care she can recover. It will depend on what hope she has to bring her back. You must not speak to her tonight.'

When Doctor Greville had gone, Eliza came out. 'I will look after her, but it is hard to say whether she will recover. She is frightened of something or of someone. Can it be —'

'Alexander Marlowe? I don't know. He was following her, but what he meant by that, we don't know. She is connected to the two men who were murdered; one we think was her lover, for whom she stole from her employers —'

Eliza's eyes widened. 'Poor girl, what on earth had she become involved in? No wonder she is frightened, Mr Dickens, and it does look as if she was attacked. Not surprising round here.'

'She 'ad a bag an' a bonnet when I saw 'er, an' they're missin' now.'

'You'll have to come back. She cannot tell you anything tonight — give it a couple of days. Let me have some time with her.'

'You'll be safe?'

Eliza smiled. 'It's just as well my neighbour, the charcoal burner, didn't see Scrap climbing over the wall or you, Mr Dickens, hovering outside the yard door. A big man, my neighbour — not keen on strangers.'

Stemp was waiting at the front door. They heard the bolts slide and made their way back along Union Street, where a fog was gathering.

The thought of trudging through the streets as far as Waterloo Bridge, or even Blackfriars Bridge filled Dickens with a sudden weariness. He'd had enough of Southwark for one day, and the idea of taking a boat across a river weighed down by fog and shrouded in mist was not to be contemplated by any sane man.

'A cab, my lads — there'll be one to take us across Southwark Bridge and thence to Bow Street.'

27: COUNSEL ADVISES

Dickens was surprised to see Mr Henry Meteyard in Sam Jones's office — Henry Meteyard, son of Sampson, Limehouse butcher, six foot three like his father, handsome built, of course, handsome face, too, handy pugilist in a dark alley, and, probably most pertinent just now, barrister at law of Lincoln's Inn. Very much at home with his feet on the fender.

However, given the travellers' return from the wastelands of Southwark, they were to take the floor first, or rather Scrap would, whose ownership of anything to do with Emma Cooper established his right to speak first. He thought that he would return to the paupers' kitchen the next morning.

'Keep an eye on things, and Mrs'll need 'elp with the dinner an' that. Mebbe when she's ready, I can talk to Emma. I know what to ask.'

Superintendent Jones forbore to give any warnings or to suggest that Constable Stemp went with Scrap. Eliza's neighbours sounded a likely lot for defence purposes. In any case, there was no evidence that Marlowe had attacked Emma Cooper. He had been in that alley behind Mrs Dryden's shop, and the description of the young woman's injuries were consistent with her having been assaulted not long before she was found on the porch. So, unless Marlowe had the power of flight, it would have been impossible.

'Good,' Jones said. 'Now, I have news of Mrs Thomas Dryden and old Mother Dunk. I called on our friend, here, at Lincoln's Inn. I thought he might have a persuasive effect on Mrs Dryden — he has a way with the ladies —'

Henry Meteyard raised his teacup in acknowledgement of the justice of the compliment. '*Amicus curiae*, at your service.'

'Not that Mrs Dryden is a lady,' Jones continued, 'but for the purposes of investigation, I'm treating her as one.'

'And Mother Dunk, is she to be raised from the mangle?' asked Dickens mischievously.

'Put through it, more like. However, don't interrupt; we'll get to her eventually. My friend of the court, with every courteous flourish at his command, persuaded Mrs Dryden to confess her part in the proceedings or it would go hard with her, especially given her history, and, of course, the evidence of Mrs Dunk and Miss Pruey. I know they haven't given anything regarding Marlowe, but she didn't know that. Henry, give them the gist.'

'She coughed it all up. Though a victim of circumstances, you must understand, deceived, of course, threatened, naturally, only an innocent dupe — being but a delicate lady — ' Henry held up his hand to silence Dickens before he had the chance to speak. 'The bones of the matter are that Marlowe came to the shop to buy some trinket for a lady, examined all the goods, and mentioned that he dealt in wax dolls and figures. Thomas Dryden came in and they were all very convivial over a bottle of brandy. Marlowe mentioned that he'd sold wax figures to a Judge Quarterman — queer stick, lived alone, wealthy. Marlowe had known someone who had known the judge years back. Married once, it seemed. Wife ran off and this someone had suggested the talk was of murder. Ripe for blackmail, Marlowe observed casually. Reputation as a hanging judge. Cruel devil, especially about women — the wax figures Marlowe had sold him were all victims, but they weren't believed because they were women. Did they remember the case of one Eliza Winton?'

'He'd done his research. He knew about the Drydens' connection with Eliza Winton,' Dickens interrupted, 'and I'll bet he found out about the judge and his waxworks. It was common knowledge, according to Mrs Flint.'

'Doctor Yarwood knew about them. All Marlowe had to do was present himself as a waxwork artist —'

'Mention an Eliza victim he'd modelled and offer it to the judge — and more, if he wanted,' Henry added. 'The judge was mad enough to fall for it.'

'And we know how persuasive Marlowe could be. A gentleman artist, of course. He fooled his own daughter for a time,' Dickens said.

'But he needed accomplices, which is where it all came apart.'

'Tends to happen with conspiracy,' Henry said. 'Someone talks or makes a mistake. However, to continue with Mrs Dryden's version. Mr Thomas Dryden was all ears at the word blackmail. As Mr Jones had said to you, Dryden had no cause to hate the judge, but the money was the thing. Mrs Dryden was, you understand, reluctant to have anything to do with it, but her husband threatened her. Just a poor, weak woman. Marlowe sent the first blackmail letter — no answer, so he and Dryden watched the house, got to know his habits. Mrs Dryden was forced to follow him, pretend to have a fit of the vapours, and plant another letter. After this one Marlowe followed him, and as the judge got into a cab he simply ran up and put it in his hand. Now, they needed to know when he would be alone in the house, when the housekeeper wouldn't be there — out shopping, for example. They watched. Mrs Dryden again forced, of course, to knock on the door — and who should come to answer but Ma Dunk, her own laundress? Naturally, Mrs Dryden leaves another note, this time with a paper purporting to be an article to be sent to a newspaper, accusing the judge of torturing his wife and murdering her.'

'A terrifying prospect for him,' Dickens said, 'because the first was true. Eliza Quarterman had told Marlowe how the judge had mistreated her. She told me that there was cruelty in him. She thought he would have murdered her. The judge would have known what the newspapers could make of that, especially if any former servants came forward to add their two penn'orth. He'd have been ruined.'

'Exactly. Whatever was in the paper Marlowe wrote made him pay up — a lot of money, the sums increasing as they always do in blackmail. Mrs Dryden meets him at Madame Tussaud's — Marlowe's picturesque idea, of course — and the judge, probably half mad by now, refuses to pay any more.'

'I thought he was angry when I met him — unreasonably so. There was a fellow eating a pie and looking at the murderers. He wasn't doing any harm, but there was a kind of mad rage in the judge. Not against the pieman, but the blackmailers. Why on earth did he force me to go to his house?'

'Maybe he thought they'd not follow if he had a guest,' Jones said.

'But Mrs Dryden had gone there already.'

'Exactly — let in by Pruey.'

'Because,' Henry continued, 'Mrs Dryden had reported Ma Dunk's connection to the judge, and so they could have someone on the inside, as it were. When Ma Dunk told them that Pruey would be on duty on that very night, they were in.'

'But what about murder?' Scrap asked. 'Did they intend to kill 'im?'

'Mrs Dryden says not — Dryden and Marlowe wanted to frighten him into paying up.'

'But in his letter —' Dickens began.

'Showing off, I wonder,' Henry said, 'teasing you with your own words, carried away by his own cleverness, boasting he'd committed a murder that could never be discovered, but, of course, he's hanged himself by writing it. *Mens rea*, *actus rea* — guilty mind, guilty act. Neat as a Christmas parcel.'

'Hoist with his own petard.'

'He will be — if we find him,' Jones said. 'He's admitted murder in the letter, whether he meant it or not.'

'What about Dryden's death?' asked Dickens.

'She swears she doesn't know what happened to him,' said Henry. 'However, when the waxworks started appearing all round town, she had a feeling Dryden was in on the caper. He and Marlowe had become thick as thieves — carousing, gambling — great pals, laughing their way about town.'

'Marlowe, drunk on his success,' Dickens said, 'recklessly swaggering on his way, sure that he'd get away with it, but, Henry, did you get any impression that she suspected Marlowe had murdered Dryden?'

'Impossible to say. She's a thorough-going liar when it suits her. Dryden left her, she says, for some other woman. The young woman who painted eyes, Mr Jones tells me, Miss Emma Cooper. Of course, Mrs Dryden didn't know anything about her. I'm sure she did. After all, she, Dryden and Marlowe were all in on it.'

'That poor young woman was just a dupe,' Jones said. 'Remember what they did to Eliza Winton? Mrs Dryden knew all about Dryden's seduction of that other poor woman. We'll never know the reason for it. They'd have been using Eliza Winton for some reason, and they were using Emma Cooper.'

'And was Marlowe living with Mrs Dryden?' asked Dickens. 'Sergeant Rogers said there was a man there.'

'Not Marlowe, she says, of course — just a commercial with his samples. Warehouse in Fenchurch Street. Name of Bloxham. I think we'll find he was there, but perhaps not in his shirtsleeves.'

'Marlowe was in that alley — didn't imagine 'im, an' 'e'd been in that cellar,' Scrap insisted.

'Mr Thomas Dryden had let him use the cellar — nothing to do with Mrs, naturally,' Henry told him. 'However, nothing to fret about, Scrap. Superintendent Jones has had speech with Ma Dunk.'

'I certainly have. I only had to tell her that Mrs Thomas Dryden was helping me with enquiries, and that she had much to tell, for Ma Dunk to tell me not ter take no notice of that 'arpy — in it up ter 'er 'igh an' mighty neck, an' no better than she should be with 'er fancy man —'

'She knew about Marlowe?' Dickens asked.

'He and Dryden were sometimes at the stable where she kept her cart, and she volunteered Tippler to do any cab driving they might want — private like, as she told me,' said Jones. 'It was Pruey who let in Mrs Dryden on the evening of the judge's death when Mrs Flint, the housekeeper had gone. It was Pruey who let her into the waxworks chamber, and, as we know, it was Pruey and Munty who delivered the waxworks to the Adelphi, and Ma Dunk was the one who dressed as a man to put the figure on the tomb in St Giles's — did it for the money. Just a lark, according to Ma. Ma didn't know anything about murder. The toffs did what they liked, and what was a poor laundress to do to earn a bit extra? No harm in it. She wasn't a bit surprised to find Marlowe serenely taking his breakfast when she went to collect the laundry. Despite Ma's pleading her innocence, there's enough conflicting evidence, enough doubt about her and Mrs Dryden's roles in the judge's death, and Dryden's and Munty's deaths, to keep them all on remand.'

'Munty,' Dickens exclaimed, 'what about him?'

'Well, it wasn't Dryden, he was already dead, and I honestly wonder now about Marlowe. Munty was very small beer to Marlowe and the Drydens and could be bought off, like Ma Dunk and Pruey, with very little. I mean a very small portion of what they'd squeezed out of the judge. Chicken feed. Munty wasn't a danger. Ma Dunk might have been, but Marlowe wouldn't have seen that — one of the lumpen masses to him, but if she'd liked she could have felled him with one blow. If we hadn't started nosing about, I think Mr Marlowe might have found Ma Dunk a formidable adversary if she'd a mind to get more money from him.'

'She didn't murder Munty?'

'I mentioned Caroline Derby to her — she started at that name. Murdered, I reminded her, by Biddy Ross, her own mother. Most indignant, she was, when I reminded her that poor Munty had been done to death in a back alley near her premises. She was more outraged by Biddy's waxwork at the judge's. What right had the old —? You can guess the torrent of abuse. She didn't care tuppence about the judge's death. Served him right. She's callous, but, on balance, I think not. Munty was more use to her alive than dead — like Pruey. She had power over those two hapless creatures. And I was thinking — remember Rogers telling us that Munty had said he was going to the Stingo to meet a gent —'

'Money in it.'

'Exactly. No money on him when he was killed, but he could have got some from Marlowe. Maybe some lounger from the Stingo saw him put money in his pocket and did for him in that alley as Munty was on his way home.'

Dickens thought about that. 'It makes sense, Sam. Munty was as a speck of dust in Marlowe's eye.'

'But 'e's to cop it fer the judge, I 'opes,' Scrap said, possessed by a sanguinary desire that his enemy should hang.

'Blackmail, conspiracy, burglary, and murder — of a judge, too. The law won't take too kindly to the latter, in particular. Never mind that nobody liked Quarterman — he was one of them,' Henry explained. 'Is that not so, Mr Jones?'

Mr Jones didn't answer. He was thinking about dogs. A dog his mother had kept, the runt of a litter — a foolish, light-hearted, thoughtless creature. Brought up soft, his father had said, his father who had kept big-jowled, broad-shouldered, slavering dogs to guard his blacksmith's shop. Hammer and Anvil, they were called. His father had a somewhat grim sense of humour. But when silly, soft Pansy had been cornered in the outhouse, she had fought for her life, snarling, slavering, lashing out, so that even Hammer and Anvil sometimes retreated. Their barking had brought his father to the rescue, but that cornered dog had shown the savagery under its petted skin. Marlowe might well realise that his clever clogs letter could condemn him.

'Cornered,' he said.

'If he were,' Dickens said, divining Jones's meaning, 'what might he do, the laughing cavalier? How might even he fight his way out?'

'That's what I'm thinking.'

'But we've gotter find 'im,' Scrap urged.

Henry Meteyard picked up the currents in the air. 'Suppose I go with Scrap to Southwark?' He looked at Scrap's street urchin outfit. 'What'll I go as?'

Scrap looked back consideringly. 'Coal 'eaver.'

They had to laugh at Scrap's pinpoint accuracy and Henry said, 'It can be done. Tomorrow morning, then.'

Sam Jones was relieved. At least he wouldn't have to worry about Scrap, and in any case, he had decided it was time to send a letter to Inspector Wells of M Division in Southwark. He wanted that chapel kept an eye on. He'd had a few chilling thoughts about all those paupers streaming in to eat their midday meal. Eliza and her assistant couldn't possibly know them all. It might be a wise child that knows its own father, but a man disguised in rags might be anyone. Wells, whose fat forefinger was always tapping his nose, could keep things close.

Dickens declared that he must go back to Wellington Street on editorial business. Henry promised his brains and his brawn should they be needed, and Scrap departed to the stationery shop in Crown Street.

28: THE MAN IN THE DOORWAY

There are fifty doors by which discovery may enter. With infinite pains and cunning, the murderer double locks and bars forty-nine of them, and cannot see the fiftieth standing wide open.

Alexander Marlowe, in his arrogance, had left more than one door at least ajar, Dickens thought, as he felt his way down to Wellington Street, having parted from Henry at the corner of Russell Street; even the substantial Mr Meteyard shrank to the vagueness of a wraith as the fog swirled about him.

Arrogance, Dickens had always thought, came with its own stupidity. Marlowe, undoubtedly a clever man in many ways, had stupidly chosen the wrong associates. He'd read Ma Dunk wrongly, Dickens was certain — just a laundress with a grudge. Perhaps he had sniffed out Ma's bad blood. Known about Biddy Ross. Divined that she could be bought; thought she'd never tell. He might not have known that Ma's brother, the cab driver, was a regular around Tavistock Square and sniffed only beer about him. Maybe it hadn't suited Ma to divulge the cab driver's identity. She'd keep her own secrets for her own ends. Marlowe would hardly have noticed simple Pruey, who had given away her guilt in the blink of an eye. Just a tool — useful as a jemmy and no tears if lost. And even Alexander Marlowe could not have foreseen the clincher for Ma and Pruey — that a glass eye would be left in a cart. And another door ajar. The crossing-sweeper huddled at his post by Tavistock House would have been beneath the notice of a gentleman. Marlowe's doors were not sealed as tightly as he had thought. All they needed was that one wide-open door. Half-open would do.

The fog was rolling up Wellington Street from the river. He'd like to go home, he thought, and forget about waxworks and murder. He stopped suddenly at an impossible sight — a man on stilts, as tall as a giant. He blinked and stepped forward, and the vision dissolved into a man walking away with a ladder — a man melted into mist. He'd been outside the Lyceum Theatre, just opposite Dickens's office. He crossed the road. "Frightened to Death", he read, feeling a touch of ice at his neck. Chamberlaine's old farce revived? He looked more closely. No, it wasn't. The ice spread. It was a poster advertising the Haymarket. A long way from home, this poster. The Lyceum wouldn't be advertising for the Haymarket Theatre, where Mr Browne was reprising his famous role as Jack Phantom.

Jack Phantom, Jack o' Lantern, the will-o'-the-wisp, Spring-heeled Jack — the devil who dressed as a gentleman. Well, he'd just seen all three in one.

A crack in the snarl of slow-moving traffic allowed him to squeeze to the opposite side of the road, where he saw someone lounging against the door post, hat tipped over his eyes — a faceless someone, wreathed in fog and eerily lit by the gas lamp above the door. Jack Phantom? Dickens gripped his stick. He wasn't going to run. Let him show himself if he dared or vanish again if he chose.

'You wanted me?' he asked sharply, though his heart seemed to knock at his ribs. *Let's hope Jack Phantom can't see through a frock coat*, he thought.

The figure seemed to unfold itself like a creaking old yardstick to appear as a tall, thin man in a threadbare coat, the sleeves of which were too short. Dickens thought he heard bones rattle. A long, thin hand reached up to tip back the shabby top hat. Dickens knew the shifty yellow face and the too-close-together muddy eyes. One of Reynolds's men. George Reynolds, publisher of that rag *Reynolds's Weekly News*, office just across the road. This fellow would want money or, perish the thought, a job.

'Got something to say about the waxworks. Something you an' the superintendent will want to know. What's the going rate?'

'Don't know until you tell, but if it's good, then something, certainly. Mr Reynolds not generous these days?'

'Me and him have parted company. A little misunderstanding about a cash box.'

Dickens did not enquire further. The man was not one he'd trust, but as a hack journalist — penny-a-liner now, he imagined — he had a nose for truffling in the dirt, a nose which was curiously askew. Someone had punched him, probably. That ferret face was made for unearthing secrets and selling them to the highest bidder. He opened the front door, turned up the gas in the hall, and took the man in — Crowquill, he called himself. Stole that, too, from an illustrator. Fancied himself a satirist. Shameless — and deluded. He looked a wreck, or more like a man clinging to the wreckage of his life. He might have been any age from forty to a hundred — he'd been about for years. Dickens heard the man wheezing like a run-down clock as he laboured up the stairs.

He took the bellows to the dying coals in the grate and put on more when it flared up. He then gestured Mr Crowquill to a chair, found two glasses and poured brandy. 'Now, tell me.'

'Simmonds,' Crowquill began.

Dickens's ears tingled. 'Waxworks, used to be in Holborn, then Finsbury Square.' He remembered then that Simmonds had exhibited Biddy Ross in all her murderous splendour, but he only said, 'Samson.'

'Saw him — terrifying brute. Fellow called William Marlowe worked for Simmonds way back. Bit of a lad. Sacked for dallying with the Mrs, so I heard.'

Dickens saw some faded letters on a sign above an oil and colour shop in Leicester Square. *Soft you now*, he thought. 'And he interested you because…?'

'Murder case I reported on. Remember the Reinhart case, years back, the German who murdered his mistress and four children up in Pentonville?'

'I do — a horrible case. One, a baby of eight months as I recall. Killed himself.'

'Cut their throats and his own, and you'll remember that some fellow took over the house, kept it as it was, complete with bloodstains, and got up a waxwork exhibition of the mistress, Ellen Leeson, the four kiddies and Reinhart. Paid twenty-five pounds for all the clothes they'd worn and dressed up his waxworks. Kiddies in their bloodstained beds. Even displayed a bloodied knife — don't know if it was the one that Reinhart used. Sixpence admission. Crowds in the street. Fifty pounds in pocket on the first day. Made a packet.'

'The devil he did. Some fellow?'

'William Marlowe, but I'm ahead of myself. There are a few more interesting snippets. A young fellow, one James Parr —' Dickens's felt the tingling like a faint electric shock, but he didn't move — 'sacked from Simmonds's, got three months for criminal damage at the waxworks. Broke a few windows and posted up a couple of scurrilous pictures of Mr and Mrs. Got an artist to draw a sketch of Simmonds hanging from a gallows. Simmonds was showing a mummy at the time, and a sketch of Mrs showed her as the mummy, ugly as sin, claiming that she was two thousand years old, just dug up from St Giles's churchyard.'

'Artist?' Dickens asked, knowing the answer, and thinking about a waxwork in St Giles's churchyard.

'Interviewed Parr in the House of Correction — he told me the name for a shilling. William Marlowe put him up to it — remember he'd had amorous business with the lady who'd accused him of assault. Mr Simmonds believed his wife, o' course. Didn't bring charges, though — too doubtful of a win, I reckon. Knew Marlowe could talk his way out of anything.'

'What happened to Parr?'

'Another dead loss. Lived with some woman near Golden Lane — she had a baby that died. Thought to be a deliberate injury to its throat. Parr was hanged for it. You'll know the case.'

Dickens shook his head. *Don't give anything away.*

'No? Well, she was Eliza Parr — or that's what she said, but who knows? Change their names a damn sight more often than they change their drawers. Whoever she was, she was transported. He was hanged. Turned out his real name was Munton.'

Dickens almost bit into his brandy glass, such was his shock this time, but he kept his courteously neutral gaze on Crowquill.

'Had a boy — orphanage, I suppose, for him.' There was an interrogatory look in Crowquill's eye in the pause, but Dickens just waited. 'Anyway, I kept my eye on Marlowe and his doings — thought there might be a good story in it when the law caught up with him.'

'It didn't, I'm guessing.'

'Not for a while. He was over in the Commercial Road for a time — tuppenny-ha'penny waxwork outfit in a tent. Knew about it because honest William gave evidence in a case. Some blighter punched the owner — didn't like the figures. Mind, they weren't much to look at. One supposed to be Queen Victoria. Looked like a pork butcher's wife. Anyway, I picked up his scent again at the Egyptian Hall — waxworks there. Going up in the world, gentleman Will. Big concern. Remember they had that centrifugal railway contraption — folk whizzing round and round, or up an' down. Ingenious stuff. Very popular. Marlowe in charge of the waxworks.

'However, he went a bit too far — seduced the owner's wife. Husband brought an action. All sorts of creditors came out of the woodwork. Spent like a drunk on Friday night, our Will, and borrowed from everybody or stole. The Commercial Road man naturally trusted the blighter. Robbed him blind — IOUs floatin' about like confetti. Off to the Marshalsea. Thought I'd leave him to sweat it out, and then he might be desperate enough for a pound or two to tell his story. That business of the Pentonville murder makes a good tale. Series, I thought. Good money in them. Life of a rogue, I thought, *Willie the Waxwork Man* — neat, eh? Like *Varney the Vampire*, only more genteel — for readers like yours, maybe?'

Dickens kept a straight face. Seeing that Crowquill's glass was empty, he lifted it and took a deep breath as he went for the bottle. He put some more brandy in his own glass, too. He needed it. Turning round, and giving Crowquill his glass, he asked, 'What happened about the Pentonville waxworks?'

'Didn't pay his rent, o' course. Action brought, but he was gone with the takings an' the stock. Valuable stuff, I daresay. Left his assistant to clear the decks and he, like James Parr, copped a sentence because he couldn't pay the rent, and he was indicted as well for keeping a disorderly house. Disorderly! It was a blooming charnel house.'

'Did you find Marlowe in the Marshalsea?'

'Interesting, that. Some do-gooding female visited him, brought comforts — very persuasive, William, though getting on a bit by now. Kept his looks, mind. Dress him up an' he'd still charm the ladies. 'Bout my age, I should think, an' I've not done so bad.'

Mirror, mirror, on the wall, Dickens thought, looking at the jaundiced face and the complacent smile, showing a few yellow teeth. 'The woman — who was she?'

'No idea, but she raised the money to pay his debts and puff, he's gone. Loved and left her, I daresay. I lost sight of him then, for a year or two. But, when the waxworks started appearing all about London, I naturally thought of him. Just the sort of stunt he'd pull.' Crowquill downed his brandy and looked straight at Dickens. 'And then there's Judge Quarterman. Visitation of God. Suppose it was a visitation o' blackmail? That business of the judge's wife. Missing for years. Vanished without a trace. Married for a few weeks. Dead, I wonder? Odd business. Quarterman had a collection of waxworks.' He paused to tap the twisted nose. 'Been following my nose. Mr Jones investigating. You by his side. Judge's laundress in quod. Very interesting.'

'Do you know where he is now?'

'Alas, no, but what I've told you is surely worth something to Mr Jones, an' if I were to hear anything more, naturally, I'd bring my information to him. In the meantime, something on account'd be fair, Mr Dickens. Keep it from Mr Reynolds, eh?'

Well, Crowquill knew what blackmail was. He'd have to give him something. One, to get rid of him, and two, the man clearly needed a good hot meal. What worried Dickens was how much Crowquill knew or guessed — even that the judge might have been murdered. And how far was he prepared to go to find William Marlowe? William Marlowe who had to be

Alexander, who might, or might not, be dangerous. He thought of dead Joshua Munton, whose father had been cheated by Marlowe. He'd bet anything that Munty hadn't known that. Unless, chilling thought, Munty had found out. Yet, Dickens could hardly warn Crowquill — that would make him all the more determined to ferret out Marlowe, and it was not his place to give out information held by the police.

'On account then, and I'll trust your word that you will bring anything you find out to Mr Jones.' He went as far as he dared. 'Blackmail's a nasty business. I'd leave it to the police. If Marlowe were behind bars, you could get his story then.'

Dickens gave Crowquill two pounds 'on account', which seemed to satisfy him, and when he added another five shillings, saying, 'Get yourself a decent dinner, sir, you look famished,' Crowquill's eyes slid away, and something worked about the thin mouth as if he were chewing on something unfamiliar. Not sure if he liked it, but he took Dickens's proffered hand.

'Compliments, Mr Dickens. Reynolds ain't right about you. Says you think — well, never mind that. Not that I thought he was right. Bitter sort, Reynolds,' he added hastily. 'Much obliged.'

And then he was gone. Dickens heard him shambling down the stairs. *Hope he's to be trusted*, he thought, taking up his hat again. He looked at his desk and all the papers piled there. King John, without crown, waiting to be dispatched for his *Child's History of England*; something from Charles Lever about living on the continent — cheap and cheerful. It would suit Alexander Marlowe. He half-wished the man had fled to France or somewhere. Plenty of waxworks in Paris. And on his desk at home, that blank child, Esther Summerson, waiting for the impress of pen on paper to give her life. And a crossing-sweeper, blank as empty paper — very dirty paper. Name of Jo. Don't know nothink.

He felt beleaguered. Too much to do, but he must tell Sam about Munty and the rest. And, of course, he'd committed himself to it. These investigations filled a need, he thought. Satisfied something in him. Case closed just as when a book was finished, but without the fret of sending the work out into the world and the critics waiting to tear you to pieces. And Sam and Scrap who asked nothing of him, but that he be there. 'One for all and all for one,' he'd told Scrap once. Sam had laughed and said, 'The three musketeers, eh?' And a frail flame of justice for someone in this blighted world where lives went all awry and there was murder planned by arrogance, by egotism, and by greed, the basest of all.

Dickens went down the stairs. *Go on*, he thought, *admit it: you're as subject to the passion for hunting as any other human being. Only hear the cry, 'Stop thief!' in the street, and the passion flames in every human breast and they are off, never mind if it's a dog that's stolen a butcher's chop, a boy who's filched a handkerchief, or the deepest-dyed-in-blood murderer.*

And at the door, he sniffed the air as a dog might, but only coughed up the fog. As he was locking the door, a sharp-eyed urchin appeared like a ragged genie from a dark lantern and gave him a note. Under the light over the doorway, he made out the words: *Where's Eliza?* And the boy was gone.

He walked up towards Bow Street. It was slow going in the fog from which shapes loomed and vanished and passed by. He stopped, for there was the lad, leaning against a lamp post, cool as you like. Someone knocked into him. He heard a sharp intake of breath and felt a weight against his back. Whoever it was lurched by and disappeared into the dark. The boy was gone, too, and another shape loomed up and passed. He was in the way, standing in the street, peering at a lamp post. He groped his way on. The boy was there again on the next street corner. Beckoning, he vanished round the corner. Dickens looked up towards the lights of Bow Street, but he turned left and almost collided with the urchin, whose impudent face was grinning up at him. He darted off again, still looking back from time to time as if making sure Dickens was following. This was madness, he thought. What was he walking into? This wasn't the way into Southwark, unless he were being led to Hungerford Bridge. That thought stopped him and he made to turn round.

Just at that moment, a woman came out of a house. As she came down the steps, he caught sight of her pale oval face, her dark curling hair peeping from under her bonnet, and her dark red pelisse. A faint scent of roses and then she was gone. His heart seemed to stop for a moment. *Where's Eliza?* Not Quarterman. Another. Who often wore that dark red. Never called Eliza. Always her full name, and somehow, he knew. His guide was waiting to cross the road into Maiden Lane.

29: WHERE'S ELIZA?

Sam Jones thought he might as well go home. He'd written his note to Inspector Wells, giving him an outline of the case, mentioning Emma Cooper as a possible connection to the criminals. He'd explained that she had taken refuge in the paupers' kitchen off Redcross Street, and that he thought she might be in danger, but only might, and he'd asked Wells to have his constables keep an eye on the place. He didn't mention the name Eliza Quarterman. The neighbours knew her as Mrs Clifford, but he wanted to keep her very much at a distance from the case — not important, just a charitable lady who had taken in the fugitive, Emma Cooper. He trusted Wells, but you never knew who else might talk.

He thought about Alexander Marlowe. Dickens was always saying what a place London was to hide your head. Hundreds, probably thousands of lodging houses, cheap hotels, private boarding houses. Some woman he'd seduced into taking him in? It was hopeless. Yes, they knew that he looked like his nephew, Seth Marlowe, but older, of course, and sometimes bearded. He thought of Ma Dunk, brick-built and bearded, passing as a man in that graveyard. Marlowe in a black skirt and bonnet — a walking waxwork? Grieving widow holed up in some genteel boarding house? Or he could be on his way out of London, dressed in rags, sleeping in a ditch, making his way to some port. And in this fog, every man was a groping shadow of himself.

No, time to go home and take supper in the kitchen, listen to the innocent chatter of his children, play trains, sit by the parlour fire with Elizabeth later with a glass of ruby wine and feel the warmth of home enveloping him as a kindly blanket. Marlowe could freeze to death in his ditch for all he cared.

The desk sergeant knocked and came in to deliver a letter. What now? An educated hand had written his name on the envelope. 'By hand?' he asked the sergeant, who told him that a lad had come with it and darted away before he had time to question him.

'What sort of lad?'

'Urchin sort — earned a ha'penny for it, I should think.'

'All right. Get back downstairs.'

There was just the one sheet of paper and two words: *Where's Eliza?*

Damn fool, he thought, recognising the writing from Dickens's letter. Not dead in a ditch, then. But no use trying to find some urchin — he'd be in some Fagin's kitchen now, gorging on his sausage or swigging a ha'pennyworth of gin.

An urgent knocking on the door. He felt his heart sink as Rogers burst in. He knew from his face that something was very wrong. Scrap? He wondered. Scrap should have been at the shop an hour ago or more.

'Mrs Jones,' Rogers gasped, 'she's missing.'

Superintendent Jones never knew how he had managed to stay on his feet, but he did, bracing himself on the edge of his desk and wordlessly offering the note to Rogers, who looked and said, 'The devil.'

'When?' Jones asked.

'A couple of hours ago. Children came to the shop with Posy. They said she'd been meant to pick them up from school. So Eleanor decided they should go home. Only Posy was there. She didn't dare leave them to go an' look. They waited an' then they came for me an' Scrap. Eleanor thought if I wasn't there, Scrap would come for us.'

'Where are they all now?'

'Norfolk Street with Mollie and Scrap — Eleanor thought if Mrs Jones came home —'

Jones was opening his desk. 'Get Stemp and Feak, anyone else available, lamps, and take one of these.' He handed Rogers a flintlock pistol. He put two more on the desk while he grabbed his coat. They went into his pocket, and he followed Rogers downstairs. Stemp, who heard everything on the wind, was already in his plain clothes. Jones knew he'd have a truncheon underneath his jacket. He met Stemp's eyes. 'Take this,' he said. 'Don't hesitate to use it.'

'Mrs Jones first, sir, questions after.'

Rogers, meanwhile, had collared five other constables who'd just come off the beat. 'Search, sir — the way to the school from your house.'

Jones and Rogers, followed by the other policemen, made as quick progress as they could up to Norfolk Street in the fog. No use taking a cab and sitting in Oxford Street for an age. Stemp stayed outside at the front of the house and Feak went round to the alley at the back. The other constables were detailed to follow the route from Jones's house to the school. Gardens, alleys, any doctors' houses. A preliminary search — in case she had had some sort of accident. It wasn't far up to Gloucester Place, where the school was situated. She'd walk up to the turning at Upper Marylebone Street, turn in there and walk along Gloucester Place. The school was on the corner of Weymouth Street, Jones told them.

Mollie Rogers was upstairs with Posy, the servant girl, putting the exhausted Tom to bed. Rogers waited at the parlour door and watched with a lump in his throat as the little girl, Eleanor, didn't move at first as Jones went into the room. Scrap was holding her hand. Frozen with fright, he thought. A little girl who'd seen her father dying of consumption. A little girl who, as time had gone on, had unfrozen from that grief and placed her heart in Elizabeth Jones's hand and in the boss's. He felt the gun in his pocket. If Marlowe had taken Mrs Jones, he'd use it. He'd heard Stemp. They could ask any questions they liked about the death of a wanted man and Rogers wouldn't care. *Just don't let the chief do it*, he thought. *Me or Stemp. We don't matter to the Commissioner.*

He had to turn away when he heard the sobbing and saw Jones sit and the child turn to his opening arms. Scrap's knuckles were at his eyes. Rogers brushed his hand over his own eyes as Mollie came downstairs, and he moved to meet her and take her hand. Her eyes were frightened.

'She'll not go to bed,' she whispered, 'but Scrap'll stay with her while me and Posy watch Tom. He shouldn't wake up on his own, an' I can't leave Posy, either. She's in a state. What'll you do?'

'Wait for one of the constables to come back and then send to the infirmary up on Northumberland Street. Just in case.'

Mollie squeezed his hand and went upstairs. He peeped into the parlour and withdrew. Mr Jones was speaking in a low voice, one arm round each child. Such trust in their looks. *We have to find her*, Rogers thought, and then he just waited. When one of the constables reported in, he sent him off to the workhouse infirmary to see if any injured lady had been brought in.

Stemp came in. 'Nothin' yet. But I've been thinkin', Mr Rogers, the judge's house ain't far away —'

'The beat constables were told to keep an eye — and the locks were changed.'

'Might be fifty doors and windows locked; it only takes one little opening to get in,' Stemp responded in his thoughtful way, not knowing that he was echoing the thoughts of Mr Dickens, but Constable Stemp had collared a lot of burglars in his time. 'Get into the yard, take a windowpane out — fifteen seconds and he's in. The back door's left open a crack for when he comes back. Break into a neighbourin' house, along the roof to the judge's house, in through a garret window —'

'Blimey, Stemp, he ain't Spring-heeled Jack.'

'Ain't 'e?'

At which question, Rogers met the challenge in Stemp's eyes and remembered the talk of the billsticker and his ladder. *Where's Eliza?* Where's Elizabeth? He made up his mind. 'Go and have a look — take Feak. I don't think he'll come here if he's got — well, you know —'

Stemp was gone. Rogers waited, hearing the low murmur of the voices, and then he heard the sofa creak and Mr Jones came to the door, his face a mask of anxiety, his grey eyes anguished. Scrap was with him.

'Won't leave 'er, Mr Jones, but Mr Rogers, can you get Mollie to bring some blankets? Nell might sleep, but I'll be there when she wakes up.'

'Keep the fire built up, Scrap. Don't sit in the cold, and when Mrs Jones comes back, she'll need warming up.'

'You'll find 'er, I knows it.' Scrap's blue eyes looked at Jones, and for that moment he believed it in his heart, though his head would tell him something else when Scrap went back to keep his vigil.

Rogers went upstairs for Mollie. Scrap went back into the parlour. Superintendent Jones stood at the front door, looking out into the fog under which the great city seemed to be held in a profound stillness, but he could feel the hammering of his own heart as if it were climbing up his throat to choke him. Out in that dark. He thought of all the winding streets, all the twisting alleys, secret back courts, yards, burial grounds. Possibly in the hands of a lunatic. The joker turned mad.

He stepped back and took a deep breath. His heart settled and resumed a steadier beat. *A stunt*, he thought, *that's what it is. He won't kill a policeman's wife — he's not cornered yet. But we have to find her, and we have to be very careful not to show ourselves.* Then he thought, *He'll have left her somewhere to tease us.* He didn't care where Marlowe was. Only where Elizabeth was. He thought of her walking along Upper Marylebone Street in the fog — it would be a moment's work for a man in a carriage to seize her and drive off to — Manchester Square, he thought. The judge's house locked up, new locks, but nowhere was impregnable. An empty house — over the yard wall, a chisel, a jemmy. An empty house next door to Mrs Dryden's. A coal chute. A trapdoor. Now you see him, now you don't.

Jones turned as Rogers came towards him. 'The judge's house,' he said.

'Stemp and Feak already there, sir. Stemp's idea, an' I've sent one of the men to the workhouse infirmary to ask if any injured lady's been brought in.'

'Perhaps we should go to Manchester Square now — see what's happening. If he's in there, we need more than two.'

They groped their way through narrow streets to Portland Street and across to Queen Anne Street, which was better lit, and eventually they reached Manchester Square, where the judge's house was in darkness. They went round the back and saw the yard door open and the back door. Jones noticed that it had been forced — Stemp, probably — and they entered. In the hall they looked up the stairs, from where they could hear the thud of heavy boots and the sound of doors being unceremoniously shoved open and closed with a slam. Rogers went up while Jones went into the library, where Dickens had taken his sherry with the judge. Dickens, he thought. He'd welcome him now, and Henry Meteyard. Scrap wouldn't be going to Southwark tomorrow — if... Not to be contemplated. Concentrate on the matter in hand. Emma Cooper could wait.

He looked about him and went into the room where the waxworks had been, but there was no sign that anyone had been here. Hearing boots come down the stairs, he went out into the hall.

'No sign of entry,' Stemp said. 'I don't think he's been here.'

'Nothin', sir, the place is empty,' Feak added.

'There's cellars,' Jones said.

'Looked, sir, an' at the coal chute,' Stemp said.

Feak had a thought. 'Ma Dunk's house is empty, an' there's that stable where they kept the cart — out o' the way.'

'The Adelphi arches — he was there,' Jones said. 'That's a warren of a place. We need more men. Feak, get back to my house quick as you can, find out what news from the infirmary, and then take two of those constables to Dunk's and that stable. If they're clear, send one to Bow Street to get a couple more lads to go to the Adelphi and send the other two from Norfolk Street to the Adelphi. Tell them to wait on the wharves by Salisbury Stairs. That's where Stemp, Rogers and I are going, unless you can think of anywhere else.'

'Yes, sir, I'll send 'em, but I'd best stay at your house if there's no sign at Ma Dunk's. They'll need someone just ter —'

'I know. Good lad, Feak. My thanks.'

'Couple o' minutes to Wellington Street,' Rogers said, 'if you want Mr Dickens.'

'He'll have gone home. Too far to Tavistock Square. We need to hurry.'

30: A DOOR AJAR

Maiden Lane. *That might mean the Adelphi arches*, Dickens thought, as he followed his ragged Pied Piper. That was where Marlowe had stored the waxworks. A man dragging in a woman. The residents of the arches wouldn't notice and if they did, they wouldn't care. The most wretched and degraded of the nymphs of the pave worked there; men took men in there — and children. His urchin probably had his home there. He'd take a penny from anyone to do anything.

But it was a maze down there, a complication of tunnels and passages — a world of its own underneath the fine Adam houses above. *Heaven and Hell*, he thought, and no passage from the lower region to the higher. What had that wretched boy beckoning him on to do with the grand folk who lived up there in marbled and gilded splendour? He'd had lodgings in Buckingham Street by the Adelphi when he was a young man — more a garret than gilt, but still not the arches where darkness thickened now as the fog met the clouds of mist rising from the river, and meagre shadows flitted to and from the river stairs where ghostly ships with ghostly sails trembled in the raw air. There was the awful sound of a foghorn, which reminded him of the dead woman on Blackfriars Bridge. There was the hollow clink of metal on the shrouds and masts, an occasional hoarse cry, an answering shout, the tread of invisible feet behind him, the shuddering sense of a cold breath at his neck, and the boy still waiting.

He followed and saw that the boy was leading him into the arches. Inside, the tramps, the pickpockets, the dodgers, the lurkers, the lags and the nymphs and their ragged shepherds were packed in. *Like maggots in a cheese*, he thought. There were the waggoners who bedded down with their horses; the cowkeepers whose cows never saw a green pasture, but who lived in the darkness and were milked in the darkness which was relieved only by the flickering of fires in braziers, and in the day, by the weakest of light peering through the loopholes which looked out over the river and the wharves. The place stank of sewers, of beasts, of unwashed humanity and its foul breath, coal dust, lamp smoke, tar from torches, frying fish, grease — every vile smell of subterranean life. It sounded with the rumble of cartwheels, the neighing of horses, the thud of feet stamping to the music of a concertina, and wild shrieks cut off suddenly to be followed by equally wild laughter. He thought of the clergyman who had been found dead down there, his throat cut, and the prostitute found starved to death in an abandoned cart. No one had noticed her.

He followed the boy through the simmering mass of bodies, looking neither to the left or right. If anyone noticed him, he knew what they'd think — a well-dressed man following a boy into the dark. He pushed his scarf up to cover his face, and eventually he found himself out in the foggy air in an open court where there were sheds and stables and haylofts, wagons piled with coal, old carts, broken wheels, stacks of old barrels, packing cases, lumps of old wood and iron twisted into fantastic shapes, coal heaps, and petrified hills of dung and dust. No scavengers tonight, but the dust heaps would be swarming with them by day, after anything to carry away and sell. His courier had vanished as mysteriously as he had arrived at Wellington Street with his note.

He waited, watching the fog wreathing itself round the buildings, watching for anything possibly human that moved. There was one gas lamp fixed to the wall above him, shedding a sickly green light, but there was no other light anywhere, only the shadowy fog and the misty vapours rising from gratings and the cold stone ground. He had no idea what to do other than prowl about the sheds and stables in the hope that he might hear something. He had been brought here for a purpose — that boy had made sure that he followed. And had his instinct been right, or did he just have an overworked imagination? Had Marlowe brought Elizabeth Jones here? It would be just the sort of stunt Marlowe would dream up, but then he thought of the judge collapsed in his nightgown and the look of terror on that ashen visage, and that letter… His heart turned over.

His eyes were more adjusted to the foggy gloom now. A movement caught his eye, a shadow by one of the heaps of barrels. It was the shape of a cat leaping down and then melting into the darkness.

He still waited, scanning the rattletrap sheds and stables. Some movement, but he couldn't tell what. Circling eddies of fog still rose and fell, making it impossible to tell if something or someone moved in the corners, or on the wreck of stairs which he made out on the outside of some ruined warehouse, but something flickered nearby the ruin. A light in an upstairs window in an opposite building. Some kind of stable with a hayloft above. A candle flame or an oil lamp. He took off his scarf and left it on the ground in the feeble gaslight. If Elizabeth were missing, then Sam would know about it by now — he and Rogers would work it out. They'd come. He fumbled his way round the court. He dared not show himself in the open, though Marlowe might well know he was there. He left a glove on a crumbling windowsill. Sam and the others would have lamps. Another windowsill presented itself. He took off his other glove and saw on his little finger, glinting even in this darkness, the diamond ring he had never taken off since the death of his sister-in-law, Mary Hogarth, fourteen years ago. But now if it were lost, then it would be so, perhaps to save a life. Sam would know it was his. He put it on the sill with the glove and carried on towards that flickering light.

There was a door ajar. He was expected. Something fluttered at his head, then he heard a scraping sound somewhere above. Dickens looked up and had just the briefest glimpse of a figure, and then it was gone. He heard a thud and then the sound of running feet. The fluttering thing now on the ground was a silk handkerchief — a woman's. He put it in his pocket. He didn't want Sam Jones to find that, but he left his hat at the door and pushed it open very slowly and stepped softly into the darkness. A dark lantern had been left on the floor. He was meant to find his way to the light upstairs. He slid open the door of the lantern and the light showed that he was in a stable. No horses, just empty loose boxes and a brick floor, and in front of him, the rickety wooden staircase. A memory came to him of just such a night when he had gone to meet a murderer in a stable in an alleyway near St Bartholomew's Church — a man who had a gun. He had no idea if the figure on the roof had been Marlowe, who might, even now, be waiting upstairs — to frighten Charles Dickens to death.

He went up on tiptoe, one step at a time. He did not want the creak of a stair to signal his presence. He dared not even breathe, but he waited on one step, listening to the silence, looking down to where the fog had slipped in behind him and seemed to be creeping up the stairs. He looked up, but there was nothing to see but darkness and nothing to hear. Even his heart seemed to have stopped. His lamp showed him another six stairs which looked too flimsy to bear his weight, but he went on, stepping cautiously until he reached a landing place

— the hayloft where another lamp was burning at a window. It was empty apart from a few rotten hay bales and wisps of straw on the wooden floor, patched with holes. He felt the draught from another open window from where the figure had got out.

Had he walked into a trap? The figure on the roof had gone, but that was not to say he hadn't sneaked back. Dickens crept down the staircase and found himself on the brick floor again. The door was closed. He tried it. Of course, it was barred on the outside. He thought of that dark and empty court under the fog. No use hammering. That window upstairs gave access to the roof where the figure had been. He'd have to try it. He stood, listening, thinking if there were a way out beyond the loose boxes — another door, perhaps, though that would probably be barred, too. He crept along, peeping into the boxes as he went, stopping to listen to the creaking of old wood in the roof. Then he heard it — the sound of the rustling as if some sleeper turned over on a bed of straw.

The last box. He lifted his lantern. A figure there, a figure completely swathed in black. One of those damned waxworks. Man or woman, he couldn't tell. Just the sort of fool thing… The straw rustled again. And still he stood, holding up the lantern and watching the shadows and the remnants of mist play about the dark shape, making it seem to move as though it might step forward, or it might lift up its black shroud.

The straw rustled again. It did move — just the slightest motion, as if a mechanical waxwork were coming to life, or a spectre. Dickens stepped back involuntarily, and his boot scraped on stone.

'Who's there?'

He was inside the loose box in a second, saying, 'Elizabeth. Don't be afraid. I'm here,' and then he was lifting the dark material from her, holding up the lamp to see her astonished white face looking at his.

'You?'

'You're not harmed?'

'I thought it was he — I thought he had come back. I don't know how long — I didn't dare move — such darkness — how did you…?'

Dickens noticed then that her arms had been tied behind her back — not enough to hurt her, but enough to prevent her trying to escape. The rope had been fastened to an empty hay rack.

He untied the knot. 'He sent a message by a boy. He meant for me to find you. Sam will know by now. They'll work it out. They'll come.'

'He mustn't see that.' She pointed to the rope. 'I'm not harmed — I don't want Sam thinking it's his fault. That man — he said I wouldn't be here long. I don't think he meant to harm me. But Sam, the children — can we get out?'

'He's barred the door, but there's a window upstairs. He was on the roof when I came up to the door. Can you bear to wait until I see if I can get out? I'll leave the lamp.'

'No, you'll need it. I'm not frightened now — I wasn't really before, more anxious and angry, thinking about the children waiting — just go, please.'

Dickens wasn't really surprised at her self-command. Elizabeth Jones had heard and seen a good deal, but as he hurried back up the stairs, he thought about Marlowe. Marlowe, so full of himself that he really believed they wouldn't find him. He didn't feel cornered yet, but he would. He'd made a serious mistake in abducting Superintendent Jones's wife — even for a joke.

31: A LEAP IN THE DARK

Rogers found a constable from Hungerford Pier on his beat along the wharves. 'Lookin' for a lady,' Rogers told him. No name needed, but he saw the constable's sceptical expression. 'I mean a lady. Kidnappin', so it's serious. Word has it she's been brought here, so do as you're told.'

The constable, somewhat sheepish now, and aware of the taller man who, he realised belatedly, was the superintendent from Bow Street, was told to wait by Salisbury Stairs for the other policemen after he had shown them which tunnels led where. Some they knew led to the streets behind the arches, but some were just blind alleys. They wanted the one which would take them into the court that Pruey had described.

The constable stopped by an entrance. 'That one's your best bet, sir — leads into Durham Street then the Strand. Lot o' stables at the back. Coal wagons and so on go through from the wharves.'

'Any others worth a look?'

'The end one leads into Adam Street — Strand again. Carter Street — a lot o' warehouses down there. George Street at the far end.'

'We'll take the Durham Street one. Back to the stairs for you. When my men come, show them the way into the others, and keep your own eyes and ears sharp. I have your number,' Jones said, looking grim-eyed at the number on the man's collar.

'This is the one, sir,' Stemp said, as they went in, 'where that Pruey said she'd been with Munty an' the cart. Remember it.'

No one paid attention to them. They were used to the police down here, and it wasn't hard to tuck yourself into a niche or under a cart if you thought they were looking for you. Stemp led the way through the crowds, the cows, the horses, the wagons and carts, and they came out at the exit which led into the court. 'Lights out,' Jones said, and they moved into the court, flattening themselves against the wall, avoiding the gas light under which Dickens had stood only a while ago. They scanned the open court as he had, wondering similarly whether any of the dilapidated sheds were holding a prisoner.

Rogers saw something lying under the gas lamp. A black woollen scarf. He picked it up to show to Jones. 'Good quality,' Rogers said. 'Doesn't belong to anyone back there.'

'A gentleman's scarf? Marlowe's?' Jones wondered.

'Bit of a light, sir, over there.' Stemp pointed, and they saw the faint flickering.

'Stemp, take the right side of the court. Rogers and I will work our way round on the left until we get to that building.'

Stemp went on his way. Rogers looked at his chief's set face and touched him on the arm. 'Sir, I'm thinkin' Stemp's got a gun, and so have I. Him or me should do it, if it comes to it. I wouldn't want it thought you'd acted wrong.'

Jones took the pistol from his pocket and handed it over. 'Obliged, Alf — you're a wise fellow.'

They crept along, keeping to the wall. Rogers put his hand on a windowsill and felt a leather glove.

'Didn't just drop that,' he whispered, passing it to Jones. 'What's he up to?'

'Leaving clues. That's what he does. Good God, Alf, I hope this isn't a wild goose chase and he's taken her somewhere else.'

Rogers couldn't answer. He thought of the time that was passing — time they might be wasting.

They crept on, feeling their way, and this time Jones touched something soft on another windowsill. Another glove, and his eye caught what seemed like the glitter of glass as the glove moved. *Not another eye*, he thought. He reached out for the little shining thing. A ring — a diamond ring. He brought it up to his eye. It couldn't be. Yes, it could. He thought of the note he'd received. The same message sent to someone else?

'A bit of light, Alf, just for a second.'

Rogers opened the slide on his lamp and in that second, Jones knew for sure. He'd seen it often enough. 'Mr Dickens is here — it's his ring. He's leaving the clues.'

'Then where is he?'

They made to go forward. A rattling noise stopped them, and they looked up to where the light was in the window to see a figure climbing out. Stemp was there already, picking up a top hat. They saw him look up, his arm raised. The shot cracked, and then the figure was gone and Stemp was already unbarring the door.

Elizabeth Jones was waiting. 'Charles,' she said. Then she knew. 'Oh, Sam —' and his arm was about her. 'That noise — Charles was —'

'Where?'

'He was going to — on the roof — he was at the window — I heard —'

Even Stemp was shaken to the core, his face suddenly falling as he realised what had happened. 'Thought it was Marlowe — only to frighten, sir, I didn't —'

'You missed, Mr Stemp, thank the Lord, if I may say so,' said a voice, 'though I blame you for a leap into a dust heap.'

At the door, they saw that Dickens was removing what looked like an old cabbage leaf from his head. His shoulders were festooned with potato peelings, mud, dust and ashes, and the rest of him was equally filthy, but he was smiling at Stemp, who was gazing at him as though he had returned from the grave.

Rogers shut the door. 'Best keep quiet a bit. In case anyone heard that shot.'

And they stood, all five of them, speechless for a few moments, looking at the gun in Stemp's hand, and then hearing the sound of running feet. Rogers opened the door to find two constables.

'Stemp fired. Fellow escaped, lads — jumped off the roof — look about you. Tell the others. Mrs Jones is safe.' He shut the door again. 'Keep Mr Dickens out of it, sir. I'll stand 'em down in a while.'

Superintendent Jones, whose face was ashen, was looking at his wife, who was looking at him. 'He didn't harm me,' she said, 'but I should like to go home. I'll tell you all after I've seen the children.'

They knew it was no use searching for Marlowe. He'd be long gone, but the dispersal of the men to carry on the search gave them time to think. Sergeant Rogers was to gather them up shortly and dismiss them and then return to Bow Street. Superintendent Jones took his wife out through the exit to Durham Street, where from the Strand they could make their way home. Dickens found his top hat, another casualty of the evening. Stemp had trodden on it as he'd stepped back to fire, but it was wearable — by a man who would rather not be recognised in his present odorous state, though anyone seeing the hefty constable escorting a muddy and bedraggled fellow through the streets would assume an arrest had taken place.

The hefty constable took Dickens home to Tavistock Square and on that long walk, Dickens was able to reassure Mr Stemp, whose habitual stolidness had taken a knock, that he perfectly understood that the constable had known what he was about, and only meant to see off the possible kidnapper, Mrs Jones bein' the most important matter just then.

'I mean, sir, Mr Dickens, we wasn't ter know where that damned dog 'ad Mrs Jones. No use killin' 'im — Mrs Jones might not 'ave been in that stable, an' if yer don't mind my mentionin' the matter —'

'You didn't expect to see me capering about on the roof.'

'Give me a turn, that, sir, when Mrs Jones said.'

'And me, Mr Stemp, but no hard feelings — a dust hill has the advantage of being more accommodating than a coal heap. I might have broken my neck rather than injuring my pride. I can smell rotten cabbage leaf still — and worse.'

32: EARTHQUAKE

Dickens, clean and smelling of soap and a dab of scent, presented himself at Jones's house the next morning. Though he had spent most of the night thinking about Sam and Elizabeth and wondering what they might have told the children, he had resisted the temptation to go round to Norfolk Street. They would need time to comfort the children and time to themselves. This would be an agony to Sam, he had thought. His life as a policeman was dangerous enough, but to have his wife kidnapped, that would be hard, probably impossible to bear, even if she were not harmed.

Jones answered the door. 'I was expecting you,' he said. 'You smell a good deal fresher than when I saw you last.'

'All well?' Dickens asked, stepping in.

'Come into the parlour. They're all in the kitchen. Scrap's still here, of course.'

'I sent a message to Henry, telling him that we'd contact him later.'

'I did send a note to Inspector Wells, asking him to keep an eye on the paupers' kitchen, but he'll know we know all about that place.'

'He?'

'Yes, he,' Jones said as they sat down. 'Elizabeth assures me she wasn't harmed in any way — not that that matters. He took her by force into a carriage, so we can add that to his list of felonies. He sent you a note, I'm assuming.'

'Some urchin brought it.'

'Same one who left a note for me.'

'I was coming to you to tell you about a visitor I had, but the lad kept beckoning me on, and I was thinking that we knew where Eliza was. He surely couldn't mean Mrs Quarterman. I nearly turned back when I thought it might be a trap, but then a woman came out of a house in a red cape — that dark red — ' Jones understood — 'and I smelt rosewater as she passed. I knew then, or, at least, I thought it might be just the sort of stunt he'd try, and when that lad took me to the Adelphi arches, I had to risk it. He was there on the roof. I heard him run off, but he came back and barred the door.'

Jones pointed to the gloves on the table and took the ring from his pocket. 'I knew when I saw that. You never take it off.'

'Ah, well, I knew you'd recognise it. And it was in a noble cause.'

'For which I thank you, and so does Elizabeth, who was never more glad to see anyone, she says.'

'Remarkable lady, your wife. She wasn't frightened — she wouldn't keep the lamp. Is she really…'

'She is remarkable. I don't know whether I am — it's shaken me, I can tell you. Made me think…'

'I know, but too soon, maybe, to consider any major steps. It's rare, isn't it?'

'Plenty of abductions happen — usually of young ladies with inheritances. I can't think of a case like this one, but I'll have to think it all over. I think I'd have done what Stemp did, though I might not have missed — that frightens me, too. Losing one's reason when someone so close is in danger. Sergeant Rogers, however, wise fellow, took my gun off me.'

'And Stemp knew what he was doing. I believe him — he knew Elizabeth was more important than chasing about after Marlowe. He really did mean only to frighten him.'

'Pity he didn't fall into a dung heap.'

Elizabeth came in. 'Thank you, Charles, for taking that risk to find me.'

'The children?' he asked, sensing a tension in the air as she came in, never before felt in the Jones household. It was as if an electric spark had flared and died down, leaving a shudder in the air. Even though Elizabeth was smiling at him, he saw a shadowy something in her eyes which reflected the anxiety in Sam Jones's eyes, despite his smiling welcome at the door.

'Told them I missed my way in the fog. Found myself in some back streets, found a policeman who took me to Bow Street. It seemed as if I were lost for hours. I know we've always told them the truth, but this time —'

'We don't want them frightened every time Elizabeth goes out, after all they've been through. I'm their father; I shouldn't be the one who brings them into danger.' The electric spark flared again and died down as Elizabeth took her husband's arm and caressed it.

'There's danger at every street corner, Sam,' she said, 'and not because you're a policeman. Pickpockets everywhere; children taken and robbed of every strip of clothing; young girls abducted; men and women robbed at knife point. It's all in the papers —'

'And there doesn't seem to be a thing I can do about it. Superintendent Jones of Bow Street, indeed, who can't even protect his own wife from some madman.'

'And that's it, Sam, a madman — someone who is so beyond reason that neither you, nor Charles, nor Rogers or any of them could have predicted what he would do. And it's only because of my name — it wouldn't have happened if I were called Ann or —'

'Or Alice, or Albertine,' Dickens supplied.

Elizabeth shot him a grateful look, and even Sam Jones laughed then. 'I don't know anyone called Albertine.'

'No more do I. An Albina, I do know — pale sort of creature, oysterish about the eyes, watery about the nose.'

'You've made her up,' Elizabeth protested.

'Not at all. Lady Albina Marchmont — I can make an introduction.'

'Oh, all right then,' Jones said, his hands opening in surrender. 'I concede your point, but still, Elizabeth, you'll be —'

'Careful. I'm always careful, Sam, and we have to go on as if nothing extraordinary has happened, for their sakes, or they will, certainly Eleanor will, be afraid every time you or I go out. You should both go. Let it be an ordinary day, though Scrap wants to stay. That's not so unusual. He'll keep Tom amused, and Eleanor and I will make a cake for Papa when he comes home — a little earlier today, perhaps, for their sake.'

Dickens and Jones walked down Norfolk Street. 'I was coming to see you,' Dickens began.

Jones didn't answer. His being, Dickens knew, was still in his parlour, though his outer form was walking along the street. *Say nothing yet,* he told himself. *Let him walk quietly across this bridge from home to business. It needs time.* He thought of Sam's anguished face in these few seconds before he had teased Stemp about the dust heap and broken the spell of shock and fright. Sam had surely believed that his wife might be dead, or even that Dickens had been shot. Elizabeth was right; it was her name — but still, Marlowe had found that out, and acted on it. Even if he had not harmed her, harm had been done. A rush and sweep of something through the air, like Death upon the wing, and the earth had quaked under Sam's feet; he felt the tremor still.

Dickens felt it himself. Uncertainty and peril written on everything, in every shop window, on every cab and carriage that passed them, on the very stones beneath their feet, on every face, in every eye that glanced their way, on the face of Sam Jones, whose grey eyes had always seemed to watch the distance, watch it without flinching, even as danger drew nearer and nearer, which it had so often. Now, he looked like a man upon whom danger had leapt like a fiend and worried at his back.

They came to an early morning coffee stall at the top of Bow Street, where Dickens stopped. 'A few minutes, Sam, to get your bearings.'

Jones looked at Dickens as if surprised to find him at his side, but he nodded and Dickens bought the coffee. It tasted of the Marshalsea, that is of roasted corn, but it was hot, and it allowed them to stand in a doorway and for Jones to come to. He looked again at Dickens.

'You were coming to see me about something — a visitor, you said, before…'

Dickens took him by the arm. 'Sammy, my lad, I'll tell you in a minute or two, but first, this blow — you are rocked to your foundations, I know it. Suddenly the world is not as it was, for he has come too near, and you think of others who might with even worse intentions. I cannot soften that blow, nor, indeed, diminish that fear — as palpable a thing as the knife's blade, but, as your Elizabeth so wisely counsels, there is danger on every corner —'

'In my very house. I tell you, Charles, I am ready to pack, lock, stock, and barrel, and flee to some hidden village, deep in a forest, to keep them safe —'

'I've thought of Siberia many times when I was ready to fly from the shoals and breakers of this world.'

Jones gave him the ghost of a grin. 'I know, and it's duty that keeps you at the wheel, as it will keep me, so my head tells me. I'll not run away. And when I think of my Elizabeth's courage and wisdom, I'm ashamed.'

'And so am I, but we are only men, after all. We have hearts as well as heads, and who are we, that we should believe that we are never to be ruled by the heart? That's what I told Scrap when he was so despondent about being followed.'

'Ah, Scrap. There's courage and wisdom, too. Well, Mr Charles Dickens, my other fount of wisdom, it's time I did my duty. As ever, you have done me good.'

'Hard word, that, duty.'

'But a plain one. And it's my duty to find Marlowe, before he does anything worse.'

'All for one, remember. Rogers, Stemp, Feak —'

'And you. Believe me, I don't forget. So, what about this visitor?'

'The Reinhart case — remember that?'

'Good Lord, I do.'

Dickens told him all that Crowquill had imparted to him about Alexander Marlowe's long career, and then he watched Jones's face as he thought about what he had heard, and saw the tightening of his jaw and the steel in his eye.

'James Parr, alias Munton, served time because of Alexander Marlowe. James Parr's son, known as Munty, was murdered. That gives another shape to things — a nasty shape,' Jones observed.

'I didn't say anything about the lad to Crowquill, but I did wonder if Munty knew or found out about Marlowe.'

'Money in it, he told that old fellow down near Bird Court. Off to meet a toff at the Stingo, where no one saw Munty meet anyone, and there's no way of knowing if Munty was on his way there or back.'

'Money in it,' Dickens pursued, 'not Munty alone. Ma Dunk? They'd all taken risks for Alexander Marlowe. If she knew about Marlowe's past, she'd see a way of making more. Put Munty up to screwing a bit more out of Marlowe?'

'And Thomas Dryden dead at Hungerford Bridge. Makes me think again about Marlowe. Not just the joker we thought. This Crowquill, is he to be trusted?'

'Said he'd come to you if he had a sniff of Marlowe anywhere about. I told him to leave it to the police, but he's after a story, and he's in want of money. I can only hope he's to be trusted.'

33: THE PENMAN

'Stemp was right,' Rogers said to Superintendent Jones. 'Adam Flack was the name. Nephew to James Flack, the wax modeller. Very thick with Alexander Marlowe when he was apprentice there. And, by the way, full name Alexander William Marlowe. He an' Flack about the same age. Fond of a drink — and the women. According to Mrs Ann Marlowe, when James Flack died, the business wasn't much good, and the nephew gave it up. Had some talent as an artist, she said, but no head for business. Went off to work elsewhere. She hadn't any idea where. Doesn't know what happened to him.'

'Thick with Marlowe, though, and his assistant in the Reinhart case.'

Dickens and Jones had gone over Crowquill's information again in the hearing of Sergeant Rogers and Stemp. Jones had wondered about the unnamed assistant who had served a sentence for keeping the disorderly house in Pentonville, where one William Marlowe had opened a grotesque waxwork exhibition of the victims and the killer in the Reinhart case. William Marlowe had escaped with the money, leaving another man to bear the blame — just as James Parr, alias Munton, had served a sentence for something which had been initiated by Marlowe.

They all remembered the Reinhart murder and the waxworks scandal, but it was Constable Stemp who had dredged from his long memory the startling name, Adam Flack, the name which had sent Sergeant Rogers hotfoot to ask Mrs Ann Marlowe if the name had meant anything to her. Not that it was much help. They were talking about a man who had served his time fifteen years ago. However, Flack was an unusual name. The Post Office Trades Directory might serve, especially if — unlikely — Mr Flack were trading in wax or other artistic pursuits as a proprietor. If he were not, then someone would have to search the street directory for the name Flack. And while that was happening, Dickens betook himself to Wellington Street.

When he arrived, he lurked for a few moments, looking over to the office of *Reynolds's Weekly News*. There he hoped to find out if anyone could tell him the whereabouts of Crowquill, cursing himself for not having had the wit to ask for Crowquill's card or address. Mr Reynolds's office was not a place he cared to visit.

An inky lad in the process of murdering a quill pen was at a desk in the first office. Ink spurted across the page and the pen made a last protest before it expired. 'Drat,' the lad said, and then, 'Sir?'

Dickens asked for Edward Blanchard, a journalist he'd met in the company of Blanchard's connection, Sidney Laman Blanchard, a contributor to *Household Words*. Edward Laman Blanchard, author of many pantomimes, including *Prince Bluecap*, the pantomime he'd seen on the very night of Judge Quarterman's death. Blanchard was sometimes an author of other things, notably, *The Mysteries of the Court of London*, on which he had collaborated with Reynolds. Blanchard was an occasional journalist for Reynolds — he'd know Crowquill. He was unlikely to be at the office, but Dickens hoped that the inky lad might be able to tell him where Blanchard lived. He did not wish to spend more than a moment on Reynolds's premises, nor did he wish to come face to face with the blackguard.

Mr Blanchard likely ter be at Drury Lane, the lad informed him. Pantomime, did he see? Dickens did. Should have thought of that, and if Blanchard were not at the theatre, then someone would tell him where the man lived.

He found Edward Blanchard in the foyer at Drury Lane, congratulated him on the spectacle of *Prince Bluecap*, told him his children had cheered the dancing vegetables, and asked if Mr Blanchard could tell him where to find Crowquill.

Edward Blanchard's eyebrows shot up at the name. 'Surely not for *Household Words*?'

'No, not at all — more the *Household Narrative* — the current events, you know?' he improvised, wishing he had thought more clearly about the implications of seeking out Crowquill. 'Mr Crowquill has some information for me about a case of poisoning.'

'I haven't seen him recently — he fell out with Reynolds, I believe. Mind you, most people do. Crowquill had lodgings in Stanhope Street — above a hairdresser's shop.'

Dickens found Mr Truefitt's establishment quite easily. There was a picture in one window of a handsome built gentleman with a waxed moustache, curling a well-dressed lady's hair with a pair of tongs. There was also a notice declaring Mr Truefitt, hairdresser to the fashionable gentry — *not Mr Crowquill*, thought Dickens, remembering Crowquill's untidy thatch of hair, too much like a haystack to be in fashion anywhere but the farmyard. The rest of the window was taken up with wigs on wax heads, ribbons, bottles of perfume, hair oil, pots of pomatum, combs, and brushes. Mr Truefitt had not succumbed to the prevailing fashion for black-clad dolls, for in his other window were displayed the wax figure of a lady of the blue-eyed shepherdess type in sprigged blue, and a pink-faced gentleman of the military type, holding a bottle of perfume — Guards Club Bouquet, forsooth — and gazing at her, glassy-eyed. Both had similarly glossy curls, the lady's golden ringlets framing her equally pink face — rather too much like a lobster's, Dickens thought.

Inside, a youth of the cherub type — pomatum not ink; curls, crisp from the tongs; velveteen suit; and guileless blue eyes — stood behind the counter on which lay a further selection of perfume bottles, combs and brushes, repeated in profusion in some neat glass cases. A faint smell of singed hair mingled with the ambrosial smell of marrow-oil from an open bottle labelled 'Lewis's Scented Marrow-Oil Perfume'. The youth recognised Mr Charles Dickens, to whom he executed a low bow — not a crisp curl out of place — and offered the services of the establishment while casting a professional eye over the distinguished customer's hair, revealed by the removal of his top hat. Dickens was conscious of something lacking and nearly took out his comb to arrange his own curls.

The cherub, seeming to read his mind, and clearly not so guileless, offered, 'A very nice line in combs, sir, tortoiseshell, mother of pearl, a lovely silver-backed pair of brushes, a lovely—'

'Thank you, but not today. I am looking for Mr Crowquill.'

'Now, there's a gentleman who'd be better for a touch of the scented marrow-oil. Rose, this is,' the cherub answered, wafting the bottle at Dickens, who wondered if he still smelt of dust heap and cabbage leaf. 'Upstairs — attic rooms. Watch your step, sir, dark as a coal hole up there, an' the stairs is none too safe.' He pointed to a door at the side of the counter.

Dickens found himself in a little airless space as he closed the door. The smell here was more of cabbage than rose, but with a whiff of marrowbone and stale grease. He went up the first narrow staircase to a landing with two doors and another even narrower set of winding stairs, rightly described by the cherub, which led him to the crow's nest. He knocked, but there was no answer. He pushed at the door, which yielded to his touch, and went into a small room, sparsely and shabbily furnished with a worn sofa, a couple of chairs at a table which served as a writing desk, a dining table, a wardrobe, a laundry basket and a pawnbroker's counter, given the miscellany of articles scattered there — pens and paper, a knife, a loaf of bread, a butter crock, several bottles of wine, some chipped glasses, a teacup, half of a smoked cigar in a saucer, some shirts, a greasy cravat, a pair of boots, a clock with no hands, a broken watch chain, and some tarnished silver spoons. No sign of Crowquill.

The congealing silence suggested that there was no one home. A door ajar took Dickens into a second room with an unmade bed, a toilet stand, a bowl with scummy water, soap, a cut-throat razor, a towel, and a tarnished mirror nailed to the wall in the green depths of which Dickens saw a spectral likeness of himself, and remembered the cherub. He combed his hair and looked out of the one window which gave out to a yard below, where a disconsolate dog chewed on a bone. When Dickens turned round, he heard footsteps on the stairs.

Darting back into the sitting room, he was just in time to see the door open and reveal a shrimp of a girl with a sharp, too old face, wearing a drab dress and dirty apron — no curls and velveteen for her.

'Ashes,' she announced, showing him her shovel, and quite unmoved by the presence of a stranger in Crowquill's room.

Perhaps the floating population in such rooms meant that anyone might take up residence, or Crowquill might have a Box and Cox type of arrangement — Crowquill inhabiting the rooms by night; by day, out pursuing his journalistic avocations while some night bird occupied the unmade bed next door.

'Ashes,' the girl repeated, with the air of a female gravedigger.

'I'm looking for Mr Crowquill.'

'So's Mr Truefitt — rent, see,' she explained. World-weary, now, and aged about fifty. 'Ain't seen 'im fer a day or two. Ashes, though.'

He wanted to say, 'dust' as the echo of the thrice repeated word, 'ashes' suggested an image of death and ruin, a reminder of the terrors of the night before and Sam Jones's face in the shadows of the stable. The judge's dead face, grey as ashes. But he stood aside while she collected the ashes of Mr Crowquill's dead fire.

When the girl and the cold ashes had departed, Dickens went to look at the papers on the table, some glued together by the butter. Crowquill had used the knife as a paperweight. There was the beginning of an article on the so-called 'wild man' of the woods in Kilkenny, who was supposed to have escaped from a menagerie in Liverpool. Just the sort of thing that Crowquill would like. Not finished, though. Not wanted by Reynolds. Crowquill had turned to crime, it seemed. A break-in at a cutler's in Gough Street; a yellowing clipping about a drowning in the Hoxton Canal; an attempted murder in Westminster. Crowquill had noted the judge's death and the disappearance of Mrs Quarterman. There were notes on Ma Dunk and Pruey. On the same page was the name 'Munton' then 'Munty' followed by a question mark. So Crowquill had known about that death. Dickens remembered the interrogatory look in his eye when Crowquill had wondered what had become of James Munton's son. The inquest had been reported in the papers. A young man known as Munty, 'killed by person or persons unknown'. But he had feigned ignorance of Joshua Munton because, like any newshound on the scent of a story, he had kept back information which might mean a scoop.

Not seen for a day or two? Avoiding his landlord? Or out on enquiries? Dickens wondered into what dark waters Crowquill was wading. There had been a shifty look about him when Dickens had offered his hand. Embarrassed about the money for a meal, Dickens had thought, but maybe Crowquill had known he was going to break the pledge that was given by that handshake.

Turning over the pages, he found some dog-eared newspaper clippings about the Reinhart case, Marlowe's name, and the address of the house in Pentonville where the waxwork show had been set up. There was a newspaper clipping detailing the case brought against Adam Flack for keeping a disorderly house. Flack's address was given as number seventeen Southampton Street, Pentonville — same as the waxworks. Flack was sentenced to nine months with hard labour. But it was fifteen years ago. Was it likely that Flack had any contact with Marlowe, who had brought about his imprisonment?

Dickens continued to look through the pages, for any note or name or question which might give a clue. There were newspaper clippings to do with Quarterman's death. And, great heavens, there was a clipping about Thomas Dryden's drowning — now, Crowquill had not mentioned that name. What was he up to?

There were lists of waxwork exhibitions, newspaper clippings about waxwork shows which had closed down, or been destroyed by fire. Crowquill had certainly been following that sharp nose of his. Waxworks in Haymarket, at London Bridge, the Assembly Rooms, the Egyptian Hall, the Cosmorama, in

Clerkenwell, in Lambeth — all over the place. The crossed-out names suggested that Marlowe had not been traced to any of those —

A kind of mania, Dickens thought, tramping all over London, in search of Marlowe. A thought struck him as he looked at the list. Crowquill had been looking for years. He'd collected newspaper clippings and followed his crooked nose, trying to trace the man. He knew about the Marshalsea. But when had he started? At the time he had reported on the Reinhart case? But why? Granted, the waxwork show of the murderer and victims was a grotesque affair, but to make it your business to look back into Marlowe's history, to follow him, all to write some penny dreadful that you thought would make your fortune… Dickens riffled through the papers again. Crowquill had not started his great work. Of *Willie, The Waxwork Man* there was no sign.

Some other motive? That gave him another thought. Crowquill — his nom de plume. Who the devil was Crowquill? Dickens had no idea. Who had been Boz? The world had wondered. Literary men and journalists often used pseudonyms. The *Punch* men were all Mr Punch at one time or another. Thackeray had been Titmarsh once.

Whom to ask? Not Reynolds — rather ask the Devil for a favour, and Reynolds would want to know why. There was that matter of a tiff over a cash box. Blanchard? Blanchard whose theatrical nom de plume had been Francisco Frost, Blanchard who had been an actor and who had written for *Punch*. His uncle Samuel, father of Sidney Laman Blanchard, had started out as a lowly clerk. Almost everyone he knew had been someone else. Mark Lemon had been a tavern keeper; Douglas Jerrold, another *Punch* man, alias Mrs Caudle, had been a sailor, as had Henry Mayhew and Dickens's old friend, the artist

Clarkson Stanfield. You could take up your pen for *Punch*, or for *Reynolds's Weekly News*, or, indeed, *Household Words*, and no one asked where you came from.

Dickens turned back to the papers, thinking about Crowquill and his motive. Crowquill had sought him out to give information about Marlowe, but had he come to Wellington Street to find out if the police knew where Marlowe was — to get information by giving? He knew about the judge's death; he knew about Ma Dunk and Pruey; and though he had pretended not to, he knew about Munty. And he knew about Dryden. It was interesting, Dickens reflected, that Crowquill had not given him the name Adam Flack either. Yet it was there in his collection of clippings. He would know that Dickens would tell the Reinhart story to Jones and that Bow Street would find the name of Marlowe's assistant. Keep them off Crowquill's scent while they scraped beneath the grime of Pentonville, looking for Adam Flack who had known Marlowe fifteen years ago.

As he pursued this train of thought, Dickens was turning over papers, stopping every now and then to listen. It would be very awkward if Crowquill came back and found him searching. There was no sound on the stairs. He gazed at the pot of feathers on the table. Mostly goose quill pens, but some black crow quills, of course, and one that looked like a swan's feather. Perhaps Crowquill collected quill pens. Of course, he was a penman — of sorts —

Penman. Penman. That rang a bell. Good Lord. Could it be that Mr Edward Penman, who had reported to the police that he knew the name of Thomas Dryden, mentioning the eminently respectable Retailers' Association, was Mr Crowquill? Mr Penman had gone away on business but had left his address. Crowquill hadn't mentioned Dryden to Dickens. Oh, yes, he had picked and chosen the information he had given. Not Dryden's name, because Dickens might have made the connection. Well, he had now. The address wouldn't be Stanhope Street. Crowquill knew about Dryden. Perhaps he knew how Dryden had come into that water by Hungerford Bridge.

Dickens slid open a drawer in the table. Old quills, bits of sealing wax, a penknife, a bent fork, letters to Mr Crowquill at Reynolds's office, unpaid bills, newspaper clippings, crumbs, and dust. He paused to listen again. Then he pulled out the drawer further and turned over more papers, as well as a card with a black border — a thin memorial card, decorated with some melancholy urns and weeping angels. The information on the card told that it was in memory of Mrs Mary Penman, who had died on September 24th, aged seventy-six years, and who was interred in the Coleman Street Burial Ground. Well, Mr Crowquill was certainly connected to someone called Penman. Mother? Dickens wondered. He saw that the name of the undertaker was engraved in smaller letters: *Mrs E. Lyus, Tabernacle Walk, Finsbury.* Another lady undertaker. Not an Eliza, he hoped.

Now, he thought, it would be possible to find out from the undertaker where the late Mrs Mary Penman had lived, and if that address, say, were the one given by Edward Penman to the police, then it might well prove that Crowquill was Edward Penman and had reported Thomas Dryden's death. And that would suggest —

What? That Crowquill knew a deal more than he had let on. Dickens slipped the card into his pocket and went out and down the narrow staircase. *Tabernacle Walk*, he thought.

34: A DEED OF DREADFUL NOTE

Sergeant Rogers and Dickens waited for Constable Feak to come back from Hungerford Pier Police Station with the address of the Mr Penman who had identified Thomas Dryden from the notices that had gone up. Dickens had thought better of a mad dash to Tabernacle Walk, having reflected that he had been gone long enough. It was not the time to be haring off alone and placing an additional anxiety on the shoulders of Sam Jones. In any case, it made more sense first to find out the address of the Penman who'd reported Dryden's identity.

Superintendent Jones had gone home, having been reassured by Sergeant Rogers that he would send immediately if anything happened. Constable Stemp had gone up to Pentonville — just in case anyone remembered Adam Flack or knew him. The stables and outbuildings at the Adelphi arches had been searched. Plenty of evidence of criminal pursuits and dossers down, some sleepers, drunks, tramps, a whole family in rags — all kinds of human flotsam, even a pig, but not a trace of Marlowe had been found.

'It's a rum do, Mr Dickens. I mean, if the address is in Finsbury somewhere near that burial ground or the undertaker's, then Penman could be Crowquill, but why should he come forward to identify Dryden, if, as you think, he was wantin' to keep things to himself?'

'That's the puzzle. Crowquill knew about the judge, Ma Dunk, Pruey, Munty, and he was after Marlowe... He told me he wanted to write a book about Marlowe's exploits, but I didn't find any trace of any book at his lodgings. No

284

manuscript, just the notes he'd made on the judge and the others and the newspaper clippings.'

'Something else in it?' Rogers asked. 'Some other motive? Marlowe done him wrong?'

'I did wonder about that. Did he know something about Munty and Dryden's death — wanted Marlowe suspected? I do think that Crowquill came to me to find out what we know on the pretext of giving information. He's after Marlowe for something. And we won't know until we find out more about Crowquill and whether he is Penman.'

Constable Feak returned. The address Penman had given was in Finsbury. Worship Street, Finsbury. Dickens remembered then. Finsbury, where Simmonds's Waxworks had been after they'd moved from Holborn. Where, perhaps, Crowquill learned about Marlowe's doings at Simmonds's, but it still didn't answer why he should pursue Marlowe.

'Worship Street, I think, Mr Rogers, and pray for divine intervention.'

Divinity was not on Mr Rogers's mind as he adjusted his belt and truncheon, unless it might be a matter of sending Marlowe to another world, preferably in a downward direction. The sergeant had not forgotten Mr Jones's face in that sickly gaslight at the Adelphi arches.

Dickens and Sergeant Rogers walked along dreary Worship Street, passing the gasworks, the stone yard, a printer's shop, the Bell and Dragon pub breathing fire and fume, until they came upon a slice of a shop squeezed between a butcher's shop and a tripe dresser's shop, as if it had got itself in there by mistake and couldn't get out to a more fragrant setting. The window bore the legend, *Mrs Mary Penman, Linen Draper and Children's Outfitter.* They went in to find an angular, elderly lady behind the counter — another woman in black. The case had been haunted by them, Dickens thought, from the very moment he had stepped into Madame Tussaud's Chamber of Horrors and Mrs Thomas Dryden had hissed by him. This one, however, looked as if she might weep rather than hiss. No blank waxwork, this face. Grief there in the drawn features, the red-rimmed eyes, lines deeply scored from nose to chin, and it was in the stooped shoulders and the listless hands turning over the sets of baby clothes that she was showing to another lady, a young lady who seemed paralysed by indecision. The older lady glanced across at them with frightened eyes as she saw the policeman's uniform, and they moved into the shadows where various articles of clothing hung to conceal them.

Eventually the young lady made up her mind — not to make up her mind. Nothing was quite what she wanted for her precious darling, whose skin was so sensitive. The angular lady escorted her to the door and put up the closed sign before turning to them with a weary sigh, looking warily at Sergeant Rogers, and asking what they wanted.

Dickens stepped forward. 'It is about Mr Edward Penman, a journalist who writes under the name of Crowquill.'

She looked alarmed. 'My nephew? Has something happened?'

'No, no, it's just that Sergeant Rogers here needs to find him, and I…'

She was staring at him. 'Good gracious, you are Mr Dickens. What on earth — oh, I see, Edward is a friend of yours — he writes, of course.'

Dickens didn't correct her about the friendship. 'I saw your nephew the other night. He gave me some information, which

I passed on to Sergeant Rogers. He wished to know more, so I accompanied him, thinking that Mr Penman might be here.'

'He never comes here, Mr Dickens. He didn't come to his mother's funeral last September, though I wrote him a card and a letter, and I sent a memorial card. Not a word from him.'

'I am sorry for that.'

'She who loved him, worked for him, hoped for him. Mary was taken suddenly — a heart attack — but he didn't answer. She missed him — her only son — her only child left on this earth — she despaired —'

The lady seemed to struggle for breath and search for her handkerchief. Dickens took her arm. She seemed to be made entirely of bone. 'Is there anywhere we could sit down? You could have some water.'

'In the back — the parlour.'

She led them into the neat, but sparingly furnished back room. Dickens could hardly imagine the untidy Crowquill sitting on the hard black sofa on which the angular lady sat down. Dickens took an upright chair. Rogers found the kitchen and came back with a glass of water.

'Mrs Penman was your sister?' Dickens asked when she had drunk some of the water and seemed to breathe more easily.

'Yes, I have always lived here with Mary. I am Miss Martha Clarke. My sister was left a widow…' She looked at him after the pause. He saw how the handkerchief twisted in her hands and then they were still, and she half laughed, the dry, satirical sound of a woman who knew that there was not much to laugh at in the world. 'No, that is what we said. In fact, he went out one evening and never came home. Oh, the striving for respectability, to keep a good name. What a society we live in. A man deserts his wife, and she must pay with lies and grinding work. A girl is ruined, and she must pay with her life. A boy is given everything his mother can spare and he barely has time for her. And I, a spinster, plain as a cook's linen apron, yet with brains enough to have done something better, must stand for hours behind a counter, be patient with silly little women like the one you saw before. Our linen is soft as butter, but I must bow my head to her whims. I must earn my bread, grieving as I am for the closest friend I had in the world — Mary, my sister, pretty Mary, who always loved me. Mary —'

Here she wept all the tears Dickens suspected she had held in since the moment Mary had died. She was alone in the world and had nothing to hope for now, except to drudge on behind her counter until death took her to that burial ground in Coleman Street. She had lost her sister, her nephew never came, and what had happened to that other child if Crowquill were the only child left on this earth?

When Miss Clarke had composed herself and asked their forgiveness for her tears, he said, 'You have had much to bear, I can tell, as had your sister. Did she lose a child?'

'That's what's wrong with Edward, Mr Dickens. Crowquill — a nasty name, I think, a bitter name. It's not that we blamed him. No one understood more than Mary what he felt for his little sister. We all loved her, but you've to grieve for what is lost, not — not throw away everything that's good. If he'd — oh, it's no use — we went to church, we prayed for her, we believed. He scorned us — so bitter, but I believe Mary is with Rose now, at last, and that's some comfort. I'll be with them — in not too long, I hope.'

She put her handkerchief to her eyes. Rogers looked at Dickens, his glance understanding that they would have to be patient. Miss Clarke must tell her tale in her own time.

After a moment or two, he asked gently, 'What happened to your niece?'

Her head was lowered, and the handkerchief twisted in her hands again. When she looked up, there was resignation in her eyes. 'What does it matter? I may tell you, I suppose. I know your books. Little Em'ly — you didn't judge. You had pity for her fall and for poor Martha who nearly drowned herself.'

Dickens knew then what Rose's story would be, and he thought he knew the name of the person who had brought about Rose's fall, but he let Miss Clarke continue.

'The scandal is old — nearly twenty years old. Oh, how people talked, but where could we go? We had to bear it, restore that good name — what use was that? Customers came anyway — you can imagine. Some even bought things; some were shameless and just came to look round the shop that was the home of the girl who drowned herself because — because she was ruined.'

'A man called William Marlowe,' Dickens said.

'Edward told you?'

'He spoke of him. I could tell that he loathed him, but I didn't know why. How did she meet Marlowe?'

'Rose was — wanted to be an actress. Heavens, Edward wanted to be a writer, Rose an actress. We had no idea where those children came from. So unlike us. Their father, I suppose, but he was only a linen draper, after all. Rose worked at the Royal Albert Saloon up in Britannia Fields — Hoxton way.'

Among Crowquill's papers there had been a yellowing newspaper clipping concerning a suicide in the Hoxton canal. Dickens hadn't looked at it, but that was why it was with all the papers about Marlowe.

'Rose was in the dancing chorus. They had dancing and musical plays and balls. She loved it because it was more exciting than church and a linen draper's shop. She was young and pretty. Not meant for life behind the counter, Mr Dickens, though it would have been better if she had stayed here. There was a play called *A Deed of Dreadful Note*. A farce, and Rose was wild for the part of Mrs Fright.'

Waxworks, Dickens thought. He'd seen the play at the Haymarket years back. Waxworks concealed in cupboards and mistaken for hidden lovers. Marlowe was surely in this story somewhere. Another piece of his history left out by Crowquill.

'Mr Marlowe was in charge of the waxworks and when someone else got the part of Mrs Fright, he was there to comfort Rose. You can guess the rest. She was expecting a child, he vanished, and she — well, she did it. Edward left home and whenever he came back, which wasn't often, he'd not let it alone. It was all Marlowe and what he'd do if he found him.'

Mania, Dickens thought, and motive, but there was no more to be said. Dickens and Rogers rose to go. Dickens said he would ask his journalist friends if they knew where Crowquill could be. He would be glad to give a message from Miss Clarke.

'Tell him that there is a home for him if he needs one. His mother would want me to say that.' She knew he wouldn't come.

She let them out by the shop door. Just as she closed it, she told them one last thing. 'Our Rose. She was in lodgings up in Hoxton. Near the workhouse. In a place called Land of Promise.'

290

They were silent as they walked back along Worship Street. Sergeant Rogers was wondering when he should tell Mr Jones, while Dickens was thinking of those delicate baby clothes and reflecting on the Land of Promise and all the lives so far entangled in this case — lives that had begun in innocent hope and had been wrenched into hideous shapes by some demon waxwork artist called Fate.

35: COALMEN IN THE CASE

The aspiring coal-heaver in leather apron, heavy greatcoat, and suitably blackened about the eyes and hands, and with his similarly accoutred apprentice, had returned from Southwark. Superintendent Jones, who was now back in business, listened with satisfaction to the news that nothing untoward had occurred at the paupers' kitchen. Eliza Quarterman, at first wary, had recognised Scrap's eyes like two pieces of sky in a black cloud, and had enjoyed the coal-heaver's gentlemanly bow. The two had enjoyed their stew, and if Mr Henry Meteyard had thought the meat lacking in some quality found in Mr Sampson Meteyard's Limehouse meat, he did not say so. A coal-heaver ought to be glad of a dish of anything; his apprentice certainly relished it.

Emma Cooper remained in her room, but Eliza reported that she had told the story of her relations with Mr Thomas Dryden, who had charmed her from her perch at Mrs Beddows's warehouse and for whom she had filched a quantity of blank eyes which she had painted at the lodgings in Porter Street. When Thomas Dryden failed to return home, she was frightened. She had no money to pay rent; she was a thief; she was ruined, and she had nowhere to go. The only place she could think of was the paupers' kitchen. The lady there did not ask questions. She was kind and would advise her what to do. Perhaps she would even give her enough money to find lodgings. Emma thought she might find employment.

A man caught hold of her in the alley leading to the pauper's kitchen — a tall man who said he knew where Thomas Dryden was, but he wouldn't tell her. She was to go with him. She said she wouldn't, so he said he'd treat her to a drink and then he'd tell her everything. He didn't seem like a bad man. He had a gentlemanly manner, and he smiled all the time, and gave her some brandy, but he said he couldn't tell her where Thomas was. It was a secret. She would have to come with him. Thomas was waiting. He kept trying to make her drink more, and then he said that she wouldn't like him to tell the police that she'd stolen glass eyes from her employer. She was terrified and she just ran. She heard him shouting, but the people in the pub must have got in his way.

Outside it was dark and she didn't know where she was. She just wanted to get away from the pub, so she ran anywhere until she thought she was safe. She wandered about, not knowing where she was, until she found a shop doorway to curl up in and there she slept. She didn't know for how long, but she was woken by someone who was kneeling beside her. A woman. She asked if the woman knew the way to Redcross Street, and the woman said she would take her. There was another woman with her. They went into an alley, and they turned on her. One cut into her cheek with a knife and the other took her bag and tried to rip off her coat. She screamed. They pushed her down and took the bit of money she had in her pocket. One kicked her in the face before they ran away. She wandered about the alleys until she found the chapel where the kitchen was and just lay down on the steps. Better to die, she'd thought. At least the lady at the kitchen would see that she was buried. She didn't care where — as long as it was out of this world.

To Mr Jones's questions, Henry Meteyard answered that Emma Cooper did not know the name of the man who had taken her to the pub. He had been a tall, well-dressed man with a beard. A toff. And she had heard the name Alexander

Marlowe. Thomas went about with him, but she'd never met him.

'But he'd seen her,' Jones said.

'He'd make sure of that,' said Dickens. 'He'd want to know everyone who was involved in his schemes.'

'Well, we can leave her out of it, and we'll forget about the theft of a few glass eyes.'

'Out of five hundred and seventy-six thousand. Drop in the ocean.'

'Don't remind me. Number of glass eyes manufactured in a year,' Jones said, seeing Henry and Scrap's puzzled faces.

'Not worth it,' Henry said, 'two months in prison and a whole life ruined.'

'Exactly. She's better off with Eliza Quarterman.'

Jones contemplated Dickens and Sergeant Rogers. 'Now, this Crowquill. What about him? From what you two have told us, he's been after Marlowe for years, and therefore if he finds him before we do —'

'Mania, I thought, when I went through his papers, even before we met the aunt,' said Dickens. 'I realised afterwards that he'd come to get information, not to give it.'

'What he would do to Marlowe, sir, if he found him, that's what Miss Clarke said,' added Rogers.

'The man on the ladder putting up the poster. Crowquill's quarry right under his nose.'

'And Marlowe's hunter standing across the street. It's an intriguing thought.'

'Pity Marlowe didn't fall off that ladder at your feet, Mr D. You could've given 'im a good whippin' with that stick o' yours,' Scrap said, relishing the thought.

'My sentiments exactly.' Jones smiled at Scrap. 'But I want Marlowe first before Crowquill finds him. He might only intend to give Marlowe a thrashing, which he'll richly deserve, but he might go further than he intends. Now, Reynolds employed Crowquill, so he needs to be questioned. We need to find out if Crowquill had any close friend, anyone who might know of his interest in Marlowe, anyone who saw him after you did, Charles. No, not you — Inspector Grove can slip down to Wellington Street.'

Henry Meteyard had been thinking. 'Crowquill. I know who he is. There was a case a week or two ago, about the time when those waxworks started appearing. Fellow called Captain Reid — captain of what, I never found out — coal merchant had up for delivering short weight. It was a habit of his, it seems. Anyway, my barrister colleague, Standish Grady, took him to court because Reid had cheated him. I looked in to see what the verdict was — guilty and fined. Reid came out looking pleased with himself. He could easily afford the fine. Grady pointed out Crowquill, who was with him. I'd seen him about court before. I supposed he'd been reporting on the case, though it wasn't much of a case for the papers. However, Reid had his business premises at the Adelphi, and his coal is stored in the arches.'

'Crowquill might have known Reid. Reid been had up before mebbe, an' Crowquill sniffin' out witnesses an' so forth,' Rogers said. 'I'll slip along there an' ask a few questions.'

'Offices in Adam Street,' Henry said.

'Mr Reid, coal merchant of the Strand,' Jones said.

'Lord, Sam, Adam Street abuts the Strand. I'll bet it's on his wagons: Adam Street, Strand.'

'Who's Mr Reid?' Henry asked.

'Judge Quarterman's coal merchant, possibly your Captain Reid who knows Crowquill, and whose coal delivery man knows the house in Manchester Square. Take Stemp with you,

Rogers. He interviewed the coal delivery man, who may well be blameless, but that's not to say he didn't talk to Reid about the judge's death, and we know Reid talked to Crowquill.'

'Newshound,' Dickens said, 'he was following every lead. He knew all about Munty and Dryden. Munty's name was given at the inquest. Crowquill said that he'd suspected Marlowe when those waxworks started appearing.'

'Earlier, maybe, when all that stuff about the judge's waxworks was in the papers. Crowquill only had to see Reid's wagon about Manchester Square to wonder if Reid knew anything about the goings-on at the judge's house. Saw that Reid's case was coming up and there he is, having a chat. What other avenues are open to us?'

'Henry Mayhew — his office is a few doors down from Reynolds and he's got staff. I'll bet one of them knows him. I've a young man, George Sala, writing for me about the back streets. He was with Douglas Jerrold in Wellington Street when Jerrold had his newspaper, and he still has lodgings in the building. They all know each other. I'll ask about.'

'I'm for Norfolk Street,' Scrap said to Jones.

'Tell Mrs Jones I won't be late.'

Rogers went out to find Inspector Grove; he was followed by Scrap and Henry Meteyard. Henry thought it was time he sneaked back into his quarters in Lincoln's Inn if he could get past the porter and re-emerge as a respectable barrister. If they needed him, however, he was ready to come out in any guise they might require.

Dickens stayed in his chair, looking at Jones. 'I'll get about my business in a minute or two, when you've told me how you are and how everyone fares.'

'Elizabeth is brisk and apparently cheerful, Tom is like Mrs Bouncer, full of spring, and Eleanor is thoughtful, stealing an anxious look at us at the tea table. Scrap is as you have just seen him, but Mrs Jones and Eleanor are as precious porcelain — to be watched for cracks.'

'And you?'

'Doing my duty.'

'And?'

'Convincing myself that had Elizabeth been your Albertine or Alice, it wouldn't have happened.'

'And?'

'You ought to go in for Henry's business — like a terrier for the questions, you are today. And, mostly believing myself, and — since we want more evidence, my learned friend, so we can get that man off the streets — be off and find a lead to Mr Crowquill for me.'

'M'ludship — humble servant — gone.' And he was.

36: AN INVITATION

Dickens had visited Henry Mayhew's office, met journalists he knew and some he didn't; he'd come across George Sala at Mayhew's; spoken to Henry Chorley at *The Athenaeum* offices; spoken to a man he knew at *The Morning Post*; popped into *The Farmers' Gazette*, also in Wellington Street North — unlikely, but some horny-handed agricultural writer might know Crowquill; that haystack of hair came to mind. He'd been down to the office of *The Examiner*, edited by his friend, John Forster. Not Crowquill's kind of paper, but the office was in Wellington Street, Strand, next door to *The Literary Gazette*. They'd hardly be publishing *The Waxwork Man* — if it existed. He had hesitated at the door of the offices of *The Spectator* at number nine. He didn't think Crowquill would have been employed there, and besides, George Brimley, their book reviewer, was an old enemy with a sneering pen. He didn't go in.

He'd even been round the corner into the Strand to ask a man he knew who worked on *The Globe* newspaper, and he'd called in at *The Illustrated London News*. When he found himself contemplating the premises of the very unlikely *Lady's Newspaper*, he knew that he had done all he could, other than visiting every newspaper in London. The Wellington Street offices all knew Crowquill by sight. It was the best bet, and there was George Sala, the young man with the keys to the street.

Now he sat contemplating the rampart of letters on his own desk at Tavistock House. A Mr Binks inviting him to address the Wakefield Mechanics' Institute; a bill for wine and spirits; a letter from his sub-editor, Harry Wills, informing him that he'd mistaken St Michael's Mount in Cornwall for Mont St Michel off Normandy — botheration; a note from his friend, Daniel Maclise about a missing magician's fancy dress costume — Lord knew where that had gone. In the cellar, perhaps, a ghostly remnant of his conjuring days, magicking ghostly Christmas puddings from ghostly top hats. An invitation to take a walk with his brother-in-law, Henry Austin; an invitation to an art exhibition. Oh, an exhibition at the Fenton Gallery, paintings by Clarkson Stanfield, Daniel Maclise, and David Roberts. He knew the Fenton Gallery — a private gallery owned by a Mr Fenton, an enormously wealthy recluse. What a coup for Stanny and Maclise. When? Oh, bother, tonight. From 7.30. Well, he could look in, he supposed, at about 8.30. He'd have to. All three artists were friends. Where had the wretched invitation been until today? In the cellar with that magician's outfit, probably.

At half past eight, Dickens was standing outside Fenton's impressive white stucco mansion in Chester Terrace by Regent's Park. Two flaming torches lit up the steps rather dramatically, and from the half-open door he could hear the sound of music drifting out. It sounded like a harpsichord. It was all very tasteful. He expected a bewigged footman in livery to appear to escort him into the gallery upstairs, but no one appeared. Well, he was late. He wondered whether he had committed a faux pas in turning up an hour after the time. Mr Fenton might be offended, but he'd offend his friends more if he didn't go in, and he hadn't responded to the invitation because it had only come today. Stanny and the others would understand.

He went up the steps of the pillared portico and pushed open the door to find himself in a handsome white marble hall, dimly lit by some candles in niches in the walls. He could see the paler rectangles where paintings had hung. A new collection coming, perhaps. Other niches where classical busts had probably stood were empty, as was a floor of black and white marble. The harpsichord still played that rather thin, tinny music. He'd have thought the millionaire recluse might have hired a string quartet or something for the occasion. A marble staircase with an intricate ironwork balustrade rose above a magnificent chandelier, candles unlit. Perhaps the recluse spent all his money on art rather than creature comforts, like light and furniture, yet there was an odd sense of abandonment about the place; even the music sounded slightly eerie, as if a ghost were playing on the keys. In the gloom at the side of the staircase, he saw where the music was coming from. A lady of the eighteenth-century type in an elaborate gown was leaning over the harpsichord on which a branched candlestick stood, illuminating her improbable wig. Fancy dress, it seemed. Had he come to the wrong party? He stepped forward to ask if the exhibition were upstairs, but the query died on his lips. She didn't move, nor did her hands. They were deathly still on the keys, and yet the music still played.

Two things happened then. He touched a hand and the door slammed shut. And in the gap of those seconds, he knew. She wasn't real. The hand was made of wax, and she had no face. The candles had been blown out by the wind, and he was in the dark. There was no exhibition of the paintings of Stanfield, Maclise, or Roberts. The music stopped. A lid closed on a music box. He stood still and waited, aware of the cold and the silence, his heart beating. He knew that he was locked in and that Marlowe had played this trick before.

After what seemed an age, a voice came from above, a voice he couldn't recognise. It sounded magnified and hollow, as if coming from a speaking trumpet, and it bade him to come and see the exhibition. *Must be Marlowe*, he thought. Or Crowquill? Which of the two was the greater danger to him? Marlowe. He shuffled away from the harpsichord, felt for the cold iron of the balustrade and made his way up the stairs. They curved away to a balustraded landing, where he stood to listen. He could see light flickering from another open door. He looked back down the marble steps, imagining being pushed from behind by the owner of that inhuman voice. And if he reached the front door in time, he wouldn't be able to get out. He stepped forward through the door.

He wasn't a bit surprised to find himself in a waxwork show. Not unlike the judge's, but with fewer figures. There was candlelight. And there were shadows on the walls, and the figures were dressed in black — women, of course. Marlowe. Was he supposed to be frightened to death?

Had he not seen the judge's chamber and the judge's face as he lay dead there, Dickens might have been frightened to death, but these figures were fairground work. The faces were crude and coarse, and seemed to grin and grimace in the flickering light, and the unpainted eyes protruded blindly from under heavy lids as if they might start from their sockets. And they were bald. It was a lunatic asylum of waxworks this time. He recognised the heads from Mrs Dryden's cellar. Marlowe, then. He'd retrieved them somehow, or had a stock of them somewhere.

Dickens wasn't terrified, but he was filled with unease. Something must happen, but he couldn't predict what. However, he only flinched inwardly when a waxwork seemed to step from behind another, pulling off the black covering from its head, but his hands were clenched by his sides. Then he saw and was relieved. Crowquill.

'I've been looking for you,' Dickens said.

'I guessed you would. I guessed you'd think it all over an' wonder why I really wanted Marlowe.'

'I know why. I went to your lodgings and found a memorial card concerning a Mrs Penman, and I remembered that a Mr Penman identified Thomas Dryden, but you didn't mention that name to me. I found your aunt, Miss Clarke, and she told me.'

'Ah, so you know about Rose and what he did to her.' Crowquill stepped to one side and twitched at the covering of a seated figure. 'As you see, I have found him. I brought him here. I set it up. I thought he should see this. Oh, the joker. He knows what it is to be frightened now.'

So, this was Alexander Marlowe, the laughing dandy. Well, he wasn't smiling now. He was gagged and bound to the chair, one eye closed. What could be seen of his face was swollen, his nose probably broken, his hair bloodied, his jacket practically torn to shreds, and his trousers all muddy. Dear Lord, he had had his thrashing. Most chilling was the rope round his neck, fashioned as a noose.

'How did you find him?'

'I followed you to the arches on the night I came to your office. I suspected you weren't telling me everything an' I saw that boy give you a note. It was easy in the fog, though I collided with you when you suddenly stopped. You felt my breath on your neck. It didn't matter. I saw you go into that stable an' I saw him bar the door. I took him then. A rope round his neck, then I left him in some wretched hovel in that courtyard while I arranged all this. I knew about the gallery closing. His wax heads from Mrs Dryden's.' Crowquill's mouth twisted into a mirthless laugh that was more like a snarl. 'I was there when she was arrested. Lost him, then — one of Mr Jones's men delayed me.'

'Why have you brought me here?'

'I hoped you wouldn't know that Fenton has sold up. I banked on your loyalty to your friends, an' so it proved. An' even if you suspected something, I knew you'd come. I'd already whetted your appetite, and Mr Jones's. The candles and the wax hand —' he picked up the noose round Marlowe's neck and pulled it tight. The choking sounds were horrible — 'remember Mrs Manning's mask and the noose? All my own work. I wanted to keep it going until I found him, an' to confuse him an' the police.' Another jerk on the rope. Another gurgling sound from the gagged man before Crowquill dropped the rope again.

'And if I had brought the police?'

'I didn't care if you brought all of Bow Street as long as someone saw him brought down, saw him fouled and bloodied, an' humiliated, all his swagger reduced to snivelling terror. I'd have liked a bigger audience. Exhibition of a scoundrel, a cheat, a liar, a murderer.' Another jerk on the rope.

'What do you intend to do with him now?'

'It's a pretty problem. He knows who I am. I have reminded him of Rose an' that he is a murderer.' At this word, Crowquill slapped his victim's head. There was a muffled groan behind the gag. 'He cannot live. I won't allow it. He's worse than the dirt under my feet an' yours.' He slapped him again. The bloodied head jerked forward with a strangled cry. It was a horrible sight, Dickens thought. Marlowe was a scoundrel, but this...

'You don't have to do it. He'll hang at Newgate.'

'But not for Rose.'

'Does it matter? He'll hang for the judge's death — he sent me a letter confessing it. He frightened the man to death, and there's Joshua Munton, and probably Thomas Dryden.'

More muffled cries from the gag. 'He says not. He says he knows nothing about Dryden, who never came to their meeting at Hungerford Bridge. He says he knows nothin' about Joshua Munton.' The ruined head tried to nod and sounds of anguish came as the prisoner strained at his ropes. 'He'll talk his way out of those deaths. He might have caused the judge's death. It'll be manslaughter.'

'Transportation, then. He'll not survive the journey.'

'Ain't good enough.'

'You can't kill him. He's not worth your life.'

'No, he's not, but I don't care much for my life anyway. It ain't worth much to me or anyone.'

'It was worth something to Mrs Mary Penman.'

'She's dead. She knows nothing now.'

'Therefore, Rose knows nothing. She wouldn't want —'

'Quite the Jesuit, aren't you? But I want him dead.'

'Miss Martha said there's a home for you in Finsbury.'

'An' what should I do in Finsbury? Take lodgings in the Land of Promise. Where poor Rose had all his promises broken.' Crowquill slapped his prisoner even harder. 'Well, I promised her I'd find him, an' he'd be paid, and I've kept my promise. He's never kept a promise in his life except to himself.'

'And after you've done it, what then? You won't wait here while I fetch Superintendent Jones.'

'Suppose you fetch him now? Will I be gone when you get back? Will he —' a vicious kick this time — 'be hanging from the staircase? Will I be waiting for the superintendent's handcuffs, or will I, tired of this life of mine, follow him to perdition?'

The silence which followed these questions was punctuated by the groans and whimpers of the gagged man whose humiliation was complete. There was the sudden acrid stink of urine. Dickens stepped back. He was thinking, too. It was a pretty problem — for him. Pretty dreadful. Impossible to solve. He had no wish to witness a murder, but suppose he tried to grapple with Crowquill now? He saw what the man had done to Marlowe. What if he tried to stop him in the act? One of the three of them would undoubtedly hurtle over that iron balustrade on the landing and onto the black and white marble below, and it might be him. Yet, if he went out to get Sam, a man might be murdered while he was gone, and he would have done nothing to save the victim or the possible suicide. Either decision meant one death or more. On his head like heaped coals.

'You should go, you know, Mr Dickens. There's nothing you can do. You can't stop me. See what I have in my pocket. I've already used it on him.' Dickens looked at the cosh, a heavy thing weighted with lead. 'Come near me an' I'll use it. I might be a sick man, but the strength of rage is on my side. Unless you'd rather be unconscious when I do for him. Painful, but you'd be out of it.'

Dickens had to try. 'Don't do it, I beg you. Leave. Make your escape. Disappear. I won't give you away. You'll be free, and the law will deal with him. He's half dead already.'

'Sick in his cell an' a doctor fetched to comfort the dying man; die in his cell an' a parson fetched to pray over him. An' if he lives, there's prayers on the scaffold. But not for him. Not a word. No prayers for my Rose. Suicide's a crime. He's the criminal. So just go. One of us might be alive when you get back.'

Dickens looked at the man's burning eyes. It was no use. All the words in the world were no good. He took a candle from one of the side tables, thought of throwing the branched candlestick at Crowquill, thought of the man catching fire, thought of Marlowe catching fire, thought of a burning Crowquill coming at him with his cosh, thought of a conflagration of wax figures and black shrouds, and a house in flames. He'd once seen a woman catch fire and turn into a pillar of flame; it had been during a case in which a boy had been murdered at Hungerford Stairs. That had been a horror, too. He hadn't been able to stop her.

Crowquill still stared at him. What else could he say?

'An' just so you know, I pushed Dryden into that water. He wouldn't tell me where Marlowe was. Didn't mean to kill him. Didn't care, though. Reported it — Marlowe could get the blame if the police found him first.'

'An accident, though, so —'

'Reynolds says you think you're God Almighty. Not this time. Just a man, Charles Dickens. I had that dinner, so go. Save yourself. Leave the devil to his fate.'

Dickens went down the stairs with his candle. The invisible music started up again, but the faceless player at the harpsichord did not move. He went out of the door, leaving it ajar. Perhaps a policeman on his beat would pass and be suspicious and mount those stairs and prevent a murder. He steeled himself to be calm; he schooled himself not to run like a madman and draw attention to himself in the serene purlieus of Chester Terrace, and he walked as fast as he could. But his heart was racing, and his breath came raggedly. It wasn't far. Down Chester Terrace to the New Road and then along and down Cleveland Street and into Norfolk Street. He had no idea of the time. He might have been in the Fenton house for hours. There was a light coming through the shutters of the front parlour window. As he usually did, Dickens leant across the railings and knocked twice on the window, but not urgently. He mustn't frighten Elizabeth or the children. Sam Jones would know that knock and think he brought news of Crowquill.

He heard the bolts drawn and the lock turned, and his heart wouldn't stay still in his breast. Sam Jones appeared at the door, took one look at Dickens's agonised white face and stepped out, pulling the door behind him. In a series of hurried, breathless whispers, Dickens told him the news. 'Came as fast as — didn't run — draw attention. Didn't want to frighten them, but quick, Sam, oh, quick — they might be —'

Jones saw that Dickens was shaking. Dear God, what a decision to make. 'Wait here, get your breath. I'll have to tell Elizabeth that I'm going to Bow Street. I daren't make too much fuss.'

Dickens waited, hanging on to the iron railings, breathing in the night air, trying to steady himself, seeing that noose and that wreck of a man hanging from the staircase, and Crowquill — where was he? A solitary figure stealing away through a twist of alleys, an outcast thing, throwing its monstrous shadow on the dead wall of the night, or —

A comforting hand on his shoulder, a moment's pause, a deep breath, some soft words spoken, and they were away, striding back to Chester Terrace and a door wide open.

Dickens was ready to rush through that open door, but Jones stopped him. Dickens had said he had left the door ajar, so the wind might have blown it open. However, someone might be in there. Someone who ought to be taken by surprise. They went up the steps cautiously and stood listening under the portico, but there was only silence, punctuated by the oddest creaking sound, as if someone in there were opening and closing a door. It seemed too regular to be the wind. Yet Dickens could not imagine Crowquill simply standing there pushing a door to and fro, waiting to be found. Jones made up his mind and stepped into the hall. Dickens followed.

Jones's lamp picked out the crumpled thing on the floor — a sack of bones left out for the dust collector, and something liquid black snaking across the tiles. He heard Dickens gasp and saw him looking up. The lamp showed an improbable thing that looked like a grotesque circus act, a man seated on a chair, suspended in the air, the chair slowly turning one way and then another. The man's head had fallen forward. Time stood still as they watched with appalled fascination something black and glistening, falling drop by drop onto the form below.

Jones recovered first and dashed up the stairs to look over the landing balustrade. He could see the stove-in head beneath him. The man was dead. Jones looked at the shape on the floor down below. It was too hazardous to try to haul up the man and the chair. He went down again to turn over the body.

'Crowquill,' Dickens said, 'so that's Marlowe up there. Crowquill did it.'

'And killed himself in the process,' Jones said. 'I wonder if he fell, carried over by the weight of the man in the chair.'

'Seems likely enough. I thought about tackling him, but he threatened me with his cosh. I thought about stopping him in the act, and then I thought one or more of us would end up dead on that floor.'

'I'm glad you didn't try. I saw Marlowe's head up there. Crowquill had beaten him senseless.'

'Still, I can't help thinking…'

'I know. It came too near, but what do you always tell me? Courage, persevere. It was between those two. Neither much use, I'm sorry to say, to anyone. But you, whose work is not yet done, to die in a vain attempt to save one of them… No, Charles Dickens, no. It's a horrible sight, as bad as anything we've seen, but they did it. So, don't dwell too much on it — and I won't dwell too much on that stable and those ropes that bound my wife.'

'You saw them?'

'I did, lying on the floor. I knew what he'd done. I won't dwell on it, but I won't forget it.'

'Scars on the heart, eh?'

'They'll heal, but we'll feel the pull of them from time to time.'

'Written on the heart like old writing on the wall. Like those faded letters on the sign at Marlowe's Oil and Colour Warehouse, where it all started. The past never fully erased.'

'Some of this will have to be rubbed out. I don't want you anywhere near this, so you'll need to get a cab to the stationery shop and get hold of Rogers. He can round up Stemp. What we need is two policemen to have discovered this and sent for me. Door open, they are suspicious, find the bodies. Recognise Mr Crowquill — we'll work out how later, but they know I've been wanting to question him about the waxworks case. In the meantime, I'm closing that door once you've gone out. Then go home.'

Dickens went out to find a cab at the stand in Albany Street. Superintendent Jones shut the door and turned out his lamp. He stood leaning against the door, listening to the creak of the chair as it turned on the rope.

37: WHEN WE PRACTISE TO DECEIVE

Dickens had slunk like a hunted thing to his Wellington Street office, hoping that when the news became current, he would not have all the journalists in Wellington Street knocking on his door to enquire why he had wanted Crowquill. On his way in, he had caught sight of George Brimley striding magisterially towards the Strand to the offices of *The Spectator* — no doubt with a sharpened quill in his pocket, ready to skewer some hapless author's work. However, he managed to slip into his own premises without anyone accosting him.

He'd come to Wellington Street because he couldn't concentrate. The fresh page he had tried to begin seemed to look back at him with a blank aspect. Esther Summerson remained a blank child. All he had managed was the opening line of his new chapter: *I have a great deal of difficulty in beginning to write…* And that, ironically, was it. Instead, his mind was full of the images of that figure in the chair hanging from the balustrade, turning on the rope, and the black blood dripping onto the man below. He knew Sam was right, and he knew he'd weather it eventually. After all, Sam had had a greater fright than he — the terror that his wife had been harmed.

Now, at his desk, he looked through the various papers submitted for his consideration for *Household Words* in the new year. Harry Wills would have already weeded out the impossibles. *New Discoveries in Ghosts* might be appealing, but not for him just now. *Penny Banks* — yes, useful. A piece on gunpowder. He thought of Ma Dunk, daughter of a murderess. *Wonderful Toys* — pity that hadn't come in time for the Christmas numbers, he reflected, turning over the front page.

Good Lord, automata — one apparently able to play chess, a clockwork trumpeter, a clockwork conjuror to be seen at Boulogne, made by a jeweller, who was also exhibiting a flute player with moving lips — the music coming from a hidden music box…

And he was back in Chester Terrace and hearing that tinny music and seeing those bloodless wax hands on the keys of the harpsichord. Worse, he thought, if it had been an automaton. That might well have frightened him to death. The article would do, though. Readers liked a touch of fancy.

A knock on the door brought in the office boy, who told him that a Mr Reynolds wanted to see him. *'Evans, 'orrors an 'ell*, he thought, the last man in the world he wanted to see. He heard heavy footsteps coming up the stairs.

God Almighty arranged his features into an expression of what he hoped was supernatural calm just in time before Reynolds, all bluster and bristle, put his large whiskered head round the door. His broad shoulders followed.

'Crowquill!' he barked.

'Yes?'

'Dead, I hear, and you were asking after him. What did you want him for?'

Dickens was tempted to say that it wasn't Reynolds's business, but he only said, 'Some manuscript he wanted me to look at.'

'What?'

'Some story about the waxworks that were appearing. Something about a waxwork man. He said he'd bring it round, but he didn't.'

'Blanchard gave you Crowquill's address.'

'Yes, I went there, but he wasn't at home. That's it. I don't know any more about him.'

Reynolds looked at him suspiciously. 'No manuscript at his lodgings?'

'I didn't look. I knocked. No answer. I came away. If you want to know anything, Bow Street's just a step away. They must know about it.'

'That Superintendent Jones on the case?'

'I've no idea. Now, Mr Reynolds, if you please, I should like to get on.'

Reynolds hesitated. Dickens thought he was probably thinking that Dickens had stolen a march on him by getting hold of Crowquill's supposed manuscript. Just as the wretch had stolen his Mr Pickwick for some miserable piece of fiction, impudently entitled *Pickwick Abroad*. He picked up his pen and Reynolds blundered out without a word.

God Almighty. More like the Devil's Advocate. Still, he'd had to lie, and he could only hope that Reynolds would believe it. Reynolds was more interested in Crowquill's story — a possible money-spinner. He was probably on his way to Crowquill's lodgings to see if he could find it. Not finding it, he would go to his grave believing that Dickens had stolen it.

More important, however, was the news from the inquest. He was desperate to know, but he dared not go to Bow Street. Reynolds's office was just opposite; he could be watching, if he were not on his way to Crowquill's lodgings. He hoped Reynolds wouldn't meet the ash girl who might tell him that Dickens had been in Crowquill's room. *Lord, when we practise to deceive, what a tangled web we weave.* And Sam, having to give his evidence at the inquest, somehow skirting over the presence of Charles Dickens. It would be adjourned, surely, pending further inquiries by the police.

A note to Sam, warning him not to come to the office of *Household Words* and telling him that he couldn't go to Bow

Street — the newspaper offices in Wellington Street were stirring — but to send back with a message about where they could meet. He went down to tell the office boy that he must wait for a reply.

And one came. A message had been sent to the coal heaver at Lincoln's Inn. The evidence needed to be very neatly arranged for the consumption of the magistrate at the resumed inquest. Noon at The Hole in the Wall, by Hatton Wall, off Leather Lane.

Noon arrived in its own slow time. *Hole in the corner, more like*, Dickens thought, as he looked at the pub skulking darkly down a passage off Hatton Wall. No one would find him here. He didn't know if he could find himself, or his way out, and he was amused to see that the sign showed what might have been a wall with a hole, or the Slough of Despond. *Abandon hope, all ye*, he thought and then laughed out loud. The landlord of this hole in the corner was, apparently, one William Hidden.

And hidden within, occupying a booth, was the respectable barrister, Mr Henry Meteyard of Lincoln's Inn, and the respectable Superintendent Jones of Bow Street.

'Came a crooked way, did you?' Jones said as he and Henry looked at the long-coated, bespectacled figure in the low-crowned hat who had materialised before them, as though conjured from the cellarage. 'Very cloak and dagger.'

'That wretch, Reynolds, came to see me earlier — wanted to know about Crowquill. Asked about you, Sam. Didn't want him seeing me scuttling to Bow Street.'

'What did you tell him?'

'I spun a tale about Crowquill offering me a manuscript — said he'd not turned up to deliver it. He knew I'd been to the lodgings. Probably thinks I've stolen Crowquill's great work. But best avoided just now. Inquest go off all right?'

Jones told him what had occurred. Sergeant Rogers and Constable Stemp had given their evidence. On the way back from carrying out enquiries on behalf of Bow Street — this imaginative detail to explain their presence in Chester Terrace, strictly speaking D Division's territory — they had investigated the open door at the empty mansion and found the two dead men. Sergeant Rogers testified that he had recognised Mr Crowquill, the journalist, whom he knew that Superintendent Jones wished to speak to in connection with the death of Judge Quarterman at his house in Manchester Square. Sergeant Rogers knew the journalist by sight. He had seen him in court reporting on proceedings. Superintendent Jones told the coroner that he had received a message from Mr Crowquill regarding the judge's death which, it seemed, the journalist had been investigating. He had expected the journalist to come to Bow Street, but he had not appeared to give his testimony. The other dead man, the superintendent thought, was one Alexander Marlowe, who was also wanted in connection with the judge's death. The case was a complex one. The superintendent did not yet know the connection between Mr Crowquill and Marlowe, but he had in custody various persons who were of interest in the case.

'The coroner obligingly adjourned the inquest, pending further enquiries by the police,' Sam concluded. 'I wanted Henry to come in so that I can give a coherent account when the next inquest comes on. We've got the events in order from the judge's death to the discovery of the bodies in Chester Terrace. Henry thinks we can leave Eliza Quarterman out of it — she's nothing to do with the deaths, but I'll have to ask Mrs Ann Marlowe to give evidence.'

'I should think she'll be glad to paint her brother-in-law in as bad a light as she can.'

'You've got Ma Dunk, Pruey and Mrs Dryden to testify to Marlowe's part in the judge's death. You can make clear Crowquill's motive for killing Marlowe. But you'll need Miss Clarke, the aunt, for the story about Crowquill's sister. Is she up to it?' Henry asked.

'I think she might be. She hadn't much affection for Crowquill, and she was still grieving over Rose and her sister.'

'I want to know how Crowquill found Marlowe,' Jones said. 'I know it's not material evidence, as only Charles knows the answer, and he wasn't there.'

'No need to explain how to the court,' Henry said. 'You've got Crowquill, the journalist, following his own leads and that should be enough, and you'll have his papers — evidence of Crowquill's long-standing pursuit of Marlowe.'

'Rogers has gone to collect them from Crowquill's lodgings,' Jones told Dickens.

'Hope he doesn't meet Reynolds.'

'Serves Reynolds right if he does. He'll think we've got the manuscript, and that should take the heat off you.'

'Sam,' Henry continued, 'you only know that Crowquill found him somehow and took him to the empty house. The magistrate will accept that, as both men are dead, it will be impossible to know the when, the where, and the how.'

'For my own satisfaction.'

Dickens told them how he had been followed by Crowquill to the Adelphi arches and how Crowquill had taken Marlowe after he'd barred the door to lock Dickens in the stable. 'What about the abduction of Elizabeth?' he asked.

'I don't think we can keep that quiet,' Jones said. 'It's bound to get out. There were a lot of policemen there that night.

Someone will have talked. And I've got the note that Marlowe sent. No need to mention you.'

'You might be prepared to speculate that Crowquill found Marlowe at the arches because he was following him. There's the Reid connection, too,' Henry said.

'Oh, I forgot about him. What did you find out?'

'Crowquill had approached Reid. Henry saw them in court, if you remember. Crowquill wanted to get into the house at Manchester Square. Said he wanted to report on the judge's chamber of horrors, and paid Reid for information about access to the premises,' Jones explained.

'Ah, I remember that Mrs Flint was approached by several journalists who offered money. Maybe Crowquill was one of them and when she turned him down, he went to Reid.'

'Probably, but whether he got in, we don't know.'

'It doesn't matter,' Henry said. 'It's only more evidence to confirm that Crowquill was after Marlowe. Keep it simple. Reid will have to testify that he gave information about access to the house. That's his look-out if the magistrate censures him.'

'Dryden?' asked Dickens.

'We don't know — only that he was drowned. No evidence of how it happened. Got what he deserved, I'm inclined to think. No evidence regarding Munty, either.'

'No justice for that poor, benighted creature.'

'An imperfect thing sometimes, justice, and each man does not always have his due. The court can act only on proof,' Henry said. 'Stick with what you have. A straightforward story of greed, blackmail, revenge, and murder. Nothing the jury likes better. You clear up the judge's death, solve a murder and a suicide. Waxworks mania put to bed. Story of the judge's wife fades away, as these things do, and the public interest turns to some other lurid matter. That fellow, Pocket, for example, who's escaped from Pentonville.'

'The one who sent a note to the governor. Presented his compliments and explained he was quite safe, and was intending to proceed to the continent to recruit his health.' Dickens had read that story.

'Impudent beggar,' Jones said, but he acknowledged the truth that it was a good story to distract the multitude.

'Masked murderers in Marylebone — read it the other day,' Henry said cheerfully.

'Criminal conversation in Camden,' Dickens offered.

'Poisoning in Peckham,' Henry added.

'And in Paddington, Portland Town, Pancras —'

'And Poplar, no doubt. Yes, I get your drift,' Jones said. 'How it goes on, though. Enough to break your heart, sometimes. But —' glancing at Dickens — 'we won't dwell. Let's be thankful it's over.'

'I'll drink to that,' Henry said, raising his glass, but his face turned a shade more serious when he put it down again. 'It's what we're here for. To use life well. To do what we can, however little. No point otherwise. Now, I'm for Limehouse and Mrs Amelia Meteyard's roast beef. See you in court.'

Dickens and Jones followed him out into Leather Lane and watched him stride away. 'Wise man,' Jones said, 'so very —'

'Stalwart,' Dickens finished, 'heart of oak.'

'And yours?'

'That ingenious piece of clockwork ticks on but brokenly — sometimes. But not today, my ancient Brave-Heart. Arm, arm! Good roast beef is what's wanted, and not at that hole in the corner.'

'And not at Mr Stagg's, if you please. We might be interrupted.'

Dickens grinned. 'Suspicious death, sir.'

'We're not available.'

And they wound their way through the city streets, sometimes speaking, sometimes not, always in step, until they reached the river where they stopped to look at the high water running fast, moving on, its own purpose certain as the purpose of the sun and the moon and the stars. The human tide flowed past them, borne by chance and change, its purpose, in truth, uncertain. But river and people had this in common: moving on to one end, the eternal shore — which rather melancholy thought made Dickens take Mr Jones's arm and steer him in the direction of Birchin Lane.

The warm fire at the George and Vulture in Cowper's Court made its frequent guest, Mr Charles Dickens, and his companion most welcome. Roast beef excellent. Landlord, Mr Whitmarsh. Wife, Eliza. Mr Dickens did not mention that to Mr Jones, whose propensity for indigestion might well have been awakened before the good roast beef was served.

They parted at Southwark Bridge, over which Dickens knew he would have to go to see Mrs Eliza Quarterman. 'Before she reads all about it in the newspapers,' he said.

38: DEPARTURES AND ARRIVALS

Eliza Quarterman listened. Dickens had to tell her almost everything. The newspapers wouldn't leave anything out. The man bound to a chair, hanging from a rope, the other crushed on the marble below, the waxwork figures in the empty chamber, the faceless figure at the harpsichord. If he hadn't been there, Dickens knew that he would have read it with the same fascinated horror as everybody else in the city. He missed out the cries and whimperings of the beaten man, the slaps, and the jerks on the rope about his neck, the broken nose and swollen face, the humiliating stench of his urine. Only he and Sam Jones knew about those now. Alexander Marlowe may not have deserved their pity, but his daughter did. His heart was wrung as he saw the pallor of her face blanch even more as she listened, so that she looked as fragile as paper. He saw how thin she was, how sorrow and grief shrank her, and how the relentless hardship of the life she had chosen had worn away her youth and beauty.

'I ought never to have been born. Nothing but tragedy has come of my life. My poor mother in that hideous burying ground. What am I to feel about the man who was my father, who did such dreadful things, and yet who died in such a grotesque way? And that other man who did it, who bore such hatred in his heart, and yet who loved his sister. The judge, too, my husband whom I could neither love nor respect, but whose death my disappearance brought about… I must bear the guilt of that.'

'I think not. The man who blackmailed him is the one who bears the guilt, and the judge who had no love in his heart to give to you or anyone. He had no heart at all.'

'Mine was already given. I should have resisted. I let them —'

'You were just a girl. What power did you have to resist?'

'I could have gone to the north as a governess. I thought, I believed that Lady Julia's grandson ... that he loved me. But his father had other plans for Francis, and ... well, even Francis had no power to resist. After Lady Julia's death, Francis was sent away. In any case, where should we have gone? Francis, disinherited, and I, a foundling. I could not blame him. And then it was too late. Sir Henry Clifford sold me to the judge.'

Dickens could imagine it. The grandson, Francis, sent away; Sir Henry Clifford and his wife using their power to bully the girl into the judge's arms. They would not have sent her north when they knew the judge would pay handsomely for her.

'The judge wanted obedience in all things. A wife had a duty to perform —' She put her hands to her face. 'I could not be dutiful. I had already... and the judge knew. He hated me, yet he insisted... I cannot bear to remember...'

Dickens didn't speak. He wished she did not have to remember, but perhaps it would be better if she could unburden herself and begin to see that she was the victim. Not only of the judge and Sir Henry Clifford, but also, he suspected, of Francis Clifford, who had swiftly married the brewer's daughter. He had not fought for Eliza, who had given him her heart and more. No doubt the threat of being disinherited had concentrated his mind wonderfully. And he, too, had probably not wanted the foundling as a wife. It was

320

not for him to speak of these things, however. He waited for her to recover some of her composure.

'I wrote to Francis. I thought he might help me ... to escape. We met once in Kensington Gardens. It was too late. I saw that. He was to be married to the daughter of a wealthy man. It was as if what had passed between us had never happened. He gave me money and to my shame, I took it. I never heard from him again. Alexander Marlowe — my father — he did not want me, either, yet I am tainted with his blood.'

Dickens looked at her fine, drawn face and clear, pale eyes in which there was truth and beauty of a kind that was different from her younger self, and so different from the sly coarseness of Ma Dunk. Bad blood there, but not here. 'I do not believe that. Alexander Marlowe is nothing to do with you. Leave him behind. Think how many have defied their beginnings to make themselves. My boy, Scrap — what a beginning he had. His father was a brute beast, yet from what glimpses I have of his mother of whom he speaks sometimes, she was a good woman. He is her child, not that violent man's. Remember that good old lady who was your grandmother, who grieved for her lost daughter, who, like Mr Crowquill's sister, was innocent. Her child died with her. You survived; you have made yourself and there is purpose in your life, as your paupers' kitchen shows. You have friends, your protective neighbours, the redoubtable Mrs Marlowe, the good Doctor Greville who came at your call. There are good people, and your life is with them now.'

Eliza looked at him and remembered Scrap, just a boy, and yet determined to put right his error, and here was Mr Charles Dickens, the light of whose intent, searching gaze seemed to see into her very soul, and to understand all that she felt and suffered. She felt the warm pressure of his hand on hers.

'And you may count me and young Scrap, of course, as your liegemen, if you need us. Time will lessen the rawness of your wounds. I do not say that you will forget, of course. The chances and changes of the world rob us of many hopes and loves. Many trials beset us, but the journey is ever onward, and we must pursue it. There is always hope, Eliza, a light somewhere ahead, however faint just now.'

'I believe it when you say it, and I shall try to believe it when you are gone.'

'Courage will not desert you. You had it when you left the judge, and you will have it yet. Give it time. All wounds need time, the wounds of the heart most of all.'

'I see that you know the truth of that, Mr Dickens, and that somehow you have found the courage to endure, to do what you do, and to bring hope to all those whose lives are so blighted. I don't know yet if I can find that courage ... and oh, the courage you had — you went to that house, not knowing what he might do.'

'Yes, but that won't be mentioned, and neither will your name come into it. No one knows that the man who called himself William Marlowe had a daughter, except Mrs Ann —'

'She won't tell. And what about Emma?'

'She did nothing except steal a few glass eyes. The resumed inquest will deal only with Marlowe and Crowquill and what brought about their deaths, and Marlowe's part in the judge's death. There are witnesses to give evidence about that, but no one knows Emma Cooper's name, nor the name of Mrs Clifford who runs a paupers' kitchen in Southwark.'

Dickens left Eliza to her thoughts. She had courage. She had endurance and she had friends; she would take care of Emma Cooper, and Mrs Ann Marlowe would take care of her.

Perhaps the good Doctor Greville would, too. There was nothing more to be done. He walked up the High Street towards St Saviour's Church, the image of which he had seen on a tin token at the Foundling Hospital. He looked at the great spire towering above the graveyard, that equal resting place for sound hearts, wounded hearts, broken hearts. St Saviour's, rising above the squalor of Southwark, equal resting place of the learned bishop, Lancelot Andrewes, the poet, John Gower, and Shakespeare's brother, and an old woman who had died in the workhouse. *Death the leveller*, he thought. They were all dust now. Dust among dust, and ashes among ashes.

He crossed the bridge, turning his back on Lant Street and the Crossbones graveyard. He left behind the taint of the Marshalsea, and the hungry boy with blacking under his nails who had gazed out of that attic window and dreamed of another world beyond the wrecks of houses — for the time being, anyway. He'd had enough of Southwark for now. He wouldn't go to Wellington Street for a day or two. Let the dust settle. Let the hunt for Pocket the Pentonville escapee be the new craze. He strode on, feeling the ingenious piece of clockwork steady itself. Tavistock House. He wanted his study, his desk, his blue slips of paper. A blank child, a woman with a secret, a dead man on a bed, a murder to be solved, a detective on the case.

On the corner of Tavistock Square, there was a man up a ladder. Another billsticker. Dickens looked up, his breath quickening for a moment, and almost tripped over the bucket of water at the foot of the ladder. He looked irritably at the offending bucket, then suddenly started to laugh. As if he were made of flesh and blood, Mr Bucket, of the detective force, arrived, conjured from the very air. And as Charles Dickens stood smiling at that air, a stout woman came by, and she looked up as well. She looked at him, too, for a few moments, nodded as one might say, 'You need watching,' and went on her way. A noticing sort of body, he thought, with shrewd, piercing eyes. Mrs Bucket, a lady of natural detective genius, a woman in fifty thousand, in a hundred and fifty thousand, and Mr Bucket's partner in crime.

My lady detective, he thought, hurrying on. *A funeral procession, and a gun tossed into a piece of water by a woman with murder in her heart. And a pair of shrewd eyes watching. Yes, yes, yes.* He didn't look back. It was just as well. The billsticker finished his job, came down his ladder, and looked up at his poster with satisfaction.

Madame Tussaud and Sons Bazaar
Taken from Life, His Honour, Judge Quarterman
In Wig and Gown
With Biddy Ross, Rebecca Smith, Mary Ann Geering
And Mrs Manning
  The Chamber of Horrors, 6d.

HISTORICAL NOTES

The scene at Madame Tussaud's at the opening of this novel is based on an article in Dickens's magazine, *All the Year Round*, in which the writer, Charles Allston Collins, younger brother of Wilkie Collins, describes a visit to the Chamber of Horrors and the meeting with the pie-eating stranger. The article appeared in 1860, the year that Charles Collins married Dickens's daughter, Katey. The article would have been edited by Dickens, and there are some unmistakable touches of Dickens's humour, especially in the meeting with the young man and his pie. I gave the encounter to Dickens as it was just the sort of thing that would have happened to him, and, of course, I imagined the conversation.

Madame Tussaud began her career in France during the Revolution and its aftermath, and she did take casts of the victims of the guillotine. She opened her Baker Street Bazaar in 1835, and it's still going. There are branches across the world, from Beijing to New York. I read the astounding statistic that 500 million people have visited the London waxworks. Charles Dickens is there, of course.

Waxworks were very popular and there were others besides Tussaud's, including Springthorpe's and Simmonds's, both mentioned in the book. Doctor Kahn and his anatomical exhibits and 'extraordinary freaks of nature' were on Oxford Street and were open on special days for ladies only. I wonder what they made of the 'famous Caesarean Operation'. Doctor Kahn was no doubt right in claiming 'nothing of the kind ever before having been seen' in London.

Waxworks were not the only popular attraction in London in that winter of 1851. There was an astonishing variety of amusements and entertainments showing off the Victorians' ingenuity, inventiveness, delight in new technology, and love of spectacle.

December was then, and is now, the pantomime season and the pantomimes were a spectacle, often praised in the newspapers for the gorgeously painted scenes of forests with trees of silver and gold, deserts, rivers, seas of sparkling azure, elfin kingdoms with flowers and crystal columns, starlit skies, fountains, floods, and fairy ballets. There were dazzling fireworks, cloud-capped towers and temples, ships, and even steam trains to the 'wonder and delight of a gaping audience' as one critic put it.

Dickens was a great fan of the pantomime. In his novel *David Copperfield*, he gives an impression of the magic created by the stage spectacle:

The poetry, the lights, the music, the company, the smooth stupendous changes of glittering and brilliant scenery, were so dazzling and opened up such illimitable regions of delight…

In December 1851, Dickens's article 'Preparing for the Pantomime' appeared in *Household Words*, in which Dickens takes his readers behind the scenes to meet the property man and the scene painters.

A number of Dickens's acquaintances, including Edward Leman Blanchard, who was called 'the king of the pantomime writers', had pantomimes showing. Blanchard's *Harlequin Bluecap* was on at the Olympic Theatre, as was Holcroft's *Road to Ruin*, and various productions of the popular farce, *Box and Cox*, were on in the year 1851. The journalist, George Sala, who is mentioned in the book, had a brother, Charles, who collaborated with George Ellis in the pantomime, *Harlequin Billy Taylor*, showing at the Princess's Theatre on Boxing Day. Blanchard's *Mr and Mrs Briggs*, set in a 'wild romantic dell', was on at Astley's Circus, complete with a scene depicting the Crystal Palace in all its glittering splendour.

Astley's Royal Amphitheatre was a favourite of Dickens's and was famous for its equestrian shows; it is the setting for a scene in my third book, *Murder by Ghostlight*. In December 1851, you could see the beautiful white horse, Taglione, dancing to the music of a piano. Horses jumped through hoops, and I found an image of a horse wearing a very large napkin and eating its dinner at a table with a man in a military uniform. And there were my two elephants, those key witnesses in *The Jaggard Case*.

The Imperial Chinese Junk, *Ke-Ying*, was still moored in the Thames where the Chinese mandarin, Captain Hesing, who appears in *The Chinese Puzzle*, was entertaining audiences with his acrobats and fireworks. Mr Wyld's 'Monster Globe' was open from 10.00 a.m. to 10.00 p.m. with lectures on the earth, the Arctic regions, and gold deposits throughout the world. There were German acrobats at Savile House in Leicester Square, magicians at St James's Hall, and for sixpence you could go to the Regent's Park Zoo to see the hippopotamus among the other 1,750 living animals.

Panoramas were very popular. In December, Mr Burford was advertising 'The Panorama Nimroud, Ancient Nineveh' where you could imagine yourself in the ancient world for sixpence. The panorama was invented in 1787 by an Irish artist, Robert Baker. He devised an apparatus in which curving lines of perspective were drawn on the cylindrical surface of a painting. Baker opened his panorama in 1793 in Leicester

Square. It was a rotunda, 90 feet in diameter and 57 feet high. The Colosseum near Regent's Park was the largest panorama, where you could see Paris by night and a view of the whole of London by day. In 1851 there were at least a dozen panoramas which took you all over the world, as far as Australia and India, to Niagara Falls. At the Egyptian Hall, the panorama took you down the Nile. Dickens's *Household Words* article 'A Voyage Round the World' celebrates the possibilities of travelling the world while staying in London.

The Cyclorama in Albany Street showed the 'thrilling and life-like depiction of the fearful earthquake in Lisbon, which two centuries ago, laid this famous city in ruins.' There were dioramas, too, a bit different from panoramas in that they were created by a picture painted on both sides of a transparent screen, and the changes of effect were created by the ingenious manipulation of windows and skylights so that sometimes the picture would be lit at the front and at other times seen from behind. There had been a Cosmorama in Regent Street, which showed visitors views of distant lands and landmarks through optical devices that used magnification. However, by 1851, the Cosmorama Rooms were more like a bazaar and a museum of curiosities, where you could see The Parisian Venus — in wax, of course — and 'worthy the attention of the Philosopher and the general public', so the poster claimed.

Mr Crowquill mentions the Centrifugal Railway, which had been a great attraction in the Haymarket. It was a kind of early rollercoaster in which the visitor entered a car on rails. The car rose to a peak on the coaster, descended rapidly, and passed through the central hoop with enough speed and centrifugal force to remain on the rails. By 1851, there was an outdoor one at St Helen's Gardens in Rotherhithe, but it was only open until October, when the last balloon ascent of the year took place and there was a great fireworks display.

I found a letter to one of the newspapers from George Sala, the journalist, the title of which was 'Balloon Mania'. Sala had nearly come to grief on a balloon flight and wrote to decry the madness of such undertakings. There were some serious accidents and deaths.

However, a reporter from *The Morning Post* wrote very enthusiastically about his balloon ride from Cremorne Gardens, one of the famous pleasure gardens, where you could listen to the orchestra in the monstrous pagoda and dance on the platform which accommodated 4,000 dancers, or see the circus, or play bowls in the American Bowling Alley, or get lost in the maze. The reporter went up with the famous aeronaut, Guiseppe Lunardini — handy name — whose coolness in the face of a near accident, the reporter praised. The balloon took them across the Thames and descended with some difficulty on account of a tear in the fabric. They landed in a field near Esher, packed up the balloon, sent it to London by market garden cart, and went to the pub, returning home later by train. The balloon flight had carried them fifteen miles and had lasted half an hour.

The pantomime, the panorama, the diorama, the cyclorama, the pleasure garden, fireworks, music concerts, magic shows, and plays were all means by which, Dickens wrote, to cherish 'the light of fancy which is inherent in the human breast.' Of course, he argued for better education, better food, fresh air, sanitation, and pure water to improve the lives of the poor, but he believed, too, that the imagination must be fed if the poor were to lead lives better than those of beasts.

However, most of the entertainments cost at least sixpence, and that was far beyond the means of many of the very poor. No wonder that the street musicians and magicians, fortune tellers, street patterers declaiming ballads and news, and the Punch shows were so popular. You could put a halfpenny in the hat, or nothing at all, and if you were lucky, you might be able to afford a pennorth of hot eels while you were watching; transported, just for a very short while, to a world beyond the muddy street and your wretched lodging house or cellar.

A NOTE TO THE READER

Dear Reader,

When I visited the Foundling Museum several years ago, I knew that Dickens had been a regular visitor, and the exhibits I saw there stayed in my mind, but I had no idea what kind of story I would write about the Foundling Hospital. However, when I was planning the story of Eliza Quarterman, my visit to the museum came back to me.

Between 1837 to 1839, Dickens lived at number 48 Doughty Street just round the corner from the Foundling Hospital where he attended the chapel. Orphans and abandoned children were on his mind as he wrote *Oliver Twist* while he was living in Doughty Street. The hospital is now the Foundling Museum, where I went to see the tokens and textiles which are part of the records of the children who were given up to the hospital from its beginning in 1740. I bought a book called *Threads of Feeling*, which gives the history of the fabric pieces the museum holds. There are 5,000 small textile items pinned to the registration documents for each child. These little pieces of fabric form the largest collection of everyday textiles surviving from the mid-eighteenth century. There are scraps of calico, linen, flannel, gingham, and satin, even silk, the costliest of fabrics, all very moving reminders of the young women who could not keep their children.

A little square of brown linen is attached to the record of Foundling 13298, a boy admitted on 2nd July, 1759. It's a rough piece of cloth, very cheap to buy and often purchased by parish overseers to clothe the poor. Nothing much to look at, but it tells the story of a young woman too poor to look after her infant. The piece of blue silk left with Foundling 1254, a girl admitted on 29th May, 1755, might tell a different story — a servant, perhaps, seduced by a master who tempted her with a silk present. There are pieces of material with patterns and stripes, perhaps cut down from second-hand dresses belonging to the mothers, and the distinctive pattern might well have been essential for identification — just in case the mother came back to see her child. Very few children were reclaimed, and sometimes those who asked for their children back were refused.

Silk was an impractical material for ordinary women, as it was virtually impossible to wash, but a working girl, a servant or seamstress could afford a printed linen or cotton if she wanted something pretty and fashionable — a dress, say, made of the flowered cotton attached to the record of Foundling 14093, a girl admitted on 4th October, 1759. The cotton is cream, and the flowers are blue and red. It must have been a charming dress, and there is something very poignant about this little scrap. I wondered who she was and what happened to her after she had given up her little girl.

Sometimes the piece of material is a ribbon, which was tied to the child's wrist. Ribbons were made of silk, but a yard could be bought for a few pence. They were often given as lovers' tokens and tied into love knots like the flowered yellow and red ribbon given with Foundling 10667, a girl admitted on 29th November, 1758. Perhaps the lover who gave the pretty ribbon at the fair had abandoned her and she was left too poor to look after her child. There's another yellow ribbon with the words, 'My name is Andrews,' printed in ink. He became Foundling 453, and then he would have been given a new name by the hospital. He became someone else, but perhaps his mother wrote the name, 'Andrews'? Did she hope that she would find him again? Many of the fabric pieces have hearts sewn onto them, testimony to the love that the mothers felt, and one token carries the message 'you have my Heart, Tho we must part', telling words which show that most of these mothers believed that their sacrifice was better for the child. There was hope for a future.

In *The Waxwork Man*, Eliza Quarterman is left at the Foundling Hospital with a token of identification. The museum displays a collection of these tokens. There are metal tags engraved with the child's name, buttons, keys, padlocks, brooches, rings, even coins, and the token depicting St Saviour's Church. I remembered that token when I was thinking about who Eliza Quarterman was to be. I knew it would be a useful clue to lead Dickens to search for Eliza in Southwark, where he had lived as a boy when his father was in the debtors' prison, the Marshalsea, the home of Little Dorrit. And I remembered the textile scraps and thinking about the stories they might tell, which is where Eliza's mother comes from.

Dickens did know John Brownlow, who was secretary at the hospital from 1849 to 1872, having begun as Foundling no. 18607. He was born in 1800, the son of Mary Goodacre, about whom nothing is known, except that she gave up her child. Brownlow began his working life in 1814 as a clerk in the secretary's office. Dickens gives an account of the running of the hospital in the *Household Words* article, 'Received A Blank Child' (1853), the title referring to the form that was filled in as each child was received into the hospital. The space for the name was a blank. Dickens obviously admires the work of the hospital, and there are some humorous touches in his descriptions of the children, whose teachers sow 'little seeds of alphabet and multiplication', and he writes of the child who tries on his hat, 'with which an infant extinguished himself, to his great terror.' And he notes that 'they were all sensibly and comfortably clothed.' However, the title does suggest some ambiguity in his attitude. He knows that these children are far better off at Coram's than on the streets, yet I think he wonders about the individuals who are taught so well to conform. Tattycoram, the foundling girl, is introduced in *Little Dorrit* (1855). Outwardly, she is the obedient servant, but inwardly she passionately resents her servitude and her name, a corruption of Harriet with the name of Coram attached. Dickens understands what feelings might boil up in the heart of a girl who is taught to be submissive and thankful to her betters.

Well, I am thankful to my readers, and I hope you've enjoyed reading *The Waxwork Man*. I thank you for taking the time to do so. Reviews are very important to writers, so it would be great if you could spare the time to post a review on **Amazon** and **Goodreads**. Readers can connect with me online, on **Facebook (JCBriggsBooks)**, **Twitter (@JeanCBriggs)**, and you can find out more about the books and Charles Dickens via my website: **jcbriggsbooks.com** where you will find Mr Dickens's A–Z of murder — all cases of murder to which I found a Dickens connection.

Thank you!

Jean Briggs

Sapere Books is an exciting new publisher of brilliant fiction and popular history.

To find out more about our latest releases and our monthly bargain books visit our website:
saperebooks.com

Printed in Great Britain
by Amazon

34382474R00185